A WHISPER TO A SCREAM

A Novel by Elissa Gabrielle

A WHISPER TO A SCREAM

A Novel by Elissa Gabrielle

Peace in the Storm Publishing

Praise for
A WHISPER TO A SCREAM

"Elissa Gabrielle does in 36 chapters, what a rapper does in 16 bars; what a poet does in stanzas. She is poetry in motion. Her new book will have you begging and screaming for more."
~JIHAD, ESSENCE best selling author of *Wild Cherry*

"This exhilarating page turner commands your full attention from the very start and never releases it. *A Whisper to a Scream* is a richly satisfying novel that you'll find yourself completely drawn into, delivered in a style that only Elissa Gabrielle can bring."
~S.D. Denny, author of *The Baker's Dozen*

"She's back and Elissa Gabrielle sets her literary pen OFF as she introduces readers to Queen Thomas, Quincy Hughes, and all the drama and chaos that surround their lives. In the midst of abuse, murder, and the fight for justice and peace of mind, is it possible for Queen and Quincy to really find true love? You want to buckle up for this ride because Gabrielle takes you on a winding ride full of twists and turns, from a mere whisper to a gut-wrenching scream! After reading this book, you'll ponder what is coming next from this amazing literary voice."
~Linda R. Herman, author of *Consequences*

"A true page turner! Expect to sit on the edge of your seat as *A Whisper to a Scream* takes you on a rollercoaster of emotions."
~Ebonee Monique, author of *Suicide Diaries*

"*A Whisper to a Scream* delivered more thrills and chills then an amusement park! Elissa's pen is equivalent to anything once can watch on *Lifetime* or *E* TV. The piece stirs joy, angst, wonder and amusement within the reader and levels the ground with sincerity and moral growth. A page turner indeed"
~Marie Antoinette, author of *A Girl Named Job*

"Intensely passionate and dramatic. *A Whisper to a Scream* will own your every emotion from beginning to end."
~Hazel Mills, author of
Bare Necessities: Sensuous Tales of Passion

"Elissa creates a new genre, Romantica, with this deliberately delicious read. An exciting, suspenseful, page-turner that is sure to leave hearts aching for more. As racial color lines are drawn, erased, and re-drawn with perfect strokes from the author's pen we experience love, sex, betrayal and trust on a level that is sure to delight and leave readers with one question. At what point of terror does a whisper become a scream?"
~LaToya S. Watkins, author of *In Love with Losers*

"A Whisper to a Scream may prove to be Elissa Gabrielle's best work to date. Deliciously disturbing, Queen Thomas' life is full of deception and desire. Dr. Quincy Hughes is a white man who is intensely infatuated with Queen, but her ex-lover Derrick may kill their relationship - by killing Queen! Interracial intimacy is intertwined with Elissa's ability to provide tons of drama. It's enough to turn *"A Whisper to a Scream."*
~Joey Pinkney, contributor to *The Soul of a Man*

"A *Whisper to a Scream* brings to life the terror of domestic abuse. People tend to believe that this happens to people who are in the lower classes, but this book demonstrates that it happens with those in the professional realms as well. It's ugly and harsh, but needs to talked about more often."
~Gayle Jackson Sloan, author of *Let the Necessary Occur*

"A *Whisper to a Scream* is first-rate suspense. Elissa Gabrielle's writing is 'good to the last drop' causing you to always want more."
~OOSA Online Book Club

"Ms. Gabrielle delivers a tale that quenches any literary thirst. *A Whisper to a Scream* is destined to become a classic!"
~Péron Long, author of *Livin Ain't Easy*

"With enticing precision, *A Whisper to a Scream* draws you in like a moth to a flame. Through relatable and unforgettable characters in shocking situations, Elissa Gabrielle has crafted a tale that makes your heart beat faster in anticipation of what will happen on the next page."
~Lorraine Elzia, Author of *Mistress Memoirs*

DEDICATION

To Paula…
Through the Sunshine
Through the Rain
Through the Joy
Through the Pain
You will Always Remain,
My Friend

He brought me back to life.
The dead had arisen.
His whispers resurrected my being.
My screams brought me back to existence.
Emboldened by his essence,
I relished in being his conquest.
~Queen Thomas

QUEEN
The Scream Within

I can taste the salty blood as it oozes from the corners of my mouth. My lips feel puffy, swollen, tender, and, as the back of my right hand touches my top lip, it aches. I'm scared. Slowly and nervously, I bring my hand into view, disgusted by the sight of my own blood and saliva mixture. Inside, I scream silently. Racing heartbeats throb so hard that my eardrums ache. I'm so scared. My eyes peer down to ripped pantyhose that lay so carelessly atop bruised calves and thighs. Purple ovals cover my legs, and the crimson-colored deep scratches, I nervously trace with my fingertips.

"You gon' make me kill you!" he screams, the bass in his voice shakes my soul.

The towering figure, I once adored, creeps further and closer into view. The veins protruding from his forehead, coupled with the tiny beads of sweat, causing tiny streams down over his brow, makes him look just as scary as he is. The man I once loved, now out of breath, pants like a jealous lover. Full of rage, Cujo is no match for Derrick. Like a rabid dog, he foams at the mouth, before opening his jaws wide, and the thunder escapes him, every ounce of him screams at me as he lands another blow.

Looking up at his towering, brown, six-foot-five frame, and muscular stature, I try to scream, "No!" but no sounds form. The word, wrapped tightly around my throat, won't come out.

I plead for dear life, crying, my tears blur my vision.

"Derrick, please, stop!"

"Shut up, bitch!"

As his punch lands against the side of my head, I hear my neck crack, and my face crashes against the maroon-colored wall in Derrick's bedroom, leaving a trail of mucous, teardrops and fear. Again, panic stricken, my heart races and beats so fast, I feel as if I may convulse. Trembling, my legs shake and ache and I scramble, literally crawling on my knees, for dear life. I panic. If I don't get out of here alive, Daddy will be burying his only child in a few days.

My bloody knees work their way over the hardwood floors in a rush to escape. My hands, bruised, and cut lead me, as I have no strength to rise to my feet.

"Didn't I tell your ass before that you'll never leave me?" Derrick questions as he kicks me repeatedly in my rib cage.

"Nooooooo, Derrick, please! I promise, I won't leave you!" I scream and beg for mercy.

And, at this moment, while I lay still on his bedroom floor, my lifeless body, covered only by a ripped beige tank top and a torn winter-white skirt, has not the strength to move one inch, let alone, run for cover. The blow of a man twice my size has taken over. And, no matter how hard I try to grasp on, I feel myself fading out of consciousness, slowly.

The jolt of Derrick grabbing my arm shocks me, briefly, as panic shoots through my being. With hatred and contempt, he drags me across the floor, pulling me to the foot of the bed. His size thirteen shoe blows dust into my eyes with each stomp, and, as I glide across his floor, I can feel the thin pieces of wood splinter into my flesh. I want to scream, but no words. The nightmare I cannot escape from has me in a trance.

What have I done to deserve this?

Derrick props me up like a rag doll, and now my head rests at the foot of his bed. Pearl satin sheets drape down to the floor. The stiffness of the box spring pokes dents into my back, which I'm sure is all whelped from the beating. Each time I exhale, and then inhale, the spring reams further into my spine. A river of tears flow down my butterscotch cheeks; the salt burns as it enters the crevices of my wounds.

I'm ready to die.

As Derrick stands in front of me, I look up to see a snarl only the devil could adorn. I want so badly to damn him and send him to Hell, but somehow, I think he's managed to take me with him. His chocolate-coated fingers, equipped with dirty, nasty fingernails, dangle near his crotch, and as he prepares to unzip his dark blue jeans, he laughs—a gothic, deadly, immoral laugh, which moves and shakes the Earth beneath me. Consternation wraps around my heart, dreading what's about to come next. He's going to rape me.

Trying again to flee, I try to roll, move out of Derrick's way, but Derrick grabs me by my hair, pulling so hard, I feel strands break free from their roots as he rips my hair from my head. I grab my head, in an attempt to salvage any hair that's left.

"Jesus," I plead.

As I pray that I am covered by the blood of Jesus, I wonder how hard it would be to murder Derrick Simmons.

"Don't look at her! That's what got your ass whooped in the first place. Coming in here, unannounced and uninvited with dinner," Derrick yells, still unzipping his jeans. Purple swollen eyes lose sight of the other woman in this quagmire. Although my vision is cloudy, I can still see her with my peripherals. Curiosity gets the best of me, and I once again turn my head ever so slightly and glance at this woman.

This woman, I've seen before. I know her. And, she's sleeping with my man, obviously. Ringlet curls dance around her face as they glide past her ears. A light-skinned, plump African American woman; late thirties maybe, unless she's early twenties and has seriously let herself go. I want to call her. What's her name? "Sherri?"

Only darkness covers me as the open-handed slap with two years of bullshit behind it, lands across the side of my head. I begin to fade as my head crashes against the bedpost. Derrick's clearing of the throat is a prelude to the wad of phlegm that lands in my hair, dripping down the sides of my face.

I scream within and my nightmare becomes a distant memory.

๛๛๛๛๛

Repetitive blunt force impacts trample my shoulder. "Girl, wake up! Queen, get up!"

Groggy, numb and motionless, I respond, "What?" Looking up to this woman I know so well, yet, I don't at all, has me confused and curious, and then I remember. Through bloodshot eyes, I expel, "Sherri?"

"Yes, Queen, it's Sherri from the courthouse. Listen, girl, we have to get out of here." Leaning in to pull me up, Sherri reaches under my arms and tugs, pulls hard and I stand on shaky, trembling legs, and weak knees. "He's in the bathroom. We gotta go now," she softly yells in an exaggerated, panicked voice. Squeezing my hand, she pulls me toward Derrick's front door, and I hesitate, take a step back. The fire in her eyes confirms her disgust and fear as she looks at me through dark brown curls of good hair. "What, Queen? We have to go!"

"Did he rape me, Sherri?"

Bowing her head in embarrassment, she answers the question I'm not sure I want the answer to. "No, he didn't."

"Thank God," I pray through swollen lips.

Our pace quickens as the sight of the brown, wood grain door becomes within reach. Our freedom is right before our eyes. Nearing the Promised Land, she looks back at me again and with the strength of a dying lamb, Sherri confesses, "he raped me," as the flood of stainless tears pour relentlessly from her eyes, landing onto the back of my hand. I cry with her, as we keep hope alive.

The faster we run, the more I see evidence of not only my abuse, via bruised feet and legs, but also of her invasion, as her skirt is partially gone and her ripped blouse exposes a purple lace bra and a bruised breast. My heart pounds fast as Sherri's hand lands on the golden doorknob. She turns it. The cool breeze strikes us in the face, as it is the wind of autonomy; under the guise of a nightly chill, freedom rings.

Amazingly, my keys are still in my skirt pocket, and I hear them jingle as we run down the flight of red-bricked stairs. "Did you drive?"

"No," Sherri grunted.

"Let's go to my truck!"

Scurrying across the street, hand in hand, resembling two school age girlfriends, we race. My right thumb presses the open symbol on my car's keychain, and the doors unlock. As we hop into my Dodge Durango, which now serves as our safe haven, the porch light to Derrick's two-story, bi-level colonial comes on, and the towering inferno, the devil himself, runs down the staircase, with the swiftness of a lion, and the calculated movements of a cheetah, he reaches my truck in record time. Sherri screams, as terror has taken her hostage, coming face to face with the man, my man, who just stole her dignity, and ripped away her identity with a single stroke.

Frantically, I lock the doors, and as Derrick's once handsome profile comes face to face with my driver's side window, I pull off, leaving a dirty villain in the dust, forever.

The wooded Pocono Mountains, while lovely, scenic, quiet and serene, is no place to attempt a fast getaway. Winding roads, fully blossomed trees, and colorful foliage makes for a great Hallmark card, but does nothing for two women, racing down and around winding dark roads at seventy miles per hour, running for dear life. Our sanity lies in my hands, as I dance with the devil, pressing the pedal to the floor. The main road is about two minutes away.

"Thank you, Queen," Sherri testifies as she grabs hold of my arm. "He told me you two were no more," she gushes, voice full of tears and bad memories. Before I can respond, flashing lights and the constant beeping of a horn distracts me. Derrick is right behind us, high beams introducing themselves to my rearview mirror and the back of my truck. My speed quickens. At eighty miles per hour, I no longer have control of this vehicle. It will be by the grace of God that we make it home alive.

"Queen! Watch out!" Sherri screams a blood-curdling scream. Bambi leaps in front of my truck with the grace of a ballerina and all the common sense of a walnut. Jerking the wheel to its far most right swerves us across the road, where the onset of a tree is inevitable. The muscles in my legs tighten as I press down on the break, with all my might, while pulling the emergency break. My heart beats so fast, it's hard to breathe. Feels like slow motion, as I rise out my seat, as my face crashes against the windshield. I fade to black.

❧❧❧❧❧

"So, you want to put the old man in the grave, huh?"

"Daddy?"

"Yes, pumpkin, it's me."

"Daddy? What are you doing here? Wait, where am I?"

Wearing a heavy heart, my dad walks over to me, lands a kiss onto my forehead, and the familiar scent of Pierre Cardin penetrates my nostrils, while the fine stubble of his salt and pepper beard tickles my skin; it's all very comforting and safe.

"You're in the hospital, Queen."

"I am?"

"Yes, you arrived last night, by ambulance."

"Where?"

"In Crystal Lakes community."

"Really?"

"You were in a car accident, Queen. The EMT says you ran into a tree."

Feeling groggy, I close my eyes as the horror returns to me. "I remember now, Dad."

As tears form in his eyes, he leans in again to gently kiss my forehead. I grab his arm.

"It's okay, Daddy. I'm okay."

As a single tear rolls down his cheek, I take on his pain as if it were my own.

"Because I don't know what I would've done without you, Queen. You're all I've got. I thank the good Lord, you're alive."

"Daddy, I'll always be with you, no matter what."

"Queen, I'm going to talk to the doctors to see if I can find out any information."

"Okay, Daddy."

As my dad walks out of the room, I see he's once again put on his favorite khaki pants, Oxford brown shoes, with his ivory button down sweater. I call it his reading attire. All he needs is a pipe, and a Lazy Boy with ottoman, to look like one of the seniors in those assisted living facilities. I must admit, Dad, although in his sixties now, still reminds me of Billy Dee Williams. He was one of those fine cats back in the day. Yep, back in the day, it was just me and my dad. Well, before my mom died.

Pain settles into my soul when I think of her. From the picture I have of her in my bedroom, and Dad still has, I look exactly like her—from the mulatto complexion and the flowing soft brown hair. Full lips and big brown eyes make me a spitting image of Mama. When thoughts of her enter my mind, I drift back to a happy place in time. I was four years old, full of enough energy to launch the space shuttle. My mom would play this game with me, and I couldn't wait for her to do it, each night before I went to bed. With pearly white teeth, her smile would light up the night; sunshine deep down in her soul. And she would sing to me.

"Whisper something sweet to me.
Whisper something sweet to me.
Mama loves her baby.
Mama loves her baby.
From the sunshine to the night.
From the darkness to the light.
Queen loves her mommy.
And Mama loves her baby.
Whisper something sweet to me."

Oh, how I held onto that last line with all my might. The anticipation of what was to come made me anxious every time. Mama would put her ear next to my mouth, and that was my cue to whisper something sweet in her ear.

And then, she'd sing it again.

"Whisper something sweet to me.
Whisper something sweet to me.
Mama loves her baby.
Mama loves her baby.
From the sunshine to the night.
From the darkness to the light.
Queen loves her mommy.
And Mama loves her baby.
Whisper something sweet to me."

And, as her long hair, which always smelled like flowers, landed in my face, I'd cover the side of my mouth with my tiny hand, and whisper in her ear, "I love you, Mommy."

And she'd sing again, "'Cause Mama loves her baby."

༺༺༺༺༺

Dad stops my trip down memory lane. "Queen?"

"Yes, Dad."

"Are you okay?"

"Fine, Dad. Just thinking about Mom. I miss her."

"Yeah, I miss her too. The doctor says you're going to be just fine. The bruising will go down in about a week and you'll be able to remove the facial bandages in a few days. Thank God he was able to save your life. I'll be right back. You need anything?"

"No, Dad. But, wait. Dad?"

"Yes, baby?"

"Where's Sherri?"

"Who?"

"Sherri. The woman with me in the truck last night. She works at the courthouse."

As my father approaches me, the pit of my stomach turns into knots.

"Baby, I'm sorry. She died."

QUINCY
Have a Nice Life

"oodnight, Dr. Hughes," Carmella sings through ruby red lips and batting eyes. The look of delight on her face is reinforced as I pat her on the hand while grabbing my briefcase to head through the emergency room at Mountain View Medical Center.

Feeling the monkey on my back, with each step, I turn around. She's watching. Jocking, hard as hell, I might add. The slightest curl of my lips exposes a grin, and I once again wave to Carmella, the registered nurse from the ER, upon my departure.

"See you tomorrow."

"I'm looking forward to it, Dr. Hughes," she shrills seductively.

If I don't know anything else, I know when a woman wants to get down. And Carmella does, in the worst way. Could it be the charm? No, as I don't personally feel I'm that charming. The looks? Maybe. Standing at a slender six-foot-three and three quarter inches, I'm a well-oiled machine, if I must say so myself. Frank Sinatra blue-eyes and jet black hair doesn't hurt the cause. I'd never admit that in public, as "modesty is the best policy" my mother would always tell me. The fact is, as an emergency room physician in my mid-thirties, I get a lot of unwanted attention, so I'm extremely careful with the ladies. Mainly a "hit-it-and-quit it" kind of guy. Miss Carmella, although sweet in her disposition, is simply not my cup of tea. She has to be in her early fifties, which is not a problem, as mature women are enlightening, but the ultra-red hair and red nail polish, with matching red lipstick, on her frail Irish frame, just doesn't light a spark in me.

Climbing up into my black Lincoln Navigator, I slide into the oversized seat, recline and put on the heat. I reach up slightly to increase the volume. *"Ready to Die"* by Notorious B.I.G. plays and will be the theme music for my ride. Ain't nothing like some ol' school Hip-Hop. And, ain't nothing like Biggie. Resting my head on the headrest, I crack the window inviting in the cool. Hard day on the job—broken fingers to broken arms, to torn retinas to sprained ankles, car accident victims to fatal heart attacks—so I'm due for a night out with my boys, just to chill, and free my mind of so much despair.

After Mom and Dad decided to follow my aunt, and a few cousins, to the Pocono Mountains, I followed suit and joined them. My best friend, Patrick, also relocated, so the change was one that was smooth. Wasn't hard to get a job as one of the ER doctors at the hospital either. It all just fell into place.

My home was priced nicely in the Winding Roads Community. Three bedrooms, family room, two bathrooms, a huge eat-in-kitchen, one car garage, and all the amenities that come with it, made the decision to purchase an easy one. Mom and Dad are in the same development, about ten minutes away, which is convenient.

All of my boys back at home in Jersey thought I was frontin' for leaving. I caught a lot of heat about it, but learned over time to just let it go. When they question me now, I always ask them, "What the fuck am I missing? The crackheads, the stolen cars, or the high taxes?" Don't get me wrong, crackheads are here too, just not on my front stoop.

As I make my way to Jasper's, a nightclub in Pocono City, I notice the colors on the leaves are changing. The area is so scenic and serene, which was a culture shock from the hectic streets of Jersey City, but after a while, you learn to let down your defenses and relax, right along with the rabbits scurrying along the sides of the roads.

I hear the club music as I enter the parking lot. The valet, a short Mexican guy, takes my keys, and as I adjust my Carhart jacket, I make my way into the club. Waving of the hands by my boy Patrick alerts me to where we'll be seated for the evening. As I make my way over, I feel the rhythm of the music, and enjoy the grown and sexy feel, the vibe, it's just right. I'm known for my serious two-step, so I definitely plan to hit the dance floor tonight. Dimly lit candles cascade, adorning each table, and the interior lights draped around the bar give it an air of New York City nightlife. I miss the city, but this here will do. A few fine honeys out on the dance floor make for nice eye candy. Little Puerto Rican Mami has my attention as she moves those shapely hips to the beat. A wink of her eye tells me I have her attention also. And if I wasn't involved at the moment, I'd step to her and tap that plump ass with the quickness. Sometimes, I think I'm just too faithful.

Patrick stands and gives me dap and some grown man love. He's got to be the coolest brother I know. People couldn't understand, when we were growing up, how we could be so cool. Patrick, originally from Newark, had it rough. I didn't have it much better in Jersey City, but the point is we made it. We were often teased with the whole black and white issue, but I love his black ass to death, and unless he's been lying to me for decades, he loves my white ass just the same. His Aunt Pam lived on my block in Jersey City, and he would come to visit every summer.

Man, I remember it like it was yesterday. A hot summer day in August. Pico and 'em opened up the fire hydrant down the block, Miss Belle, a new lady to our block, pretty as hell, and Aunt Pam, Big's aunt, were serving food during our annual block party. Everything from hot dogs, to cheap grape soda, Pop-rocks, watermelon, hamburgers and cotton candy was on that table.

Big's Aunt Pam would pile my plate so high, I'd be stuff for hours. On that one day in particular, something changed. I met Big.

"Quincy, why don't you go over there and meet my nephew, Patrick?"

"Sure, Aunt Pam, where is he?"

She pointed to her porch and Patrick sat there, blasting his boom box so loud. I wanted to touch it so bad, as I always dreamed of having one like that, but my Pop's couldn't afford it. I was ready to run over, but, I took my time getting to him.

As I moved closer to Patrick, I noticed how black and how heavy he was. He was a scary motherfucker to look at.

Appearing to be about 19, Patrick was massive. I kept my cool and walked toward him.

Nodding my head, I introduced myself.

"Wassup man, my name is Quincy but they call me Q. Your aunt Pam told me to come over."

"I didn't know white boys lived in the hood," he replied, smiling from ear to ear. He laughed out loud.

"The hood has a little bit of everything in it, man."

Reaching his hand out to greet me, he confessed, "I'm Patrick, man, nice to meet you, Q. Oh, by the way, everyone calls me Big."

I laughed out loud.

"Why they call you that?"

"Well, look at me, Q. I'm big as hell."

"Yeah, you are, but you cool peeps."

Running my hand across the top of his boom box, I admired the shiny silver machine, and the bass that came from it.

Blasting "My Adidas" from Run-DMC, Big seemed cool as hell. From his velour sweat suit to his shell-toe Adidas, the same pair I had on, left me admiring him even within those few seconds of meeting him.

"This radio is so fly, Big. How much this set you back?"

"Not much, Q, I just saved til I could get it."

"Word?"

"Word is bond, man."

We've been close like Starsky and Hutch, stick to clutch, ever since that day.

҂ ҂ ҂ ҂ ҂

"What's up, baby? My man," he barks, grinning from ear to ear.

"One hundred grand. What's up, Big?" I pat him on the back.

"Baby, all is good. What took you so long?" he questions while taking his seat.

"Man, rough day. Bad, bad car accident, lost a young one tonight."

"Man, sorry to hear that."

"Yeah, me too."

As I take my seat, my eyes peer over to Raj, a new cat to the community. Patrick met him on the job, some construction site for new homes they're working on. I've never seen an Indian working on new construction. The shit amazes me. But he's cool. Same age as us; mid-thirties, single, looking for love and ass, or maybe just ass, like the rest of us. I have my steady ass in Tina, but nothing concrete or serious. Something about her just doesn't ring "love and marriage." But, she can slob a knob with the best of them, so she'll do for the moment.

My eyes move past Raj to Angelo; one of those Eric Benet types, all into the Earth and holistic shit, a poet, performing spoken word when he can, and on Friday nights, he's right here at Jasper's doing his thing. Never met a black man named Angelo, but there's a first time for everything. The women love his metro-sexual looking ass. The short dreads, high cheekbones and the seashell necklace around his neck, along with the tie-dye shirts, drive the women wild. I just don't get it, but he's cool people.

"I see the United Nations is here again. Your usual Friday night drinks, fellas?" Lana questions as she prepares to take our drink orders. She's a cute little black girl. Flat chest and even flatter ass doesn't cut it for me, but she's got a cute face, and is nice enough.

I look up at her to respond. "Yes, Ma'am, I'll be having my usual Heineken, but I may go for my rum and coke later."

Big jumps in. "Baby girl, bring me two Coronas with lemon and your phone number."

"Damn, Big, every week you ask for the same thing and every week all you get are two Coronas," Raj chimes in as he laughs at Patrick.

"Shut the hell up 'fore I send you back to the nearest 7-Eleven, Raj," Big cautions and laughs. "If I keep asking, she'll give in one day."

"Or, she'll have you served with a restraining order," Angelo jumps in. "What you need to do is learn how to speak to a lady, Big."

Angelo takes Lana by the hand. He kisses the back of it. She smiles. "Now, Lana, if I asked for your number, and told you that you were my world, would you give it to me?" A single finger is placed over Lana's mouth as Angelo rises from his seat, and moves in closer into Lana's face. "If I told you that I wanted to lick your lips, pinch your hips and rock you all night and then some, 'til the moon meets the sun to make the horizon cum, would you give me your number then?" Angelo looks back to Big, winking his eye with a proud look on his face.

Lana smiles as the curvature of her top lip shows a hint of mockery. "Not sure Angelo. I would need to get permission from my girlfriend first. Would you be interested in a threesome?"

"OOOOOOOOH SHIT!" We all yell in unison. Not sure if Angelo is flattered, embarrassed or a little bit of both. That's what he gets for trying to be as smooth as Blair Underwood.

As he takes his seat, Big throws in his two cents to add salt in his wound. "Yeah, maybe you can recite some of that bitch ass poetry to her girlfriend. You such a bitch, man."

"Big, shut your gorilla ass up. You just mad you ain't smooth like me."

"Okay, fellas, I'll bring your drinks back in a moment," Lana laughs as she walks away.

"What's up for the night man?" Big asks me.

"Not much. I'm going to stop by Tina's on the way home, then call it a night."

"Is that right?"

"Yeah, Big. Why?"

"Man, I don't trust that girl."

"Me either," Raj implies.

I glance over to Angelo, who throws his hands up. "What do you want me to say, Q? Something ain't right about that girl."

I rise to my feet, and with an accusatory stance, I point to each one of them and tell them how I really feel.

"Raj, you just mad cause you jerking off seven days a week. And Lo, you, you, well, you just shut the fuck up. And Big, I thought you were my man?"

"I am your man, brother. And man to man, I'm telling you, I don't like that girl."

"Something about her reminds me of a stripper," Raj explains, as he drinks his martini.

Taking my seat, I reveal, "Man, how the hell someone gon' remind you of a stripper?" I throw my balled up napkin at Raj's head.

Big cannot resist the opportunity to profess on this one. Leaning his fat ass onto the table, he props his elbows and looks me dead in the eyes. "Well, why are you messing with her, Q? It's not because she looks like a nice girl, is it?"

I laugh. He's got a point.

Big pushes on. "It's because she looks like she can suck five golf balls through that straw, right?"

"Shut the fuck up, Big!"

As we all laugh, Big gets up from the table and dances. Pointing to me, he sings, "You know that girl a ho boy, and you gonna find out the wrong way, boy!"

As he hands his pretend mike –otherwise known as the spoon, over to Raj, he gets his 7-Eleven ass up and starts to dance, an off beat, wanna have rhythm two-step, and continues in song, "Yes, and you know boy, that girl you messin' with is a ho, boy!"

Raj hands the pretend mike to Angelo, and he gets up, begins to dance, starts to shout and stomp and brings the fire and brimstone, like a black reverend at a down south church on Easter Sunday. "And you know ah, when the man tells ya, that ah, the girl is a ho ah, then ah, she's a ho ah, a whole lotta ho ah. Can I get an Amen?"

"Amen, brother," Raj and Big sing in unison.

"Alright, alright, damn. I ain't tryin' to marry the girl."

"Thank God!" Big yells.

I get up from the table and point to each one of them. "Fuck you, fuck you and fuck you."

Lana approaches, amused at the dumb asses I call my boys. "Have you boys decided on dinner?"

Big is a glutton for punishment it seems and its déjà vu all over again. Same question, same answer, different week.

"Girl, you know I'll sop you up with a biscuit, you 'lil tenderoni."

"Ha, ha, yes, I know, Patrick and I'll be sure to keep that in mind," she laughs.

"Lana, just some wings for me, and um, make me a to-go salmon dinner," I tell her with thoughts of Tina on my mind.

"Who's the salmon for?" nosey ass Raj questions.

"None of your damn business, Raj."

"Damn, man, just curious. I bet it's for your girlfriend, right? The ho, right?"

"Right, bitch."

"Don't do it Raj," Big encourages.

I'm curious so I ask. "Do what, Big?"

"Nothing, man."

"Did y'all bitches leave your balls at the door?" Angelo questions.

"What they want to know, but are too scared to ask is, are you surprising Tina with dinner tonight?"

"Yes, I am, Angelo." I point to Raj. "And the next time your Indian ass has something to say, say it, bitch, with your turban wearing ass."

I point to Big.

"And your big, black ass knows better. Don't keep shit from me. Y'all jackasses are paranoid. Yes, I'm surprising my girl with dinner tonight, bitches."

೩ ೩ ೩ ೩ ೩

Cruising through the wooded roads, only the headlights of my ride illuminate the street and provide light to guide me on my journey this evening. A twenty minute drive, on a crisp and cool night in the Pocono Mountains can be so serene. My light jazz plays softly throughout, which definitely sets off the grown and sexy feeling to equal the sexy mood I'm in this evening. And if Tina allows me to have my way, I'll be exploring every crevice of her mahogany brown skin, discovering its firmness as I find my way to pleasure.

As much as I try to relax and release from all of the confines of work, I can't help but to think about my patients. Some days are easy, while others are unbearable. In my many years of being a doctor, I've witnessed the best and the worst of what people and God has to offer. And this morning, one of the worst presented itself right before my eyes in the form of a young African American woman, begging and pleading for me to save her life. The car accident she was in was so bad that the trauma to her body was one of the worst I'd ever witnessed. Her intestines had protruded from her body and dangled on her side. Half of her right leg was torn, and yet, in the midst of dying, she said to me, "Do what you can doctor, and if I don't make it, tell my mother that I love her with all my heart and that I'm going to see my daddy on the other side." When those words came from her mouth, I wanted to cry, but had to fight to keep her alive. Two minutes later, she was dead.

೩ ೩ ೩ ೩ ೩

As I park my truck a few houses down from Tina's first floor apartment, and for the surprise factor, I turn off the ignition, and make my way down the street. Salmon dinner in tow, I glance up to see Tina's living room window. Funny, there are no lights on, so either she's sleeping or she's not home. I've come this far, so I make my way up the stairs to this two-family walk up, where Tina rents out the first floor. She's still in school, training to become a medical assistant, so this is all she can afford. But, shit, a nice two bedroom apartment in the Poconos averages about six hundred a month, so she's good.

I remember how I met Tina. It was about six months ago. Her class had come to visit the ER at Mountain View and I happened to be working that day. Thank God the ER was light and I was only treating an allergic reaction. She stood out in the crowd. They all wore white lab coats, and Tina's was tight as hell. Her smooth and supple brown skin offset the white coat something serious. Cleavage for days, Tina has to be about a 40DD, and every ounce of those babies was on display that day. My eyes immediately connected to her sultry and shapely figure, and glanced up to her face which was equally delectable. Her weave needed some tending to, but hey, no one's perfect. Our eyes immediately connected and it was on from there. It would have been unethical for me to say one word to her, so I left it alone. A few days later, I got her phone call. She introduced herself, reminded me of whom she was and asked for a date. I immediately, and eagerly, accepted. At the time, I couldn't remember the last time I was on a date with anyone. It was ass here and there, so the invite was a welcomed one.

"This is Dr. Hughes," I anxiously said to the caller. I had so much work to do, phone calls at work were not in the schedule.

"I can't believe you're actually on the phone," a sexy voice greeted me.

"Who's this?" I impatiently questioned.

"Ha, ha," she laughed seductively. "This is Tina," I met you a short while ago. My class visited Mountain View."

I couldn't believe she called, and her confidence did turn me on, I must admit.

So now, I stand here at Tina's doorstep. As I look over my shoulder, only porch lights greet me on this quiet, moonlit street. A black and white cat scurries across the road, which serves as the only source of any living creatures tonight.

Propping the salmon dinner on the brick landing, I pop my collar and close my jacket a bit more, as the cool night air has settled into my bones. After blowing warm air into the palms of my hands, I rub them together, and then take my index finger and press it into the amber lit doorbell for the first floor. My eyes peer upwards and after about a minute and two additional rings of the doorbell, Tina's hallway light comes on. A smile crosses my face, as it is the grin of lust, confirming my desire to have my way with "Miss New Booty." A slight chuckle escapes me, because I know this so called relationship isn't going too much further than the bedroom. Tina is very good for a nut but I can't see much more happening. Love and marriage is definitely in my future, as I'm looking forward to sharing my life with that special someone. But my gut tells me that Tina is not the one. Maybe Big, Raj and Lo were right. Time will tell.

Time told.

Well, well, well, I guess they were right. As the front door opens, I'm greeted with what appears to be an escape convict, straight out of Attica. Big, bold and black, this man has to be about six-foot-five, and weighing in at about two hundred eighty-five pounds of pure muscle. The sweat pouring from his burly brow gives me all the answers to any questions I may have had. And the fact that he's in boxer briefs, and nothing else, solidifies the fact that Tina has already had dinner for the evening.

"Can I help you?"

"Uh, yeah, just delivering dinner," I reveal, handing the platter of food to him.

"Okay, thanks, but Tina didn't say she ordered dinner," he replies, taking the platter from me.

"I don't have cash for a tip, man, sorry," he tells me as beads of sweat roll through the nappy hair on his chest.

"Baby?" Tina makes her way to the front door, in an oversized white-T.

Disgusted by the sight, I make my exit, and hastily walk down the stairs.

She calls out to me. "Q? It's not what it looks like!" she shrills.

I don't respond.

"You know this dude?" the big, black buck questions.

"Q!" she runs behind me, grabbing my arm.

"Tina, really, it's okay. Have a nice life," I spit, snatching my arm away from this whore. I laugh out loud.

Looking her in the eyes, then to the horrible shape her night of fucking left her weave, I laugh again.

"Yep, have a nice life."

QUEEN
Wake Up Angel

"Mommy, where are you going?"
"Whisper something sweet to me.
Whisper something sweet to me.
Mama loves her baby.
Mama loves her baby.
From the sunshine to the night.
From the darkness to the light.
Queen loves her mommy.
And Mama loves her baby.
Whisper something sweet to me."
"I love you, Mommy."
"Cause Mama loves her baby."
"Bella, you don't have to do this! Stay home! We can work this out!"
"Frank. I can't do this to you or my Queen. This is for the best. Queen, take good care of your daddy, okay?"
"Okay, Mommy."
"I love you, Queen."
"I love you too, Mommy."
"Daddy? Why are you crying?"
"Because I'm sad, Queen."
"Why, Daddy?"
"Because your Mommy is not here."
"Mommy told me to take good care of you, Daddy. And that's what I'm going to do."

An all too familiar smell of White Diamonds penetrates my senses and pulls me from the depths of nowhere, or maybe

Heaven, or maybe my subconscious, or maybe I'm just being too prolific at what the clock reads as eight in the morning. My foggy eyes register the time, and as I prop myself up onto my pillow, I see a sight that makes me smile from the inside out. My best friend, Paula. Long black eyelashes bat "Good morning," and a smile as warm as the sun somehow assures me that everything will be all right. Paula's full-figured face, and butter soft skin is complimented by a glow, a radiance only God can bestow, and is often not found in contemporary women of modern society. She has the radiance and depth of our ancestors; Our "Nanas" and "Big Mamas." She is one of a kind; a strong black woman who in her own right disproves this myth that we can not get along, that we somehow can't and won't support one another. For me, Paula has been that rock, and I'd like to think I've been the same for her.

"So, you finally decide to wake from your beauty nap, eh?"

"Good morning, Paula. I was having the weirdest dream about my mother."

"Again?"

"Yeah."

"Was it a good one?"

"I went back to the last day I saw her. She sang my favorite song. I remember my father crying."

"Have you spoken to your Dad about this?" "I try, but he shuts me down when I bring it up."

"I see."

"So Paula, what brings you here so early?"

"I wanted to see your progress. I wanted to come by and spend some time with you before work. And to talk to you about the Bevens case."

"Shit!"

Trying to prop myself up a bit more, confirms that I really need to be in this hospital bed. My body aches something terrible. My legs, still shaky and weak, are so sore, but thank the good Lord I'm alive. My fingers reach my face slowly and I feel the bandages still wrapped firmly around my face.

"The doctor said your facial swelling is reducing considerably."

"Really?"

"Yep. And you have no major scars."

"Praise God."

"Praise."

"Queen, I knew God would not allow anything to happen to that gorgeous face and winning smile. That face is going to make Michael Bevens a free man."

"I surely hope so. He's innocent, Paula. I know I say that about all of the firm's clients, but this one, I know in my heart. He's innocent. I just hope I'm able to return to work to be there in court to defend him. If not, who's on the calendar to fill in?"

"George Royce is available."

"No, I have to get out of here. George is a dynamite defense attorney, but he doesn't know this case like I do. When is the trial set to begin?"

"Next Thursday, which leaves you one week and two days."

A lovely, soft and plump nurse walks into the room with breakfast for me. Her colorful scrubs, accompanied by her full hips, with limp to match, makes Paula's eyebrows raise with amusement. Her blonde, gheri curl hairstyle is totally unbelievable as those curls have been out of style since the late eighties. What's even more unbelievable is that the nurse is a white woman. Pleasant enough, so I simply say, "Thank you."

"You're quite welcome, Ms. Thomas. Let me know if you need anything else."

"I will."

Taking a glance at my breakfast tray makes me lose my appetite actually, as runny grits, micro-waved scrambled eggs, oven baked bacon, and watery orange juice has done what I've not been able to; put me on a much needed diet, which tells me that these extra twenty five pounds I carry with me for dear life, we will soon be departing.

"Queen?"

"Yes, Paula."

"How did you crash?"

"From what I recall, a deer ran in front of the truck."

"I see."

"Well, your Dad said the doctors told him you had multiple bruising,   and   wood   pieces   in   your   back."

"I ran into a tree, Paula."

"Some of the injuries were not consistent with the crash, Queen."

Going from first to third gear, I shift immediately, as the path of this conversation has me strolling down memory lane - dark memories that I wish would have faded upon impact.

"When is Sherri's funeral?"

"Not sure yet, Queen. Why?"

"I would like to go, Paula."

"I'll get the info and let you know."

"Thanks."

"How did you end up in the truck with Sherri? You hardly know her."

"Long story."

"I have time."

"I'm not putting another black man in jail, Paula."

"Just what I thought."

Not sure I want to know what Paula's thought is or was, so I circle my fork around the eggs and grits, pretending to be sincerely interested in how they'd taste together.

"He can't and won't get away with this, Queen."

"I'll deal with it."

"I've dealt with it, Queen."

"What do you mean?"

"I convinced Judge Owens to execute this TRO. She said she'd keep it under wraps. All you have to do is sign and I'll take care of the rest, Queen."

"Paula!"

"Queen, I love you with all my heart and soul. I know what's going on and I'm not going to allow this to happen anymore."

"Allow what?"

"You think I don't know that Derrick is beating on you?"

My head bows in shame and I want so badly to return to my dream; to fall asleep again, but really, that option is not a sound one, as my dreams as of late have all been about my mom. Maybe just sliding under the covers would be best, or pressing the distress signal for the nurses to rush in here to save my life would serve as a great distraction. None of that is plausible, however, so dealing with this now, is my only option, unless, of course, one of us drops dead in the next two seconds.

"He has hit me a few times, Paula. And trust me, its over for us. This last time, confirmed that officially."

"Is that right?"

"Absolutely."

"How do you plan to break the news, Queen?"
"I'm just going to tell him. Besides, he can't possibly think we're still together after what happened."
"And what was that?"

"He raped Sherri, Paula. I didn't see it, but Sherri told me right before the accident. Problem is, there's no way to prove it."
As Paula's eyes widen large as silver dollars, I can see the goose bumps rise on her arms, as they rise on mine-the realization of what occurred is still too horrifying to deal with completely.
"Oh my God! Poor Sherri!"
"Like I said, long story, Paula."
"You need to have him arrested."
"On what charges, Paula?"

"For beating your ass? For raping Sherri? For causing this accident?"
"Where's the proof, Paula? Five expert witnesses will testify that I got my injuries from the accident. And he'll simply deny the rest."

"I swear to God, I'm going to bring Derrick Simmons to justice, Queen. For you, for me and for Sherri."

"God speed, Paula. Right now, I just want to focus on getting out of this hospital and making Michael Bevens a free man."

"Promise me, Queen, that you will sign this restraining order. This will at least start the process."

As Paula places the restraining order paperwork on the sliding wood grain table before me, her eyes once again widen; a glossed covering reveals tears in her eyes. I feel her pain, take it on as if it is my own, well, it is my own agony. Never thought in my wildest dreams, and sometimes they are wild, but you couldn't pay me to believe that I would suffer from domestic abuse. An educated, fulfilled, strong and powerful black woman, an attorney for that matter, getting her ass beat? No way. Well, yes way. Thankfully, the abuse has not gone on as long as it could've, the abuse is not a vile as I've witnessed. Okay, who am I kidding? I got tossed like a salad one time too many, in the name of love, I suppose, although when I think about it, it wasn't love at all.

"You're right, Paula. I need to get this straight. It's over for Derrick and I. Now, I just have to let him know."
"How do you think he's going to take it?"
"I'm not sure. But he has to know after this ordeal, that this relationship can not go on."
"Queen?"
Paula takes my hand into hers, rubs it gently, providing much needed comfort.
"Yes, Paula," I smile, returning her comfort.
"What about the accident and the rape?"
"God will lead me in the right direction."
Leaning closer to become face to face with me, Paula gently kisses my forehead, I inhale to get another whiff of her White Diamonds perfume as it mixes with her radiant smile, her warm embrace as she hugs me, and it all melts my hard heart, making me whole.
"If God doesn't lead you in that direction, I'll ask Jesus to let me take the wheel."
"Ha, ha, ha. You're funny, Paula. I'm going to be fine. This situation will work out."
"I know, Queen, but you have to let go of the whole black man thing."
"What do you mean, Paula?"
"I mean, you can't allow a corrupt system, which houses all of our black men in jail, to keep you from doing the right thing here. Your work as a defense attorney is contribution enough. Please do not continue to take on that burden."
"I feel you. Love you, Paula."
"Love you, too."
"Get some rest and I will check on you later. Don't forget about the restraining order."

ھھھھھ

"When is Mommy coming back?"
"She's not, Queen."
"I miss Mommy."
"Me too, Queen."
"But it's my first day of school."
"I know and I'm here with you. You're going to do fine."

"Daddy, my ponytails are crooked. I can't go to kindergarten with crooked ponytails."
"You look fine, Queen."
"Daddy!"
"Trust me, Queen, your ponytails are fine. Besides you'll be the prettiest girl in the entire school."
"Okay, Daddy."
"Now, you walk in there, and make me proud. I'll be here waiting for you after school."
"I love you, Daddy."
"Love you too, Pumpkin."

❧❧❧❧❧

"Wake up, Angel," he sings as his rustic mustache brushes the little bit of face that is not under bandages.

My heart races, shoots and pounds through my chest as I am startled, like never before, and awakened by the man who tried to take my life, steal my existence, threaten my livelihood and sanity-he's here-evil in its most pure and deepest form.
"What are you doing here, Derrick?" I question while sliding the restraining order papers under my food tray.

"I'm here to check on my favorite lady," he reveals, taking my hand into his.

"Derrick, I know what you did," I confess, removing my hand from his, snatching back my dignity.

"And what is that?"

"Get out, Derrick."

As Derrick's fist presses against my rib cage, he bruises it on impact, pressing firmly into my side, causing excruciating pain and deep down terror. Leaning over, his massive chest hovers over me, and the stench of cheap cologne and funk penetrates my senses, making my skin crawl with disgust. A single kiss to my forehead is preceded by his eminent threat, "I'm not letting you go, Queen."

Pressing the distress key, I pray the nurse comes in with the swiftness. And she does.
"Is everything okay Ms. Thomas?"

Derrick gets out of the beige visitor's chair, faces the nurse and tells her, "All is fine. I was just leaving."
"Okay then. But let me check you out anyway, Ms Thomas. Just to make sure. You know, you're really quite blessed that

you survived such a horrific accident. God must really have you in his favor," she tells me as she attempts to make me more comfortable.

My eyes go from the nurse and up to Derrick, and back down to the nurse.

"God is on my side," I reveal looking Derrick square in his eyes, "He's my protector."

QUINCY
I Ain't No Joke

Flipping through the pages of *King* magazine reminds me of why I'm attracted to the women I'm attracted to. Ain't nothing better than a bangin' set of ass cheeks coated in caramel. I happen not to give a shit what anyone thinks-we all have our preference, and mine is what it t-i-s. I don't discriminate, however, as I've had a nice piece of vanilla ass in my day.

A Saturday morning with no hours on the board at the hospital at all is a rarity in my life, one that I would gladly accept on any given weekend. Sitting still is one of those things I believe we all happen to take for granted. I have no problems resting my ass comfortably on the couch and watching old Kung Fu flicks as the day passes by. Just as soon as I return from a trip to the gym, I'll happily spend the day with the remote, some take out buffalo wings and fries, a few Heinekens and the fifty-inch plasma. Shit, I may not even shower when I get home.

No sooner than my fantasy of being a lazy glutton for the day almost becomes my reality, does the phone ring, and I swear, this better not be a call about work, someone requesting a favor, Tina's whore ass begging for forgiveness or anything else I don't want to be bothered with today.

As my silver razor dances a jig on my glass and stainless steel coffee table, Michael Jackson sings one of my favorite tunes, and I reach over, escaping my comfort zone to pick the phone up. Opening the flip, I place the phone to my ear, "Hello?"

"Wassup, baby?" Big yells loud as all hell in my ear. Love my boy to death but I am too tired to run around town with his ass today.

As I prepare to come up with a quick and believable lie to get me out of whatever my man has in store for me today, Big beats me to the punch.

"Don't even try to lie, man. I know you ain't doing shit. You have the weekend off and yes, you're coming with me today."

Exhaling all of the air out of my system, I lean up and expel my true feelings to Big.

"If I didn't love yo' black ass, you would be doing this shit alone today. Where the hell are we going anyway?"

"Listen, you blue-eyed bandit…"

"Damn, Big, you just don't know how much I DON'T feel like doing anything today."

"Just listen. Man, Auntie is having trouble down there in J.C. I need to take her some food and get some things together in the house for her."

With a look of disbelief written all over my entire face, I sit up more as this shit has my full attention.
"Are you serious, man? What the fuck are your cousins doing down there?"

Big's sigh greets me on the other end of this phone. I can feel his disappointment in the question I posed.

"Q, my cousins ain't shit, you know that, you lived it with me. Ree-Ree is still on that shit and all of the rest of them ain't worth two nickels."

"It's too bad, man. But yeah, I'm down. Let's go handle this."

"Thanks, man. I'll swing by and pick you up in about an hour."

"Ha," I laugh and stand up.

"What are you laughing about, Q?"

"Big, your black ass never gets anywhere on time. You say one hour; that translates into about two. So, I'll see you when you get here."

"Fuck you, Q!"

"Yeah, ditto, bitch! Oh yeah, Big?"

"What, man?"

"Clean that dirty ass truck before you get over here."

"Yeah, Q, fuck you, man. But, will do."

"You have got to be the dirtiest motherfucker I've ever met. You live like a pig, man."

"Damn, Q, I said, I'll clean the shit! Damn!"

"Big?"

"What, bitch?"

"Uhm, how are you ever gon' get a wife living the way you do?"

"Look you blue-eyed-black-man-wannabe, everybody ain't tryin' to get married like you. Lookin' for love in all the wrong weaves…"

"That's fucked up, Big."

"Yeah well, you asked for it. I'ma get me a mail-in order Russian bride who will clean my house, there, feel better now?"

"If you say so, fool, I'll see you in a bit."

"Thanks, man. See you in a minute."

"Alright, brother."

☙☙☙☙☙

Crossing the bridge which connects New Jersey and Pennsylvania boasts timeless beauty as green grass and frosty mixtures cover sides of rocky mountains. Big cracks his window slightly to allow the fresh, crisp, mountain air in, as it blends with the heat that blasts within this massive truck, that keeps us from freezing. A nice blend of chill and warmth, on this winter-kissed Saturday afternoon.

As my eyes roam, I see that my man has actually taken the time to clean the car. From the new air-freshener dangling from the rearview mirror, to the Armor-All wiped dashboard and the freshly vacuumed floor, Big listened to my plea for him to clean his shit before he picked me up. His black, extended Suburban has enough room to fit ten motherfuckers in here; it's like a living room on wheels, equipped with navigation, DVD player, heated and cooled seats-the works. Not that my ride is a piece of shit, but dayum, he went all out for this one. Had to set him back about seventy-g's. I'm a minimalist and cheap, so my stuff is nice, but standard. A black Navigator sits in my driveway, and its just fine in my book.

As Big drives, we listen to classic old-school Hip-Hop, the kind we grew up listening to. Eric B. & Rakim set the mood for our ride to Jersey City, with the classic, "Paid in Full" and provides a trip down memory lane. Perfect time for me to fuck with my boy.

The radio sings with heavy bass, "thinking of a master plan."

"Yo, Big, remember when you came over the summer of 1987?"

Big smiles that big ass gorilla smile and turns to face me quickly, before looking back at the road, which is a good idea, since he's driving today.

"Yeah, man, I remember that! Lisa and Hanifah, I remember them so well."

I laugh out loud because I was hoping Big would remember those tricks. He throws in two additional cents for good measure.

"Yeah, Q, I remember how Hanifah didn't want to give you the time of day with your white ass," he jokes and laughs out loud.

"You know man, I was hoping you would say something about that."

"And why is that, Q?"

The fucking with my man begins. A grin that exemplifies the word "cheese" overcomes me as I rev up to spit fire at my man this afternoon.

"Yeah Patrick," I call him by his real name for this one, "We were listening to this song right here, "Paid in Full" by Eric B. & Rakim. You remember that?"

"Yeah, Q, I remember that and now I'm sorry I said anything."

Laughter consumes me whole.

"Ha ha, yeah, you remember, right?"

"Yeah, Q, I remember," he confesses with a shit-grin on his face.

"You got paid in full that day, right man?"

"Yeah man, damn. Next subject."

"Lisa gave you the clap, syphilis and gonorrhea, man?"

"Yes, Q, you were there, you lily white bitch!"

"Ha, ha, how the hell does anyone get all three?"

Suddenly the look in Big's eyes change from embarrassment to empowerment, as he looks at me, noticing how loud I'm laughing, he tells me, "Bitch, he who laughs last, laughs loudest."

"What?"

"Yeah boy! Uh, Q, while you are having a ball laughing at my black ass, let us not forget that shit you pulled on Hanifah."

"Awe, fuck you Big!"

I throw my hands up.

"Yeah, its fuck me now, right?"

"Man, whatever."

"Your ass was so hard up for some black punany, Q, that you told the poor girl that you were black!!!!" Big yells and laughs.

"Yeah, whatever man."

"Yeah, Q, now laugh at that shit!"

"Yes, I am laughing, because I got that ass, didn't I?"

Placing his hand on his chin as if he is deep in thought, Big responds, "Yeah, as a matter of fact you did get that ass, and just the ass. I got the ass and the crabs!"

Big's face immediately turns from joy to sorrow, so I inquire.

"Big, what's up, man?"

"Five-O, brother."

"Awe, damn."

"Why are you awe-damning?"

"It's five-o, Big."

"Yeah, but your blues ain't like mine, Quincy."

"I realize that, man and I'm sorry."

"Nothing for you to be sorry about, man. Just hand me the registration and insurance out of the glove box. They tryin' to catch me ridin' dirty, man."

Reaching into the glove box, I pull Big's insurance card and registration out and hand it to him as he pulls to the shoulder of the road. Turning my head, I look behind us, out of the back window to the truck, and see a state trooper in full uniform and matching hat, walk up to the driver's side of the truck. The nervous look in Big's eyes, confirms what he always says, that no matter how successful, rich, and a good citizen you are, and whether or not you break the rules or live life to near perfection, a black man will always have a cross to bare. As Big rolls down the window, the state trooper remarks, "License and registration, please."

Big hands the trooper both cards.

Through a set of thin Caucasian lips, the trooper cynically questions, "Nice truck. How long did you have to work for this?"

Big nervously and angrily responds, "A few years."
The trooper laughs out loud. "Yeah, right. Probably a few months, and let me guess, you paid in cash?" He begins to walk away, and heads back to the police car.

Big looks at me with a look of disgust on his face. I try to make him laugh.

"Man, did you see that hat? And that tight ass uniform?"

"Nah man, all that's on my mind is, is this cop going to harass me? Plant something in my truck? Pull his gun out? Arrest me? Will I be on the news tonight? Will my name legally change to Rodney King today? Nah, Q, gots bigger things on my mind at the moment."

"Damn, Pat, sorry man."
Big takes a look at his rearview mirror.

"He's coming back. I know my shit is straight."
As the trooper approaches, Big's rather large body cringes.
The trooper hands him the cards and Big hands them to me. I hold on to them, and will return them to the glove box after we pull off. Don't need to give this pig any reason to do anything.

"You're clean," the trooper tells Big.

"Thanks, officer," Big responds between clinched teeth.
The trooper offers an explanation.

"I pulled you over because I thought your tail light was out."

"Well, is it?" Big questions sarcastically.

"No, it's not."

"That's good to know."

"What do you do for a living?"

"I own a construction company, officer."
The trooper laughs out loud.

"Oh yes, and this man next to you is one of your workers, right?"
My compulsion prompts me to jump in right away, in defense of my best friend.

"No officer, my name is Dr. Quincy Hughes, and I am an emergency room doctor at the medical center in the Poconos. My friend here, my best friend, owns Exclusive Home Construction and builds quality homes in the Poconos. We're both listed, and active members of our community. And for the record, my man did pay for this car in cash, as I paid for mine, and it's an economical decision made by two professionals, not because we're drug dealers. I've taken down your badge number and will be forwarding a letter of complaint to the state, sir."

"Son, I suggest you watch your mouth, before you and your black friend are locked up for the weekend under suspicion of illegal contraband."

"Just shut up, Q. Leave it alone," Big implores.

"Yeah, Q, leave it alone," the trooper throws his hands up like a rapper would when he remarks the letter "Q."

"Nah, Big, see, I have 911 on the cell now, so they're listening to this whole line of questioning and harassment coming from state trooper, uh, is it McElroy?"

"Uh, you all have a nice day. And if I catch you speeding again, you won't be so lucky next time."

Big rolls up the window in the middle of the trooper's sentence, and pulls off the shoulder of the road, and proceeds down the highway.

Eric B. & Rakim's *"I Ain't No Joke"* appropriately plays and I turn the volume up to its capacity. We both look at one another and laugh in unison.

ೞೞೞೞೞ

Crossing over another bridge, this time it leads from Big's hometown of Newark, to mine of Jersey City, and what a difference an hour makes. Stale air replaces fresh and easy breathing, concrete everywhere, zombies walking through the streets and a liquor store on every corner, highlights all that is negative in inner city life. Balancing it all, is quite frankly, the inner city. Nowhere in Pocono City can you get an Italian cheeseburger, full of fatty French fries, laced in onions, peppers on a long sub roll, the calories equivalent of two day's worth of what a person needs. Nor can you find a mile-high corned beef on rye, with coleslaw and Russian dressing, or fried fish, macaroni and cheese and all the other artery clogging eating that makes the inner city worth driving to on a Saturday afternoon. And holla, you won't find lovely Latinas, or beautiful black women of all shapes and sizes and hues, walking the streets, on their way to the gym or train station or corner store, whether they are a round-a-way girl, or a corporate Mami, they provide rich eye-candy for all of us.

The inevitable occurs.

"Q, you wanna stop and get something to eat?"

"Yeah, Big, but man, you need to slow down with all this fatty food, man."

"Yeah, I know, but shit, I ain't been down here in a minute and I want me a double Italian cheese steak from Roberto's. You down?"

"Hell yeah, I'm down."

"Alright man, let's eat, then we can head to Auntie's house."

"Cool, and while we're there, I want to stop in and see Miss Anna."

As Big parks the truck on a corner in Jersey City, right next to Roberto's, a pizzeria and sandwich shop that's been here since the 1960's, he smiles and sighs.

"Yeah, Q, I ain't seen Miss Anna for a good while. I remember having the craziest crush on her when I was younger, man. That long hair, and fat booty, shit man, I was like, when I grown up, I'm gonna marry Miss Anna."

"Word, Big? I felt the same way. Something about the way she looked in those skirts when she would go to work, had me feeling some kind of way. And don't forget about them big tits either."

"Shit, can't forget about the tits, man. I just wanted to run up to her and put my head right in the middle of all that glory."

"Man, you crazy, Big!"

"Yeah, you too, Q."

৵৵৵৵৵

My cell phone dances a jig, as the tight sounds of Marvin Gaye's *"I Want You"* interrupts my date with this turkey and cheese sub. I opted to take the lesser of the two evils, and not do the fried food thing today. As my phone rings, it reminds me that I never took Tina's number out of my phone, nor erased her special ring tone. Can't believe I ever messed with that trick. I must've been out of my mind. Well, no, I wasn't out of my mind, just horny, I suppose.

"Q, who's that, man?"

"Tina."

"Aren't you going to answer that?" Big questions through greasy, heart-attack-waiting-to-happen lips.

"Nah, man."

"Trouble in Paradise?"

"Fuck you, man."

"What?" he again questions as he wipes his mouth.

"Man, Tina is full of shit."

As Big places his gigantic hand next to his right ear, he gets up, right in the middle of Roberto's and starts a dance. Still with hand to ear, he jokes.

"Did you say something, Q?"

"No, bitch, I didn't."

"Oh, that's funny, because I thought you said, Big, you were right about that ho."

"Nah, I ain't said that you big, black, fuck. But since you said it for me…"

"Yeah, I knew it. So tell Daddy what happened," he smiles as he sits down from his dancing Fame moment.

"I went by her house to surprise her with dinner. You remember that night."

"Yeah, I remember. I told your white ass not to go."

"Yeah, man, should have listened."

"Yeah, I…"

"Shut the hell up, Big. So anywho, this big ass black dude answers the door. Sweaty and shit. You could smell all that ass as soon as the door opened."

"Word, Q?"

"Yeah, man, then her nasty ass comes to the door, weave-a-licious, looking like a dick just dropped out of her mouth."

Big's laugh sends thunder through the eatery.

"Yeah, Big, I ain't fucking with her no more. I'm waiting until I find true love, man."

"What?" Big questions and he places the back of his hand on my forehead. I knock his hand off of my head.

"Man, I'm serious. I need me a woman. A good woman, one woman to love me. That's all I want."

"Well, you are a doctor, you got a little paper, no babies, and you white, so you should have no problem in that area, bitch."

"We'll see."

"But Q, what prompted the sudden realization?"

"I think the E.R. is getting to me, man. Seeing all of the lives changed in the blink of an eye, man it's fucking with me. I'm ready to share my life with someone, man. I realize that one day, I'll be dead and gone, but until that day comes, I want to be with someone. Granted, I save many lives, but the one's that I can't, those people have a story, a history, and I just feel real fucked up, mostly with the ones who have no family coming in to claim them. I don't want to be alone, man, my playing days are over."

"Damn, man, that's deep. So, let me ask you something, Q."

"Sure, man, what's up?"

"What you gone do about getting some ass? What's going on with that lady in the hospital, uh, what's her name again?"
"Who you talking about, Carmella?"
"Yeah."
"Shit, man. She's not my type. You know what I like."
"Oh yeah, man, growing up in Jersey City has got you with a permanent case of Jungle Fever."
"Fuck you, Big. But on the real man, I don't see it that way. You know Mom and Dad never played the race card. Yeah, I'm white, but I don't look at people that way. I like women of color, not because I don't like white women, it's just because I like what I like, that's all."

"I hear that, man. More people need to be open-minded like that."

"I think so."

"But, Q, it's never gonna happen."
"I know that, too, Big."

ଈଈଈଈଈ

Many luxury condos, skyscrapers and office complexes are going up like Leggos in Jersey City. Endless brick row houses located in the Harsimus Cove district of Historic Downtown Jersey City, boasts a commuters dream with a very short walk to the Grove Street PATH station, for those who work in Manhattan. I did the Manhattan hospital scene for a few years myself, then opted to follow my family to the Poconos, and haven't looked back.

Stepping further into reality, takes us from touring the city's growth, to what's really going on here. Making a left onto the block where I grew up, and where Big spent most of his summers, reveals that too many things have changed, mostly for the worse. The block is just not the same, as many crack addicts roam without purpose or direction; gang members have marked their directory via graffiti on garage doors and street signs, and have sprinkled in a few murders for good measure. No, the 1970's have come and gone and the innocent, urban struggle we all endured, with trips to the corner store for penny candy, walks home from public school, and a few, clean fist fights, have all been replaced with drive by shootings, middle-class families scraping to pay for private school, and no more fighting like a man, you'll get shot like a dog first.

"Damn, Dr. Hughes, this ain't your Mamma's Jersey City," Big remarks and he pulls into an empty parking space in front of his Aunt's home.

"Yeah, I know, Big, this is some sad shit to witness, man."

Glancing to my right, I see so many sitting on Auntie's stoop, and all are not relatives. Sure, there are a few of Big's cousins, but who are the rest of these motherfuckers? My head shifts to the left, and I don't have to say a word, as Big looks at me with the look of disdain in his eyes.

"Yo, Q, what the hell is going on here?"

"Shit, beats the hell out of me. Let's go in and do what we can."

"No doubt."

As Big and I get out of the truck, all eyes are on us, from the little children running up and down the street, to the onlookers hanging out of windows, being nosey as fuck, to the people on the stoop, and we still haven't figured out who the hell these bitches are. Big's massive presence, commands attention from all the lurkers as he walks up the brick staircase to his Aunt's house, and I follow suit.

"Who y'all is?" the obvious junkie with the burgundy micro braids question.

"Who the hell are you?" Big asks. If he was any angrier, smoke and flames would begin to shoot out of his nostrils.

"Don't worry about who I am fat boy," junkie girl replies.

As Big leans over to get in her face, the remaining people on the stairs move out of the way. "Listen here. You get the hell off of my Aunt's porch, before I call the cops. Matter of fact, I'm calling the cops now. Get the fuck off of the porch. Ya heard?"

Everyone scatters like roaches with the lights on.

"Pat? Pat? Is that you?" Big's aunt questions as she looks out the window. He tilts his head up and sees his aunt. "Yeah, Auntie, it's me. I'm coming up now."

A smile crosses her face.

"You got Quincy with you, Pat?"

"Yes, m'am."

"Oh, good, y'all come on up."

Entering Auntie's apartment on the second floor, reveals what I thought all along. She's being taken advantage of because she's getting old. Her hardwood floors are still pristine, as is her living room, where I have a seat. Auntie approaches me, leans over and gives me a kiss on the cheek.

"Hey, Auntie."

"Quincy, you look good son."

"Thanks, Auntie."

"Auntie, where's Ree-Ree and everyone?" Big questions as he paces from the dining room to the living room.

"Ree-Ree, well, I haven't seen Ree-Ree in days, and ain't nobody else done came around. Ain't got my social security in the mail this month, ain't bought no food, lights 'bout to go out and everything."

"What, Auntie?"

"You heard me, Patrick. That's why I called you. You's the only one I could call."

"Well, I got you, Auntie. Go and get me the bills that need paying and I'll write out checks and get them in the mail today. And give me your last social security check stub, we're going to get direct deposit for you. What's going on with the mortgage?"

"Mortgage paid, baby."

"Thank God, Auntie. Next time, don't wait this long to call me. You need food?"

"Some. Anna in the kitchen making some tea right now for us. You know we gone watch the food channel tonight and drink our tea."

"Miss Anna?" Big questions and looks at me. We both go back to our jokes from earlier.

"Yes, Patrick, ain't that what I said? Miss Anna Belle in the kitchen. Here she come now."

A smile comes over me as I get up from my seat to greet Miss Anna also known as Miss Belle with a hug and a kiss. Big leans in to give her a hug, and lifts her off of her feet. Even though she's aged, Miss Anna still looks good. And if I was twenty-five years older, I'd step to her.

She still adorns the most beautiful white teeth, with a smile that will melt your heart. Smooth, butterscotch skin, with long flowing brown soft hair, pouty full lips, I'm instantly reminded of why all the boys in the neighborhood loved her so when we were growing up.

"Y'all boys are looking good!" Miss Anna says with that big, bold and beautiful smile. She continues. "How's the Poconos?"

"Oh, Miss Anna, it's beautiful. You have to visit," I tell her. "I want to. Me and your Auntie will have to come one weekend."

"We have plenty of room, Mom and Dad are there too, Big has a huge house, come when you're ready."

"Me and Miss Anna will do, son, will do."

QUEEN
Bloody Murderer

Homemade signs that scream "Bloody Murderer" in bright and bold crimson colored blocked letters are carried proudly by protestors who were anxious for the day when the court would confirm my client's guilt and put him away for life, throwing him under the jail and flushing any keys to his emancipation down the drain. If they only knew, what I truly believe in my heart, that Michael Bevens is innocent, they'd pack their pick-it signs and go home, apologetically, with their judgmental tails between their legs. All defense attorneys believe in their client's innocence, I suppose. I know, for a fact that Michael didn't kill those two little girls in Pocono almost eighteen months ago. Knowing is only half the battle.

I glance at my light skin, which adorns goose bumps that crawl up my forearm as I put the rental car in park. The protestors fill the parking lot to the county's federal courthouse. Hip-Hop has taken me through some of my darkest hours and today is no different. Public Enemy's "Fight the Power" blasts and reverberates throughout the car – this is my food for thought, my drug of choice, my reminder that there is definitely a battle ahead of me. Staring out of the window of the Nissan Altima my insurance company provided while my truck is being repaired, I see the faces of anger and hurt, rage and contempt for a man they believe is guilty of slaughtering two innocent girls. The thought of those two, precious white girls, savagely beaten and thrown out like two-day old trash, has turned part of the community into the modern day war of the roses. Black, Latino, white, and any other race you can dare to imagine, are among the protestors, as this heinous crime has surpassed racial, political and even socio-economical barriers. I even cringe when I think of the crime scene photos; two friends, on their way home from school, walking innocently and carelessly through unpaved streets, and quiet calm, heading home from a school, much better than the one they went to previously in the inner city. Skipping through life without a care in the world, through a community which boasts all of the joys of living, a safe haven from the world of drugs, alcohol and crime that torments so many living in the ghetto. The streets of Pocono, were like streets of gold, lined with cookie cutter houses that many could afford, low taxes that made relocation a dream, and the safety and comfort of knowing that your little girl can walk home from school with her sister, without a care in the world.

Snap back into reality, and the world as I know it, as a criminal defense attorney, has seen up close and all too well the unforgiving truths of life. Being quite familiar of the pains and pleasures and heartaches of the human experience, I've come to learn one thing from being on both sides of the inner city and suburban fence; crime is crime, horror is horror and no matter how many white picket fences, or perfectly landscaped lawns, or beautiful walks in the nearby park will ever change humanity. There are devils everywhere, no matter how low the taxes are.

Pablo, a bailiff spots me and comes over to the car, walking his way through the crowd to assist me with getting into the courthouse. I hand him my briefcase as I slowly get up from my seat, still sore in many spots, but determined. Determined to defend this man to the best of my ability, busted lip, swollen face, limp and cane in tow.

"Queen, are you okay?" Pablo questions through soft and pretty Latino lips. The batting of his eyes exposes his long eyelashes.

"Hey there, Pablo. Thanks for the help. Yes, I'm fine. Was in a car accident," I reveal, downplaying recent events through a parting of red, swollen lips.

"Wow, sorry to hear that. You should be home resting, Queen," he tells me as he gingerly tries to escort me through the insanity.

As he gives me much needed support, Pablo escorts me through the chaos and leads me into the courthouse, where the true madness begins today.

"Will you be okay, Queen?"

"Sure, Pablo and thanks."

I politely take my briefcase from Pablo's hand. He opens the door to Room 38, the room where the trial, State vs. Bevens is set to begin.

"Should I tell Derrick you're here?"

Panic consumes my entire being and knots take over my insides when I'm reminded of the horror that stands in the way of me and freedom. Derrick Simmons. In my mind, body, soul, spirit and with every breath I take, I pray he's out of my life for good, but since nothing in my life has ever been easy, the truth slaps me boldly in the face when I realize just from Pablo's question alone that Derrick is not out of my life, he is very much in my existence as he is the reason for my current circumstance, and has proven to be an inevitable certainty.

A crooked smile takes over my face. "No, Pablo. That's okay, but thanks anyway."

Perhaps going out with Pablo when he initially pursued, would have, without a doubt, been the better choice, but Derrick's charm coupled with his big, black presence made him quite irresistible. Somewhere, deep down in my soul, I knew Derrick was the wrong choice for me, but when I stumbled upon this reality, I was in too deep.

"Okay, Queen. I'll look for you when the day is over to get you out of the courthouse," Pablo confirms with the sexiest grin. I return his smile. "Thanks, Pablo."

My sore behind shifts side to side just as sexy as it had swayed prior to the accident, in a navy blue knee-length skirt, with matching single-breasted jacket, which overlays an ivory colored satin chemise which drapes just above the double-d's seductively, and not inappropriately. My mother left me with a few things; beauty and brains, so I use both, on a daily basis. Walking down the aisle of the courtroom, I look down, staring at the burgundy standard carpet as to avoid the crowded room of onlookers, lurkers, protestors, observers and reporters.

"Nice of you to join us this morning, Ms. Thomas," Judge Randolph teases as I approach the defense table. I look up to him with a sly smile, hoping that my charm will prevent any further embarrassment. Because if my life gets any more complicated, I'll be forced into early retirement, via a padded cell, vanilla colored walls, and a black floor mat which will replace the living room sofa.

Brushing my hair from my shoulder, I look up to Judge Randolph, "I apologize, your Honor."

"So, Ms. Thomas, may the court inquire as to what happened to your face?"

"Oh, your Honor, I was in a car accident and am still bruised and broken sort of."

"Okay. And you're well enough to proceed with trial?"

"Yes, your honor, I am."

"Very well."

"Thank you, your Honor. If I may have just one word with my client?"

The courtroom's overhead lights shine off the top of Judge Randolph's salt and pepper, silky hair. Pale, white skin, a clean shaven face, and piercing blue eyes, makes me think that Judge Randolph used to be the shit in his day. Tall and slim, he's known throughout the small legal community in this county as a good catch, if older, rich, and sexy, oh yeah, and white, is what you're looking for. As for myself, I've only been with a black man, so I have no interest. Besides, it's unethical for me to even have this conversation, even if it is with myself.

"Very well, Ms. Thomas," he slams his gavel, "Court will resume in ten minutes."

Approaching my client, Michael's eyes connect with mine, and his fear carries over to my spirit. When I glance at the rows behind him, I see the face of his mother, Patricia Bevens, whose been by her son's side since day one, professing his innocence also. On both sides of her are Michael's siblings, Felicia and Renee, his younger sisters, ages twenty and twenty-two respectively, and his younger brother, Patrick, age nineteen. It's admirable, the support Michael has, and I love how his younger siblings admire him so, even in the midst of this unimaginable horror. They are all too familiar with how society views black men, how they are often times guilty until proven innocent, and realize the unsympathetic veracity of Michael committing two very deadly modern world sins; fucking a white woman, which most people suspected, one that he was dating at the time and being suspected, and charged with killing two little white girls.

Michael's appearance is typical in some respects to what some of our younger black men wear as attire these days. His covered in corn rows in his hair, which are done nicely, but leaves room for people to assume he's up to no good. His dark skin is majestic, but makes some people uncomfortable. He sorta reminds me of Michael Vick. Very pleasing to the eye.

We have an uphill battle. God is on our side.

Reaching the empty seat next to Michael, I sit down; take his hand in mine, now they're both trembling. Looking to my right, I gaze into the windows to Michael's soul, and witness the vulnerability and fear that many black men face when falsely accused of wrongdoing.

"Michael, we have to have faith. I'm going to do the best I can for you and for your family," I tell him as I rub his hand in an attempt to provide comfort and reassurance.

"You didn't kill those girls, right, Michael?" I question, demanding an honest answer.

"I didn't kill those girls Ms. Thomas, you have my word," he expels convincingly between clinched teeth and eager eyes.

"Okay, so we're going to get through this, Michael." Before I can catch my breath and get in another word edgewise, Patricia leans in, "You're so smart, Ms. Thomas. Thank you for helping my child."

"Thank you, Mrs. Bevens; I will do my best for your family."

"You're so smart, chile. You talk so good and white," she ignorantly reveals.

"Thank you," I say, managing not to confess my disdain for her last comment.

My Dad spent an immense amount of time and effort convincing me and teaching me that becoming educated is not the equivalent of "Acting white." He often told me that when people tell you that, they're really giving white folks too much credit. So, that's what I've come to believe. It's a God-damned shame that in the twenty-first century that we still equate being well educated with being white and reaching the promised land.

QUINCY
Liberation

O kay, fella, you have to listen to your Mommy, and let her take good care of this cold, okay?" I tell little Roger, who's come into the emergency room today, full of snot, a terrible head cold, fever and aches and pains. No true emergency, but I get where Mom is coming from. Speaking of Mom, where is she coming from? Honey-dip has been eyeing me since I pulled the curtain closed to examine her son. And why is she in the emergency room with four-inch stilettos? A wannabe Anna Nicole Smith, yes, she could get the business, but I'd be bored an hour afterwards, so I'll pass. Cut kid though.

Glancing at the paperwork again to get little Roger's last name, she beats me to the punch. As she reaches out her hand to shake mine, in an attempt to thank me, I noticed the full cleavage that sits up just as perky. Again, a bit inappropriate for an emergency room visit.

"It's Cassandra. I mean, Ms. Cassandra Manahan. Thanks so much for taking care of my little Roger."

I return her handshake. "Sure, Ms. Manahan, no problem. Make sure he gets plenty of fluids, orange juice, apple juice, water, hot tea, if he'll drink it."

Looking once more to recap little Roger's age. "Yep, since he's seven, there's no real danger here. He'll be just fine. Ms. Manahan, is he allergic to anything?"

Through pursed lips, and blue eyes, which look like Halloween contact lenses, bleached blonde hair, and long red

fingernails, Anna, I mean, Ms. Manahan seductively replies, "No. He's not allergic to anything."
I smile.

"Very well," I pull my prescription pad out of my lab jacket pocket, "have this filled, and in about a week, he'll be back to new. Do follow up with your son's regular physician as soon as you can."

Reaching out her hand to grab the script, she bends, leans in slightly to give me a sneak peak of her well-endowed bosom, entrapped in a tight-ass Chrissy from Three's Company sweater.

"Thank you, Dr. Hughes."

"You're welcome."
Patting little Roger on his head, I open the curtain and make my way out of the makeshift exam room. Placing my pen and prescription pad back into my white lab coat, I hear her say, "Uh, Dr. Hughes?"
I turn around to face Ms. Manahan.

"Yes?"

She moves in closer to me and whispers, "Um, I was just wondering if you'd like to go out for coffee one day?"
I grin from ear to ear in flattery. "I really can't, Ms. Manahan. But thank you, I'm flattered."

A look of disappointment crosses her face as she reaches into her purse and pulls out her card.

"Well, here," she hands the card to me, "If you have a change of heart, the offer will always stand."
"Thank you," I reply as I take the card and make my way out of the exam room, this time with a pep in my step.

Walking across pristine white floors, throughout an emergency room that boasts no real emergencies today, I glide toward my office, and in the process, my hip vibrates just a bit as my phone rings. Pulling my white lab coat back, I reach down to my right hip and retrieve my phone. Looking at the screen to determine who's calling, only leaves me with a question in my head, as the screens says "Private." I normally wouldn't answer a call that registers as such, but I've learned, as a doctor, to pick up each and every call, so I do.

"Good afternoon, this is Dr. Hughes."

"Q?"

"Yes, this is Quincy."

"Q! Why you playin' like that? I been callin' you for weeks."

Little does Tina know that if it weren't for the fact that I am at work, she'd really get a verbal slashing. I smile, to maintain my composure, as I walk pass Carmella, and Georgia, a physician's assistant and make my way into my office.

"Tina, what do you want?"

"Oh, baby, I miss you, Q. I'm dyin' to see you baby."

"Ha, ha. You've got to be kidding me, Tina. Sorry, but I thought you got the message that our so called relationship is over."

"What?"

"Yes, Tina. We are no longer a couple, or fuck buddies, or whatever you want to classify us as."

"And why not?"

"Tina, I don't have time for this today. Later."

"You bet not hang up on me, Q. I ain't did nothin' to you but give you some good ass, now you trippin' fool."

"Tina, maybe your recollection is different from mine, but as I recall, the last time I saw you, you were, what appeared to be, uh, fucking Paul Bunyan or was it Andre the Giant?"
I had to throw that in there for comic relief. This shit is truly unbelievable.

"That was my cousin, Q."

"So, you're fucking your cousin, Tina? I thought people did that kind of stuff down south somewhere. What, my dick wasn't enough for you? You sure acted like it was."

"Quincy, come on, you know I love that long dick you got. You funny, Q. So, when can I come see you? What time are you gettin' home? Let me taste that big dick again."

"Tina, actually, I'm glad things happened the way they did. I realize now that I don't want someone to fuck that I can't trust. I'm gonna wait and see what happens. I ain't messin' around no more."

"Ha, ha, ha, you crazy, Q. You a crazy white boy! I know you want some of this ass!"

"Me being white has nothing to do with it, Tina. And no, to be honest, I don't want any of your ass. Not anymore. I'm going to tell you something, Tina. Being in this emergency room, day in and day out, has shown me that life is too short. The next woman I get some ass from will be the woman I'll spend the rest of my life with. You need to grow up, get serious, and stop fucking around. Later, Tina."

"You done lost your fuckin' mind."

Click.

Opening the door to my office, I look out to see Carmella staring in. Placing the phone back into its holster, I continue to walk out of the office, and to the nurse's station only to find Carmella waiting and wanting me to justify her love. It's not happening, though.

Batting her eyes, Carmella stares at me as I reach over to grab the next record of admission. She hands it to me, and I pull the paperwork from her hand, and slide the papers from her ruby red fingertips. She smiles. Through fire engine red lips, she smiles, exposing a mouth full of perfectly bleached teeth.

"Here you go, Dr. Hughes."

I return her smile. "Thank you, Carmella."

"You're more than welcome. Anytime, Dr. Hughes."

I laugh silently on the inside. A few more weeks of abstinence and I may have to put a paper bag, with Halle Berry's picture affixed, over Carmella's wrinkled face, and give her the business. I'm reaching, but it could happen. Not really though.

"You're very kind, Carmella. Thanks again."

At least four nurses stand by Carmella's side, and, as I make my way to the next examining room, I can feel the heat on my back, as their eyes try to pierce me from behind.

My cell rings again, vibrations pound my hip, reaching down I pull the phone from the holster, and read the screen once again. Reading the infamous "Private" once again, I decline the offer to engage once again in a verbal assault from a former, now jilted ex-lover, and make my way on to more important things this afternoon, one of which is to save someone's life.

I quietly whisper, "Go to hell, Tina."

And with that one statement, I feel liberated.

QUEEN
Everlasting Life

"For God so loved the world, that he gave his only begotten Son, that whosoever believeth in him should not perish, but have everlasting life," the church's pastor says softly as mourners enter the doors of Jerusalem Baptist Church. Glancing around the church, I see mahogany pews full of heartbroken people, to pay honor to a woman, a life, long gone, too soon. Grief-stricken family members hold on to one another for dear life, as they cry, deep-hearted sobs full of unbearable grief, as today is the day of their daughter's, sister's, cousin's, friend's final rest. Today is the day Sherri goes home to meet the Lord.

And what a deeply sad day it is. Feeling faint and dizzy, I manage to take another step forward, as I stand in line. The line to view Sherri's body is long, full of all races and creeds, people from the courthouse and various law enforcement entities from up here on the mountain have come out in droves to pay respect to a woman, a sister, so full of possibilities and laughter, promise and energy, hope and light, one whose path to righteousness was darkened tragically and brought to an abrupt halt in the wonder years of her existence.

I look to my left, and as I turn my head, my neck stiffens, the remnants of being broken and bruised in the car accident in which God spared my life, but called on Sherri to come home.

I remember Sherri and although we weren't close, I remember seeing her in the courthouse and she would tell me how she wanted to go to law school. I encouraged her, told her to go, don't let nothing stop you. She was excited about the possibilities.

The deep pain and guilt threatens to make me weak in the knees, but I need to remain strong as those here who know of the collision have expressed how grateful to God they are that at least I made it. But as the line moves forward, and this time I glance to my right, I see the pain that a mother endures when she outlives her child. My heavy heart cries for Sherri's mom. She will never see her daughter alive again, and as I move up another step, I glance down to see my black leather heels, and my eyes trace up my leg, staring at my off-black pantyhose, as if I'm sincerely interested in them. Anything beats looking at Sherri's mother. But, I have to. The guilt I carry in my heart won't let my eyes leave her again. I want to die and take Sherri's place, if only for a moment, so her mom can once again be comforted, be full, be happy. When your child dies, I'm sure you lose a part of yourself, not only because Sherri was her child, but also because of the way Sherri and her mom have become entwined with each other's identity. What is she going through right now? I wonder and my heart aches thinking about her. Is she experiencing an overwhelming sense of failure because she thought she could protect Sherri and keep her safe forever? She is witnessing, in the harshest way possible, that she was wrong. As a mother, she couldn't protect her, well, at least, not on that fateful, dreaded night, and, neither could I. Is she feeling the unfairness of her death? Because God knows I am. The natural order of things is that parents die before their children; anything else is misery, full of anguish, sorrow and unbearable pain. Sherri's death goes against nature, as it is a disaster; an immutable truth that is devastatingly, a catastrophe.

When I look at her mom, I see Sherri in her, from the bubbling brown skin, to the full cheeks, even her lips, Sherri is her mother's daughter in every sense of the word. And as I witness her grief, I wonder if I was lying in that casket, and if my mom were here, would she grieve the same. Seems like I've grieved for Momma since I was four, so that means I've felt a void in my life for thirty years. I've grieved every day since the last day I saw my Mom. When she told me to take good care of my Dad, I wore that instruction like a badge of honor, and even at that tender age, I knew it my duty to stay strong for Dad. But, oh, how I miss my Mom. From the touch of her soft hand to the silkiness of her flowing hair. I'd sacrifice my soul just to smell her once more. I often wonder if her funeral was as big as this. Whenever I question Dad, he always blows me off, I guess the pain is still too insufferable for him.

My eyes peer to what's directly in front of me, and as I draw nearer to Sherri's body, I feel weak.

Two mourners are at Sherri's open casket, touching her face, rubbing her hand, they speak to her as if she is still alive. Then, one woman's grief takes a hold of her, and as her head drops, her legs weaken, and ushers rush up to her, to provide her with the strength she needs to make it to her pew. Ushers with black suits and white gloves escort her away from the body.

My legs move in slow motion as I remember the fear in Sherri's eyes on that fateful night. She literally tried to save my life, when she could've just fled and left me there with the devil. My feet won't move from the place I'm in, and I recall my last moments with Sherri. The panic and fear in her eyes, Oh God, this is too much to bear.

"He told me you two were no more," she gushed, voice full of tears and bad memories. She was so scared that day, I remember. I place my hand over my eyes, as the tears pour fluidly from them, as if they too are running, fleeing from this nightmare and stream down my cheeks. As I take a step closer to Sherri's casket, the memories surface once more.

Through bloodshot eyes, I expelled, "Sherri?"

"Yes, Queen, it's Sherri from the courthouse. Listen, girl, we have to get out of here."

My head drops as I take another step forward. She wanted to make sure I got out of Derrick's house, alive. For that, I'm forever grateful.

But, Oh God, he raped her! I silently yell on the inside. My heart races, ascending to my throat and I want to frantically run out of here, to somewhere safe, where death and despair are not allowed. A place where all of the cruelties of the world can't creep in. I want to be in a world where mothers don't leave daughters, alone, and where daughters don't die before their time. He raped her, I think to myself.

Nearing the Promised Land, she looked back at me again and with the strength of a dying lamb, Sherri confessed, "he raped me," as the flood of stainless tears poured relentlessly from her eyes, landing onto the back of my hand. I cried with her, as we kept hope alive.

My final step allows me to see Sherri again, and the flood of tears profusely pour into puddles of pain. My fingertips hesitantly glide over her hand, as I touch her skin. She looks so peaceful, resembling nothing like her last moments alive. Her all white dress, with gold jewelry to match makes Sherri look like the angel she was. Her soft, pink makeup is done to perfection, is delicate and almost pure. I pray she finds happiness at home with our God.

"I'm so sorry, Sherri," I softly whisper as I bend down to kiss her on the forehead.

Leaning up to prepare to take my seat, I feel an arm around my waist. As I'm firmly pulled into the arm of someone, the intense pressure in my rib cage makes me want to cry in agony, but I remain quiet. Looking down at the brown dress shoes, I suddenly realize who holds me hostage once more. Goose bumps appear all over my arms and my heart races so, I feel it pounding through my chest. Looking to my right, I'm face to face with the devil reincarnate, the one responsible for Sherri's untimely demise. Swiftly turning my head, I look at Sherri.

"You know, getting her to finally shut the hell up was hard. I had to make sure I didn't wake you before I killed her," Derrick expels with venom behind his every words.

Trying to pull away, Derrick presses further into my side, pinches me, making me want to scream from terror, panic and pain.

I manage to remove my arm and my hand glides into my jacket pocket.

"I picked up the biggest rock, well, it was more like a boulder, and I bashed her head in. Poor thing. I had to take her out of her misery. Besides, I couldn't take a chance that she'd ever say anything about anything, ya know?"

"You're going to hell, Derrick," I whisper in disgust.

"Baby, I'll go anywhere as long as you're coming with me," he tells me as he pulls me closer to him.

"I told you, it's over."

"Naw, Queen, it ain't over. You don't really mean that. I messed up, I'll make it up to you."

"No, Derrick, it's over, like I said. Don't make me…"

"What, Queen? You ain't gonna do nothing, but remain my woman, and we'll get through this."

"Get off of me, Derrick," I softly yell as I pull away.

Kissing Sherri once more on the forehead, Derrick leans in to reveal, "She yelled like a baby with that final blow. What a shame."

"You're a murderer, Derrick."

"Yeah, and you love me, Queen."

"It's over, Derrick."

"Never, Queen."

"You raped and killed Sherri, Derrick. You're going to hell."

"You know, I did. Yes, you got me," he whispers and continues. "Yes, I killed Sherri, and I raped her too. Her pussy wasn't as juicy as yours though. Damn shame, she was a pretty girl."

Looking up at his face once more, he blows me a kiss, and smiles, just like a psychotic maniac would.

"I see your face has healed quite nicely, Queen. But I'm not surprised. You're a gorgeous woman."

"What happened to you Derrick?"

"Nothing, ain't shit wrong with me, Queen. Not a damn thing."

"You're going to regret every word," I confess and walk away.

Walking toward Sherri's family, her Mom gets up and greets me. Reaching her arms out to touch me, I return the gesture, and give her a hug. Her plump, yet petite frame holds me tight, and my emotions get the best of me. Crying like a baby, I look Sherri's mother in the eyes. "I'm so sorry for your loss, M'am."

"I know you are Baby. But God is good."

"Yes, He is."

She hugs me once more. "I thank God you survived chile. My Sherri admired you so, Queen. She said she wanted to finish law school and be like you."

"She did?"

"Yes, Queen."

As tears continue to stream down my face, Sherri's mom wipes my tears away, and as her hands touch my skin, I feel her comfort and wished my own mother was here to comfort me, to love and protect me, the same way Sherri's mother would, if only she could.

"You come by the house later on. Come and get some food, you hear?"

"I'll try, M'am."

"Yes, we will be there, Mrs. Wright is it?" Derrick questions as he barges into the conversation with the boldness of a cobra and the evil of Satan himself.

"And you are?"

He extends his big, black hand to shake hers.

"I'm Derrick Simmons, Queen's man, I knew your daughter."

"Is that right?" Sherri's mother questions.

"Yes. She was a beautiful woman. Now, I see where she got her beauty."

"Thank you, young man."

Giving her a final kiss on her cheek, I offer my condolences once more and proceed out of the church. Derrick's presence forces me to remove myself from anything remotely close to him.

"I'll be in touch, Mrs. Wright."

"Okay, Queen. You take care of yourself."

As I swiftly walk down the hall and head toward the door to exit Jerusalem Baptist Church, Derrick follows me, and as I turn to face him, I expel, "I'll call the cops if you don't leave me alone, Derrick."

The pastor's voice rings and the words settle deep into my spirit.

"And she went, and sat her down over against him a good way off, as it were a bowshot: for she said, Let me not see the death of the child. And she sat over against him, and lift up her voice, and wept."

QUINCY
Witnessing The Misery

I'm calling it, Stephanie," I tell the nurse on duty with me today. "Sure, Doc," she solemnly replies. Glancing up to the clock in surgical room 30, it reads 12:39, so, I tell her, "Time of death is twelve, thirty-nine in the afternoon." After removing my cap, I remove my gloves and throw them to the floor. Stephanie senses my frustration. "Doctor Hughes!" she yells and walks after me. "Stephanie, I'm fine. I'm headed to tell the parents."
"Okay, Doc."

Placing the surgical soap into my palm, I begin to scrub, vigorously, in an attempt to wash away the horror of the last hour. "Life shouldn't be given and taken away so suddenly," I fuss and stress out loud. Looking up to the mirror, I stare at myself and wonder why I'm here, witnessing this misery yet another day. But then reality strikes like an empire and I'm reminded of why I'm a doctor. It is to save lives, but as with anything in life comes the bitter with the sweet, so with life comes death. We are born to die. I think of Quinton. The death part I haven't grown accustomed to yet, and I probably never will. There is an unwritten rule for doctors that suggest it is not wise or possible for us to feel emotions over a patient's death because there is always another patient to help. Granted, I look forward to saving another life, as I do it almost every day of the week, but the pain of losing a patient never leaves me and any doctor that prescribes to the emotional detachment philosophy doesn't need to be a doctor.

Cupping both of my hands together, I place them under lukewarm water, and toss the water onto my face. Taking the hand towel, I dry my face and smooth my hair back into place and make my way into the emergency room to find the parents of the patient whose life just slipped through my hands. Walking near the nurses' station, Carmella points to the exam room where the parents are sitting. I nod to Carmella as a token of my gratitude. She smiles.

Pulling the curtain back, I see in their faces, nervousness, anxiety, grief and fear. How can I tell them that their grown daughter has passed on before them? Quickly, and as tenderly as I can, then I'm out of here.

"Hi, I'm Dr. Hughes," I say as I extend my hand to Dad's. He returns the shake and stands, and now faces me eye to eye. Mom is too distraught, too full of hope, will not leave her seat, instead, she clutches her purse, and rocks softly back and forth. She doesn't even look at me.

"You know, Doctor Hughes, she always suffered with asthma. But we did everything we could doctor," she yells, eyes full of tears and regret as she tells me about her child.

Dad puts his arms around her, tries to console her. "Let the doctor tell us what's going on, honey."

"Mr. and Mrs. Sullivan," I address them as I sit on the gurney.

"No, God, No! Please! Lord have mercy, No!" Mom yells a heart-wrenching yell.

"Go on Doctor Hughes," Mr. Sullivan instructs.

"Well, your daughter didn't make it. The attack was just too severe and I'm so sorry," I expel, trying to hold back the tears from falling from my own eyes.

"Thank you, Doctor Hughes, I know you did all you could," Mr. Sullivan remarks as he shakes my hand. I accept his hand into mine, and give him a light hug. At this point, I don't know if I'm trying to seek comfort or provide it. Taking my hand, I pat Mrs. Sullivan on the back, turn around and walk away.

Hurriedly, I walk into my office, and quickly wipe away the tear that has managed to escape my eye. I grab my briefcase, my gym bag, lock my office door and head out of the emergency room.

"Doctor? Doctor?" Carmella questions. And as nice and sweet as pie as she is, I turn to face her, still walking, only to tell her, "I'm off for the rest of the day. Page Doctor Keith. See you tomorrow."

I clock so many hours for the hospital and clinic that one of my perks, even if it is one I designed, is to come and go as I please. The hospital sometimes gets one hundred hours a week out of me, so shit, I'm out of here.

As I place my briefcase into the truck, along with my gym bag, I take my seat, turn the heat on full blast and sit in the parking lot while the car warms. Memories of what just occurred enters my mind. The fact that I could not save that woman's life instills a pain in me that forces me to frantically hit the steering wheel, repeatedly, to let out my frustration. The tears flow, just like the pain I'm feeling.

"Damn!" I yell as I punch the dashboard over and over again.

Neo-soul sounds along with a hearty vibration interrupt my moment of self-pity and I pick up the phone to see who's calling. If it's Tina, I swear to God, she'll want to kill herself immediately after our conversation. I ain't in the mood to hear none of her lies and her begging will fall on deaf ears, for sure. Thank God, it's Pat, my man, couldn't have called at a better time.

"What's up, brother?" I smile, hoping my sorrow won't be apparent through this phone call.

"What the hell is wrong with you, man?" Big questions. This man knows me way too well.

"Nothing, man, just a rough day at the hospital," I respond, while taking a momentary look in the rearview mirror. I look just a pitiful as I sound.

"Sorry to hear that, bro."

"Yeah, I'm sorry too, man."

"Well, listen, Richie Cunningham. Let's meet up tonight."

"Nah, you didn't just call me that, Ving Rhames."

"Yeah, I did, Eddie Munster, but anywho, Jasper's tonight, man?"

"Yeah, I guess."

"Awe, come on, White Boy. You have one of the most noble jobs on the planet, Q, don't forget that. While I'm building homes, you're saving lives, man. It's important."

"Yeah, yeah, yeah, I know. Just don't feel that important today. Well, I'm headed to the gym. Why don't your fat ass join me?"

"Nah, bitch, I'm still working, but I'll catch your Jack LaLanne ass out later tonight."

"Okay, Big, I'm telling you, you need to take better care of yourself."

"Yeah, I know, you honkey. I'll get to it."

"Soon, Big, make it soon."

"I will, Q. Yo, man, keep your head up."

"I'll holla, Big."

"Me too, man. Peace."

Popping my jazz compilation CD into the CD player, I recline in the driver's seat, and prepare to take a long, slow ride over to Power Steps, the biggest gym in the area. Doing my usual, cracking the window to allow some fresh air in, and look to my right to find my bottle of Fiji water resting in the cup holder. As I pull out of the Medical center's parking lot, I pick up the bottle, twist the top, and take a large gulp. The weather allowed the car to serve as a cooler, as the water is ice cold, and feels so good as it goes down. I pull the gray skully off of my head, run my fingers through my hair, and turn right, and begin my drive down the winding wooded road that serves as a main artery throughout these parts.

Smooth jazz plays softly throughout my ride, and as I tap my fingers against the steering wheel in beat to the melodic track, I wonder what my life would be like if instead of going to the gym, I was headed home to my lady or better yet, my wife. Maybe I'm losing my mind, as the loneliness kicks in every now and then, especially during difficult times like today. My new found revelation may have been prompted by Tina's infidelity also, which is crazy because we weren't serious. Or maybe, I'm just getting older, and it's just time. Time to be a real man, and to engage in real things, other than medicine.

But it seems like all the women I meet are out to get something. Once they find out I'm a physician, that's all she wrote. They see dollar signs – perceive me as eye candy, and better yet, arm candy, like I'm some fucking trophy or something. Where are the real women? The women who shout out to the mountains that they need a good man in their lives, that they would give a kidney for a husband. Where are they?

The infamous vibration on my hip interrupts my chill moment, and as I press the speaker button, I say a silent prayer that this is not Tina again, and hope to God it is not Big, calling again, after I told him I'd see him later on. He's good for that shit.

"Yes?" I question as I turn the music down.

"Q?"

"Yes?"

"Q! Where you at?"

"On my way to the gym. Why?"

"I wanna see you, Q!"

"Tina, why? There's no need."

"Why not, Q?"

"Because we are no more."

"What the hell is wrong with you, Q?"

"Nothing, Tina. I'm trying to be nice."

"What? You ain't got to be nice. I know you miss me."

"Bye, Tina."

"You ain't leaving me that easy."

"You sound nuts, Tina. Hey, how about you go and fuck your new man?"

"Fuck you, Quincy. You ain't shit, you know that?"

"Well, first Tina, you already fucked me, remember? And apparently you're fucking a lot of people. And maybe I ain't shit to you, and that's cool."

"Whatever, Q."

"Yeah, whatever, Weavalina."

My last comment gives me the much needed comic relief I so desperately needed today. Actually, the shit is funny as hell for some reason, and I can't stop laughing.

"I know you didn't call me Weavalina, bitch! You got some nerve. Yo ass was loving every inch of this weave too. Remember that shit, bitch?"

"Ha, ha, ha. Whew, girl, you are funny. Love is a strong word, baby, and I was not in love with that weave. You need to handle that. Ha, ha ha, shit, girl!"

"Go to hell, Q."

"Yeah, you too, Tina. But get rid of that nasty weave before you do. You don't want that shit catching fire! Ha, later."
Click.

QUEEN
Remnants of His Filth

Glancing over to my left, my eyes, cloudy and full of sleep, see, through blurred vision, the alarm clock, which is about ten minutes from ringing a loud, obnoxious tune to wake me. I never understood the purpose for alarm clocks, as I've always awakened before the ring, well, in most cases. But when I slip into another sleep-filled coma, that annoying buzzing drives me mad, which makes me think that my body wants to wake sooner rather than from the assistance of a five dollar annoying piece of shit. Nevertheless, about seven minutes and counting. Pressing the snooze button prior to the ringing will allow me to have another twenty minutes of sleep, for which I am extremely grateful.

Turning to my side, I prop the extra large down pillows, and roll over, and in doing so, smell the breath that signifies "morning" and I've disgusted myself. "Whew," I say aloud and I nestle my face into my burgundy comforter. The sunlight sneaks into my bedroom through a set of floor-length blinds, attempting to steal my last few minutes of funky mouth glory. The inevitable is upon me, as I must wake up, get ready and get moving for another day. This day in particular is so crucial as Michael's trial is underway and I have to fight like tooth and nail to free this innocent man.

Staying up half the night, me, my laptop, loads of case files and three glasses of cheap red wine, has my head spinning. Multiple calls from Derrick's crazy, abusive ass has my nerves in a frenzy. Reluctantly, I answered the phone once last night, just to get him to stop calling. Well, my pleas went on deaf ears as he went on and on with the "I love you's" and the "Please, baby, baby, please" begging.

When Derrick was good, he was truly good, however, slowly but surely, he became violent, disrespectful, unstable, and after the first three ass-whoopings I endured, I should've gotten out of the relationship, but black women sometimes have this belief that we can somehow change the world, when we put on the Superwoman cape, and try to solve the world's problems, with focus and utter emphasis being on saving our black man. Well, some problems need more than a black woman's touch, and with Derrick, I had to learn the hard way. No longer could I get away with the obvious excuses, like, "I fell." Coworkers, especially, my best friend, Paula, were growing hip to the game.

Crimson toes escape fluffy linens, as I manage my way out of my king-sized bed. Sitting up, I place my feet into my slippers, and stand up, stretch and make my way to my bedroom window. The sky is bright, and the sun is shining. As I look out of my window, up into the sky, I speak to my Savior and thank him for another day.

"Dear Lord. I know that you will never forsake me. I thank you for all things, Lord. God, I love you, because I know you first loved me. Lord, please take care of Sherri. And if you see my Mother, Lord, please cover her in your precious blood. Let her know Lord, that me and Daddy are doing the best we can, without her here. Lord, please protect me as I travel through the highways and byways, and give me traveling mercies today and always. God, I thank you for forgiveness. In your Heavenly name, I pray, Amen."

After I open my eyes, I look down and see something that makes my world shatter. There's a truck parked down the street, strikingly similar to Derrick's, which makes my heart beat rapidly throughout my chest. My nipples harden, as I feel them growing ripe. My soft pink chemise fits loosely on my size fourteen frame, and the butterflies in my belly cause me to feel nauseas. Goosebumps travel up one arm and down another, and my soft, brown, curly hair feels like it is standing atop of my head, along with the hair on my neck. Nervousness, and utter fear in its most deep and pure form, sets an alarm deep down in my soul, as my world just doesn't feel right. Instability, consumes me whole.

Grabbing my matching pink robe from the Lazy-Boy recliner in the bedroom, I put it on as I rush down the stairs to make sure the alarm is on and all the doors and windows are locked. My heart ascends to my throat, with rampant thoughts running through my mind as I race down the flight of stairs, recalling the night of horror, in which I witnessed Derrick at his very worse, and on that same night, my life almost came to an end. The fear leaves me unbalanced and my slippers, allow me to slip on one step, as the new plush carpet, provide a luxurious walking experience, when barefoot, but when running in an attempt to save yourself, proves only to be a health hazard.

Holding on to the banister for dear life allows me a moment to regain my composure and continue running down the stairs. Reaching the front door, I can see that it is still locked, and I say a silent prayer, thanking God for yet another blessing this morning. "Thank you, Jesus," I whisper. No sooner than I turn around to check my windows, does my whisper turn to a scream, as the keypad on the alarm system has been disarmed, and as I proceed from the front door, through the foyer, and into the kitchen to retrieve any weapon and to call 911, the devil reincarnate appears, grinning from ear to God damned evil ear, as he moves in close to me, rudely invading all of my space, he grabs me, I want to scream, but I can't. Panic and fear is at an all time high, and as he holds me tight, I look up to him, eyes full of tears and regret, I expel, "Get out, Derrick."

"No, baby. Queen, you know I love you. You know we are meant to be. I ain't goin' nowhere baby girl. So get used to it," he tells me with contempt in his eyes.

My eyes travel down the dark skin on his arms, the skin I once adored, that smooth, ebony satin that made the sugar of my walls melt with desire, and witness the veins protruding from his muscular arms.

The slithering of his pink tongue, as it dangles from mahogany lips once tantalized and made me yearn, as the initial foreplay was only the beginning. As it stands now, as he moves nearer, I pray like hell, he doesn't try to kiss me, and instead wish him an immediate heart attack, or stroke, or even an act of violence by the police, whichever would bring this black man to his quickest and most painful demise. What I once loved about him, I now despise, and the thought of him disgusts me and to look at him makes my insides cringe with repulsion. Hatred and contempt breeds within the depths of my being, but more so an unprecedented fear consumes me, and as I try to pull away, his massive arms hold me tight, preventing any movement, and I'm stuck, in the arms of a virtual stranger, as I really do not know Derrick at all.

"Get off of me, Derrick!" I yell like a mad woman.

Pulling me into the living room, Derrick throws me onto the sofa, and as I kick and yell, he commands my silence.

Putting his hand over my mouth, I smell sex, his filthy musky order, nasty and vile, and I want to regurgitate. "Shut the fuck up, Queen. I done told you, if I can't have you, ain't nobody gonna have you."

By the grace of God, one of my kicks lands across the side of his head, and he falls to the side of the sofa. His dirty brown Timberland boots leaves remnants of his filth on my floor.

In a hurried panic, I scuffle, and move from the sofa, and make an attempt to retrieve the kitchen phone to call 911. Falling to the floor, I trip as Derrick grabs hold of my right leg. I'm so scared right now! Flashbacks of the accident surface and the tears fill my eyes. If I breathe any faster, any harder, I'm going to have a stroke.

Banging my knees on the floor, I crawl, fast and furious, trying to get away from this mad man, this monster, he's nuts, and as I fight to save my life, I fantasize about killing this son of a bitch. The Lord moves me to kick, and frantically my feet flurry in mid air, as I turn to face him, my foot lands across the side of his head and he falls. I manage to get up in what seems like hours, take seconds, and I run into the kitchen to retrieve the phone. Constantly looking behind me, I can still smell his nasty ass on my hands, on my skin, the dirt of his fingers leaves my psyche stained. He is unable to hide the fact that he has been jerking off all night, and I can smell it, taste it, he makes me sick.

Pressing the phone to my ear, I raise my trembling hand to dial 911, but there's no ringtone. Oh my God! Did he cut the phone lines? For the love of God, I pray he didn't because this means that one of my worst fears will be reality today. My Dad will be burying his only child. Pressing the button over and over again, I try to get a dial tone. I scream, "Hello" into the receiver only to have my heart skip a beat.

"Queen? Baby? You haven't left for work yet? Doesn't your trial resume today?" Daddy questions.

Turning around, I can feel Derrick's hot, nasty breath on my neck. The smell of it makes me want to throw the hell up. Pulling me close to him, he holds on for dear life, squeezes me tight, and places the knife to my throat. Placing his single finger over his ashy lips, tells me that he wants me to be quiet.

"Hello? Queen? You okay, dear?"

"Uh, yes, Dad. I'm fine. I will call you later, okay?"

"Queen?"

"Yes, Dad?"

"Is everything fine?"

"Yes. Dad. I will talk to you later."

Derrick guides my hand as I hang up the phone on the kitchen wall. Goosebumps take over my body.

Grabbing my face with his hand, Derrick squeezes hard, so hard in fact that I feel my face go numb. A slithering tongue comes out of his disgusting mouth and draws nearer to my face. He proceeds to lick me, from forehead to nose to lips.

"Mmmm, you still taste as good as you look, redbone," he tells me as he pants, looking like a bat out of hell.

"Get off of me, Derrick," I scream.

"Why, baby? Don't you miss me?"

"Hell no, I don't miss you. What happened to you Derrick?"

Moving away from me, Derrick allows the kitchen knife to fall to the floor. As if he jumped out of himself, and another person jumped in, Derrick's head drops, and he stumbles back into the kitchen chair.

Placing his head into his hand, he answers, "I don't know."

"Well, you need to fix it, Derrick. Get out now, or I'm calling the cops."

Looking up to me, his persona changes again, and from sorrow to vengeful he sprints, at record speed, into that monster again.

"What the hell you say?" he questions as he approaches me. His massive stature hovers over me, as he questions once more, "What the fuck you say, bitch?"

I slouch down, to brace myself for another blow.

"I said, get out, Derrick.. Go get some help, before I call the fucking cops!"

As he clears his throat, I can hear the mountain of phlegm and spit building up in his throat and before I can move an inch, the wad he spits onto my face is both degrading, and demeaning, and I want to kill him.

"Fine, bitch, have your way," he whispers after spitting in my face and walks out of the front door.

After I gather my composure, I race to the front door, lock it, and peep out of the window to see the fucking psycho walk to his car. What to do next is a mystery as I have two choices. Destroy a black man's life, by calling the cops, or rush to court to help save a black man's life?

QUINCY
Doctor Love

Feeling myself just about to wake up, I thank God for small blessings. I mean, I know I'm sleeping, yet, I know I'm about to wake up. Can't quite figure that out, as I didn't study neurology in medical school. No matter the case, I'm glad to be on the side of waking up. Today is the anniversary of Quinton's death. And while my parents, and Big and other family have dealt with my brother's death, which happened twenty years ago, the grief still lingers on in my world.

Having just dreamt about him, I still picture his face. I was fifteen, and Quinton was seventeen. Funny, when I dream of him I see him at thirty seven, as an older version of me, since we did look almost exactly alike. But, unfortunately, I remember his death, his life, like I remember to breathe – it's something that is constantly on my mind. I'm better than I was, but I'll never get over losing my big brother. And while Big is my best friend and I'm grateful to have him in my life, and he does seem like a brother, nothing or no one will ever be able to replace Quinton.

It was the summer of 1989, and I was just about to enter my senior year in High School. Quinton had saved up enough money to buy a little piece of nothing car. He put all his money into the music system. A 1979 white Ford mustang with beat up red leather seats. The engine was nice, and the system was boomin'. Quinton washed that car every day damn near and put every dime he had into that ride. Big and I were so hyped about it, and I was so proud of my big brother.

We were coming home one night from the movie theater – this real beat up spot in Newark – rats and shit used to run over our feet in the theater, but we didn't care. We were funky fresh dressed and ready to party – me, Big and Quinton in high top fades. Quinton had a job, he treated his brother and his brother's best friend to the movies. "Batman" had just opened on the screens. Yes, the Adventures of the caped crusader had me so excited. We were in awe at how Quinton was able to Mack the ladies, all of them – Spanish, white, black, all of them would flock to Quinton, because he was the super-hot, super good looking white boy with piercing blue eyes and a nice ride, albeit a 1979 Ford mustang.

We left the movies, and Big and I were yelling out the car window at all of the honeys riding by, on Broad Street in downtown, Newark. This was during the time when you could hang out all night in Newark and wouldn't have to worry about a thing, nothing, except for maybe someone trying to take your girl or something. We were riding passed Club Zanzibar, just about to get on the highway to head back to Jersey City. Big was spending the summer with his Auntie, and Quinton and I were headed back home. Riding up the ramp, Quinton yelled, "Oh Shit!" Most of what happened next is still a blur to me. I wonder if that's my brain's way of protecting my heart, by blocking out the memory, of if I truly can't remember.

A drunk driver was flying down the one-way on ramp as we traveled up, hitting us head on. Our car flipped backwards and landed right side up after a few turns. Neither Big or I was hurt in a major way, but Quinton…

Quinton suffered head trauma, lacerations all over his body from the broken glass. All I remember was screaming and yelling as onlookers drove by, some of them stopped, I kept yelling, "Somebody help us, call 911." Big ran to the nearest pay phone and called 911, then ran back over to me as I pulled Quinton's body out of the car. I laid him flat on the ground, and talked to him. He was bleeding from his eyes, his mouth, his nose, his ears, and I just remember crying, telling him, "Quinton, it's gonna be okay."

When the paramedics finally arrived, which was almost twenty minutes later, they were so lax in their response. I kept screaming to them, "Save my brother! Do something!" They worked on him, but could have and should have worked harder, faster, they should have been there faster, quicker, gave a damn, they should have cared.

When the cops arrived, they asked if we had been drinking and just treated us like criminals. I yelled to them, "It was a hit and run!" as the driver who hit us was no where to be found. But they kept scrutinizing and questioning us like we were the guilty ones. Fucking cops.

I'll never forget the look on my mother's face when her and my dad got to the scene. I truly believe in my heart, it was that moment, that time when my brother lay there lifeless on the street like some fucking animal that I told myself, I'm going to do everything in my power to prevent another mother from looking the way my mother did when she hugged her dead son – dead at the age of seventeen, life taken by a hit and run, drunk driver.

᪣᪣᪣᪣᪣

Who the hell is this ringing my damn phone on my day off? I think to myself, as I put my gym bag into my truck. The cold air sneaks into my sweats and makes my ass shiver. But it's okay, because I am not at work, not looking at any snotty noses, not dodging Carmella's horny ass, and, well, just not dealing. I plan to get my workout on this morning, then head home to relax, and hopefully sit on my ass for the remainder of the day. But, it is Friday, so something tells me, it's not going down.

Reluctantly reaching, I find my cell, affixed to my hip, and as I pull it up into view, I see it's my man, Big, meaning, once again, he's going to find a way to fuck up my plans. However, it is my man, so I need to answer.

"Hello, wassup, bro" I question, planting my ass firmly into my car seat.

"Wassup, white boy?" Big greets me.

"I don't appreciate your racial epithets today, man. On my way to the gym. You wanna bring your big ass over there to meet me?"

"No, bitch, some of us do have to work today. You have the day off, right?"

"Right, but…"

"But what, Richie Cunningham? No, I'm not going to ask you to do anything. Well…"

"Well, what, Big? I don't feel like being your errand boy today. Aiight?"

"You gotta come to Jasper's tonight, Q."

"Well, I figured that, dumb ass. We go to Jasper's every Friday, don't we?"

"Yes, we try, retard, but don't miss tonight."

"Why, Big? What's so fucking important about tonight? I'm there, by the way…"

"Lo is doing his poetry tonight. They are going to have poetry nights on Fridays now, and Angelo is performing tonight," Big reveals while breathing heavily on the phone.

"Why the fuck are you breathing so hard, man? And that's what's up about Angelo. I can't wait to see his punk ass do his thing."

"I'm breathing so hard, bitch, because I have a cold, and it is cold as shit on this construction site. You should see Raj. Have you ever seen an Indian freeze?"

"I'm sure the sight of Raj's Indian, curry ass is hilarious. Take care of that cold, man. Go and get plenty of green tea, make it hot with honey and lemon. Dress in layers."

"Damn, you lily white ass is always the doctor, huh?"

"Always, brother. Can't have anything happen to my big black friend, right?"

"Right!"

"Alright, Big. I'll see you tonight. Call me if you need."

"Wait, uh…"

"Wassup, Big?"

"What's the deal with you and Tina?"

"Not a damn thing. Why?"

"I saw her yesterday, all hugged up on some big ass black dude. Big brother too."

"Yeah, sounds like same giant I caught her with."

"Alright man, just wanted to make sure you weren't still fucking with her."

"Nope, not at all. I wouldn't let her suck your dick at this point, and she can suck the hell out of a dick, too. Whew, I need me some ass."

"I heard that. Yeah, man, ain't like you to be so long without gettin' some."

"Yeah, Big, but like I told you, I'm trying to catch my wife. I'm tired of fucking around with ass here and ass there. I'll just be jerking off till I find Mrs. Right, or if my balls turn blue, I'll settle for Mrs. Right Now."

"Ha, Ha, Ha, I heard that. Alright man, see you later."
Click.

Every now and then, I think about moving back to Jersey. Although I love this area, for its simplicity, quiet and serenity, I often miss the hustle and bustle, the rush hour traffic, the pavement, and the gunshots. Can someone really miss gunshots? I guess I miss the inner city life that I grew up in. It's nice to start anew, and I am thankful I did, besides with the fam moving up here and my best friend; I really didn't have much choice.

Cruising through the town, I see another business has closed, while another one has opened. That's the thing up here in the Poconos. Great opportunities to run your own shit, but keeping it going is an entirely different ball game. Reaching nearer to my destination makes me anxious because it's more than time for me to get my workout on.

Pulling up into the parking lot, I luckily find a spot near the entrance and pull right in. The lot is pretty full today, which is unusual for a weekday. Most folks up here on the mountain commute back and forth to New York and New Jersey to earn those hefty paychecks. Guess people took off this Friday. Who knows?

As I make my way out of my truck, I see a familiar face. Can't place the name, but the face definitely rings a bell. Politely, I nod my head, and give her a slight grin to acknowledge her, then reach into the back of my truck to grab my bag. We both moved at the same time as we headed toward the gym's entrance. Looking into her eyes forced a tingle down my spine, and then I remembered, that I don't remember where I know her from, or that I'm truly attracted to her. I'm horny, that's for sure, and she looks like she is the perfect fit for a horny man. My gutter and dirty instinct tells me to say hello and demand that she pulls those sweats off, however the wanna-be-good side of me says to fall back, as only true love awaits. My dick is singing another tune, however, and is boldly pleading to slide into something sweet.

"How are you?" she questions, through reddish-pink lips.

"I'm good, thanks," I respond as I hold the door for her.
As she walks passed me, I see her tits bouncing, in rhythm to her stride, she moves, slowly and surely, sure of herself that is,

and I try not to wonder what she's like in bed. But my imagination takes on a mind of its own.

"Don't you remember me, Doctor?" she inquires.

As I follow her into the gym, I watch her from behind, no ass rests in those sweats, which is a big turn off for me, but for what she lacks in the way of a bangin' set of ass cheeks, she sorta makes up for in the size of her breasts. I sound like a mad man. She turns around, as she awaits my response.

"Uh, your face is very familiar. I know I've seen you before, but can't pinpoint the time and place. But, you did call me doctor, so I'm guessing we've met at either the medical center or at a seminar?"

"Yes, well, you're almost there. You treated my son, some time ago. You were cute then, and you're even more handsome in your workout gear. My name is Cassandra. Remember? Cassandra Manahan. My son is Roger."

Flashbacks of her snot-nosed runt play in my mind. She was pretty then, just as she is now, and I remember them tits now, just like I did then.

"Oh yes, I remember now. How is little Roger?" I probe and smile as he pats my shoulder.

"He's fine, Doctor…"

"Oh, Doctor Hughes. Well, my name is Quincy."

"Quincy, huh? Nice name. It fits you."

"Does it?"

"Yes, Quincy. It's a distinguished name. A sexy and regal name. Just like you," she taps my chest in jest.

"Thank you, Cassandra. I appreciate that. You're going to make me blush."

"Now that would make you even more sexy and I don't think that's possible, Quincy."

Okay, if she keeps talking like this, she's going to get it in the worst way.

Trying to break the obvious sexual tension, I politely excuse myself. She's cute, in a sort of country western star kind of way. I must be really horny, or maybe she is attractive.

"Okay, Cassandra, so good talking to you. I guess I'll see you another time."

"Are you married?" she boldly probes.

"No, I'm not, are you?"

"I'm separated, heading for divorce."

"I'm sorry to hear that."

"Don't be."

"Okay, then I'm not sorry?"

"You're adorable, Dr. Hughes."

"Thanks, Cassandra. Talk to you soon."

As I pry myself from Cassandra's verbal clutches, I move closer to the treadmills to get a little running done before hitting the weights. While walking over, two of the gym's regulars walk past, eyeing me from head to toe. They remain in their scantily-clad gym attire, which they are notorious for wearing; skin tight biker shorts and matching tops. Leaves nothing to the imagination.

"Hi, cutie," the short one remarks.

"Hi," I respond. But with little enthusiasm. Don't need these tricks getting the wrong impression.

"Afternoon, Doctor," the taller one exclaims.

"How are ya," I respond.

Placing my towel onto the treadmill, I gear up for a good run. White, fragile earpieces, go into my ears, and I put on some old Jay-Z to get me going. One can never go wrong with *"The Black Album,"* and this will be the day's theme music.

QUEEN
Fight the Power

The lobby of the courthouse is filled with the repugnant stench of voyeurism. I wave my attorney badge at the security guard, he smiles and nods, and I walk briskly by the vultures waiting in line to get through the metal detectors. Anxiety and anticipation cloak their faces as they pray and hope to get a seat in the courtroom for an up close, personal glimpse at the dead meat the media is portraying my client out to be. I roll my eyes at each and every one of them for their cynical and judgmental views. I shake my head in disbelief. What ever happened to *'innocent until proven guilty?'* The curiosity associated with this trial has turned it into a media event with all the people and paparazzi attached. A media event in this uneventful area – yes, only a double murder could wake the folks in this town.

Once in the courtroom, I see Michael has already been brought in and he's seated at the defense table. I quickly reflect on the first time he was brought into the courtroom, in hand and ankle shackles – modern day slavery, I thought. He hangs his head in shame and as I look deep into his eyes, I am more convinced than ever that I must make everyone see they've fingered the wrong man. Thank God Michael's Mom chose the dark navy blue suit for court today. It brings out his hazel eyes. Aesthetics play a major role in everything. I'm convinced juror number four has the hots for him. She's an attractive, red-headed white woman in her thirties, and I can sense a Mandingo fantasy dancing around in her thoughts as she stares at Michael. Hell, looking his best just might help us win a much needed vote or two from the jury.

Cletus Jackson walks in right after me and places his briefcase on the prosecutor's table. The smell of his cologne equals his presence, strong and arousing. I must admit, I wish we were on the same side of this case instead of vigorously playing a game of offense and defense against each other. Cletus is a tenacious, skilled litigator and handsome as hell. Well-equipped with a majestic stature, Mr. Jackson makes heads turn when he enters a room. Part of me is proud, I must admit – a black man serving as lead prosecutor, with a commanding presence, amazingly articulate, and brilliantly intelligent. I've really had to step up my game in this case because nothing gets passed him and it's clear he's waiting for me to make one mistake so he can fry my client.

"Ready for round two Ms. Thomas?"

"I was just going to ask you the same thing Mr. Jackson, especially since I've yet to bring you my 'A' game."

"I'd really hate for you to waste all your skills on a guilty man."

"I've just been warming up. But once I get Mr. Bevens a Not Guilty verdict, I'll be happy to give you lessons about jury trials."

I wink at him and he smiles back at me through a small, but sexy gap in his teeth. This man is not going to ruffle my feathers today; I'm ready for the fight ahead of me. My knees are weak from all the kicking and fighting with the devil this morning and I massage my legs as I sit down and mentally prepare myself for war.

Judge Randolph takes the stand and the courtroom becomes silent. There is something about a black robe that makes even adults sit real still and quiet.

"Counsel, are you ready to continue?"

Cletus stands and adjusts his tie. "Yes, your Honor, I am. I'd like to introduce into evidence Prosecution Exhibit A. It's the jail psychiatric report for Mr. Bevens."

I was glad my trial preparation had been thorough last night. I knew he would try and bring in Michael's psych report. I would have tried it too if I were him. But not today; I'm not going to make it that easy for him.

"Objection, your Honor. Relevancy?"

Cletus didn't see that one coming. I blindsided him and feels so good. He's shifting through the pages of the report trying to camouflage that fact, but I can still see it even as he tries to rebut my objection.

"Your Honor, the Defendant's state of mind is very relevant to this case. The mental thought process of this killer of two small children is a relevant issue and the jury is entitled to hear it."

"With all due respect to my esteemed colleague here; Mr. Jackson is failing to recognize that a report done *after* my client was in custody does not go toward his state of mind at the time of a crime he *allegedly* committed."

Frustration seeps from every pore in Cletus' face which is just the fuel I need to continue.

"I submit that foundation has not been laid here to prove my client's guilt, so therefore, a report done while he was in jail after the crime is not relevant at this stage of the trial. A report of that nature, if admissible at all, would be relevant only during the sentencing phase, not during the case in chief."

Judge Randolph raises his eyebrow indicating he is impressed. "She has a point Mr. Jackson. Objection sustained."

Michael shifts in his chair next to me and cracks a smile. He can tell we are gaining ground and he is thankful for it—so am I. But I know we have only won a battle and Cletus is more than prepared for battle and will continue on with the war, which he does.

He calls the medical examiner to the stand. I'm searching my brain as he testifies, but I can't find anything to refute his testimony so I decide to leave cross-examination of him alone. Cletus winks at me as his witness leaves the stand. He's being smug and we both know he just scored one in the win column. Next he calls the father of one of the murdered girls to testify. Even though the father only wants justice for his daughter and is out for the blood of my client whom he feels took his daughter's life, I just can't attack this man who has lost so much.   I hold back the tears while listening to his emotionally-filled testimony. This man is hurting, and I feel his pain. He's biting his lips as he talks. The anguish is all over his angered face as he describes how hard it is to out live his baby girl; especially since she was snatched from him so early in life.

I listen to his stories of watching his princess jumping rope in the backyard and dressing dolls with friends the day before.

The witness yells, "You bastard!" and points in Michael's direction.

"Objection!" I yell in defense. The judge sustains.

His testimony is tugging at my heart, but I am managing to hold it all in. I can't cross examine him either, that would be like pouring salt into very deep wounds. I won't be another jab at his heart. As I look in the eyes of the jurors, the most important people in the room when it comes to Michael's fate, I can see that Cletus gets to chalk up another battle won by him.

"Lord, give me something. Anything. Michael is innocent, help me help him." I pray the words as Cletus calls the lead detective to the stand. Detective Spencer is old school police. Cut from the breed of officers that actually believe in solving crimes not just in finding someone to arrest and pin a crime on. I could tell he got his hair cut just for his appearance today in court. I can tell he's anal that way—appearance first. From the perfect knot in his tie, to his impeccably tailored suit and his highly shined shoes, he looks like the poster child for law enforcement; very respectable. I listen intently as Cletus questions the detective and I wait for him to leave a hole for me to crawl through when it's my turn on redirect and he does.

"Detective Spencer, did you take a statement from the Defendant?"

"I did."

"And what was the extent of his statement to you?"

"When I questioned him, he admitted to being in the area that the bodies of the girls were found in, but he said that he never touched them or the murder weapon."

"So he admitted he was there? Did he have an excuse for being there?"

"Well sir, he seemed to be very confused about his whereabouts because he said he is often in that neighborhood. His actual words were that he could not remember if he was there at that particular time or not."

"So let me get this straight, even though his prints were on the murder weapon and he admitted he might have been in the area, he still said he was innocent?"

"Yes, sir."

"No further questions your Honor."

My intuition tells me there's something here, so I'm going to follow my gut. I get up slowly and walk toward the witness stand asking God to lead me as I hand the detective his written report.

"Good Morning Detective Spencer."

"Good Morning ma'am."

"Detective Spencer, is everything my client told you included in your report?"

"Yes, ma'am it's very detailed."

"And is your statement the only place you have indicated your impressions about this case?"

"Ma'am?" He hesitates, so I repeat my question.

"Is everything about this case, as you saw it, included in this report?"

"Actually no ma'am. I also sent a memo to the prosecutor's office separately."

Cletus jumps to his feet. "Objection, your Honor. Foundation?"

Judge Randolph says, "I'll allow it," and then it's on in my mind—my foot is in the door and I'm coming in whether Cletus likes it or not. I'm fueled right now so I move closer to the detective.

"Detective Spencer, what did your memo to the prosecutor say?"

"It questioned the motive of Mr. Bevens."

Cletus is angered and rises again.

"Objection your Honor. Relevancy?"

Judge Randolph looks at Cletus through eyes of irritated frustration. "This line of questioning seems very relevant Mr. Jackson; don't interrupt again. Continue on Ms. Thomas."

I can see in Detective Spencer's face that he would rather not be sitting in the witness chair at this moment, but I can also sense that he is a truthful man, so I continue to press him.

"Exactly how did your memo question his motive, what about it bothered you?"

"Well ma'am, I indicated in my memo that I didn't think Mr. Bevens had a motive to commit the crimes he was charged with."

My eyes become wide and the people in the courtroom gasp and a few whisper among themselves. I'm on a roll now, I can feel it and I push forward in my momentum.

"Your Honor, the Prosecutor never submitted Detective Spencer's memo to the defense and The Brady Doctrine clearly indicates that suppression of evidence which is favorable to the accused violates due process. I move for a mistrial."

Cletus rises to his feet, fixes his jacket and adjusts his tie. He addresses the judge.

"Sir, we might have received the memo from Detective Spencer; I really don't know if we did or not, but even if we did receive it, our office did not, and would not ever knowingly withhold evidence from the defense."

"Well, Mr. Jackson, if you did not knowingly withhold evidence, explain to the court why Ms. Jackson didn't receive it?"

"Your Honor, I really don't have an excuse. We operate under a State run agency your Honor; I don't have to tell you that. Our office is wall-to-wall paper and we are understaffed. It might have slipped through the cracks."

I interject, "Your Honor, that doesn't make a difference. The point is that all evidence was not provided to us. The Brady Doctrine specifically addresses the fact that irrespective of the good or bad faith of the prosecutor, where evidence is material to the guilt or punishment of the accused, such evidence is exculpatory and must be presented to the defense. Since we have not seen the memo of Detective Spencer, which is clearly favorable to my client, I move for a mistrial."

My underarms are warm as I speak. I know this is the break I was waiting for. Thank God, He's still in the prayer granting business. Cletus puts his hand on his chin and shakes his head in disbelief as the Judge speaks. "Court will be in recess as I take the motion for mistrial under advisement."

The judge leaves the bench and Michael begins to hug me.

"I don't know much about the law Ms. Thomas, but what happened just now was a good thing; right?

"Hopefully Michael, keep your fingers crossed. The judge will probably be out for at least an hour or so getting advice on my motion. Relax for a while, and if I were you, I would go somewhere and say a prayer. No, make that a series of prayers. I'm going to go take a break and I'll be back shortly."

As I grab my briefcase, I feel a pain shoot down my shoulder from the weight of the case in my hand. I guess I am sorer from this morning's boxing match than I thought. Half of the courtroom gives me the evil eye as I walk out the doors of the courtroom. I need a minute to myself to regroup. I see an interview room at the end of the hall and decide to go there to prepare for whatever decision the judge may come back with.

The door is closed so I knock, there's no response so I turn the rusty antique knob on the door and go in. My eyes meet those of Cletus. He's alone just sitting on a table top staring out the window.

"I'm sorry. I didn't mean to interrupt you. I'll leave. I didn't know anyone was in here."

"That's okay. I'd actually enjoy the company. Come in please."

Cletus walks toward me and slowly closes the door behind me. He places his arm around my waist and guides me to the middle of the room. His touch soothes me much like Derrick's did in the beginning, but I don't allow myself to physically respond. Maybe I am enjoying his touch because I take it as a sign that I am better than him. A sign that his smug arrogance is subsiding due to my actions in court.

"I must say, I'm impressed Ms. Thomas. That was a smooth move you just pulled in there. I'll admit you caught me off guard with that one." He looks me directly in the eyes and I notice, for the first time, that Cletus has a dimple. Just one, it's on the right side of his face. Each time his lips move, so does the dimple and the joint movement of both is extremely sexy.

"I told you before we started this morning that I had yet to bring my 'A' game. I guess you thought I was just delivering lip service huh Mr. Jackson?

"Please call me *Cletus* and what an interesting choice of words Ms. Thomas."

"Since we are being informal, you can call me *Queen.*" And what choice of words do you find interesting?"

"The choice *lip service.* I like the way that sounds coming from you." He moves in closer to me so that our faces are within an inch of each other. It's awkward but comfortable at the same time.

"I was talking about the case Cletus; I didn't mean anything by that comment."

"What if I wanted you to?

I make myself turn away from him. It's getting hot in here and I know it's because I'm too close to him. Cletus towers over me and I've always been a sucker for a tall man. But I will be damned if I let him know it so I change the subject.

"Are you nervous about my motion?"

Cletus looks me from head to toe and licks his lips. "Actually your body in motion does make me nervous, but I sure enjoy watching the moves."

"Cletus, I was talking about my motion for mistrial. Are you nervous about what the Judge will decide?"

"Not much makes me nervous when it comes to my job. You have proven yourself to be a worthy adversary. I truly underestimated you. If Judge Randolph comes back and says that he is granting your motion and he declares a mistrial, it will be the first loss on my record. But if it had to be delivered to me, my ego can stand it being delivered by a pretty lady. So I'm not worried about losing the case. I can handle that. What I am worried about is putting a killer back on the streets. I'm worried about letting a guilty man go free. This is personal to me Queen; I want your client to fry for the brutal killings he committed. So with that in mind; with the prospect of a brutal killer back on the streets—you bet your pretty ass I am worried—worried as hell."

"If my client was guilty, I wouldn't have worked so hard, but you've got Michael all wrong. You have this case all wrong Cletus. Michael is innocent and what I worry about is that you can't see it. I just hope Judge Randolph is smart enough to see what I see."

He's pissed me off royally with his holier than thou speech about my client. I need to leave. I pick my briefcase up from off the table and Cletus grabs my hand halting me in my steps.

"Don't be mad Queen. I hate to see you go, but I love watching you walk away."

He smiles and winks at me as I snatch my hand away from him.

"Go fuck yourself Cletus."

"It would be much more fun if you'd join me while I do."

I hear his words as I slam the door behind me.

QUINCY
The Quick Fix

Sweat beads form at my hairline and begin running down my face and neck. I look down at the control panel on the treadmill only to see that my warm up is coming to an end. I wipe my face, get off the machine and as I take a sip of bottled water I hear her voice again.

"We've got to stop meeting like this Quincy or people will talk." Cassandra bats her eyes and sways side to side flirtatiously as she moves closer to me.

She won't give up, I think to myself as I try not to stare at her breasts. "It's a small gym Cassandra; people are going to gossip no matter what. Are you finished with your workout already?" I try to make small talk as I gather my things and continue the effort to divert my eyes.

"Not really. I just finished my spin class; I saw you and was hoping to strike up a conversation with a friendly face. I really don't know anybody else in here." She smiles and reaches for the end of my towel to help me wipe my sweat. Big tits and attentive…that's a plus. After she pats the back of my neck dry she hands me back the towel and runs her acrylic nails along the side of my face, slowly and seductively. Then she licks her lips for added effect. I get a tingle down my spine and can feel my dick throb, so I step backwards to put some much needed space between us. I'm trying real, real hard to be good and this chick isn't making it easy for me.

"Well, you'll have to excuse me Cassandra, but I'm kind of in a hurry, I still need to hit the weights." I know I am being rude, but getting a piece of ass is not on the agenda right now, working out the frustration of my day is.

"Mind if I spot you? I could use some weight training myself, besides I'm good at carrying heavy loads." She winks at me and makes a gesture of moving her breasts side to side to emphasize her point, which her tight shirt and perky breasts make sure is not lost on me. She's persistent, I'll give her that. With all the stuff swimming around in my head, I resolve within myself that a little adult conversation might take the edge off my thoughts.

"Well, if you think you can hang then you're more than welcome to join me."

"You bet your fine ass I will."

I walk ahead of her in the direction of the weight room. I hear her skip a little behind me as she tries to catch up. This place reeks of body sweat and musk, but in a good way, or maybe it's not a good smell and I am just horny; probably the latter. It's the battle of the bulge in every direction I look in and everyone is trying to win. I pass the stair climbing machines with Cassandra following close behind me, but all I can see is jiggling ass after jiggling ass. Watching each cheek move up and down, stride after stride in slow motion confirms it for me. Yep, I'm horny.

It's a meat market in here, but I'm not interested in what's on sale. I instantly begin to regret allowing Cassandra to spot me now, but I can tell from her endless chatter and jubilant smile that it's too late to renege. It's clear she wants to persuade me into a game of hide the salami and although she's hot and I'm horny, I'm also tired of that game with random chicks. I want something real; something that will last. I hold the door to the weight room open for her and vaguely notice that her lips are still moving as I look around the rest of the room. There's only one other person in here lifting weights and besides him, the room is empty. I'm not sure if I like that or not; having more people in the room might make it easier to avoid Cassandra's come-ons. She continues to babble next to me like a love-sick puppy as we approach the weights, but my mind is elsewhere. Under different circumstances I might be flattered and make moves to tap that ass, but chasing tail is getting old. I want more than just a nut; I want a partner for life and I know Cassandra is not the one. I begin to think of the patient I lost today. She had a world of possibilities ahead of her and now they are all gone. Unrealized. Why is life stolen from us so easily like a thief in the night? My mind is going crazy right now realizing that we are born alone and we die alone, and if we are lucky, we get to spend the time in between with someone we care about. Life is too short to be alone or unsatisfied. I pray I won't be either for too much longer.

I hear Cassandra talk about her plans for the future of wanting to get involved more in community service and how she is taking night classes to better herself in pursuance of that goal. She actually will make some man happy one day; that man is just not me. I smile and feign interest in what she is saying as I lay down on a weight bench and begin to try and raise the weight of both the dumbbells and my thoughts above my head.

"So Quincy, why isn't there a Mrs. Hughes?"

Her question hits me hard. Am I wearing my thoughts on my sleeve or is she just that observant to what's going on in my head? Why isn't there a Mrs. Hughes? Even I don't know the answer to that.

"I guess I just haven't found the right woman yet." I exhale extra loud from the weight of the barbells and out of frustration at my situation.

"Are you taking applications?" Cassandra stands above my head with her crotch in my face pretending she would be able to lift the weights should I need assistance. The sight of her camel toe inches from my nose arouses me again, but I'm trying to suppress myself even though I can't help but stare at the plump pussy right in front of my face.

"I hadn't given it much thought." I lie as I continue to push the weights in the air. Cassandra walks from the head of the weight bench and around to the side of me. Before I know it, she is straddling me on the bench and running her fingernails down my chest. I almost lose my balance trying to place the dumbbells on the bar above my head.

"What are you doing Cassandra?"

"Applying for the job." She grinds on top of me, moving her hips back and forth. Momentarily, I'm transported in time and vision her naked and that this is the real thing with her breasts bouncing up and down as she rides me. I snap out of it and try to sit up. I can see the other guy in the room trying to act like he isn't watching us, even though it is very clear that he is.

"Hold up girl. This is neither the time nor the place for this."

"This may not be the place, but the most important part of your body says it's definitely the time." Cassandra squeezes my crotch and rises up off of me. She is right; I'm getting hard.

"Come on Quincy, stop playing hard to get. You know you want it."

She's right again.

Cassandra stands over me with her hands on her hips in some sort of dominant Wonder Woman stance as I sit on the bench looking confused. She leans down close to my ear with her breast an inch from my eyes. She puts my hands on her breast and forces me to squeeze them as she whispers, "Look, I only live a few blocks from here, follow me home and let's both get a real work out."

At first I can't say anything, I just stare at her. I know she's not what I'm looking for. I want a wife, but I'm lonely and I'm tired of thinking right now and just want some action. I'm sexually hungry. I much rather have a steak in the form of a loving life-long companion, but at this point, the hamburger of Cassandra will have to suffice.

"Shit girl, you ain't said nothing but a word, let's do this."

We gather our things and walk out of the gym. I watch her as she goes to her car. I can tell she is switching her flat ass with extreme vigor because she knows I'm watching. It's a sexy effort, but one that isn't needed because I'm ready to tap that ass, flat or not. Caucasian booty ain't Black booty or Latina booty, but I'm desperate and any booty right now will do.

We pull into Cassandra's apartment complex. It's not as lavish as I am used to but it's quaint nonetheless. She parks in a spot right in front of her door and I park next to her. She is inside the apartment door before I can even get out of my car. I initially think she is just in a hurry to get our freak on but as I enter her apartment through the door she left open, I know the real reason she rushed in first. Once I get in I see that she is removing clothes from the floor and dishes from the living room table in an effort to make it more presentable. The apartment is not bad, but does need a good maid.

"Have a seat; I'll get us some wine." She goes into the kitchen and I look around at the place she calls home. I see her son's toys in the corner and smile at the comfortable, hominess of the place. Cassandra returns with two wine glasses, takes a sip from hers and before I can even put my glass to my lips she sits on my lap, straddling me again and begins kissing my neck. I lean back not saying a word and sip my wine instead.

"You smell so good." I hear her say as she tries to remove my shirt. I can feel my heart beating faster, yet I stare around the room. Cassandra is aggressive and on a mission to get my clothes off of me with as few distractions as possible.

"Where is your son tonight?" His picture on the fire place mantle reminded me that she is a package deal.

"He's with his father; it's his weekend for custody, so we have all night to ourselves." She begins to kiss me passionately. Well, as passionate as a kiss can be delivered when one person is all into it and the other is merely luke warm. Her lips are soft; her breath warm; her tongue inviting. I allow her to ravish my mouth.

"Damn girl, slow down a bit, what's the rush?" I'm about to get a piece of ass and I'm feeling like a bitch right now because I want to be more intimate. I want to feel more of a connection.

"I can slow it down Quincy if that's what you want. I've just been so turned on by you since the first time I saw you in the hospital, so I feel like I am playing catch up." She begins unbuttoning my pants and kissing down my stomach and chest.

This isn't right. I want more. I can feel Cassandra rubbing my thighs as I sit motionless like a spectator to what she's doing. Is this what my life will always be like? Aimless one night stands one after another? I want more than that. I don't want to die never having found the right one. This isn't right; she isn't right. I need to get up out of here. I try to persuade myself to leave but as I try to muster up the nerve to stop Cassandra from fondling me, she places my dick in her mouth.

"Awhh Shit that feels good." I moan and lay back on the sofa.

"That's right baby, relax and let momma soothe you." She's on her knees, staring straight into my eyes as she runs her tongue slowly up and down my dick before inserting it into her mouth again. My eyes roll back in my head and I can feel my tension seeping out of my body with the suction of each stroke of her mouth. I'm relaxing now. The weight of the world seems lighter. Each movement of her tongue takes out thought after thought of why this is wrong. Cassandra begins to suck my balls one at a time while stroking my dick. Damn this bitch knows how to slob a knob. I want a wife, I want a fulfilled life, but I'll take what Cassandra is doing and doing well. As muscle after muscle within my body becomes jelly I feel myself about to cum.

I'm a doctor so I believe in the sayings that, an apple a day keeps the doctor away and milk does a body good, but a whole lot can also be said about the healing powers of a good nut.

ﮎﮎﮎﮎﮎ

Cassandra keeps the change, as she captures all of my essence with her mouth. Looking up to me with pride, she smiles, and I'm instantly repulsed, feeling good on one hand and like a used piece of meat on the other. I know there's more to romance than this. Busting in her mouth, and witnessing her red lipstick on my thighs and underwear is proof that I can score, get a piece of something when I need to, but, unfortunately, it doesn't say much more.

"You know, I could get used to satisfying you this way," Cassandra tells me as she gets up. Pointing toward my left hand, she tells me, "Besides, I don't see a ring on your finger, so you're available."

I really hope this bitch doesn't think that me coming in her mouth is the equivalent of us getting married. She must be a fucking nut.

"Ha, ha, ha," I laugh off her out-of-this-world comment and blow off her fantasy. Suddenly, I'm bored and feel the need to step and get home to a hot shower and the comforts of my own bed.

I get up along with her, stretch and yawn, and lie my way out of this situation. I got what I came for, no need in wasting anymore of her time, and I definitely have no time to waste chasing ass that well, quite frankly, I didn't have to.

Moving in close to her, Cassandra seems excited as her eyes open bright and wide. I tell her, "Listen, tonight was great, and I will call you. I'm beat." A sadness covers her and she replies, "Going so soon?"

Grabbing my jacket, I make my way to her front door.

"Yes, early morning hours and I have tons of patients."

"Oh, I see," she tells me as she removes her clothes. Big, full silicon injected breasts scream at me. And while there are no hips or curves that appeal to me, the carefully cared for hairs on her pussy look appetizing. But not enough to make me stay.

"Quincy, don't you want to fuck?" she questions as she pulls me back to the sofa.

"Come on, I know you do. I have a nice vagina with your name all over it."

Vagina? Oh, she is so not sexy talking that way.

"I'm sure you do," I respond, second guessing my decision to leave. Maybe one more nut will get the job done.

She pulls me into a kiss, and I back up quickly, because if I don't know anything else, I do know that women grow attachments fast.

"Okay, girl, let's get it on," I tell her as I shove her toward the sofa.

"Oooh, you play rough, huh, Quincy?" she asks as she smiles.

"No, just ready for that vagina you just described." My dick is struggling with becoming hard, but I vision a sweet, wet pussy, and voila, I stiffen right up.

She lays back on the sofa, and spreads her legs wide for me. Skinny pale thighs, with no hips, and big, fake tits, is not what I imagined for the night, but she has a pretty enough face, and my dick is hard again, so she'll do, but not this way.

"Get on your knees," I command, and she quickly follows my orders.

"Oooh, Quincy, I like it when you talk dirty," she tells me as she gets propped on her knees on the sofa.

Her pale, flat ass greets me, and just as I'm about to go limp, I think about what's going to happen after a few minutes – I'm going to come once again and all will be well.

Reaching into my wallet, I pull out a condom, and put it on, stroking my dick to an acceptable hard on in the process. Leaning in, I grab the flatness that is her ass, and with my other hand, my fingers roam to find her hole. I insert deeply, and begin to gyrate with force. I grind harder, then faster, the quicker I do this, the quicker I can ejaculate, and get the hell out of here.

"Oh my God, you're so big, Quincy," she starts yelling and screaming. I rock and roll her hard and fast, and barely feel the condom getting wet.

"Quincy! Quincy! Quincy! Quincy!" she yells to the top of her lungs.

Hurry up and come, I say to both myself and my dick.

"Oh my God, Quincy, Quincy, Quincy, Quincy," she shrills loudly, looking back to see me, her hair is wild and a mess, and she looks as if she is in pure ecstasy.

Is she in the same galaxy I wonder?

I force a smile.

"Quincy, oh Quincy, Quincy, Quincy, Quincy, you're so big, so long, so good, Quincy!!!" she continues.

Would you shut the fuck up, damn, I think as I try with all my might to come. I need to come, now, and get the fuck out of here.

"Q…" she attempts to yell again, and I grab her by the hair, and push her face into the pillow to muffle the annoying sounds.

"Shhh, just let me fuck you. You're so good, Cassandra," I lie but it calms her vocals down for a moment. Need to focus, gotta concentrate on getting off.

Visions of Sanaa Lathan enter my mind and I move with a swiftness. The closer I get to reaching orgasm, the more anxious I become. As I thrust harder and harder, Cassandra yells louder and louder, and as the air becomes thin, my head spins and the dry condom now fills with essence of my jism.

So happy its over, I smile that I was finally able to reach orgasm. Cassandra looks back at me like she really put in some work. Happy is the expression she beholds, and relief is written all over my face.

QUEEN
Check and Check-Mate

y chicken bacon wrap from the sandwich joint down the street from the courthouse hits the spot. I'm now fueled for whatever Judge Randolph has to say once he takes the bench again. The message left by the bailiff on my cell phone indicates that we have about twenty more minutes before court resumes and best case scenario, this is all over and done with, or worst case scenario, I will have to prepare myself to go forward with plan B. I'm nervous, but confident and rooting for it all to be over. I got this; I can feel it.

I open the doors of the courtroom and announce my presence with a slight pompous stride as I glide down the aisle. I want this moment to be one that Michael, his family and I will all remember forever. There's a chance this won't go our way and Judge Randolph may deny my motion, but that's only a slight chance and I like to think positively.

"You look real good Queen. Others couldn't pull it off as well as you, but gloating becomes you." Cletus is both flattering and obnoxious.

"This ole thing? It's my victory suit; I want to make sure I look good for the TV cameras once the case is dismissed."

"Don't count your eggs before they're hatched Queen, the judge hasn't announced his ruling yet, he could deny your motion and this might turn out to be a very long afternoon for you and your killer client."

"You may be right Cletus; but I doubt it. I told you my client is innocent, and in a few moments, Judge Randolph is going to come out here and reiterate that fact for you and all the other people here who can't catch a clue. Face it, it's the final round Cletus, I hit you with an upper cut and I'm ahead on the score cards. This match is over. Excuse me while I talk to my client." I snicker as I walk off.

Slightly brushing pass Cletus, I make my way over to Michael. Before speaking to him I notice how bright the courtroom looks this afternoon. It may just be my imagination, but as the sun's rays shine over the jury box, I'm convinced that it's a sign of a brighter day for my client; things are looking up and I take it as a sign from above.

Michael's mother looks at me as if I am the next Messiah, a position I'm not comfortable with but one by virtue of the nature of this case I have taken on as my own. They've placed all their confidence in me. I pray I can deliver.

"Do you think this is about to be over Ms. Thomas? What do you think the judge will say?"

I can see they are worried yet hopeful. I try to ease their fears. "This is the break we've been looking for. I can't foresee any reason why the judge won't rule in our favor. But until he hits that gavel and states what his ruling is; you should continue to pray." I sense concern and anxiety in their eyes and I say a prayer of my own. It's already hard out here on a black man; I'm determined not to let another one succumb to the system; at least not on my watch.

I glance over at Cletus and his legal eagle team. They are reviewing their next moves as if the case will proceed. As they shift through paperwork I continue to pray. *Lord be with me and Michael today. Please let this be the end of this madness. Let Michael be set free.* Almost as if a sign from God, the bailiff announces the arrival of the Judge.

"All rise. The Honorable Douglas Randolph presiding."

The entire courtroom stands like soldiers at attention waiting for permission to be at ease.

"Be seated." Judge Randolph opens the case file in front of him on the bench and stares at it a few minutes before speaking.

"Counsel for the Defense has entered a motion for dismissal based on prosecutorial misconduct and failure to disclose exculpatory evidence. After taking the case under advisement and after careful consideration, I am granting the Motion and this case is dismissed. The Defendant is to immediately be released from custody." He hits his gavel and leaves the bench as abruptly as he took it.

The look on Cletus' face is priceless. I wink at him to rub it in. "Check and Check Mate." I mouth in his direction from my Counsel table. Cletus makes a point of making sure his response is audible for all to hear.

"I won't cry over spilled milk, but if you can sleep at night knowing you set a killer free, more power to you Ms. Thomas." With that Cletus picks up his documents and his briefcase and abruptly proceeds to leave the courtroom. He's pissed. I know it, he knows it and everyone in the room knows it. Several reporters leave behind him in a hurry, hoping to get a statement from him outside the courtroom.

"Is it really over Ms. Thomas?" Michael's mother grabs my hand, holding it deathly tight as she looks me directly in the eye. "Is my baby really free to go?"

A mother's love for her child never fades, even in the face of criminal charges. The love of a black mother is even stronger because it has added obstacles to overcome. In Mrs. Bevin's eyes, I could see the struggle of every black mother; the fear of uncertainty of the future of her son under the hands of the white man. I empathize with her pain. Even though I don't have any black men in training of my own, I have seen the carnage of more than my share of black men at the hands of the law. I've viewed enough black history accounts of lynches based solely on skin color to recognize Mrs. Bevin's fear for her son's life and rightfully so. Thank God I get to be the messenger that change can happen. Justice can be color blind.

"Yes, ma'am, it's over. With this dismissal by the judge; the Prosecution can only re-file the case if they have brand new evidence. So barring that they find something new, this is over. Michael is free."

Mrs. Bevens hugs me tightly and I have never felt so connected to another human being in my life as I do right now.

"Hallelujah and thank you Jesus." She cups her hands around Michael's face pulling his six foot frame down to her level so that she can kiss her baby boy.

After returning his mother's kiss, Michael steps forward and shakes my hand. His gesture is lukewarm and not what I was expecting, especially since his mother's response was more loving and the fact that I had just saved his life. I chalk up his lackadaisical gesture to him being a loner, standoffish in nature and unable to accurately express his feelings. Women are better at showing their emotions and the look on Michael's mother's face was payment enough to me for both of them.

"I don't know how I can ever thank you Ms. Thomas. You definitely are a great lawyer. With all the evidence they had, I was sure the jury would find me guilty." I find it hard to read his statement or his reaction. I want more from him on my victory, but I'll settle for the self gratification of having saved the one on my watch.

"You're welcome Michael; I was just doing my job."

Michael hugs his mom and I give them all a moment of family time together as I gather my things and walk out of the courtroom.

The madness starts as soon as I hit the steps of the courthouse doors. All I need is a podium for this to be an official press conference. I stop at the doorway, run my fingers through my hair to make sure it looks its best and I confidently walk down the stairs to the mob of news reporters and camera crews awaiting my arrival so that they can make the nightly news.

"Ms. Thomas, can you give us a statement concerning the judge's ruling?" The microphone is in my face before my feet could hit the last step from the building.

"I'll make this short. Today justice was served. Michael Bevens is an innocent man who was wrongfully accused. While it is tragic that two girls were brutally murdered, it is also tragic that the State chose my client to be the scapegoat for a crime he did not commit. The real perpetrator of this crime is still out there, my client was a victim of racial profiling and hopefully with the dismissal of the charges against Mr. Bevens, the police will take this opportunity to put race aside and concentrate on solving this crime and find the real murderer. Judge Randolph has made me proud today. He saw passed the song and dance performed by the prosecutor and made the right decision. Today the judge proved that liberty and justice extends to everyone; not just white America or rich America but to all in America, even those wrongfully accused."

I make my statement and superciliously walk off amongst the earsplitting sound of reporters calling my name wanting me to give them more. I am so proud of myself with this victory, but I know it's best to end things on top so I don't say anything more. If there's one thing my father taught me, it's to always leave them wanting more.

QUINCY
Taboo Tango

"**Y**o' Bro, how about picking a brother up tonight? Parking at that bitch sucks on poetry night. You would think that they were giving out free cheese at Jaspers instead of just some tired ass people taking the stage, spitting out rhymes." I urgently plead with Big on my cell while searching my closet for something to wear.

"You know what white boy? I don't know how many times I have to tell your pigment challenged ass that you ain't a brother before it sinks in, but yeah, I'll pick you up. At least if I come and get you, I know you'll be there on time. Lo would kick both our asses if we missed tonight. You know how much this means to him."

"I'm there. Just pick me up, and quit your trippin'."

"I'll be there in about an hour and try and look decent. Save the Dockers and sweaters for another time, look fly if you can. I got a feeling Jasper's will be hoppin' tonight." Big acts like he needs to chastise me.

"Even when I don't try, my fronts are up man. I look good with very little effort. You on the other hand…why don't you work on pulling all yo' shit together so this white boy doesn't outshine you. See ya in a minute."

I hang up the phone and start laying out my gear for the night. Damn, I wish I had a honey that could help me out with this shit. Big was right, sometimes I do dress kind of uptight. I'm always fresh to death, however. If I had a woman in my life she could keep me on track about things like that. Cassandra was a much needed distraction for the day. That piece of ass was tight and welcoming, but she was and is just temporary. Just like an aspirin, she relieved what ailed, but she's not a long-term cure.

My phone rings, I look at the number. "Damn, speak of the devil." It's Cassandra. Why did I give her my home number? Better yet why did I tap that ass? Oh yeah, I remember my hard dick was the culprit and built up sperm on the brain had dictated my actions.

"Call me baby." Her voice is sexy on my answering machine, but I don't feel like, nor do I have the time to deal with her right now. What ever happened to no-strings-attached relationships? Why can't she recognize that what we did was a tune up at best, it is what it is…sexual maintenance, nothing more. I let the machine continue to take the rest of her message and I dash off to the shower.

"I can still smell you, Quincy. Can't wait for round number two."

By a quarter to ten, Big was true to his word and sitting in my driveway honking his horn like crazy.

"I've told your ghetto ass about disturbing my neighbors." I chew him out while opening the passenger door.

"Keep talking and you will be walking. Shut the hell up and get in the car." Big revs the engine as if to threaten me.

The weather is nice and we make small talk until we get close to Jasper's. We circle the block a few times looking for a spot to park. A line is already forming at the front door and the bouncers are being choosey about who they let in.

"Damn. Look at that hottie in the mini skirt. She has legs for days." Big's tongue is practically hanging out of his mouth.

"She's all right if you like 'em thin. You know me. I like a sistah with some meat."

"Yeah, the key word for you is "sistah." You need to quit being so discriminating against your own people. White girls need loving too." Big laughs at his own statement.

"I'm not discriminating. I just like what I like."

"Call it what you want, but in searching for chocolate all the time, you are going to miss out on a whole lot of vanilla loving."

"Well, for your information, fat boy, I had a vanilla bitch suck this vanilla dick today, thank you very much."

"Vanilla Ice, my man, okay, you got that off, you multi-racial loving bitch."

Damn, this bitch is off the chain tonight." Big adds after circling the block a couple of times.

"Now yo' black ass see why I had you come and get me. Park down the street, we'll just have to walk. You ain't going to find anything closer, besides, you need the exercise."

"Fuck you Q!"

"Yeah, fuck me. But you need to walk around this bitch about ten times, for real."

"Hey, don't be mad at the big sexy boy."

We park about two blocks away and luckily for us we're on the guest list so we don't have to wait in the line to get in. Lo had reserved a table and him and Raj are already waiting for us when we get pass the security guards that patted us down at the door. I'm still confused as to whether we just went through airport security or the front desk at a club due to all the hand-held metal detectors. But even though I feel inconvenienced and violated from security groping me, I have to admit; I'll take that over worrying about a shoot out occurring inside the club.

It's dark and mysterious inside with candles lit on every table. The smell of Black and Milds and cigars seems to envelope the room. The DJ announces his presence and the upcoming poetry slam in between jazz and sultry R&B tracks.

Tonight's performer, Andre', a smooth cat, singing R&B and driving the ladies wild while gyrating and taking off his shirt, is leaving the stage. His song, *"What I Gotta Do"* was hot and the ladies agree. I swear if they could, these ladies would throw their panties on stage.

The MC begins to speak.

"Tonight is smooth and mellow and we have some spoken word artists here to help keep you in the mood. Get ready to have your senses enlightened tonight as our poets take the stage."

"You ready Lo? You betta make us proud after all this hype." I give him a nod of respect as I fuck with him just a little bit.

"Do you want me to sign a napkin or something for you now white boy? It might be worth something later." Angelo's air is confident, it always is, and I envy that about him.

"I would ask for an autograph, but that would entail you signing your name and we both know your ass can't spell." I laugh as I try and bust his bubble, but all he does is flip me the bird in response.

The club photographer walks up to the table and Raj stops him and peels off a few bills for his services.

"Let's at least get a picture." Raj interjects kissing a little of Lo's ass. "When you make it big, I might be able to sell it to one of those trashy tabloids, or at least get a little change for it on EBay."

We all gather and get into position for the photographer. Onlookers give us attention as the uniqueness of our presence commands it. Big's fat ass kneels down in true convict fashion and the rest of us pose as if we're in a '90's rap group.

Our usual waitress walks up right in the middle of the four of us posing for our picture.

"Awh, how cute is that? The Village People decided to reunite once again. Do ya'll want to order something in between prison shot poses?"

We laugh and head back to our seats.

"That's cute. How about you join us sweetheart? I have a warm spot right here on my lap with your name on it that you can sit on." Big starts gyrating in his seat while pointing to his dick.

"You're inappropriate and rude as always man." I let Big know he is getting on my nerves just as the waitress says her comeback.

"If your warm spot was bigger, I might give it a thought."

"Damn!" Raj, Lo and I say in unison as we laugh at Big. Lo decides to lighten the moment by taking her hand. "I'll have a double shot of Courvoisier; no ice."

"Grey Goose for me." Raj chimes in.

"Rum and Coke." I add my two cents.

"Icehouse on draft." Big says with a crooked smile and a wink.

She writes down the orders but only seems to notice Lo.

"They say you can tell a lot about the class of a man by what he drinks." She leans in flirtatiously towards Lo.

"Courvoisier screams confidence and power. Very sexy." She is staring in his eyes as if the rest of us are not even in the room. She then runs her fingers in a circle in the palm of his hand before announcing that she'll be right back with our drinks. Lo kisses the top of her hand and winks at her as she walks off.

Big yells in her direction, "So what does Icehouse say about a man? You know you fucking with your tip right? This Eric Benet wannabe is not the only one with money at this table."

She smiles, but keeps walking.

"Give it up man. You ain't her type and your tired lines prove it." Raj sarcastically interjects.

We look at the pictures from the photographer and our drinks arrive at the same time. I take a couple of sips and soon a pretty blonde comes to our table and asks me to dance. She's not my type, but cute nonetheless, and I love the boldness of her move and hey, it's only a dance, so why not? Not to mention my rum and coke is starting to kick in and has me feeling no pain. I watch her shake her backside in front of me and I rub my hands down the side of her body in rhythm with her moves. She's got a flat ass but she's still sexy. I forgot to get her name when accepting her proposition to dance. Mental note to self: get her number before last call, just in case. I can tell from her moves that she can probably ride a mean dick. She might be just what I need if my sexual drought continues for too much longer since I've made up my mind that Cassandra's ass is history.

I watch the blonde intensely, not with my eyes, but with my lust. But suddenly, I'm distracted. SHE walks in and everything else seems to stand still. The corner of my eye saw her first and then the rest of my senses respond to her presence. She seems to float across the room like an angel to my begging eyes. Even though the music is playing, I have a buzz, and a hottie is shaking her ass against my dick; SHE has my total undivided attention even without trying.

I want to lock her up in love for days. She's enough to penetrate my dark world.

I want her in the worst way. The parting of her luscious pouty, Faith Evans lips reveals her gorgeous smile; one that melts my heart. Her pretty, caramel-coated skin glows and is flawless to my eyes. Mmm, something about the way she moves. Shit, I don't know how to act. I love a woman who doesn't even know me – now I know I've had too much to drink. Her intensity has me drunk, intoxicated by her beauty. My breath is taken each time she moves. There's a whole lot of things she and I could do.

She glides by both the dance floor and me in total disregard of my existence. Damn, that makes me want her even more.

A song plays with the words, "Beauty was her name" and I listen to the lyrics and drink in the words in recognition of her. The blonde in front of me grabs my hips trying to recapture my attention towards her. I feign interest while watching my queen find a table and take a seat.

Her gracious glide has me gearing with gratitude. Compelling, celestial, cool and conniving, she is contentment and comfort all rolled into one hell of a woman. Pretty, like Apollonia, yet, beautifully comforting, majestic even, warm – that smile, sweet like Jill Scott, lips, sexy, like Faith Evans, fuck-able, like Vanity, back in the day. Dark, brown hair, soft like cotton, flowing like The Nile. Honey-colored, almond-shaped eyes, visible from a half a room away. They're piercing. Her aura, radiant. Skin – kissed by the sun.

Her beauty is flawless to me, not a strand of hair out of place or a blemish to her sweet face. I move to the beat that I hear in the room, but my mind is on her. Scoping and jocking; I watch as she swings her head to the side to get her hair out of her face as she orders a drink. Oh how I would love to caress that Carmel skin. Chocolate lips – damn, I'd kill to kiss them. The song ends and I can't get away from the blonde in front of me and back to my table fast enough.

"Can I get your phone number?" I hear her words but I can't form any of my own in response.

"Excuse me, cutey, nice dance; can I get your number?"

Snapping back to reality, I give her the courtesy of a reply. It's lame and the best I can come up with.

"Oh yeah, sure. Later though. Thanks for the dance," I reply, and shoo her away like an annoying fly on a hot summer day.

I see her once more and I close my eyes. Gradually, my eyes open, and the silence of my existence screams an all too familiar tune in my ear. It screams, "You must have her." My eyes close once more, and I envision her beauty again, because if I lose sight of her, my dream, I'm afraid my heart would not only break, but the fear of not having something I crave more than life itself, will force me into psychosis.

Sitting down and wiping the sweat from my forehead, I hear the boys ragging each other, but mentally I can't engage. Pretending to listen; I watch her. My wet dream shifts in her chair and laughs with her girlfriend. She is an image that men, white men instinctively think about and are careful to desire. Seeing the seductive slit in her dress, which is exposing her sexy thighs, I'm envious of the fabric that has the pleasure of touching her skin. Her thighs look soft, supple and delicious even from a distance. She's sitting on the edge of her seat and I can see the fullness of her ass. Perfection. I long to rub my hands along the silhouette that is hers.

I want to feel myself inside of her, over and over and over again.

She raises her glass to her lips and I take a sip of my drink simultaneously with her, imagining our lips are one. My nose is wide open by the mere sight of her and I can't stop myself from staring.

"Snap out of it! What's got you all wrapped up man?" I can barely hear Big.

"I've got to meet her."

"Who?"

"Who? How did you miss her? That girl over there." I point toward my obsession only to see that there are several people standing at her table and some are shaking her hand. I guess her beauty has captured everyone in the room.

"Don't you know who that is?" Big throws his hands in the air as if to say I am clueless.

"No, I don't know who she is, but I want to know."

"Man, that's the attorney that got that guy off for murdering those two girls. It's been all over the TV today. She's like a female version of Johnny Cochran or something."

"You're shitting me! That was her?" I smile as I watch her more intensely than before.

"Yeah man, she's practically a celebrity. Oh wait... are you sweating her?"

"No, I'm not sweating her." I lie unconvincingly.

"Looks like you sweating her to me."

"Looks can be deceiving. I just want to get to know her." I glance at her table again and I swear I can smell her skin from here, even half a room away. Yeah, she has my nose wide open for sure.

Big's voice fades to black. I know he's talking but I can hear no words.

A dark night coupled with the slightest chill in the air makes it a time to be best spent making love, passionately and ferociously to the one you love and lust for. There is an aching in my groin which is in the deepest need of attention. Real attention from someone who not only lights my loins on fire, but from a queen, my queen who my heart begs for. The fire down in my soul will soon erupt, kick into overdrive from the cravings, the daydreams, night fantasies, the want, need and desire. Yes, I've only known her for ninety seconds, but I love her already. Yet and still, I sit here, and I'm sure my careless whispers will ultimately fall on deaf ears.

I need you...

Those three words are what I've been dying to tell her. Wishing they would graciously part from my lips, in the heat of the moment, while in between kisses, I would tell her, "I need you." But my naughty thoughts, carnal fantasies and careless whispers would only fall on deaf ears.

I want her...

Deliciousness dares me to deliberately devour all this is so divine about her. What I'd give to taste the tender goodness that sits between her thighs.

"She's out of your league. You're not her type. Let it go Q. I don't want to see you get hurt."

"Why do you assume I'm out of my league? What am I chop liver or something, I'm a good catch." Try as I may to hide my irritation at Big's comment. I can't.

"Damn man. Calm down. I was just trying to save you some drama. I didn't mean anything by it. Quit trippin'."

"What makes you say, I'm not her type?" I take another sip of my rum and coke and motion to our waitress for another round.

"Because she don't do white boys, Fonzi."

"Maybe she just hasn't met the right white boy."

"Man she's like the poster child for affirmative action. You don't stand a chance."

"Aren't you the same man that told me if I only concentrated on chocolate I would miss out on a whole lot of vanilla loving?"

"Yeah, Q, that was me." Big rolls his eyes.

"Well, I'll just use that same logic on her." I smile and waive again for the waitress.

"Yes, cutie?" the waitress questions.

"What's she drinking?" I point in the direction of my queen.

"White Zinfandel."

"Send her another one on me. Add it to my tab."

"Will do. Any message for her?"

"Yeah, tell her it's from me and give her this message." I write the words on a napkin allowing my heart to guide the pen.

"The room got brighter once you walked in."

The waitress reads my message, smiles and walks to the bar and then over to her table. I try to act like she's not in my veins, but she is. She's in my system. The butterflies in my stomach threaten to take complete control. I can't take my eyes off of her, no matter how hard I try. Anxiously awaiting her smile, I'm like a kid bringing home a report card to his parents and awaiting approval of my grades. My dick throbs, my heart races and I readjust myself as I watch her listen to the waitress.

"Down boy! You only sent her a drink." I say to both my dick and myself.

Big and Raj are looking through Lo's poetry book helping him decide which pieces to recite. I'm useless to all of them. I can't hear them, I can't see them; my whole being is engulfed by her and the head that's doing the thinking for me right now is the one that lives south of the border. Trying to hide my anxiousness as the waitress returns to our table, I contemplate what my next move should be. "I've got smooth lines as long as I have a minute to think about them." I chuckle to myself. Then the waitress puts the drink down in front of me.

"What's that?"

"It's your White Zinfandel. You paid for it. I thought you should have it."

My heart ascends to my throat.

"I ordered it for the lady. What happened?"

"She told me to tell you, Thanks, but no thanks." The waitress wipes moisture off the table and removes our empty glasses before telling me that the unaccepted wine is still on my tab.

Thanks but no thanks? What the hell is that about? I don't think I've ever had a woman refuse a drink from me before. That has always been my signature move and would at least get me to first base. Leaning forward in my chair, I rub my hand across my chin confused by her actions and stare at her more intently than before. For some reason, the fact that she did not accept my drink makes me want her even more. Does she know that? Is this some sort of head game? Pondering the possibilities of the mystery that is her arouses me. Entering the point of no return, my mind drifts off once again to a time in space where only she and I exist.

"I told you that you man…you're out of your league." Big whispers his observation in my ear and I'm thankful that he did not bust me out in front of the guys.

She slowly stands, straightening her clothes in the process. Looking at the voluptuousness of her thighs, I instantly get visuals of her riding me hard while working those hips. A delicious body – Tyra Banks, the new, thick version – substantial in the hips, legs for days, big, round, full breasts that sit firmly above her core, she's built, perfectly, wonderfully, deliciously. A whole lot to offer – satisfying. Wanting to ride that till the wheels fall off makes me anxious as I notice again the thickness of her frame - makes me envious of her very skin, but in a complementary kind of way. I would love to be wrapped around her. The sight of her ass swaying so majestically from side to side, up and down, as her hips coincide with perfection, makes the tip of my manhood as solid as a rock. Tracing the curvature of her thick thighs with my eyes, I imagine them wrapped securely and seductively around my waist, and with each blow, my manhood delves in deeper into her righteousness, further into her faithfulness and takes my breath away. Her pretty, pulsating, pussy would give way to every one of my bold, blunt blows – even if only in my dreams.

I sense that her and her friend are going on a ladies' room run. Why do women always go in pairs? I don't think I will ever understand that concept, but I welcome the opportunity presenting itself for me to talk to her face to face by intercepting her journey. I adjust my shirt and pants and walk in the same direction that she is walking in.

What are you going to say? I ask myself as I pop in an Altoid for fresh breath, but I don't have an answer because I don't know. Wing it man…but make it enticing. I reprimand myself through internal interjections to just "man up" to the situation. Anything worth having is worth stepping out of the box to fight for. I watch as they walk by table after table on their way to the bathroom. Quickening my steps, I try to catch her before she enters the small stank-filled room that is more of a heaven for female gossip and makeup re-freshening than it is a pit stop for relief.

Man up. I caution myself again as I watch her seductively use her hands to push her shoulder length hair behind her ear on the right side

Fucking sexy. Is all I can think as I make my approach. It's now or never bitch. Step up or shut up. I tell myself.

"A real man improvises according to his circumstances. Flowers would have been a better gift for someone as beautiful as you, but we're in a bar so I sent the drink instead. If you're not thirsty, help me figure out another way to make you smile." My words seem to catch her off guard. I like that. A burst of confidence went through me like a power surge. I want to get up on the stage, drop the microphone and scream, "sexual chocolate."

The personification of beauty just stares at me. I can tell she is inventorying her words before speaking. I'm uncomfortable for a minute realizing I'm being mentally and physically scrutinized.

"Thank you for sending the drink, but thirst of any kind is an awkward need; one I do not posses in any sense of the word. Nothing personal, your generosity is noted, but not desired. Thank you anyway."

Nothing personal? Nothing desired? As sophisticated as her rejection is, it is still a rejection just the same. But I don't quit that easily. She takes a few steps closer to the ladies room and I caution myself to walk the fine line between admirer and stalker.

"You may not thirst now, but you intrigue me, so I'll lay in the cut until you do."

I grab her hand and kiss it before walking away. Seeing Lo do that same move earlier made me snatch it as my own.

She smiles. Even though her smile was all I needed, I pretend not to notice as I walk away. My swagger has a little more rhythm in it as I return to our table.

"You pissing up against a wall." Big scolds me.

"Yeah, maybe so, but at least I painted my name in the process." I reply with satisfaction. I've made an impression on her and that was my goal.

Lo, uniquely laced in oversized brown shades, a sea blue linen button up shirt, turquoise beaded necklace which stops at his oily, exposed chest runs his fingers through his dread locks and moves his head side to side warming himself up in preparation to take the stage. On a high from cracking the wall my queen had tried to build, I feel a sense of vigor to cement my presence in her thoughts more deeply and Lo's poetry is just the material I need. Pulling him to the side away from the table, I implore, "I need a favor."

As the honeys walk by, winking and blowing kisses at him, he diverts his attention back to me. "I'm about to go on stage, can it wait man?"

"My favor needs to be done while you are on stage." Lo raises his eyebrow suspiciously at me.

"What kind of favor is this? What do you need? I got you, just tell me, quickly."

"I know you have already picked your poems, but do you have anything that's sexy that you could recite for me to a lady here in the club?"

Lo smiles and says, "I have lots of sexy poems, which lady is it? That will help me pick the right one." I point toward my queen.

"Damn, you picked the best looking sista in here, and I emphasize the word, 'sista', but I think I have one that fits your situation. You're reaching with her, by the way, Q, just letting you know."

"So I've been told. Nothing beats a failure but a try, and Lo, I'm damn sure gonna try."

Lo smiles, "It's like that, Q?"

"Yes, man. Do me proud, please. Tell her that I want to quench her thirst. Or better yet, tell her the room got brighter when she walked in."

As he walks toward the stage, Lo confesses, "I got you, bro."

I take my seat and Lo takes the stage. He takes a sip of his drink and without introduction, he spits his first rhyme. I barely hear it in between watching her and imagining the possibilities that I need to make reality. His first rhyme is short, but something about Lo seduces both seeing and hearing. He could be reading from the dictionary, but the delivery from his lips always seems to work, especially with the ladies.

Feeling like a cast member in the movie, Love Jones, I await Lo's next rhyme.

"I'm Angelo. Simply 'Lo' to my friends, some of whom are here with me tonight." He raises his glass to our table and Big, Raj and I all lift our glasses right back at him. I look out the corner of my eye and see that she was watching Lo's acknowledgement.

"Speaking of friends, one of mine would like to dedicate my next poem to a lovely lady in the room. The room got brighter when you walked in. You know who you are, and this one's for you."

"I'm in your zone
Watching you
Drinking your aura
Daydreaming of getting it on

Roadblocks in lifestyles
More importantly
Skin color collides

You captured me
imprisoned my mind
intoxicated with your beauty
I can't deny

Brown skin
You're my master
White skin,

I'm your slave
Does pigmentation matter
When it's you I crave?

Let's cross the barriers
Ignore the impulses we're supposed to subdue

Open the door
Invite me in
And let the
Taboo tango ensue.

Initially our eyes met briefly and implored for the chance
to welcome heavy breathing,
hunger,
needing.
May I kiss the brown flesh and begin eating?

I beg you to discard all your uncertainties,
and we'll wet together
as the taste of your sweet skin between my lips
ignites and intoxicates
then our heated tongues will meet in the midst
of hot and quickening breath
as I fill you up with all I have left

saturating you with me
dance to my rhythm baby
you can have all you want
-if you just ask
Do you want me?
Let me take you from a whisper to a scream
While chocolate dreamin."

QUEEN
Forbidden Fruit

At Paula's tenacious insistence we're going out tonight. She says we need to celebrate my victory from this morning, but I know she really just wants to help me take my mind off of things. Michael's trial and Derrick's obsession have both taken their toll on me. My mind has been bombarded day and night with nothing but heaviness and widespread drama and it's time to lighten my load, unwind and let my hair down. Paula reminded me that I owe it to myself to put both events behind me and listening to a little poetry in a club with distinct, diverse, and eclectic smiling faces coupled with friendly flowing vibes is just what the doctor ordered.

Poetry is definitely cool, although I'd rather be at a Jay-Z or Mos Def concert. I'm a true Hip-Hop connoisseur at heart. No one ever believes it until I recite the *entire Ready to Die* album from Notorious B.I.G. Jay-Z's music has set the tone for my life. Yes, I'm a lawyer, and yes, I have a life – somewhat.

I remember right after the victory earlier, immediately after the brief press conference, I was escorted to my rental. It was there, even as the press persistently pounded on my driver's side door, in an attempt to get more out of me than I was willing to give – my first phone call was to my father.

No one will ever be able to convince me that when my mother gave me those instructions to take care of my father, that I somehow managed to translate that command into taking care of all who had something in common with Daddy – the black man. Yes, the win was great, but for all black men, all men wrongfully and unjustly accused. I like to think that my actions today contributed my two cents into the pot of racial equality. Just like Barack's win was validation, this too signifies validity, even in the most small and minute form.

Placing the cell to my ear, I anxiously awaited Daddy to pick up.

"Hey Pumpkin."

"Hi Daddy." Tears did well up in my eyes as soon as I heard his voice. It's something about that man that just does it for me. I can't imagine my life without him.

"I'm proud of you Baby Girl," he revealed, choked up with his confession.

That was all I needed to hear from him. Those words were my substantiation.

"I love you, Daddy."

"Love you too, Pumpkin."

As I prepared to pull out of the court's parking lot, my phone rang. It was Paula – my girl, my rock, my best friend for life, my everything. I do credit Paula with keeping me grounded and sane throughout my life.

"Hey girl," she shrieked loudly.

"Hey Ma."

"I know you can't talk. Just wanted to tell you that I am so proud of you. I love you, sis."

"Love you too."

Not too bad. I think to myself as I check out my luscious silhouette in the mirror. Oh the struggles of the black woman. For many years, I was insecure about my frame, aesthetically, I felt in debt, as I don't look like a supermodel. Even with my stature, being above average in height, and with my weight, being curvier than most, it took me some getting used to. But over the years, I developed more and more into what I remember my mother being – a brick house, so I accepted what God gave me and have been working it ever since. Everyone is not going to be a slender stick figure and I'm cool with that. Besides word on the street is that men don't want to feel like they're fucking a teenage boy; finesse is in the voluptuousness.

Opting for a longer skirt than usual to cover up the purplish bruise Derrick left on my thigh, I'm frivolously pleased that it's just tight enough to accentuate my assets, and the slit up the side is mouth watering if I do say so myself. Just one more final touch and I can leave. The bottle is almost empty, so I spray sparingly. It's her scent—Jasmine. My zealous dedicated way of staying connected to my mom. I can't have her with me in the physical form, so the nostalgic aroma of her smell will have to do. It keeps me grounded—keeps me sane. As the flowery fragrant fog hits my skin and the lingering scent fills the air, I can almost hear her softly and gently sing…

Whisper something sweet to me.

Perfection. Now, I'm ready to go. Heading toward the door, my cell rings. The number is restricted, but I answer anyway. Could be another request for a television interview about Michael's case. Placing my hand on my hip, I tilt my neck to the side, and answer.

"Hello, this is Queen."

Silence.

"Hello. Anybody there?"

More silence, with the exception of faint breathing.

"Sorry, but I don't have time for this shit. Goodbye."

I grab my keys and I'm out the door.

Finally, I find a parking spot near Jasper's. I lucked up as someone was pulling out, thank God, because with these heels, I can't afford to walk more than ten feet at a time. Paula, dressed in the tightest of black turtlenecks, and black leather pants with boots to match looks like she's trying to catch a new husband or she's going to rob this place. Crazy, sexy cool, Paula is smiling and waiving frantically at me when I arrive at Jasper's. She has saved a place for me in line and she gives me a hug as I approach. With the face of a cherub, she smiles and tells me. "There's my superstar, lawyer, sister-friend!" She yells like a maniac. She's been my sister by choice from the day we met, we just seemed to click. I love her school-girl quality which is mixed with a hint of Rockweiler when needed and I'm glad she made me come out tonight. She always seems to know just what I need, when I need it and how I need it. I thank God for bringing her into my life.

With the infamous hand-on-hip, she tells me, "I was just about to send out a search party for you. I thought you were going to stand me up."

"Quit tripping, you know if it ain't work related I run on CP time." We both laugh at the surreal truthfulness of my statement.

"True dat! Well, I'm glad you made it. You look good girl, I think I'm jealous."

Paula has a way of always making me smile.

"You don't look bad yourself. I'm loving those boots."

"Ain't they tight? These are my 'hook em' boots. I plan on hooking somebody tonight. My oil is running low and I need some lubrication so I thought I would dress for the part."

"Well those boots are definitely a start."

The line is long but the bouncer recognizes me and moves us to the front of the line and we get in pretty quick.

"Damn girl, it's good to be you. I ain't mad at you. You be Oprah, I'm happy being your Gayle." Paula lightly shoves me as we are let in ahead of others.

"Yea, sometimes the job has its perks." I lightheartedly and humbly add.

We find a table and sit down, as I place my keys and cell down, the phone starts to vibrate across the table. The little envelope on the screen signals I have a text message. I open it.

There's a hole in my soul now that you're not around.

Just like the phone call earlier, the number from the text is restricted. Paula notices the look of confusion on my face.

"What's up girl?" She asks as she dances side to side in her seat.

"Nothing. Somebody's playing games with me, that's all."

"Who?" Paula stops moving in her seat and I can see that she is worried and ready to go into attack mode, but I don't want to tackle the topic right now.

"I don't know; let's just leave it at that." I put my hand in the air to signal that we ain't going there, I'm through discussing it. I turn my phone completely off.

"Hi, I'm the manager here at Jasper's," an Italian guy greets us. We want to offer this bottle of the finest bubbly for you and your friend. We love to treat the local celebrity every now and then," he says as the waitress pours a glass for me and a glass for Paula. Paula smiles, I do the same. Looking up to him, I extend my hand, shake his. "Thank you very much, Mr.?"

"Mr. Nicastro, mam."

"Well, thank you so much, Mr. Nicastro. I appreciate this wonderful gesture immensely."

Mr. Nicastro bends down, leans into the middle of our table and smiles. "Ms. Thomas, do you really think that guy was innocent? Don't get me wrong, its brilliant how you got him off on a technicality, one that only a skilled lawyer could pull off, but I'm curious, is he really innocent?"

Wow, I didn't see this coming. People have really paid attention to the case of State vs. Bevens. Careful in my words, I think before I speak.

With a gracious smile, which almost leads to a chuckle, since Paula is tapping my ankle with her boot, I tell him, "Sure, Mr. Bevens is innocent. Justice is a beautiful thing."

Mr. Nicastro stands to his feet and smiles. "In the words of John McCain, 'Touché'. Good work, Ms. Thomas and thank you for coming to Jasper's, we're honored to have your presence."

"What about the phone call, Queen? Who was that?" Paula's nosey ass questions again.

"Not tonight. I'm not letting anything ruin my night." That affirmation is solidified for me when a small crowd of people gather around our table and begin shaking my hand and congratulating me on Michael's case.
"Great work today, Ms. Thomas. I knew that Michael was innocent," a tall black man, dressed in a black suit tells me.
"Yes, sir, it was a great day. And, justice was served."
"You knew what I knew all along. That boy ain't killed them girls," a short, stocky, chocolate coated woman reveals.
Smiling, I reply, "Yes, justice prevailed."

Apparently the bouncer has a big mouth, or people recognized me from TV today. I don't know which lead to my new fame, but I have to admit, I like the attention.

A waitress comes to the table with a drink. Finally, after a few seconds, the sister tells me, "Great job today in court, by the way. See that cutie over there, you know, at the United Nations table," she chuckles as she points to a table across the room from ours, where there are four gentlemen seated. "Oooh, that Maxwell, look-a-like?" Paula infuses as she interrupts. The waitress laughs. "No, that fine ass white boy over there, you know with the Matthew Mcconaughey-Eric Dane-Robin-Thicke swagger." To say I'm flattered would be an understatement. I could get used to this star treatment. At least that is what I think until she points in the direction of the sender. He's tall and handsome, just not 'dark'. Is it too much to ask for all three; tall, DARK and handsome? Life's complicated enough without opening the racial door. I send the drink back.

"Tell him thanks but no thanks." The waitress looks shocked at my words, and walks away from our table.

"What's wrong with you? Why are you sending that drink back?" Paula stares at me as if I've lost my mind.

"I don't want it and I don't want to lead him on by giving him the wrong impression that I'm interested, because I'm not."

"And you're not interested because…?"

"Because he's white! I don't get down with jungle fever. Ain't never had the fever and don't plan on coming down with it anytime soon. Can we just not do this right now?" My answer is short and to the point.

"It's just a drink, Queen. He didn't ask you to marry him. You could have taken the drink. Hell, you could have given it to me. I ain't turning down nothing but my collar. He's sexy too, shit, girl, you done got high-falutin' on me."

"Will you hush? I'll buy you a drink if that's what it takes for you to drop this subject. Just come with me to the ladies room first." I change the subject because I don't need Paula swimming around in my head analyzing my thoughts.

We make our way to the bathroom slowly, enjoying the sights of all the fine men in the club. In between glances, HE approaches me. He catches me off guard and I can't help but stare. He's got to be about six-three with the bluest eyes I've ever seen with my own eyes. Eyes that look like spacious swimming pools inviting someone to dive right in. The windows of the soul never looked so desirable and debonair. He's very attractive even if I'm partial to dark meat and don't ever plan on crossing the racial line.

He surrenders his soul to me, served up in a manner I am not used to having it delivered. Unlike Derrick, he's a breath of fresh air in concept, but I keep my guard up just the same.

With a grin that reveals his pearly whites, and deep-pitted dimple in his cheek, he tells me, "A real man improvises according to his circumstances. Flowers would have been a better gift for someone as beautiful as you, but we're in a bar so I sent the drink instead. If you're not thirsty, help me figure out another way to make you smile."

I can't believe this white boy. I think to myself after he skillfully macks to me with a style and finesse that I haven't seen in some brothers. I'll give him an 'A' for his efforts. He's smooth, and very likeable, but daddy would kill me if I even entertained the thought of dating a white man. Society may be changing in its views concerning interracial relationships, but, what would my father say? It may be chic and politically correct to be color blind; but I'm just not there yet on that ideology.

I turn him down yet again, but I can't help but watch him return to his table. Built like a well-oiled machine, "Whitey" could star in a Bowflex commercial. Those strong thighs should be on display in a storefront along with those well sculpted guns. For a brief moment I think, what if, but I shake that notion from my head.

"Earth to Queen, newsflash, he's gorgeous, are you crazy? See if it were me, I'd be down on my knees right about now. Damn, look at him, Queen. Look at that fine ass white boy! Do you see him? Shit, girl, you crazy. You are crazy with a capital C."

"Shut up, Paula."

A hot, humid, sensual and sultry aura fills the room as the poets begin to perform. I find comfort in their words and the creativity of their dialect and delivery. It always amazes me how people can paint images with words in a way that makes you view life differently; more positive, more clear. One poet, entrances my mind to the point of rapture. His final poem was intended for me, and I am beguiled by the gesture. Intensively listening to the expressive lyricism of the verse, I am catapulted to a romantic place that touches my heart.

The words of Lo, as he said his friends call him, were delivered on behalf of my vanilla admirer. I soak them in and allow them to permeate my brain. I am drenched in feelings of unbridled and unobtainable desire. Confusion arrests and seizes my soul.

The poem hits home, detailing the type of relationship I envision as my own. Had a chocolate Adonis sent it, I would probably be accepting a booty call right now. But as luck would have it, my Adonis is colorless and therefore off limits; right man, wrong shade.

The words however keep replaying in my mind, as I glance over to HIM, all I can hear is, "Let's cross the barriers. Ignore the impulses we're supposed to subdue. Open the door. Invite me in. And let the Taboo tango ensue."

In a day that has included abuse, a trial, and confusing and unwanted communication, how can I possibly handle the fact that the only silver lining of the day lies in forbidden fruit?

QUINCY
Skeletons in the Closet

Queen bends over making her ass checks clap a melody that only a woman with her assets could pull of in the way of booty tricks. I playfully smack her ass as she shakes it in my face before raising her leg and turning over to ride me. In appreciation of the lap dance, I throw dollar bills into the air screaming with excitement and a feeling that I am about to bust a nut in my pants at any minute. An annoying sound rings in my ear. It gets louder and soon the sound of my cell phone ringing on the night stand next to me awakens me out of my dream right as I was about to pull Queen's hair while pretending to give it to her doggy style. I glance first at the clock on the stand next to me then at the caller ID on my phone as I fervently try to rub my hard-on down in submission to a limp state.

"You sure know how to fuck up a wet dream. This better be good, Big, and why are you calling me so early on a Sunday morning?"

"I know your cracker ass didn't forget what we are doing today did you?"

I can tell that Big is driving from the loud ass music that is playing in his truck. I swear if the volume isn't busting eardrums, Big acts like he can't hear it. Unless he is shattering windows of everyone around him as he drives by, I think he feels slighted some how.

"Can you turn that shit down long enough for you to hear me loud and clear as I tell yo black ass that I ain't going anywhere today."

"Well, if you just made the promise to me that you would hang out today, maybe you would be off of the hook. But it wasn't me that you made the promise to. You told Auntie you would visit today and you can't break her heart by reneging now can you?"

"Shit is that today? Damn, I forgot we said we would come back today."

"Sure is, and you know she has probably already started Sunday dinner before leaving for church."

"Damn, I forgot all about it."

"Well, remind yourself and get dressed. We got a long ride and you don't want to disappoint an old lady now do you?"

"Low blow man. Shit! What time are we supposed to be there?"

"You have about two hours to yourself and then I'll be there to get ya."

I rub down my throbbing dick again and sit up in the bed.

"Alright man, I'll be ready. Your trifling ass cousins need to step it up because you and them are fucking with my sleep and my fantasies. Peace out. I'll see you in a few." *Queen, hold that thought and keep that spot warm, we'll pick this up later. I say out loud to myself as I wipe my sleep-filled eyes and stand up to yawn. Damn, the things we do for family. Big and Auntie may not be family by blood, but they are family in my heart. I run my fingers through my hair and walk to the closet. She better have made some greens and cornbread.*

❧❧❧❧❧

The ride from Pocono City to Newark is uneventful. I stare out of the window watching the scenery change from green and tranquil to gray and cold. I find myself drifting into the significance of the world around me, contemplating the meaning of the transition of the environment around me and I liken the change to life itself. On one side of the bridge is hope and prosperity on the other loneliness and bitter despair. I may physically live on the side where hope springs eternal, but mentally, I live on the side of despair. I relive the sight of Queen in my mind and try and imagine that there is a way to cross over to the side of hope.

"What's up with that stupid grin on your face?"

"What grin?"

"The one you can't seem to hide while sitting over there in la-la land."

"Never mind Big, you wouldn't understand and I don't feel like explaining it to your sorry ass. So you said we're just going there to check on Auntie and leave right? Nothing more?"

"Yeah, you know I can't just rely on Ree-Ree to make sure my kin is living right. I promise man, we'll drop in, eat some home cooking, peel off some Benjamins and bounce; in that order. You'll be home before the evening news.

"I'm going to hold your punk ass to that Big."

"Quit ya bitchin, we're here."

The stairs to the apartment is absent of the gang of ghetto vermin that was sitting on the steps when we visited before. Thank God for small favors. We smell Auntie's cooking the moment she opens the door.

"You boys are right on time. Dinner's almost done. I hope you don't mind but I invited Mrs. Belle to join us." Auntie makes her announcement while setting the table, and her words are more of a courtesy than asking our permission. Something about being around her made the trip seem worth it.

"Mrs. Belle's here?" Big spoke the words, but the excitement is on both of our faces like two teenage boys peeking into the girl's locker room. There's no denying what the sight of Mrs. Belle does for both of us.

"I sure am! You boys come over here and give me a hug." She lights up the dining room with her smile as she walks in from the kitchen with her arms opened wide, welcoming us into her bosom.

We both oblige, but my hug lingers a little longer than Big's. I love the way she smells, I can't place it, it's a mixture of Jasmine and happiness, if happiness had a smell to it. Very unique and soothing.

"Boy, you better let go of me. Those types of hugs are reserved for my man or my child."

"I didn't know you had children Mrs. Belle, and you know if I was just a few years older you would need your running shoes because I would be chasing after you." I smile and release my hug feeling a bit like I was out of line.

"Child. I have a child, and I've got a lot of secrets in my closet that you don't know about boy, and I got a little cougar in me as well, so don't tempt me." She waves a potholder in my direction as she helps Auntie arrange the food on the table.

"What do you know about being a cougar Mrs. Belle?" Big chimes in as he sits down at the table and practically shoves a cornbread muffin in his mouth."

"Less than I'd like to, and more than I let on."

We all laugh.

"You boys quit being all up in grown folks business and leave Mrs. Belle alone." Auntie scolds us and we sit down to eat. Big fumbles through saying grace over the food after Auntie gives him a raised eyebrow that indicated he had no other choice than to say it as the reigning male of the family in the house. Some traditions never change in black households, I think to myself as I smile, glad that she didn't make me do it instead. Big makes his plate and begins to ask her about her bills. I listen, but only half hearted. My eyes are focused on Mrs. Belle. There is a sadness about her that is in the background of her beauty. Her caramel-colored skin is smooth and supple, but I sense sadness in her pores. Maybe it's the doctor in me, which forces me to look beyond the surface of a face in order to see deeper inside. Her eyes meet mine and I can see the sadness even clearer.

Abruptly, Mrs. Belle gets up from the table and walks to the kitchen. I watch as she reaches for her purse on the counter and removes two small orange colored medicine bottles. She shakes the contents from each bottle, one at a time, and before she can replace the caps on the bottles, Auntie calls to her, "Can you bring in the peach cobbler from the stove on your way back to the table so these boys can have some dessert before hitting the road?"

"I'll help her." I announce and walk quickly toward Mrs. Belle. She gets startled as I approach and drops the bottles of pills as if embarrassed to be taking them, worst yet, letting someone see her take them. Tiny white pills scatter across the kitchen floor and I help her pick them up. I notice the prescription drug name of Geodon on the label, but pretend not to see it or recognize what it is. Mrs. Belle hurriedly puts the bottles back in her purse and I grab the cobbler off the stove and take it to the table. My mind wonders through the rest of the dinner conversation. Geodon is for the treatment of schizophrenia and I'm curious as to how long Mrs. Belle has been taking it. I watch her laughing and talking to Big and Auntie as they prepare a doggie bag for me and Big to take home with us. Her mannerisms are so normal, she looks the same as she always has to me, but knowing what I do now, I can't help but be impressed with the composure she has given her disorder. Even as a doctor, I didn't suspect her psychiatric diagnosis. I guess she wasn't exaggerating when she said there's a lot about her we don't know.

My hug with Mrs. Belle on our way out the door lingered even longer than the one I gave her earlier. Now I have a clue as to the sadness I see behind her eyes and in her pores. The mystery of her history dances in my head as Big and I begin our trip back home.

"Where's your mind at man?" Big breaks the thick silence surrounding us in his truck, but I don't want to air Mrs. Belle's little secret, so I lie.

"I was thinking about that beautiful lawyer from the other night. I've got to figure out a way to get to know her better."

"Man I haven't seen you sweat a girl like this before. What is it about her that has you so whipped and you haven't even smelled the pussy, let alone gotten any?"

I chuckle since I don't even know the answer to that question myself. "Somehow, that makes it better Big. The fact that getting between her legs is not the only thing that turns me on about her."

"Well, damn, if you're that sprung then go see her. I usually don't make it a habit to advocate chasing a woman since you know my philosophy of 'so many women, so little time' but why don't you go see her and get some closure on this one way or the other."

"I wouldn't know where to start in trying to reach her, even if I wanted to."

"Play games all you want, but we both know you want to reach her. And that's why it pays to have friends with connections." Big has a sinister grin on his face like he wants to say, "I know something you don't know." So I bite on his need to one up me.

"Exactly what connections you got Big?"

"Only the address of where your crush works."

"How did you get that?"

"Her office is downtown in the same building where I get my construction licenses from. Pretty swank office if I do say so myself."

"Man you ain't shit. If you knew all along where she worked why didn't you tell me?"

"One, because you didn't ask, and two; because I gotta treat ya like the rest of my bitches and make you beg." He smiles as he hands me one of Queen's business cards. "Just don't make a fool out of yourself Q, but go see her so you can return to normal, I'm sick of you in this love-sick puppy mode.

I fold my hand around the business card and smile; maybe I do have a chance to change my history towards hope.

QUEEN
Daddy's Little Girl

I love my daddy with an admiration that is only magnified with special days like today. His call this morning suggesting lunch left me feeling thrilled and yearning for some much needed father-daughter time with him. La Frontera, is my favorite restaurant and he is here waiting for me as I walk in. The papa bear hug and kiss he gingerly gives me on the cheek are more comforting than a flannel nightgown and thick socks on a cold winter's night.

Always the gentleman, daddy pulls my chair out for me as I admire the ambiance of La Frontera. Low lights, pastel colored walls, abstract art pieces, and Duke Ellington and John Coltrane tunes playing in the background have a soothing affect on me. No matter how many times I come into this place, I still find something new about it to love.

"Baby girl, you sure made your papa proud winning that Bevens' case. They said it couldn't be done; yet my baby girl did it. You're a regular female Johnny Cochran and you never cease to amaze me Queen. Your momma should be proud," he says while unfolding his linen napkin and laying it gracefully in his lap. His one of a kind smile is warm and endearing; one that I will never grow old.

"I'm sure she would be daddy, if she were here, but somehow I know she saw me today."

Daddy just smiles back at me and looks down at the menu. He is distinguished in every fiber of his being. Dressed in a chocolate, Wale Corduroy Sports coat and a taupe Eddie Bauer sweater, which offset his hazel green eyes; I'm glad he's all mine and that I don't have to share. With the perfectly aligned gray streak in his hair, which is wavy and curly, he looks like a university professor even though he is a simple and unobtrusive man. His skin has aged well, proof that *black don't crack* and he is a walking poster child for handsome and debonair. I catch a few old hens at an adjacent table giving him the eye. The local retirement home must have had a field trip or something of that nature, to let the old fogies out for some fresh air, and the ladies are enjoying the sight of daddy, giggling amongst themselves as they stare. I nudge him and point in the direction of the flirtatious old ladies.

"Seems like you have an audience daddy. Guess I can't take you anywhere without you causing a commotion." I wink at him while opening up the menu and pondering what to order.

"Although their eyes are burning holes in the back of my neck, I'm not interested in the Geritol Pep Squad.'"

"Daddy…that's just wrong." I chuckle.

"Well, it may be wrong to say, but its true none the same. Women who smell like Bengay and roses don't float my boat."

"I really don't need to know what floats your boat daddy. I could go the rest of my life without that visual in my head. I'm just lucky you only have eyes for me or I would be sitting here starving right now, waiting for my turn in line." I smirk as I feel my phone vibrating in my purse. I take it out and see that I have a text message from a restricted number.

I miss you. Is all the text says. I turn off the phone completely because I am tired of all the head games.

"Can't I have a minute alone with you sweetheart? Who was that?"

"Nobody daddy. What are you going to have?"

Before daddy can answer, HE arrives standing with one hand behind his back and a napkin traced over the folded arm in front of him. He is mimicking a waiter and it would have been amusing if I weren't terrified and about to pee my pants from seeing him.

"Are you ready to order?" He says the words as they should have been said, but in my mind venom spewed from his mouth and smoke erupted from his nostrils with each syllable. Daddy barely looks up from his menu and begins to speak.

"I'll have the…"

"Save your breath daddy, this is not our waiter."

Daddy looks at me confused while I roll my eyes towards Derrick.

"Well, if it isn't our waiter, who is it?" Daddy looks up in Derrick's direction, but does not return the stupid grin that adorns Derrick's face. Daddy was waiting for an explanation and wouldn't let down his guard until he got one.

Derrick removes the napkin from his arm and sits down next to me on my side of the booth. He is too close for comfort and I can smell alcohol on his breath. It is barely noon and he already has a buzz, I know anything that follows will be awkward at best. The stench of the liquor and his entire being both engulfs me and makes me want to puke. Moving a little to the side, Derrick moves closer to me. With each inch that I put between us, he closes the gap and drunkenly smiles while doing it. Before I can answer daddy's question, Derrick answers for me.

"I have been dying to meet you for a very long time, but I was respectful to baby girl's wishes about keeping us on the downlow until the time was right."

With a look of concern, daddy asks, "I'm sorry young man, I still did not get your name, and I'm not following you. What are you keeping on the downlow?"

Hearing the word, "downlow" come out of daddy's mouth sounds almost vulgar; and the feeling of Derrick's body so close to mine in a confined area is repulsive. I need air. Resuscitation of another time and place; anywhere but here, anywhere but now.

"I'm Derrick. Queen's man." He announces at a level that even if whispered would still be too loud for my ears to hear.

Daddy raises his eyebrows and looks at me. I communicate with him through facial expression. He's known me for thirty-plus years so he'll be able to figure it out.

"Queen, you did not tell me you were involved with someone." Daddy's eyes examine me in hopes of clarification and all I can do is pray really hard to be beamed to any place other than La Frontera right now.

"He's not my man daddy. That's just wishful thinking on his part." I snarl as I move an inch to the right again.

Derrick kicks his heel into my ankle and his size 12 dress shoes hit the spin of my heel with a crushing force. The pain makes me grit my teeth.

"That's our Queen. Always the bashful one." He smiles in daddy's direction while putting his hand on my thigh and squeezing it with all his might while digging his fingertips into my skin with a vengeance. I wince in pain but say nothing. "I love your daughter and she loves me, but she didn't think you were ready to hear that she had another man, besides you, in her life."

I can tell daddy is trying to read me. Trying to get some inkling as to whether Derrick is serious or not. The grip on my thigh gets tighter. I want to SCREAM that the man sitting next to me is an abusive, raving maniac, but I can't form my lips to do it; instead of screaming that, I Whisper, "its okay daddy. I meant to tell you about Derrick, I just never had the chance to." It's not quite a lie, I did want to tell daddy about Derrick, but not in a complementary way. So my statement wasn't a lie, but I figured it would serve the purpose of the moment. My answer seems to calm Derrick and he lessens his grip on my thigh and thus my pain begins to subside.

Daddy tries to read my eyes and apparently I am convincing in camouflaging my true feelings because he buys the line I am feeding him. Or at least, he's playing the game well. Time will tell.

"It's nice to meet you Derrick." Daddy stretches his hand out toward Derrick. I see the sinister grin of satisfaction form on Derrick's face as he shakes my daddy's hand. I vomit a little in my mouth at the thought of Derrick's skin touching my father's. They are from two different worlds that should never meet. Cut from different cloths or different textures. Clean vs. Dirty; Right vs. Wrong; Good vs. Evil. Juxtaposition of what a real man should be; reverse sides of a corrupt mirror that should never be looked into.

I watch the look in Derrick's eyes as he begins to charm my daddy into thinking he was my man; that he was normal, that he was everything except pure evil. I feel lost on how to change what is unfolding before my very eyes. I feel trapped in what to do. I feel the need to puke.

"Excuse me gentlemen, I need to go to the ladies room." As I stand up, Derrick grabs my arm tightly and the pain, once felt on my thigh, has traveled the distance to my arm.

"Why are you leaving honey? We were all just starting to get to know each other." He smiles as he speaks, but his eyes scream to me that I better hurry my ass back to the table because he will only play this game for so long.

"It'll only take a minute. You boys enjoy yourselves and I'll be right back." As I walk to the Ladies room, daddy's words a few minutes earlier of feeling eyes burning a hole in the back of his neck, seemed true about me because I could feel Derrick's eyes throwing swords of flames toward me. But I need air. I need to breathe air that has not been contaminated by Derrick.

I splash cold water on my face from the mosaic bathroom face bowl in the ladies room, dry my hands and nervously call Paula. Thank God for sidekicks, since right now, I need mine. Before I can dial, a new text appears.

Need help in the bathroom?

Wait. How is Derrick texting me, when I just left his sick, sorry ass ninety-seconds ago. To this day, I can't believe I ever got involved with Derrick.

Meeting him at the courthouse some time ago, I remember the day well. Derrick, dressed in a Gucci suit, shoes to match, and fresh button-up, approached me one day after a case. He introduced himself and said that he was a corrections officer and that he admired the work that I was doing. Blessed with a gorgeous smile, and rich, smooth, dark chocolate skin, Derrick looked and talked the part. He revealed his true colors quite some time after we started dating, and I've been trying to break loose ever since. He is a raging lunatic, one that is in desperate of psychological help. The thought of what he did to Sherri haunts me most nights. I am on constant prayer to God, praying that He leads me and guide my steps on how to bring Derrick to justice.

Two big-boned white women make their way into the ladies room. The red-headed heavier one looks at me longer than what I am comfortable with. My eyes don't leave hers.

"Do I know you?" she questions as she raises her finger.

"Yes, Carla, that's the attorney who got that man off for killing those poor little sweet angels," the older, much lighter blonde reveals.

Disdain crosses the red-head's face. "Oh. Are you in here to wash the blood off your hands?" she asks, with a tone that I do not appreciate.

Surveying my words before I expel them, I desperately want to tell her fat ass to kiss my ass and go to hell, but I instead put on a happy face and tell her, "No, actually, justice was served. I'm in here to use the ladies' room, as I assume the two of you are. Justice is a wonderful thing. Don't you love the American Justice system?" I smile and they leave.

I dial Paula's phone. "Hello, what's up girl?" Surprisingly Paula answered her phone, even though she rarely does during work hours on a workday.

"Hey girl. I need your help. Call me back in about 2 minutes."

"What's up? Trying to ditch a man?"

"Something like that. Don't ask too many questions, just call me back."

"Girl you know I got your back. Consider it done." Paula hangs up and I rock my head from side to side to remove tension before leaving the bathroom. I exhale loudly before opening the door and walking back to the table as if life were as it should be.

"We missed you honey." His words drip in false affection and underlying sarcasm.

"Sorry I took so long. Did you boys miss me?" I play Derrick's little game while contemplating my next move.

"Don't worry about it Queen, Derrick and I were just getting to know each other. He seems to care about you an awful lot and it was refreshing to hear him talk about his feelings for you. Feelings you never told me about." Daddy looks at me as if disappointed that I had not shared my relationship with Derrick with him. But how could I? How do you share a mistake with your father?

I take too long to respond and the sadistic foreplay of my thigh begins again. This time he adds a twist to his grip, much like an Indian burn I received as a child; quick, yet painful. Derrick reminds me that he is in charge. Things would always go his way, at least if he had a say so in it.

"Well, I'm glad you two had a moment to get to know each other." I lie as I count the seconds till Paula's call; till the moment of my rescue. "Let's order."

"Yes, let's do that honey, I'm starving." Derrick smiles with an arrogant air of winning the game of taming his dog, i.e. me. "Waiter!" Derrick says louder than needed to catch the attention of the one assigned to our table. As the waiter approaches my phone rings. Right on time.

"It's the office, I better answer this." I lie as the waiter pulls out his pad to take down our order. "This is Queen how can I help you?" Paula breathes heavy into the phone, acting like a stalker, but not saying much else. It takes everything in me not to laugh at her gestures as I fake a conversation.

"How did that happen…you're kidding me. We have to be in court when? I'll be right there." Paula giggles on the other end of the phone at my one-sided conversation before hanging up.

"Daddy…Derrick, I am going to have to skip lunch. We've got crises at the office and I have to get back right now. I'm sorry for doing this, but I have to go. Daddy…since I drove with you, I need you to take me back."

Daddy looks at me strangely, but follows my lead. He and I both know that we came in separate cars, but thank God he catches my clue and plays along with me.

"Okay baby girl, if you have to go, we'll just have lunch some other time. I'll take you back to work." He literally jumps up from the table and reaches his hand out to Derrick once again. "It was nice to meet you young man, and maybe I will see you again."

I can tell by Daddy's actions that even he knows that if I have anything to say about it, it will be a cold day in hell before he and Derrick are in the same room together. I am relieved at him following my lead.

"Hold up. What's the rush Queen, can't that stuff at work wait? Don't they know you gotta eat? Come on girl don't run out now." Derrick reaches over to abuse my leg again, but I stand and move out of his reach before he can get me in his clutches.

"No, this can't wait. Sorry Derrick, but Daddy and I have to go." We walk toward the door and my body is tense as I await Derrick to make a scene. But he doesn't and I am relieved. Derrick stays in the restaurant and daddy walks me to my car, which is parked close to his.

"Sooner or later you will have to tell me what that was all about Queen. But I'll let you off the hook for now. Something tells me to let it go right now, so I will."

"Thank you daddy and I'll make today up to you. That moment did not need to happen, so I had to stop it. Thanks for not making it out to be more than it needed to be. I'm going back to work and I will call you tomorrow."

I kiss daddy on the cheek, and place the keys in the ignition while looking over my shoulder, prayerful that Derrick has not followed us. He hasn't. God is good. He watches over the young, the elderly and fools. And try as I might to avoid it, fate, or in this case Derrick, has a way of trying to place me in the category of the fool. I put the car in reverse and smile at my ability, at least this time, to sing, "It takes a fool to learn, that love don't love nobody."

QUINCY
Heart Rates Climbing

Clinic duty usually leaves a bad taste in my mouth, but today is different. Twice a week I am a one-man show as the doctor in charge of the clinic, which entails direct contact, observation and diagnosing of walk-in patients. This duty is done in conjunction with making my normal rounds of my regular admitted patients in the hospital, and covering the ER on those selected days. It's usually hectic running from one end of the hospital to the other, trying to do everything from wiping runny noses of snot-nosed toddlers in the clinic to checking the statistics of my patients before and after surgery. Throw in a couple of pregnant women waiting to drop their loads any minute and it's enough to leave even a superhero confused and feeling like they are spread too thin.

Mrs. Robinson came in the clinic complaining of heart pain, but I look at her chart, and immediately I know she has all the symptoms of pyrosis, or in plain language; heartburn. I diagnose the pain in her chest and neck before even entering the examination room. I'm mentally prepared to tell her my diagnosis and to prescribe the simple over-the-counter remedies to fix what ails her, but as I stroll into her room surrounded by the God-like prescience my white coat exudes, it is me that gets a life changing diagnosis.

The small examining table that I expected to see covered with the body of one was cradled by two elderly people; Mrs. Robinson and her husband. I can't believe my eyes as I walk in to see them spooning one another and holding hands on the small table. My entrance startles them and Mr. Robinson jumps to his feet.

"What's wrong with her doc? She's gonna be alright; isn't she?

"She's fine. I assume you're her husband."

"Yes. Pearl here is my wife of forty two years. I don't know what I would do without her. She means the world to me."

"Mr. Robinson, she's fine." I say while making notes on Pearl's chart.

"Are you sure? She was having chest pains. It's not a heart attack or a stroke is it?" He gently rubs the top of Pearl's head and she leans into each stroke. Like a cat being rubbed by its owner, she purrs at his touch.

"No,. Mr. Robinson…" I say as I take her pulse recognizing that she is my patient, but he is the one feeling the pain. "…she will be fine; it's just a serious case of heartburn."

"Are you sure doc? Be honest with us, we can take it." The look of concern on his face is only over-shadowed by the aura of love around the two of them. Each word uttered from his lips is directed at me, but his eyes, his feelings and his actions are directed and surround her. He's attentive; more than a mere care giver, he's a lover of her entire being.

"I'm one hundred percent sure Mr. Robinson. Her symptoms may mimic the feelings of a heart attack, but she just has acid reflux which is a regurgitation of gastric acids. It's very uncomfortable sometimes, but definitely not anything to be concerned about." I write a script for Pearl and tear the prescription slip from my pad and hand it to her.

"Take this and you'll be back to normal in a few days."

She smiles with a ray that only age can deliver. She's a woman of little words but I feel her "thanks" in her body language. For me, that's enough.

"Honey, did you hear the doctor? It's nothing. You'll be fine. God is good all the time…"

"And all the time God is good." Pearl finishes her husband's sentence and for the first time, I hear her voice. Mr. Robinson crawls back on the examination table next to his wife once again. I feel like my presence is intrusive. I'm not supposed to be here. I'm not supposed to be a third wheel in their moment. It belongs to them, so I leave. But not before digesting the expression of true love that I am witnessing and inhaling the specialness it presents. As I watch Mr. Robinson showing his appreciation for still having his wife in his life, I am touched by the abundance of love between the two and I want it for myself. I need it. Mr. Robinson is only complete by the inclusion of Mrs. Robinson; I want that same feeling of wholeness.

I slowly and silently close the door to the examining room, giving them their privacy as I focus on their hands clasped within one another. Witnessing the Robinsons and their love of each other makes clinic duty today worthwhile. Feeling their attachment to each other today is the appetizer I need to get me prepared for a meal of love of my own. Luckily for me it's 2:45, only an hour and fifteen minutes left in my duty and still early enough for me to order a main course of love for myself.

I sign off on all the hypochondriacs in the clinic, diagnose the patients with real problems and show my face at the doors of my long-term patients. Everyone in my care is momentarily fixed except me. As I take off my white coat of importance, I transform into a regular man. One in need. I have to get my time in now, because back to the hospital I go once I'm done.

Her card is in my wallet, where it has held residence since Big gave it to me. *1010 Sunset Drive, Suite 302.*

I stare at the numbers paralyzed until I am shoved by my heart.

Nothing ventured, nothing gained.

I pop the red, plastic heart awareness bracelet on my arm. The pain always shocks me back to reality of the shortness of life and this zap is no different.

"Life's too short for caution. Just do it." I say out loud to myself as I grab my sports jacket and head for the door.

Sunset drive is only about 15 minutes away. I check my hair in the rearview mirror and pop an Altoid as I park. The building her suite is in is impressive; five-stories high of offices of entrepreneurs, each sharing an address, but making their mark on society in individual form. I flip my collar and straighten my suit jacket.

"It's now or never," I say to myself as I press the button for the third floor button in the elevator. I have no idea what I will say to get in to see her, but that doesn't matter to me.

"Get in the same room with her and worry about the rest later," my heart screams. Upon exiting the elevator I feel my heart drop.

Man up! Just do it! Man up!

My mind tries to psyche the rest of me to action and I follow the lead.

It's now or never.

I hear my mind and weakly answer…"It's now."

The secretary greets me first.

"Legal Offices of Queen Thomas, attorney at law, how can I help you?" She smiles. As a first business impression, I'm impressed with her professionalism. She represents Queen well.

"I'd like to see Ms. Thomas about using her legal services."

Paula stares at me before speaking further. I know her name from the name plate on her desk. I can see the mechanical wheels moving in her brain as she sizes me up. "Damn." I think to myself, she remembers me.

Paula giggles and makes a sucking sound with her mouth. "So, you're here for legal services, Mr. …?

"Hughes. It's Doctor Hughes and yes, I need Ms. Thomas' help."

Hearing that I am a doctor seems to impress Paula slightly, but not enough to stop her from smirking at my tactics to see Queen or for lying about why I am here.

Paula smiles again and gets up from her desk. "Okay Doctor Hughes. Wait right here and let me see if Ms. Thomas can help fix what ails you."

I smirk right along with Paula and her play on words. Hopefully, Queen will give me a chance to show her that she is just what the doctor ordered for me.

Nervously, I sit and wait and wait and sit. What is she doing in there? I wonder as I admire her cozy, quaint office. Seems like Queen is a solo practitioner, fighting the wrongs of the justice system all by her lonesome. See, she needs a man like me to rub her feet at night, someone to listen to her trials and tribulations when she's had a hard day. She needs a doctor in the house to, "fix what ails" as Paula would say.

Finally, after what feels like an eternity, Paula exits Queen's office, and approaches me. She's a cute, pint sized woman, with flawless skin. She has a comforting nostalgic vibe to her – the kind of woman you take your problems to, the woman you want in your corner if some shit goes down. Powerful is what I get from her, even if the package is less than intimidating. Dressed well in a white linen top and black slacks, high heels, and nice jewelry, she represents Queen well.

"Ms. Thomas will see you now," she tells me, smiling hard and wide. Dressed in to the nines- looking fly for this woman leaves me anxious. I know I look good, but is it good enough? Following Paula, I'm nervous inside because I don't know what greets me on the other end of that door. On one hand, I could be walking into Paradise, and unfortunately, on the other, could be Queen singing, "Fight the Power" and she could tell me to take my cracker ass home.

Just as we're about to enter her office, Paula turns around, whispers, "Good luck, Doctor."

"I don't need luck, I'm just here to retain Ms. Thomas' services."

"We both know why you're here Doctor, and I'm rooting for you. Don't tell her I said that!"

"Your secret is safe with me."

Paula opens Queen's office door for me and shuts it right after I enter Queen's office. Her office is classy, just like she is. Mahogany wood desk, plush carpets, with warm salmon colored walls, a nice art covering makes the office very appealing and comfortable. Light jazz plays very eloquently in the background. As I make my way over to her desk, Queen's eyes follow me, and never leave mine. I pray this is the sign of a connection brewing. Wow, she's even more beautiful in the daylight that creeps in from her office window.

Her purple silk button down shirt is open down to her soft and full breasts and I can see them cupped together. Her hair cascades down her shoulders and soft brown bangs are swept over one eyebrow. Luscious lips covered in pink part as they greet me, "Hello."

"Hi, Ms. Thomas." I lean in to shake her hand, wishing the desk did not separate the two of us. She stands, and her hips speak to me in a tight, wool skirt in charcoal gray. She has to be wearing stilettos, because her legs go on for days. I lose focus for a moment, then my eyes rejoin her face. I stare her in the eyes, those honey-colored eyes that watch every move I make. I can't figure her out.

"Nice meeting you, officially," I joke as her hand leaves mine. Her skin is so soft. Her hands, so pretty. Nails, manicured in some sexy burgundy color. No wedding ring – hot damn.

"I received your flowers."

"I'm glad."

"Do you like them?"

"Very nice."

"I'm Quincy Hughes, by the way."

"I know."

We stare awkwardly for a moment. A slight smile escapes her beautiful lips.

"Have a seat."

"Thanks."

"So, you're a doctor?"

"Yes, Ms. Thomas."

"You can call me Queen. I don't bite."

"Be nice if you did."

"Excuse me?"

"Nothing."

"I've been a doctor for about ten years."

"I've been a lawyer for that amount of time also. But enough of the small talk. How can I help you? Just telling you right now, I don't really dabble in malpractice cases."

"Funny, I've never been sued, thank God. I'm very careful with who I put my hands on and how I do it."

She smiles. *I'd kill for that smile.*

"How can I help you Doctor?"

"I have a parking ticket."

"Ha, ha, ha. I needed a good laugh today. Pay your ticket, Dr. Hughes."

"No, Queen, I can't, I refuse, this is injustice why I received the ticket and I'd like to retain you to defend me."

"Look, Dr. Hughes. I think I know why you're here, and while I'm flattered, I really must ask you to leave now."

She gets up from her seat, and walks toward me. I admire her three inch heels, and love the way her body moves in that skirt. I'm ready to kidnap her and run off to some island with her, even if only in my dreams.

Queen stands next to me, places her hand on her hip.

"But I need your help."

"All you have to do is pay the ticket."

"I was wronged, Queen, I'd like to retain you," I tell her as I hand her the ticket. She takes the ticket from me, but I hold her hand before she has a chance to remove it from mine. "Doctor. How am I supposed to look at the ticket if you won't let go of my hand?"

"May be the only chance I get to hold your hand. I'm just experiencing a once in a lifetime treat, Queen, that's all."

"That's nice."

"You're beautiful."

"Thank you."

I stand up, position my body right in front of hers and she backs up slightly.

She smells so good. The tension in the room is thick, but not bad, it's present, however, and I wonder if this is yet another sign of something good soon to come.

"Dr. Hughes..."

"Call me Quincy."

"Quincy. Pay the ticket. If you have a real legal matter, I'd be happy to discuss that with you. If not, time is of the essence and I have real clients to see today."

Moving in closer to her, the man in me wants to kiss her pretty lips, but I remain calm. Stepping to her, I invade all of her space and pray my body language will deliver bold messages to her, even if I don't say a word. She doesn't back down – no longer does she move away from me, she stands her ground, unapologetically, staring me back in the eyes, she's my match, have I met mine, I wonder. My face reaches closer to hers when I ask, "May I leave you my card? Will you call?"

"Sit the card on my desk," she tells me as she looks up to me. Damn those eyes.

Her lips are mere inches away from mine – we're so close, I can hear her heart beating, smell her sweet breath. I stare in her eyes and she does mine, for a moment and then she looks away.

"You know, some things in life, we can't control, no matter how odd the circumstances."

"Right."

"Please call me," I beg as I take her hand, and kiss the back of it. I walk out of her office feeling like at least I came; at least I got to see her in the flesh. Whether she ever calls or not, at the very least, I got to kiss her hand.

"Have a great day, Paula."

"Thank you."

I hear Queen close her office door and before I make it out of the lobby, Paula scurries behind me, and questions, "What's the deal with you doctor?"

"Not much, just following my heart."

"Don't give up, Doctor."

"I don't plan to."

                    ॐ ॐ ॐ ॐ ॐ

"Are you ready for your next patient Doctor Hughes? Doctor Hughes? Are you alright doctor?"

Jean, a heavy-set nurse in her fifties taps me on the shoulder and I snap back from my thoughts.

"Are you ready Doctor?"

"Yes, I'll be in shortly. Just give me a few minutes to make notes in the file."

Nurse Jean looks at me strangely. I stare at her blue eye shadow, fake lashes and stiff hair before smiling back at her to let her know I am all right. It's just Queen on the brain, but I can't share that with her. It's been a whole day since I left her office and I can't seem to shake wondering if she will call.

I make notes on the chart of my last patient and go through the motions of a competent doctor even though my mind is that of a lovesick beyotch.

"Get your shit together man, she'll call." I try to reassure myself as I walk towards exam room number three. The chart says the patient complains of chest pains but no other symptoms are noted. I look at her vital signs, mentally noting the statistics of her height and weight in case that information is important to my diagnosis.

Sitting with her back to me, I can tell she's wearing a weave, and a bad one at that. It's down to the middle of her back and tangled in some spots. She really should have gotten a better grade of hair if she even wanted to pass it of as the real thing and as her own hair.

"Hello, I'm Doctor Hughes." I introduce myself in standard form.

"I know exactly who you are Quincy." Turning around, my eyes meet the voice and face of Tina. Damn, I should have known that fucked up weave, even from the back.

"What the fuck are you doing here?" Filled with anger and venom, I slam the chart down on the exam table right next to her thigh hoping I hit her by accident on purpose.

"Come on baby, I had to see you, it's been too long and I really miss you." Her arms reach out to me, but I step back out of her reach. This bitch ain't trapping me that easy. Not this time, not again.

"Tina, this shit is ridiculous, girl it's over, I've told yo' ass that a thousand times. Catch a clue, recognize it for what it is and get out the hell out of here so I can deal with my real patients."

"Come on Quincy, don't be mean. Talk to me." She pleads and bats her eyes. Actions that used to work on me, but no longer do. They've lost their sucker punch.

"We don't have shit to talk about Tina. If you want conversation, go back to the Big Black Buck that was in your house that day. Oh, shit...my bad; that's right, the two of you weren't talking, you were fucking." The anger spits out before I can control it.

"I told you, it wasn't like that. Let's make up. Make up sex is the best and you know I know how to make you feel good." She licks her fingers and rubs them along her legs.

"You used to make me feel good. Used to! Past tense. And even then, it wasn't all that...just a nut and any piece of ass can do that." Insulting this tramp makes me feel good.

"You don't mean that Quincy." She leans back on the table and spreads her legs wide open. Her skirt is short, I can see she doesn't have any panties on and the camel toe between her legs is winking at me. Her chocolate thighs scream for me to touch them and I can't help but stare.

Tina smiles with a grin that presumes she can sway me. "Yeah, quit playing hard to get Quincy, you know you want some of this." She takes two fingers and taps her plump, exposed clit in an enticing manner, and then she unbuttons her shirt, cupping both her 40DD breasts with both hands and squeezing them to taunt me. If the sight of her did not repulse me, we would be fucking right now.

Queen enters my mind. A vision of real, natural beauty on a woman with sophistication and class. I picture her smile. Remembering her smell, and how she liked the flowers I sent is enough for me to deny this tramp.

"Button your shirt back up girl; I'm not interested." I turn my back to her and abruptly walk toward the door.

"Quincy!" She is practically screaming with anger. "Are you really just going to leave me here, horny with a hot pussy calling your name? I need you!"

"You don't need me, you need to get your skank-stanking ass out of here, that's what you need. Oh, and make sure you cover up that hairy ass pussy of yours, it's attracting flies and you might scare somebody."

"That's fucked up, Q. Well, can I at least get some money? My rent is late again. I'll pay you back, Boo."

Laughing out loud. If I was an abusive man, I'd be choking the shit out of this bitch right about now. "Is that the real reason you're here? Money? I paid your rent two months in a row. Go find another fool to pay your bills, you gold-digger."

Closing the door behind me, feeling vindicated and grateful that I came to my senses about this hoe before it was too late, has me smiling. What the hell was I thinking getting involved with this trick in the first place? I question myself as I walk back to the nurse's station.

"Jean, ask Doctor Tremmel to cover for me. I'm out."

Jean tries to question me if anything is wrong, but I don't listen, nor do I respond. I just need some fresh air. I need to get the fuck out of here. My coat is hanging behind the door of my office and I can't grab it fast enough on my way to the elevator. Too much drama and not enough stability. I start my engine and race toward the levelness I need. Not knowing where I am going I just cruise with jazz music and green scenery as my guide. Tranquility, take me away. Before I know it, I am sitting outside of my parent's house, thinking about happier times.

Instinct guides my feet to their door. I need to feel like a child again and wrap myself in yesterday and the comfort and security of being taken care of. Mom answers the door. She is in her seventies but still the finest woman on the planet. She places both hands on my face and kisses my cheek. One peck on each side. My little drive-by visits always bring her happiness and I love to see her smile.

"Baby, what are you doing here?" She ushers me in the door while holding my hand in the same manner a mother does with a toddler. I chuckle to myself at her protective gesture. Even though she is the one I should be protecting, her motherly instincts are still the same and I love and welcome them.

"I just wanted to see you. Is that a crime mom?"

"If it is, then arrest me."

As we walk through the foyer of their home, my eyes are trapped on the pictures on the wall of Quinton and me. A picture perfect existence of childhood tranquility. I exhale at how simple life was back then and wish I could return to it.

"Nellie, who was that at the door?" Dad shouts from his recliner in the living room.

"Henry, its Quincy. Our boy stopped by out of the blue. Isn't that a wonderful surprise?" She rubs my face as she hollers in the direction of my dad.

"I have some peace cobbler in the oven, can you stay long enough to have some."

I'm not hungry, but how can I say no to her?

"Of course mom. I was hoping you would say that." I sit down in the recliner next to dad. It belongs to my mom and although it is a matching piece of furniture that completes a set, it is reminiscent of my parents, one is out of place without the other, there's a need for both in order for the set to be whole. I love that about them and pray I can have a little piece of what they have for myself.

Mom makes my father's plate, it is not done out of an obligation of her role as dad's wife. She does it because she loves him and she wants to. As she brings his plate to him, she kisses his bald head. I watch with admiration as he kisses her hand and tells her how much he loves her for all that she does.

"Watching ya'll makes it hard on a single man. I don't think my life is lacking until I look at the two of you."

Dad speaks in between shoving forks full of cobbler into his mouth. "Nellie is all I need in this world. I would be less of a man and less of myself if it wasn't for your mother. When are you going to become respectable and join us in the world of matrimony?"

"One day daddy. One day. I'm working on it. I just need Mrs. Right to see that I'm waiting on her."

"Well boy, don't make us wait too long. Since Quinton is gone, you are the only hope we have. Give us some grand kids before we are too old to appreciate them."

"Why did he have to bring up Quinton? If he was here, I would not have to be their 'end all and be all" concerning leaving a legacy. If he was here, there would be someone else to share the load of being an outlet for them. If Quinton was here, I'd have someone other than Big to share my thoughts and dreams with, if only Quinton were here, if only he were alive. But he isn't and he's not. His dreams and his assistance with mine are like his life…gone too soon. I stare at my parents and flashback on my day and the events with Tina instead of Queen. Why can't I have a sliver of what they have? Quinton is gone, I am alive, but I just wish I could resuscitate my love life and remove it from the grave, which I was unable to do with my brother. Is it too much to ask for happiness? Is it to much to ask to be complete, or am I destined to live a life in which love can only be described in past tense in the words, "Gone too soon."

QUEEN
Call of the Night

The wind rattles the trees outside of my windows adding a sense of eeriness to an already mysterious night air. I don't know why I feel uneasy, but I do. Instinctively, I close the curtains and grab a blanket before sitting down on my chaise lounge with some peppermint tea and a good book, *Mistress Memoirs* by Lorraine Elzia, to enjoy my wind down time. I don't know why these steamy novels do it for me, but they do. I love a cat and mouse chase. The mesmerizing soulful vocals of Jill Scott on my CD player begin to drown out the barreling of the wind outside and relax me momentarily from the stress of the day. "It's a cold mid-summer night hour and I'm thinking about you," she sings so seductively, putting me in a mood all my own as HE crosses my mind, forcefully and unapologetically. I can't seem to shake him as he has taken up permanent residence in my psyche.

Coming by my office, unannounced, after having flowers delivered prior, caught me off guard. I've never met a man who's done something like that. His name is Quincy. I likes. Quincy and Queen sound good together, but doesn't look good or acceptable. If only he were black, he'd get the business, as he's a much needed distraction, very intriguing and oh so fine, and I don't look at white men that way, but I must give credit where it is due, and it is definitely due in this case. The doctor is sensationally well built and is quite pleasing to the eye, even if it is a biased one.

I entertain the idea of being a black sex slave to a white handsome doctor for a moment, since my private thoughts belong only to me, and quickly dismiss them. Gazing at the night stand, HIS card sits there and I'm tempted to give him a call, but this is just night time fantasies, and my lonely urges kickin' in. I'm sleepy, horny, I suppose, since it's been ages since I've been loved, and well, that all has my mind a bit crazy right now, really. Yet, the visual of his blue eyes refuse to leave my mind.

That night at Jasper's – he macked to me so melodically, so skillfully. I wonder how many bitches he's controlling on a string.

The house phone rings twice, "Damn, who could that be?" Glancing down at my crimson toes, they glide into soft fuzzy pink slippers as I get up to answer it, but before I can pick up the receiver the line goes dead. "Shit." I sit back down and the ringing begins again as if timed in rhythm to when my ass hits the chair. "It's just going to ring this time, I'm not getting up again." I say to myself as I settle down further in my chair, sipping my tea and letting the machine answer for me. The caller does not leave a message. "I guess it wasn't too important if you can't leave a message." I say out loud as I try and comfort my mind and get lost in my book. I'm successful for about thirty minutes before there is a knock at my door. It's after nine o'clock p.m., anyone who really knows me, knows I don't answer unexpected calls to my door after eight at night, I think to myself before walking slowly to the door. As I peer first through the beveled glass of my front door and secondly out my adjacent window, I notice that no one is on the porch, just a small package on the doormat. "What the fuck is this?" I exhale as I slowly open the door. Side to side is my glance as I pull my robe tighter to shield my breasts from the night air, which is merciless in its delivery. Against my better judgment, I pick up the box, shake it and praying it doesn't explode. The rattling sound from inside tells me that there is a solid object inside. I close the door behind me and listen further to the rhythmic sounds playing in the background as I walk back towards my lounge chair to open the package. Quickly, I glance around the room once again. Curiosity makes me second guess opening the package, but curiosity also killed the cat, so I can't help myself in wanting to open it and see what's inside. As I tear off the thick, see-through tape, my first thoughts are that someone took a lot of time and patience in trying to secure whatever is inside. Unraveling layer after layer of brown packing material, I finally get to the contents protected inside. The prize is a picture of my father and me, but not just any picture of us, but the exact one I keep on my bed stand. The one in the heart-shaped frame I bought in Jamaica. The one that I kiss every morning before leaving the house. The one that was on my nightstand this morning when I left home. In the bottom of the box is a newspaper clipping from the *Pocono Times,* and one from the *Black Weekly Times,* both with write-ups about my victory in the Bevens case..

Dropping the box after I review its contents, I grasp the frame in my hands and run up the stairs in a world wind, unable to believe what is happening. As I reach the top landing, I stop and steady my stance. This gift cannot mean what I think it means. I slow my steps and walk in my bedroom. As I stand with my hands in the prayer position over my lips I initially close my eyes and after prayer to the contrary, I open them seeing what I hoped I would not see. The frame is gone; an empty space remains in its place. I place my hands on my heart and sit down on the bed perfectly aware of what the gift means. Someone had been in my house. Someone was watching me. Someone was fucking with my head. The Whisper of doubt was becoming a Scream of reality. After a few moments of trying to get my shit together mentally, I decide to call in the Calvary, my soldier, the one who will help me figure this shit out. I push speed dial to Paula.

"What's up girl?" Her voice is bubbly and full of cheer, a tone I would normally welcome; except this call was not intended to be your usual sista girl chatter.

"You're not going to believe this shit!" I am screaming even before I realize it.

"Believe what? Calm down, are you okay?" I sense worry in her words.

"I just got a package."

"Did you forget you ordered something online and now you're mad cause you have to pay?" She jokes not knowing the severity of the situation.

"Paula someone has been in my house. Someone is messing with my head."

"What do you mean someone has been someone has been in your house? Slow down and tell me what's up. Have you called 911?"

Until she said it, the thought had not crossed my mind. "No, I haven't I called you first."

"Girl I can't do shit for you from here, you need to call the police. Were you robbed or something? You said you got a package, now you are saying that someone was in your house. Tell me what happened."

"The doorbell rang and when I went to the door there was a package on the porch, inside was the picture of me and my father that I keep on my nightstand. And a newspaper clipping of me. That means someone has been in my house and took my picture and left it for me outside my door so I would know that they had been here." Saying the words out loud to Paula made the whole situation scarier to me and I finally knew why I had that eerie feeling minutes before. It was my women's intuition trying to warn me.

"Queen, this ain't nothing to play with. Hang up and call the police right now. I'm on my way over. That nigger done lost his fool ass mind. Get the cops there NOW." She was in straight up road dog mode and in my head, I could see her putting on her tennis shoes, tying her hair in a pony tail, removing her earrings and putting Vaseline on her face to get ready for an old school fight.

"Paula, I don't even know who did this, what am I going to tell the police?" I say the words to her as I wipe the picture frame in my hands and place it back on the nightstand where it belongs.

"Have you lost your freaking mind Queen? It doesn't take a rocket scientist to know who did this shit. That's Derrick's ass. Head games like this have his name written all over it. How much longer are you going to let him do this shit to you? If he ain't whipping your ass, he's fucking with your head. Call the police right now, or I will!" She's forceful in her words and I know she means business.

"I can't do that Paula. If it is him, I just need to ignore his ass. He'll drop it if I do. Besides, I told you, I can't be part of the wheels of motion that put more of our black men in jail."

"So you would rather your daddy bury your ass before locking him up? I don't get you Queen."

"I can't do it Paula. I just can't. Besides, we don't even know that it is Derrick."

"Who the hell else could it be Queen? Quit deluding yourself and wake up and smell the gawd-damn coffee. Didn't he just have lunch with you and your father? Who else would use the significance of that moment to fuck with your head? This is that sick bastard. I can smell it. And you need to nip this shit in the bud."

I'm beginning to recognize that Derrick is probably the one behind this, but I can't call the police. I have seen too many of my brothers become a part of the system because of stupid choices. I won't contribute to that. Derrick will get me out of his system, I just need to lay low and give it time. "I'm better now Paula. Thanks for talking to me. I needed that." I try and blow her off because my mind is made up.

"What the hell does that mean Queen? You going to let him get away with this shit? Did you forget about the restraining order against him? If nothing else call the police because he violated that."

I had forgotten about that too. Paula's ass remembers everything when it comes to Derrick. "I just can't Paula. I won't have his blood on my hands, no matter how much he plays games with me, I won't be the one to put him behind bars."

"Well, you might not have his blood on your hands, but it seems like he wants to have yours on his. Queen, I don't like this. I don't like it one bit. I will respect your wishes and not call the police, but you've got to be more careful and watch your ass." Her words are received in the "I care about you" manner that she intended them. I know she is right and that I should do more to protect myself, and I will. But I can't be the one that gets another black man in trouble. I rub my fingers along the frame and recognize the significance of how close he was to me tonight and what that meant.

"Paula, if he wanted to do me harm, he could have. He was in my house. If he wanted to hurt me he would have, but he didn't. He wants attention. If I don't give it to him, he will seek it somewhere else. Thanks for your love, but don't worry, I know what I am doing, and I know I am doing the right thing by not putting a noose around his neck."

"I don't agree with you Queen. And I will be bringing the restraining order to you in the morning to remind you of what his boundaries are. I think you need to look at them again in order to recognize what everyone "but" you seem to see. He's dangerous Queen. Please don't make me bury my friend just because she was stupid. I don't think I could handle that."

"I love you for your concern, but I will be alright. I allowed him to control my actions for too long. I control them myself now. He wants a game, but it takes two to play. If I don't participate he will have to find another player. This move was a weakness on his part Paula and he is too stupid to know it. I won't be part of his demise, but I am also smart enough to get into his head just like he thought he got into mine. I will win this stupid head game Paula. Mark my words and don't worry about me. Anything he can do, I can do better."

I hang up knowing that my answer was not good enough for Paula, but it satisfies me. Making a big event of this is what Derrick wants me to do. It would give him satisfaction knowing he had gotten into my head. And if I were to involve the police, I could never live with myself or the notion that I was the nail in another black man's coffin of jail. I can't do that. I won't. There's more than one way to play any game, and I am going to play this one with a poker face. That will piss him off more than any other reaction, and even though I know that is not the role Paula would want me to play, I've known the sting of his violence long enough to know that no reaction   hurts   him   more   than   fighting   back.

QUINCY
The Sweetness of a Black Woman

The butterflies in my stomach are at an all-time high. I can't get her eyes out of my head; they're hazel in color and mesmerizing to my core. She just does it for me. I don't think I will ever know one hundred percent why, but she's captured my every thought. From her pretty, pouty mouth to her honey-glazed skin to the fact that she's six-feet in heels is killing me softly. That warm, sun-kissed brown hair that flows as her tits bounce all around when she walks, no excuse me, glides across a room has got me in a trance. Something about her is so familiar. I feel like I've known her all my life. I would love to say I'm pussy whipped, but that's not a description I can own. I haven't had the pleasure of tasting her juices yet, but I'm her slave just the same. My mind says don't chase her, man up, let her come after me, but I can't wait. I'm out of control. I don't know how to act. My heart can't compete and does not want to. For some reason, all that "man up shit," leaves me when it comes to Queen. "Punk me baby, I'm game." My head says wait for the chase, my heart says go get what you want, so I follow my heart and go to her office. Laced in a fresh pair of Ecko jeans, my signature Carhart jacket and tan Timberlands - my appearance is unplanned, unannounced and unscheduled. I have to wait my turn, and I eagerly do so.

The tight sounds of Talib Kweli blast throughout my truck as I pull up to the building where my soon to be wife works. He rhymes, "Just to get by." This is what true Hip-Hop does. It elevates you mentally.

But Jay-Z said it best when he declared death to auto-tunes.

Paula is not in the office which is to my benefit as I am able to sit with my back to the door of Queen's office and hear what's going on behind the door. From the conversation I can tell there's a man in her office with her and he's trying to make a move on her. Can you believe this shit? Some man is trying to make a move on my lady. I laugh out loud because this woman has made me lose my mind. Just when I think he's the reason she hasn't called - I hear him giving her compliments but they are delivered like tired ass lines used in the club.

"So Queen, when are you going to let me get some of that brown sugar? You may have won at court, but I can win your heart if you let me. Stop playing hard to get. You know you want this."

What a jerk! How dare that asshole talk to my baby that way. With each deep bass syllable from his lips, I hate him more and more. He's a fucking playa with a mission and even I can appreciate the magnitude of that goal. Shit, I'm here for the same reason. Only difference is, I plan to win. It's an untapped natural energy if you ask me. I'm not a playa, but I know the game. Panty removal 101 seems to be the course he's majoring in and as I listen, I pray Queen will give him a failing grade.

I lean my chair backward almost falling as I try to get closer to the cracked door to eavesdrop better on what's going on in the room behind me. I take a mental note of what's working and what's not. His errors will be my clues; all I have to do is study the game as I should. And I'm grateful for the opportunity to observe and be schooled by his failures.

"Look Cletus, yes, I tapped that ass in court. You damn right I did."

Cletus? Did she just say Cletus?

"And Cletus, just because you look nice in a suit, doesn't mean I'm going out with you," she tells him with that sassiness and arrogant air that has drawn me in like a moth to a flame.

"Queen," he laughs out loud, "Do you realize how many women would want all of this here?"

Idiot.

"I'm sure there are many, Cletus. Why don't you go and bullshit one of them."

That's right baby. Tell him to get to steppin'. Sounds like she's escorting him to the door.

"What are you doing?" Paula catches me and I almost fall again.

"I'm just waiting my turn." I try to act innocent.

"Waiting your turn?" She laughs at my choice of words. She looks lively today with that smooth caramel skin. Her round face is comforting. But she is a firecracker for sure.

"What I meant was that I am waiting to see Queen." I try and clean it up with a shit-grin on my face.

"No, you meant exactly what you said. It seems like Queen is pulling all the men today."

I stand up and walk over closer to Paula to make sure that Queen and the man in her office can't hear my conversation. Bending down, I get close to Paula and whisper, "Who is that? Is that her boyfriend or something?"

She smiles. "He wishes. That's Cletus Jackson, he's an attorney. He was on that big case that Queen had some time ago."

"They sound like they are having a good time in there. Does she like him?"

"You sure ask a lot of questions Dr. Hughes, just not the right ones." Paula crosses her hands in front of her like a school teacher scolding a child. "What you should be asking for are insider tips."

"What?" I'm confused and don't mind showing it.

"Insider tips. If you ever want to know the way to a certain woman's heart, ask her friends and let them help you out." She walks around to her side of the desk and puts her feet up as if to say she's in charge.

I move closer to her desk anxious to hear what she has to say. "So you're willing to help me? I just need to know how to lower her guard long enough for her to see the real me. How can I do that? How can I get her to give me a chance?"

Paula smiles and I can't figure out if it is a grin of satisfaction because I am groveling, or if she's smiling because she's happy to get to be helping Queen; but either way, I'll take the silly grin from her because I need Paula's help and I'm not afraid to show it.

Paula begins telling me some of Queen's favorite things, her likes and her dislikes. She tells me her hopes and her dreams and her love of animals and miniature angels.

"Her favorite flower in the world are Magnolia's. She wears skirts all the time. Her mom told her that only true princesses where dresses. I swear, I've never seen Queen in pants. Except for jeans on the weekends. Let's see. She's a daddy's girl for sure. She's a sweetheart, she loves to be loved but hasn't yet received that unconditional love that I believe she deserves. She has a heart of gold. She will give you the shirt off her back. Let me warn you though; she has taken on the role of saving the black man. Uh, lessee…oh she loves music. You can always tell what type of day she's having, depending on the music she's listening to. If she's hyped, she's listening to rap, maybe Redman, Jay-Z or Keith Murray. If she's feeling sexy, it's Maxwell or Marvin Gaye. If she's sad, oh Lord, it's Billie Holiday for sure. Take her out of here, one of her favorite drinks is mocha latte with honey, cinnamon and a splash of milk. But, I'm her best friend, so of course I would tell you that."

I interrupt. "So you two are best friends?"

"Yes, doctor. For life."

"Cool. So Paula, tell me, do you think I have a chance?"

She chuckles this time. "Quincy, with Queen, ain't no tellin'. Every time a bouquet of flowers comes from you to the office, she blows it off. But I catch her later in the day, smelling those roses, and smiling. One time she twirled the card between her fingers and blushed. She thought I didn't see that shit, but I did. And that one arrangement you sent; the red roses with the one white one. She did read that card to me. Something about her being one of a kind. She didn't admit it, but I know she was flattered."

Paula just gave me the boost of confidence I needed to help me to break down the wall of China.

I take it all in making a mental inventory of future plans to use the information I've gained to win her heart. Paula smiles with satisfaction and walks toward Queen's door.

"Okay, that dog has had enough time sniffing my girl, it's your turn." She winks at me and opens the door.

"Ms. Thomas, your next appointment is here."

"Thank you Paula." I hear Queen's voice and I can't help but smile. "Thanks for coming by Mr. Jackson, and I hope the next time we meet in court we will be representing the same side." She remarks to Cletus as she walks him towards the door. I can't help but grin again at her sassiness.

"Yeah, you spanked me in court, I was hoping to get you to spank me flesh to flesh as well, but you won't take me up on the offer. Too bad really, it's your loss." Cletus says a little too loudly as he walks past me in the lobby. I give him a what-the-fuck-you-wanna-do-look. *Fucking prick,* I think to myself as I stand up to go in Queen's office.

"Dr. Hughes, what brings you to my office this time? Oh, let me guess you have a jaywalking ticket this time."

Smiling, I enter her office, and catch a glimpse of her full hips swaying in a tight skirt. She has to have on three inch heels and they look damn good on those thick legs.

"Oh wait, Dr. Hughes, you were caught stealing flowers and need a defense attorney, right?"

"I didn't think it was possible, but you are even more beautiful when you are sarcastic." She blushes, cheeks rosey, skin – honey - coated and flawless, and I take that as an opportunity to press forward. "This time I need your help with preparing a Will. No pretense, no games, I just need a Will." I lie a little but feel that a white lie is okay since my white skin is our barrier.

"Are you okay?" I sense worry in her voice. "Or are you just doing the responsible, adult thing?"

I rub my chin and lean in closer to her. "Do I sense concern for my health in your voice? Can I take that as a sign that you might be interested in me?" My rhetorical question is not so rhetorical.

She smiles and sits down in the chair in front of me.

"Quincy, I'm just asking questions I would ask any client needing a Will. Nothing special Quincy." She lies and we both know it. She won't even look me in the eyes. My confidence level rises.

"Well, Queen, your mouth may not want to humor me right now, but I can tell the rest of you likes me, even if only just a little bit." I use my fingers to show about an inch of space.

"Quincy, let's stay focused. Can I get some preliminary information from you so I can prepare your Will."

"Your wish is my command." I begin to fan myself and walk towards the window. "Can we do this outside? It's really hot in here and I need some fresh air."

"Outside? Why do you want to go outside?"

My back is to her and I stare out the window. "The magnolias are in bloom. Don't you just love the smell of magnolias?"

"Yes, I do, but how do you know that?" I can feel her stare upon my back, but I won't reveal my source.

"Life's too short to ask why or to question fate." I turn around and take both of her hands in mine. That tight sweater demands my attention and I try not to stare, but it's getting harder by the second. My eyes move from her breasts to her lips, damn, those lips, painted in some sort of radiant chocolate color; they look delicious, and appetizing.

"Come smell the magnolias with me Queen. You've been cooped up in this office all morning. Let's throw caution to the wind and enjoy this beautiful day. I promise to keep it business; but please indulge me and let's talk outside."

Her hands are soft, just like her eyes and the warmth of touching them raises my confidence level a little higher.

"Quincy, I don't have time for this." She tries to resist, but I'm gently pulling her towards the door and I can feel that her resistance is weak at best; she just needs coaxing.

"One latte in the park. That's all I ask, then I will leave you alone. Come on Queen, you owe me at least that. I promise, if you don't want me to come around after that, I'll leave you alone and never show up again. Albeit, it will be hard as hell but I'm a big boy so I will try. Just a few minutes in the park; come smell the magnolias with me and if you want me to stay away after that, I will."

Queen stares at me for a minute; her hand in mine, before speaking.

"Okay, we will continue your consult in the park."

"Damn, that was easy. What's the catch Queen?" I question her as we walk thorough her door and pass the winking eye of Paula.

"Well, I look at it this way Quincy, you are going to keep showing up with minor things for me to do until I give you the time of day. So since time is money, and this will be on your dime even if under the pretense of preparing a Will for you, then I will do it. In the park or in my office, what difference does it make? I'll hear you out, prepare your Will, and then we're through without all of the "what if" hanging over my head. Besides, you're kind of cute and I do owe you. So let's go."

"You are one of a kind, just like that white rose."

She smiles, never letting go of my hand.

We stop at the Coffee Shop on the first floor of her building. Queen gets ready to place her order, but I do it for her instead.

"My lady will have a mocha latte with honey, cinnamon and a splash of milk. I'll take a regular coffee, make it like I like my women; strong, black and with a lot of sweetness."

The cashier smiles at my order and so does Queen and as she does, the crowded coffee house seems to get brighter.

"Two questions Quincy."

"Fire away beautiful, I'm all ears." I say as I put coffee stirrers in each of our drinks.

"One; how did you know what I wanted?"

"A real man anticipates and fulfills his woman's needs. I consider myself a real man. Next question?"

She smirks. "Was your order true of your taste? Do you really only like black women?"

I turn and stare at her directly in her eyes. I knew that the question would come; I just did not anticipate it so soon.

"It could be that you're the finest thing that I ever saw, or it could be my imagination running too far. I could give you a bogus line about how I was raised around black people and since it's all that I know, it's all that I'm attracted to, but that would be a lie. While it's true, I did grow up around black people, that's not the source of my attraction. I do prefer black women, but honestly, I prefer a GOOD woman over anything, no matter her ethnicity, but it has nothing to do with my environment or my upbringing. It has everything to do with the character of a black woman. No creature is as strong, as resilient, as nurturing or caring. No mother would kill to protect her young, like a black mother. No wife will stand behind her man, like a black woman. No woman is as resourceful and passionate as a black woman. That's not to discount my own mother, who happens to be white because she is, without a doubt, the reason why I am who I am. I give her credit for giving my life broader meaning and perspective by not instilling in me discrimination of any kind. Like my Umi says, "shine your light on the world" and I plan to, with the right woman, no matter what shade."

Smiling, she sips her latte, grins from ear to ear with a smile only an angel could adorn. "That's Mos Def, Quincy. What you know about Mos Def?" she questions and sips her latte once more.

"What you know about Mos Def, Queen?" I respond, "I'm a Hip-Hop junkie for your information pretty lady. But, in all seriousness, I want that passion. I need it. For me, nothing short will do. Others can take the sugar substitute, but I'll take the real thing and for me, only the sweetness of a black woman will do. I think you're the one, Queen."

She lowers her eyes and I can see the wheels turning in her head. I may not have clinched the deal with Queen just yet, but I can tell that at least the foundation is laid.

QUEEN
Have Mercy

A Will was the pretense he used to get some alone time with me, yet we aren't discussing it at all. I must admit I find him attractive and intriguing in a pigment-challenged kind of way. Who am I kidding? It's more than that. From the night in the poetry club to him showing up at my office unannounced and unexpected has intrigued me more than a little bit. The sincerity in his conversation combined with the sexiness in his grin – yep, I'm afraid this white man has been on my mind. The more he talks, the more I want to hear his thoughts. Delicious is the word that comes to mind when I look at his mouth as he speaks. I try not to stare but he has the whitest teeth I've ever seen in my life. He's like a breath of fresh air to me. Not the usual dog and pony show that I'm used to. He seems sincere, but it could all be a game. If it is, he's a pro. I haven't heard a man talk about a woman, a black woman at that, so highly unless she was his mother, and I've never heard those words from white lips at all. He keeps my attention and makes me wanna drink him in; problem is he's in the wrong skin. I'm not sure I can get passed that. *Damn, I really want to.*

Quincy bends down, and I trace his broad shoulders with my eyes. My eyes continue down his strong back and as he kneels, I witness his long, strong thighs. I'm a sucker for a tall man, and that he is. Quincy has to be about six-foot-three, maybe four, and he must work out as he's got body for days. He picks a magnolia, which is my favorite flower and somehow he seems to know it. Looking at me intensely as he rises to his feet sends a rush through me, one that I didn't see coming. I think my panties are wet.

"May I?" he questions softly in my ear. His sweet lips are so close to my face, I feel his breath on the side of my cheek and it penetrates me. In the words of James Evans of *Good Times,* I want to scream "Hammercy!" but I can't, he's white.

Glancing up to return his glare, I whisper, "Sure."

His smile is approving as he appeals to my heart, but I won't let my guard down – he's not black. Placing the flower behind my ear, he moves closer to me, as he invades all of my space, his broad chest commands my attention, the smell of his cologne is strong and sensual mimicking his presence as he gingerly moves my hair from my face letting his hands linger on my jaw. His hands are soft. They feel so good. I question myself as to whether that's because he's a doctor and constantly aware of his touch on others or are his hands soft just because that is just what white skin feels like? I've never felt the touch of a white man before, so I can only guess and wonder as to which one it is.

"Are you a conservative?" I question and his eyes light up.

"Why do you ask?"

"Well, aren't all of you types, conservatives?"

Seems like my question disturbed him a bit. But he doesn't let me see it. Quincy masks it very well.

"Actually, Queen, I'm a registered independent."

"I see."

"So, who did you vote for?" he questions.

"Obama, of course."

"Smart girl."

"Didn't you vote for the republican?"

"No, mam, I didn't," he tells me, staring deep into my eyes.

"I'm surprised."

"And why is that?"

"Because I just assumed you would. Didn't that lady running float all of your boats?" He sighs and smiles.

"No. I voted for the person who presented the most promise for the country. Isn't that the reason you voted?"

"Absolutely."

"See, we have something else in common." He changes the subject.

"Is there a story behind your name? It's quite unusual and unique, just like you." Quincy smiles, that smile that melts my insides and breaks the awkwardness of the moment by beckoning my participation in the conversation.

I get that question all the time, but usually just as small talk, not from anyone who really cares about my answer. Staring deep into my eyes, he patiently waits for an answer. I can feel him paying attention to the smallest details that make up – me. Looking up to him, I respond, "My father named me. He said that from the first moment he saw me, the name just seemed to fit. He would always tell me that every little girl is a princess, but even from birth, I was destined to be a Queen."

Quincy's hand moves to my face once more, his fingers gently glide across my cheek again, and as he smiles, he tells me, "And that you are." Quincy keeps staring at me. I can tell he's feeling me, but I can't return his glance any more, I just stare at the ground and the people around me on our path, to see if they are staring at us. I feel like a fish in a bowl with all eyes on me. Although I have given men with less going on in their favor a shot, opening myself up to Quincy is something that's hard for me to do, so I avoid eye contact. He's fighting against the odds, I'm afraid to allow his blue eyes to seduce me, so I stare at the ground as we walk.

"Seems like you were daddy's little girl. What about your mother, I bet she treated you like a queen too."

"Mom spoiled me, we had a great relationship. The kind little girls dream of."

"That is so sweet, Queen. Are you still close to her?"

"She's dead," I respond, pulling my jacket tighter together. The wind in the air has made it more chilly out here.

"I'm sorry, I didn't know." I can tell by the look on his face that he is embarrassed about asking.

"It's okay. It happened when I was very young, so it's just been me and daddy for quite some time. I really don't remember much about it. I know she went to the hospital and one day daddy came home without her and told me she was gone. She was a beautiful woman and I still have my memories so she's always with me."

"If you look anything like her, then beautiful is an understatement. Do you have any relatives in the Poconos? Or Jersey?   You look just like this woman from my old neighborhood."

"Not that I know of in the Poconos, some of my family are from Jersey, but then again, I bet you think WE all look alike." It came out of my mouth before I realized I had said it. I stare at him, awaiting his reaction. He seems to analyze his words before speaking them.

"If you mean I think all attractive women look alike, then you would be wrong. She was the most beautiful woman I had ever laid my eyes on until the night I saw you."

Not bad, I think to myself. He didn't let me rattle him. It takes a strong man to handle me and he is showing that he's not weak in that area.

Stepping closer to me, Quincy wraps his arms around me.

"You're cold, right, Queen? Let me warm you up."

His massive hold on me feels so right. But I am who I am so I question him.

"So are you this presumptuous with all your ladies, Quincy?"

Grabbing my face, his thumb moves to my chin, while he lifts my face toward him. I'm forced to look up into those blue eyes. Mmmm, those eyes. He simply stares.

I whisper, "Well."

"Well, what, Queen?" he smiles as he returns my question. My face and body still unable to break free from his command. Comfortably, I am trapped in his abyss.

"Are you this audacious with all of your girlfriends?" A slight grin escapes me.

"You're so fucking pretty, Queen."

"Thank you," I reveal as I exhale slightly. Synergy moves through me, on a journey from my breasts to a roaring flame that has a safe haven between my legs.

"So?"

Quincy pulls me closer to him. Damn, he smells good. Enviable confidence covers him immensely.

"So, what, Queen?" He smiles that sexy grin that has the power to make me drop to my knees. I can't believe what I'm feeling.

"I guess you're not going to answer my question, right?"

"I'm single at the moment. There's only one woman on my mind."

"Really, well, who's the lucky lady, Dr. Hughes?"

Quincy leans in and plants the most endearing kiss to my forehead. His lips, so soft and smooth. His touch, so gentle. As he pulls back, I scream inside, "No," as I want this moment to last forever.

"You are, Queen."

My cell phone beeps indicating I have a new text message. Quincy moves back giving me just enough space to check my phone. I pull it closer into view. I don't know the number of origin, but I read it anyway.

That flower looks pretty in your hair.

I drop my phone out of shock and begin looking around to see whose watching me.

"Are you okay?" Quincy bends down to pick up my phone off the ground.

"Someone thinks it's funny to play head games with me." I am vague in my answer to Quincy and I continue to look at the people around us. Two college girls run by and begin giggling, or at least in my mind they were giggling at us. Quincy wipes my phone off and hands it to me as I say "Thank you" to him, I notice a black woman on a bench to our right and she raises her eyebrow as we walk by. My mind shifts between wondering who sent me the text and wondering if everyone around me is staring because of the company I am keeping.

"Queen, what's up? All of a sudden you seem so distant."

"Quincy, this has been nice, but I need to get back to the office." I turn back in the direction from which we came and head back to work.

"Did I say or do something wrong Queen? I thought we were having a good time." His puppy dog eyes beg for an explanation, but I'm momentarily paranoid. I know for sure at least one person is watching me, and I begin to wonder if everyone in the park is staring and asking themselves, "What's that black woman doing with that white man." I walk faster and Quincy lengthens his stride to keep up with me.

"A penny for your thoughts. Hell, I'd give all the money in my wallet right now just to know where your mind is." Quincy is trying really hard, but how can I tell him that right now, I feel like a sell out. My head is telling me I am a traitor to my race. My heart is telling me that I want him to run away and hide with me. How can I say to him that although I like him, I don't think I could be in a relationship with him because I couldn't deal with the stares, the whispers and the ridicule? I can't say any of that to him, so I punk out instead.

"There's nothing wrong Quincy, I just remembered that I have one more client coming in this afternoon, so I have to get back to the office and prepare for that. " I lie and walk even faster. Quincy talks the whole way back. Unlike a few minutes earlier, this time I can't hear a word he is saying. My mind is chastising me. What was I thinking putting myself in a position to be subjected to the opinions of others? I can't do this! I can't handle the stares. I stop Quincy at the doors to my building. Damn, I want to kiss him so badly. It's written all over his face – his concern for me, his care for my well-being, his state of confusion, its all there. I know he wants to come up, but I won't allow it so I stop him in his tracks as he opens the door for me.

"Queen, please tell me what's the matter."

"Quincy, thanks for the walk in the park, I enjoyed it. I'll see you later; I still have your card, so I will call. This was fun."

I practically run into my building without giving him a chance to talk me into another date. Once inside my office I brush past Paula and grab my purse and keys. A sight that surprises the hell out of me adds more of a *Twilight Zone* element to the day's events. Michael Bevens is here, chatting it up with Paula. He's shaven his head bald, and has cleaned his appearance up drastically. I guess freedom does wonders for a man. His suit is tailored almost to perfection and he has roses in hand. Michael rises to his feet, and smiles. "Thank you again, Ms. Thomas, for saving my life."

I smile. Although phoney, I, at least offer something. Michael moves closer to me, gives me a hug and it lasts way longer than I want it to. A confusing look comes over my face and I glance at Paula. She throws her hands up as if to say, "I have no clue."

I remove myself from Michael's embrace. Hurriedly, I pace. "Thank you so much, Michael," I tell him as I pat him on the shoulder.

"Paula, I'm leaving for the day. I'll call you later." Paula looks confused and I leave her that way. Right now, I just need to be alone. I don't remember the drive home. I was on auto-pilot and as I closed the front door of my house behind me, he grabbed me.

"You think you can ignore me bitch?" I feel the back of Derrick's hand across my face before I can even catch my breath. My knees hit the hardwood floors in my foyer and I try to crawl toward the door. Derrick stares down at me and his eyes are bloodshot red. As I continue to crawl, he circles around me like a mad dog. I reach for the door handle and he grabs me by the shoulders raising my body from the floor and pushes me up against the wall. Tears pour down my face.

"What do you want from me Derrick? Why can't you just leave me alone?" I tremble as I say the words looking at my own feet dangling at least two feet from the floor.

"I'm never going to leave you alone baby girl. You are mine. I came to see you today and saw you leave with that cracker. Is that your boyfriend now?" He holds me in place with one hand and begins to unbutton his belt with the other. "If that's your idea of a real man, let me remind you what good black dick feels like."

I whimper louder. "Derrick don't do this. Please just let me go."

"I'll let you go right after I get that jungle fever out of you and replace it with some good monkey love." His pants fall to his ankles and he lowers me to get me in the right position for entry. I try to fight him as he begins kissing my neck and grinding on me to get an erection. He's going to rape me and I don't have the strength to fight back. My kicks and punches don't faze him one bit. I just cry and close my eyes praying God will make it all stop. With his body weight he keeps me pinned against the wall while he lifts up my skirt and rips my panties until they fall. "You know, I'll kill you, right?" I'm inches from the door but I can't move, I try to resist, but fueled by anger, he's too powerful for me to make a move. He grinds harder on me and I can feel his dick rising, I know it is only a matter of time before he rapes me and all I can do is cry. I manage to reach inside my pocket and click the button on my trusty friend. Stroking his vile dick and looks me in the eye, "What's that white boy got that I don't? Nothing bitch;

absolutely nothing. Mine is bigger and better. Why would you want that shriveled up little dick when you could have all this? It's time I remind you how good my shit is." He is about to enter me when the door bell rings. Praise Jesus. Through the frosted glass, I can tell its Paula. She rings the bell again and knocks on the door.

"Queen, are you alright? I know you are in there, let me in."

She knocks harder.

"Queen. Queen. Don't make me make a scene, let me in."

I look in Derrick's bloodshot eyes. "You know she can be persistent, I need to let her in before the neighbors call the cops from all the noise she's making, and you really don't want the cops here do you?"

If looks could kill, I would be dead. Derrick grabs his pants and walks towards the back door.

"We ain't hardly through Queen; believe me, this shit ain't over."

"Derrick, I pray the wrath of God comes down on you something horrible. You're going to hell. I just want you to know that." Riding the tail of those last words, Derrick walks through the kitchen and I hear the door slam over Paula's knocking at the front door. I pull my skirt back into place and open the front door. The look on Paula's face tells me that I better not even try to lie because she knows something is going on.

"Queen, are you all right? Your mouth is bleeding." She puts her arms around me and walks me to the living room.

"Derrick was in my house when I got home." I wipe the bitter taste of the back of his hand from my lips.

"Did he hurt you?"

"He was about to rape me when you came."

"You mean that nigger just left? I'm calling the police; this is getting out of hand Queen." She picks up her phone and I place my hand over hers.

"Just let it go Paula, I'll change my locks and it will be alright."

"You have lost your damn mind. You think changing the locks is going to stop him? What set him off this time?"

"He said he saw me leave the office with Quincy and he wanted to show me what good black dick was."

"All this was over Quincy? Derrick has issues Queen, you need to recognize that."

"It won't be a problem again, because I am not going to see Quincy anymore."

"Why? Because some demented, abusive man told you not to? Derrick thinks he owns you, and you are letting him run your life."

"No, I'm not letting Derrick run my life; it has nothing to do with that. I am not going to see Quincy because I don't think I can be involved with a white man."

"Answer this for me Queen; do you like Quincy?"

"Yes, I do." A smile comes across my face for the first time since leaving the park. "Something about him feels so comfortable and so right." The mere thought of Quincy eradicates all of Derrick's madness in an instant.

"Well, if you like him, then why not give him a chance? Why can't you give both of you a chance?"

"Have you been listening to anything I have said concerning him Paula? He's white. I don't think I can get passed that. I don't think I can deal with the looks from society, the racism, the discrimination. Black people have been through so much to be treated equal. Black men have had to deal with being second class since slavery. How can I turn against my race and be involved with the tool that has kept us degraded for centuries?"

"Oh, so let me get this straight, now you are the symbol for all black people? The fate of our race lies in who you open your legs for? Girl, get over that. Love is color blind, and it's hard to find. Quincy seems like a good man, instead of focusing on what color his skin is, you should be focusing on how he makes you feel."

"I just don't know what to think Paula. I enjoy being around him, but I don't know if I could see myself with a white man."

"Does he turn you on?"

I laugh out loud. "Girl, yes!" I scream, "He's so alluring, so sexy to me, it's weird, but girl, he is just scrumptious…But I just can't see myself moving forward. Besides I have to get rid of Derrick and he's white, remember?"

"Oh, I'ma take care of Derrick, trust and believe. Keep tripping over nothing Queen, and before you know it, someone not so hung up on color will have taken your good white man while you are still being beat up by your bad black one."

❧ ❧ ❧ ❧ ❧

The stars are dim as the dark of night rests outside my window. As I toss and turn in this bed, I can't help but imagine and wonder what Quincy is doing. His tender, tempting and tasteful touch was just what I needed. The thought of him, even the fact that he crosses my mind, blows my mind, quite frankly. There's something about him, even from day one, he's proven to have staying power. Paula would giggle like a piglet if she knew of my internal fantasies about that white boy. It's funny, the "white" part of him seems to fade whenever he's near. Saying that I'm torn would be a severe understatement. I'm hungry; hungry what whatever Quincy will feed me.

The violet-colored chemise caresses my curves in all the right places, and the silk brushes against my nipples, turning me on even more. Could it be the bedroom attire turning me on this way? Absolutely not. It's Quincy. Should I call him? Nah. Maybe tomorrow. Can I call him? No way. He only needs a Will drafted. Taking another glance at my alarm clock, I realize it's time to get some sleep. The threat of Derrick has left me, thanks to Paula who had all the locks changed earlier and arranged for security to guard my front door. She is my gift from God, I know it. Sometimes, I believe God placed her in my life to watch over me like my mother would have if she were here. Nevertheless, an early morning tomorrow for me as the day will be consumed by depositions. Okay, now its midnight and I must get some sleep. Off goes the repeat of *Law and Order*.

The light from the half moon peers ever so slightly through the bedroom window, making it easy for me to see my nipples rising. My fantasies kick into overdrive. The squishing sounds of lust formulates between my thighs. I envision his lips – his perfectly chiseled jaw, the deep dimple in his chin – his eyes, his delectable mouth. Did he say, *"you're so fucking pretty, Queen?"* He's got a potty mouth. I likes. He delicately balances the street and professional. From him being a doctor to his Carhart jacket, to his Timberlands and Ecko jeans, he's indescribable really.

Restless at twelve-thirty a.m., where now my pillow attempts to extinguish the roaring flames between my thighs, and its soft, plush edge rests against my bulging clit, pulsating in anticipation of him.

My phone rings, interrupting my flow – the one in my mind and that pours fluidly from my righteousness.

Paula urged me to keep my phone turned on. Reaching over to my nightstand, my eyes peer to raised nipples that need and want attention. I read the screen, and it's Mountain View. Panic sets into my soul as I pray my father is not sick or dead or a call about him doesn't reside on the other end of this line.

"Hello?"

"Good evening, Beautiful. Did I wake you?"

"No, I'm trying to get to sleep, not there yet. Who's calling?"

"How many men do you have calling at midnight?"

"None, which is the reason I asked."

"Queen, its Quincy. I'm sorry to bother you so late."

"It's no bother at all. I was just thinking about you, actually. Well, about the Will situation. How did you get my cell phone number?"

"Your secretary, Paula, gave it to me."

"Oh, I see."

"You see what, Queen?"

"Nothing."

"So, is it a bad time? Of course, it is, I do apologize. I'll call you tomorrow. Again, I'm…"

"Don't apologize, I can't get to sleep."

"Me either."

"And why is that, Quincy? Maybe you need to drink some hot tea or take something to soothe you."

"That could be true, or…"

"Or, what?"

"Maybe I can drink you. That will soothe me."

"Is that right?"

"Yes."

"Quincy, I'm really flattered and I think you're a nice man, but I'm going to be honest with you. I don't see myself dating a white man. I really don't. I mean, I defend black men who've been wrongly accused of crimes. I do that for a living."

"It's very noble of you. My best friend is black. I grew up around a plethora of different races, so I know and understand the inequality in the system. I'm proud of the work you do."

"Are you? I'm in shock that you would be."

"Queen, look. I know you are aware of the Newark riots, right?"

"Yes."

"My family, although we lived in Jersey City didn't want to move to the so called white neighborhoods. We stayed there, to prove a point. This happened before I was born."

"Right."

"Yes, that's right. Yes, the country's history of race relations is deplorable Queen, but I'm not the culprit. I save lives on a daily basis no matter what the skin color."

"Why does your phone say Mountain View?"

"Well, you know I work for the hospital. It's just easier to use their phone sometimes, while my phone is on the charger. I could use a new battery."

"Well buy a battery."

"I will soon, for sure. Hopefully, you'll run the battery low every night while we spend hours on the phone?"
I giggle.

"You're very charming, Q."

"Oh, only my future wife is allowed to call me Q. Did you know that?"

"Maybe I should hang up, Quincy."

"I'm yours for the taking, Queen. You've taken up all of my mind, my heart, everything, since the first time I laid eyes on you. I can be anything you want or need."

"I'm flattered, Quincy."
"You're feeling me, right?"
"Quincy."
"That wasn't a "No." So, you must be feeling me, because I'm definitely feeling you."
"Quincy…"

"Tell me, Queen, what are you wearing."

"A purple nighty."

"Do you have panties on?"

"Is that what this is? You just want some ass from me?"

"Ass comes in offers by the truckload to me, Queen."
"Why aren't you on the phone with one of those hoochies then?" *Damn his voice is so sexy, so deep and intriguing.*

"Because I only want you, Queen. I know what I like. Because I know what I want. And I know what I need. When are you going to get that?"

"I got it now, Q."

"Good. Don't ever forget it."

"Okay, Quincy."

"Do you have panties on?"

"No, Quincy. I don't."

"Mmmm."

"Mmmm, what?"

"Just sounds so good to me."

"Why is that?"

"I can just imagine tasting you. You look so good and if you look good, you must taste good. Right?"

"I guess."

"Do you taste good, Queen? You look good enough to eat."

"Mmmm, Quincy, I have to go."

"Don't make me waste my time."

"Q..."

"Don't make me lose my mind, Queen."

"I don't know what to say, Q."

"Why, Queen? I know you're feeling me. You deny it in your mind. I see the way you look at me. You let society dictate who and how you should love. Throw all of that bullshit caution to the wind and give me a chance. Let me give you all you deserve. I'm not about games, Queen."

"Right."

"So speak to me now. Tell me your thoughts. What makes you happy and how can I fit into that equation?"

"I can't right now. You caught me at an awkward moment."

"Why is that?"

"I was just thinking of you, Quincy."

"Oh yeah?"

"Yeah."

"I want you, Queen."

"I want you too, Quincy."

"Can I have you now?"

"You can't come over this late, Quincy."

"Put your phone on speaker."

"Why?"

"Just do it, baby, for me...please. I won't tell a soul, Queen, I promise. If you want to keep me locked away, and hidden from the world, I will accept that if that's what I need to do to have you."

"You're making this hard for me."

"Good, because I'm not giving up on our love. I want you for myself, to keep, to honor, to cherish. I want you to be my woman."

"Is that right?" *I'm drenched.*

"Put your phone on speaker."

"Okay, it's on speaker."

"Take off your clothes."

"Why?"

"Do it now, Queen."

"You're very demanding, Q."

This man is too much.

"You like it?"

"My chemise is off."

"Lay on your back, baby," Quincy commands.

"Now, bend your knees."

I exhale with pleasure.

"Queen, spread your legs, nice and wide, for me."

Silence.

"Just imagine me there with you, Queen, and my lips kissing you softly all over your beautiful body. Can you imagine that, Queen?"

"Yes, I can, Quincy. But I can't do this, Q."

"I told you only my wife can call me Q. Now, picture my tongue gliding over your nipples, and then I suck them, real slow and long. Rub your nipples for me, Queen. Get them hard for me."

"Mmmm. Quincy, I can't do this. Mmmmm."

"Put your tongue on your nipples and think of me."

"Mmmm."

"Do you like the way I feel, Queen?"

"Yes," I whisper in satisfaction.

"I dream about you every night, Queen. I see you in my dreams. I taste you on my lips."

"Quincy…"

"You're so pretty, Baby."

"Thank you, Quincy."

"Now, take your hands and rub your thick, pretty thighs. Spread your legs, gorgeous. Suck your fingers and start rubbing my clit, Queen."

"Quincy…"

"Let me hear it, Queen."

"Hear what, Quincy, I can't…"

"Let me hear you suck your fingers."

Taking each finger, one by one, I lick and suck on them for dear life, as if ordered by a sergeant to do so. Sucking sounds are loud, lustful, loving – longing.

"Your lips sound so sweet, Queen. Kiss me, baby."
I blow a kiss softly.

"I bet your lips taste as good as you look. I've being dying to taste those pretty chocolate lips. You gonna let me taste you, Queen?"

"Quincy, this is too much for me."
 "It's not enough, Queen, kiss me again."

Another kiss leaves my lips and I swear if I could follow its path, it land right on Quincy's delicious mouth.
"You want me don't you, baby?"
"Quincy," I whisper.
"Take those wet fingers and gently rub my clit, Queen. It's mine, right?"

"Quincy."
"Is it mine, Queen?"
"I want it to be, Q."
"Are you wet?"

"Yes."
"That sweet pussy wet for me, baby?"
"Q…"

"Is that delicious hot pussy ready for me, baby?"
"Yes, Quincy…"

"You know I can make you feel good. You want me to, honey?"

"This is too much, Q…"

"You've been thinking about me, haven't you baby? You've been wanting to get to know me, I feel it, I know it, you want me to love you good, you want me, I can taste your sweet ass now…Don't lie, Queen."

"Yes, I think of you, Quincy."

"Rub it nice and slow, then stick your fingers in all that sweetness for me. Pull it out then in, over and over again, as if I'm inside deep inside your love."

"Mmmm, Quincy."

"How wet is it, Queen?"

"It's so wet, Q, so damn wet for you right now," I cry through whispers.

"Let me be your lover, your friend and your man. I can go real deep, as deep as you can stand it. Let me take you there, I promise I'll take my time, Queen."

"Is that all you want from me, Q?"

"You called me Q again. Are you going to be my wife?"

"Stop playing, Quincy."

"I want to stare in your eyes, look deep into your heart, pass the façade you hide behind. Tell me which wall you want to climb."

"You're making me too wet, Q."

"Can I taste it, Queen, please?"

"Quincy…please, this is not right. I don't date outside of my race."

"Oh, its right, and you know it. You know it, don't you baby?"

"Q…"

"Its right, isn't it baby? This white boy is right for you and you know it, don't you baby?"

"Yes."

"I want to taste it, baby."

"Quincy."

"You gonna let me slide my tongue in it, baby?"

"Quincy, stop…"

"Baby, are you gonna let me slide my tongue in that sweet pussy?"

"You're so nasty."

"Only for you, Queen. You want me to?"

"I do."

"Tell me you do."

"Quincy, please," I beg.

"Tell me you want me to slide my tongue in and out of that hot pussy baby, because I want to suck it so damn bad."

"Q…"

"I know you want me, just as bad as I want you, Queen. Don't deny it. Now, tell me you want me to taste you."
"Quincy…I…I want…"

"Tell me, baby. Tell me what you want. Don't be scared, tell me."

"Quincy, I want you to taste me. I want you…I want you to slide your tongue in me," I exhale as my hands roam while following his commands.
"Yeah, I love to hear you say it. Tell me what else you want, baby. I want to give you everything you want, Queen."

"I want to feel you deep inside of me, Quincy. I do."

"Good girl. Real deep, baby?"

"Mmmm, real deep, baby."

"I'll take my time. Real slow, long, deep, slow strokes for you, baby. You want that?"

"Ahh, Quincy, mmmmm, baby…"
"That's right, baby. Get that pussy ready for me."

"Quincy!" I yell as the rain comes down. "I need to smell it, Queen. The thought of touching you drives me wild. The thought of having you…Can I have you, Baby? I want all of it, all of you. I want to taste it. Fuck it. Suck it. Spank it. Love it. Empty myself inside of it, please," he whispers. Sensing that he's satisfying himself, the same way I am pleasing me turns me on crazy.

"Come with me…Oh baby, I'm almost there, Queen. Shit, I'm coming now. Oooh, damn. I can't wait to get my hands on you girl."

"I'm there too, Quincy. Oh God, mmmm, this feels so good."

"Don't shut me out, Queen. I can be everything you need."

QUINCY
After the Rain

After weeks of phone calls, love letters and flower deliveries, I finally hit a home run. Yesterday was a day of possibilities; I chased my dream and couldn't be more satisfied with my actions. I had some time alone with my Queen and even though I went home alone, talking both of us through an orgasm was just as good. I know I made up some ground in her head; ground my skin color was holding me back from trotting on. Funny though… she's never "said" that because I'm white, she won't give me the time of day. But it is the reason, and I'm praying it's the only reason she has left. Just like a person won't quite say, "hey, I don't want you because you're fat." She's being polite, and not trying to be obvious about my race being that roadblock that leads to her heart. Besides, like Big said, she's a poster child for affirmative action, so I knew going in that this would be an uphill battle.

Nevertheless, I woke up this morning with a smile on my face and a Queen-induced hard on. She sounded so sweet and tender on our phone call. Getting her pussy wet was a major deal for me as it confirmed what I've known all along; that the night we first laid eyes on each other at Jasper's, it was chemistry, love at first sight, if you will, no matter how hard she tried and still tries to not acknowledge it. There's something about the way she looks at me that tells me all I need to know. That twinkle in her eye. The sexy smile that lights up the night. She's feeling me, just as much as I'm feeling her, and

I know it. And, I plan on proving to her that she will be mine. In my arms is where Queen belongs.

Holding my pillow tightly as if holding her, I roll over and hump it two times as I reminisce about our encounter. I remember putting that magnolia in her hair. Her eyes penetrated me, almost burned a hole in my back as I kneeled down to pick her favorite flower. She didn't know that I caught a glance of her checking me out, but I did, and her actions sent a power surge of confidence through me. The touch of her skin, the tension in the moment, her whispers…shit, she's fine.

"You want me don't you, baby?"

"Quincy."

Replaying last night's events in my mind over and over again makes me feel as if I'm going to bust. I can only imagine how delectable she looked while thinking of me. The thought of it makes me want to fill her up with all of my goodness. I'm ready to boldly enter her wonder.

"Tell me which wall you want to climb."

"You're making me wet, Q."

"I need to smell it, Queen. The thought of touching you
drives me wild. The thought of having you…

Damn.

The gym is the only thing on my agenda for today and Big calls as I'm in the middle of my…damn he can fuck up a wet dream.

"What your sorry ass up to today? It's Saturday and you know we gotta hang out."

"I'm getting ready to jerk off, Big, then, I'm on my way to the gym but after that I'm free. What ya got planned?" I'm in a good mood and actually glad Big called to get me out of the house. Just wish he would've let me get one off first.

"You nasty bitch. Its boy's night *mutha* fucka, yo ass is at Jasper's tonight. No excuses!" Big gives me an order and for once, I'm glad to hear it and willing to accept.

"All right, quit ya whining, I'm there. Shit I need a little relaxation tonight."

"Cool. See ya at ten. And Q?"

"Yeah man?"

"Wash your hands before you get there tonight, you filthy scoundrel."

Big hangs up and I go get my workout on.

❧   ❧   ❧   ❧   ❧

Just when I thank God there's no distractions this time and I actually get the chance to do what I came to the gym to do, Cassandra's ass walks over to me. Dressed in a tight leotard which makes her breasts scream for mercy, Cassandra, still very attractive in a hit-it-and-quit-it kind of way, approaches. "Hi Quincy."

"Hey there, Cassandra," I respond with the shittiest grin on my face. I'm dead wrong and I know it.
She knows it too, apparently.

"Why haven't you called?"

Searching frantically within my heart and soul to find something decent to say, I'm distracted by her bouffant hairdo and fire engine red lips. Did I really let a country and western superstar go down on me? The thought alone makes me laugh out loud and Cassandra doesn't appreciate my sense of humor.

"What the hell is so funny, Quincy?"
"Oh nothing, Cassandra. How's life?"

As she places her hands on her snake hips, I can feel the anger emoting from every fiber of her being.

"How's life? What the fuck do you mean how's life? I've been calling you for weeks now and you don't have the decency to return my phone call? If you're not interested, just say so."

Working 9 to 5. I hear the song singing in the background of my mind.
The stupidest grin escapes me and I know I've pissed her off even more.

"Well, Quincy?" she awaits a response.
If she only knew that Queen is all that's on my mind.

"I'm not interested, Cassandra," I respond in a respectable low tone.

"Fuck you, Quincy!" she screams and walks out of the gym.

"Damn," I say to myself. I'm not in the business of hurting feelings, but there's absolutely nothing there for Cassandra. I wouldn't even let her suck Big's dick at this point. It was just a nut, nothing more and nothing less.

❧   ❧   ❧   ❧   ❧

The feeling of sweat and sore muscles is pre-orgasmic to
me when I get back home.
Removing my sweat-soaked clothes, I hit the play button on my
answering machine. Three messages await.

"Message number one. Beep. Hey Quincy, it's me, Tina.
Stop playing Boo. I'm sorry. Let me make it up to you. Let's
start all over again, Quincy, baby, I miss you."
I can't believe that nasty ass Tina is STILL calling me. Damn.
Dick must be good, but I gotta feeling that my checks feel a
whole lot better.
I laugh out loud as I think about whose bed I've been crawling
in lately.

"Message number two. Beep. Quincy, you know what,
you're a piece of shit! You know that? I thought we had a
connection. But now I realize you're just a dog, Quincy. You
thought you were so cute in the gym today, trying to laugh me
off, didn't you? Well, you're not that cute. Any man would
want this Quincy? You must be crazy for turning this down.
Anyway, good riddance you sorry ass excuse for a man!"
Cassandra screams on my answering machine.
"Damn, she must be really mad," I laugh out loud.

"Message number three. Beep. Hi, uhm, Q. It's me,
Queen. I feel a lil silly for calling you. Well, uhm, I guess I
don't even know why I'm calling. What am I doing? Ha, ha. I
feel like a teenager. Uhm, anyway, Q, I was calling to thank
you for last night. Wow, am I really thanking you via voicemail
for making me… well, anywho, I hope all is well in your world.
Take care, Quincy. Bye."

"That's right, Baby! Thank your man for taking you
there, girl!" That woman knows she does it for me. Trying not
to be desperate, I take all the strength I have left in me to not
call her and offer me on a silver platter to Queen – one that she
could have for the rest of her life if she chooses. Instead, I run
to the shower and turn on the water. As the droplets hit my
head, I lean forward placing one hand on the dark blue tile in
front of me and the other hand on my hardening erection. As it
swells in my hand widening my grip, I chuckle to myself, "Not
bad for a white boy." The water runs through my hair, down my
body and hits the pulsating veins in my dick; I add lather and
exhale deeper with each stroke. Visions of her pretty lips enter
my psyche.

"I was calling to thank you for last night."

My breath fogs the glass door. Closing my eyes, I see her face, then her juicy thighs and then the outline of her full breasts. I try to visualize how she looked last night as her fingers invaded her pussy in a manner my mouth was designed to do. The blood rushes faster from my brain to my dick. It hardens even more and gives my thoughts a standing ovation.

"Take those wet fingers and gently rub my clit, Queen. It's mine, right?"

"Quincy."

"Is it mine, Queen?"

"I want it to be, Q."

With each stroke, I whisper her name until the strokes get faster and the whispers become screams. As I release my load down the drain, I try and shake off the feeling of "Queen" on the brain.

Busting a nut always knocks my ass out. Just like a good meal, once it's done, so am I. Its mid afternoon, I've had a workout and an orgasm, so I wrap a towel around me and lay across the bed. Before I know it, I've fallen asleep and wake up only after the sun goes down. I have just enough time to get dressed and live up to my promise to Big, so that's what I do.

Jasper's here I come.

The boys are already there when I arrive.

"See, it's not just the brothas that run on CP time." Big waves his hand in the air in approval of his own words as I approach the table.

"Don't hate on me Bro. It takes a hot minute to look this good." I strike a pose in my Gucci shoes, fresh white button up and a pair of Rockafella jeans, with a mean belt that coincides with the diamond stud in my ear, for emphasis. Lo and Raj give me dap. I love these boys. My mans n 'em; they are like brothers to me and sometimes make me long for my blood brother more. As I take the one seat left at the table, I look around the club and my eyes are fixated at a table across the room to my left.

She's here. I can't take my eyes off of her. A black skirt which holds on to her ass for dear life, and black high-heeled thigh-high boots, and a white low cut sweater makes me shake my head to regain my senses. Big breaks my stare by waving his hands in front of my eyes.

"So what's up man? What's new and poppin' in your world? We haven't hollered at each other in a while, what you been up to?" He throws a few brotherly sucker punches my way and I feel the love as only brothers do.

"I'm gone bro. She's got me."

"Who? What the hell are you talking about?" He laughs as he takes a sip of his beer and stares at the waitress.

"I had a date with her man and I'm hooked." I swirl my drink so the liquor can settle better with the ice.

"Her who man? Can you be more specific?"

"My wife."

"Who in the hell is your wife, Man? I ain't never heard you talk like this."

"Queen." *I can't take my eyes off of her.*

"You mean the chocolate hottie lawyer? Awh shit, look at Richie Cunningham chasing celebrity booty. Damn, I'm impressed. How did you score that one? Wait. You're lying, Robin Thicke."

"I upped my game and she seemed to like it."

"Well, I ain't mad at you." Big takes another swig of his beer using two fingers to grasp the bottle. I take notes of his swagger, but would never let on that I do.

"Yeah, she's got my nose wide open. I think I got my foot in the door, I just have to figure out how to reel her in." I play it cool in my words to the boys as I stalk her across the room with my eyes. Everything about her catches my attention. From the way her hair hangs around her face to the color of her nail polish, I study it all from afar.

"You know what Q? I'm happy for you. When it's the right time, it will all fall into place." Big is sincere in his words and our brotherly connection deepens because of it.

"The way I see it Big, now is the time and this is the place." Big looks confused at my statement.

"Maybe so, man. But I still don't know how you got that off."

I reach in my pocket and pull out a piece of paper and slide it to Angelo.

"I need you one more time Lo. I wrote this for my girl. She's here tonight. It's kinda lame, but says what I want to say to her. Can you spit shine it for me and then deliver it like only you can do?" I look at my boy in a pleading manner, knowing what I want to be said, but recognizing I need someone smoother to be the messenger. If Queen and I were alone at my house, I'd put on a CD and let Marvin Gaye speak for me; but we are in a club so I'm using Lo instead.

Lo takes the sheet of paper from my hand and reads it.

"You're right Q, this is pretty lame, but I get what you're trying to say. Give me a few minutes and I'll fix it for you." He pulls a pen out of his jacket pocket and begins crossing out words and adding new ones. I watch as he quickly sinks into an artistic trance. He no longer seems to be sitting at the table with us because he is lost in concentration. I bet the place could catch on fire and he would still be sitting in that chair writing. Artists amaze me with their unbreakable attention to their craft.

"So lover boy, just how far did you get that warrants you enlisting Lo into your plans?" Big has a stupid grin on his face and rubs his hands together in anticipation of juicy details. I contemplate telling him everything since he's my boy; but Queen is different from the hoochies of my past and I don't want him thinking of her as just another score for his buddy, so I remain vague.

"Man, I got far enough to tease me enough to want more."

"Well, I still don't know if you hit it or not; but I'm happy for you either way."

I smile, still focusing my eyes and lust on my wife.

"So, did you?" Big asks me.

"Did I what?"

"Did you tap that ass, man?"

"Big, ass like that is not meant for tapping. It's meant for making sweet love to, man. Nah, I didn't tap that ass, but I'm planning to get in where I belong in her life."

"You done lost your mind, Quincy."

Big's attention is diverted by our waitress walking by and he tries to catch her attention. I decide to go over to Queen. I stand up, crack my neck, straighten out my shirt and walk to her table. As I approach I can hear her laughing and I feel the warmth of her smile.

"Good evening ladies, you look lovely tonight." My words are spoken to both of them, but my eyes are on Queen.

"Thank you." They answer in unison grinning from ear to ear. I may be paranoid, but something tells me that they were talking about me before I came to the table. They have that 'deer caught in headlights' look, which is a dead give away.

"Your ears must have been ringing Quincy; we were just talking about you." Paula spurts out that piece of information and I see Queen hit her leg under the table.

"And exactly what where you talking about?" I smile and move closer to Queen, taking the seat next to her. Queen's eyes don't leave mine.

"I told her you picked magnolias for me in the park. That's all." Queen is lying and we both know it.

"The walk in the park was only the beginning Queen, why don't you dance with me now?" The closeness of my face to hers allows me to smell her and I feel an urge to have her body pressed against mine.

"No thank you Quincy. We just got here. Besides, maybe you should spend some time with your friends over there." Her eyes dance away from mine and I try to search her face for the reason why. She's playing hard to get, and I'm a sucker for her every move.

"I see them all the time. Tonight I want to see more of you so dance with me."

"Not right now Quincy, maybe later." She seems persistent in her answer, so I decide to leave it alone for now.

"All right. But I will be back." Having been shot down, I walk back to the table with the boys. My ego is bruised, but I hope Angelo will be able to be the Calvary that saved the day. I return to the table and make my plea to Lo.

"How is it man? She's getting colder today; I need to warm her back up, immediately. Can you do it for me Lo? If you turn up the heat, I'll be able to take it from there."

"I got ya man. Watch and take notes." Lo nods in the direction of the DJ to indicate that he is ready to take the mic. He has a celebrity presence in Jasper's and words are not needed for him to make things happen. He walks up to the stage as the lights dim. The room is quiet, and a single spotlight shines on the stage. He whispers a prelude to the poem: "Sometimes a woman touches a man's heart and holds it captive. And when she does, he is a slave to her every whim.

Tonight that slave is Quincy, and this is to his Queen, the cherry in his chocolate covered dream."

    Lo steps back from the mic for a brief moment, licks his lips and seductively begins to speak...

May I inhale the ambrosia of you
    Pheromones so enticing,
        I have no will

        I'm compelled to partake

Please allow me to swallow
    Of nectar so sticky and sweet
        Quenching and reliving the multiple orgasms
        Only you make

I need to smell the aura of your sex
    To excite and calm me
        At the place where
        Sexuality and sensuality intersect.

The animal in me yearns for the
    The gratifying liquid of your loins
        Along my thighs
        Wrapped around me
        On my tongue

I want to be intoxicated by your fragrance
    Like a forest after the rain
    Stimulating
        Invigorating
        Keeping me sane.

Greedily, I yearn for the pungent scent of your skin
    To return me to the place
        Where I can climax
        Yet again, and again, again, baby, again.

Only one thing can complete me
    Filling my life with joys unforeseen
    That one thing is you, Queen.

*The cherry on top of my
Chocolate covered dream.*

As each word comes from Lo's mouth, I watch her reaction, and like a flower, her smile blooms with each line.

Well done Lo, well done. I think to myself as the crowd shows their appreciation with the sound of snapping fingers filling the room. The DJ begins the music again as Lo leaves the stage and I take that as my clue to get a second chance at Queen.

Queen stares at me intently and my eyes refuse to leave her. She seems antsy in her disposition, rocking in her chair; maybe the pussy that belongs to me feels a tingle. Everything tells me to walk over to her right now, but instead, I wait a moment. Although I'm as desperate as a crackhead, I control my out of control desires and patiently wait for a cue.

"Damn, Quincy, you're feeling her huh?" Raj questions as he gives me dap.

"Yes, sir," I respond, barely paying attention to Raj. Continuing in my stare of Queen, I try to emote love rays to her, photosynthesizing my eyes in sync with hers. She returns my glare once more.

She's inviting me to that tingle in her spine. I walk back to her table with an air of confidence, knowing she was impressed.

"My feelings for you were delivered from his lips to your ears…beautiful lady, please tell me, now have I earned a dance?"

I search her face for approval and pray the wall has been chipped down if only just a little. The answer comes in the form of her smile.

"I must admit, I am impressed Quincy and you have earned at least a dance."

Something tells me I've earned much more.

"Excuse us, Paula. I'm taking my wife to the dance floor."

Paula smiles and Queen looks astonished.

I extend my hand to hers and as she accepts it, and walks with me to the dance floor, I see all eyes on us. In my grown man stance, with a hint of confident swagger, I look at my table only to witness Lo, Raj and Big stare at me in amazement. I mouth the words, "WHAT" to them. The stares at her beauty and my audacity to chase her, and I say to myself, "Not bad for a white boy."

QUEEN
Use Me

The bass makes the club jump. The candles lit on every table sets the mood. I rock side to side in my chair as I sip on my drink. What else can I do at this point? What started out as curiosity unfolded into intrigue. I'll admit it, in spite of my apprehension of giving Quincy more than the time of day; a smile creeps across my face every time I see him. His gorgeous face runs through my mind more and I can't control it. Lovely, lust-filled, and lively – I think of him almost daily and it's not right. It can't be. Could it? There's just something about him that seduces every part of me into wanting to give him a chance.

I can't believe I had phone sex with him. Was that what it was? Phone sex? My goodness. What the hell was I thinking? I'm still not sure how he got me to agree to that, but it was nasty and naughty, yet felt so right. His voice, low and sexy, made me wet as I followed the sexual instructions he gave. It's hard to believe he made me cum just with words, but he did and I can't help but smile each time I think about it. His ability to bring me to the point of climax over the phone is sexy to me and I couldn't wait to get to Jasper's to relive the experience while telling Paula all the details. As I was just about to get to the juicy parts, he walked up. His eyes were penetrating me and the closeness of his body to mine gave me a quiver down my spine and reminded me of my orgasm last night. But from the moment he sat down, I began to feel awkward, wondering what others would think. Shifting in my chair, I declined his request for me to dance with him. Somehow, I didn't mind our secret attraction, but I just didn't feel ready to have everyone see me dancing with a white boy. I could sense his disappointment as he left our table, and my heart broke as he walked away. He's so fine. Really and it takes a lot for me to say it. He's damn fine. I don't mean to play hard to get, I'm just not sure yet if I want to allow a relationship to unfold between us.

Intensely, I watch him talk to his friends and wonder what's going on in his head. *Damn, he's sexy. Why does he have to be white?* Paula breaks my concentration.

"So finish the story girl, I want to hear all about it. You mean to tell me that you really had phone sex with him?"

"Yes, and girl he had me screaming his name at the end," I tell Paula as I blush with embarrassment. I chuckle at the visions in my head of me squirming in the bed, breathing hard as he asked me to rub my clit.

"Well, it's about time you got some real loving instead of that abusive shit Derrick was dishing out."

Glancing over to Quincy again, I notice that his eyes don't leave me. He looks delicious in that fresh white shirt. Damn, he could be a Calvin Klein model. Mmmm, forbidden fruit has never been so tempting. Caught like a deer in the headlights, I hear Paula speaking but I can't respond. I stare back at my illicit lover.

"Queen, this is so against the grain of who you are. When you graduated top of your class in law school, the first black woman to do so, you didn't care what others thought then. You're five-nine or something and you wear stilettos! You don't care, right? You let this man whoop your ass, yet, you care about him? And finally, a man comes along, one who admires you for the beautiful, strong and powerful woman you are; one that is secure enough in his own skin to celebrate you, and because he's white, you won't allow yourself to be loved? You're crazy, Queen. I love you. You're my best friend, but you're crazy."

"It was just a phone call Paula; don't make it out to be more than it was. Besides, I don't think I can do this."

"Do what? Enjoy yourself with a good man?" She rolls her eyes at me and I can tell she is tired of my excuses.

"You don't understand Paula."

"You're right. I don't. I don't get you and all this hesitation bullshit. What will it take for you to get with that man? Are you waiting for some sort of sign? Girl if he got you wet over the phone, imagine what it would be like in bed."

Paula has a point. I do wonder what the real act would be like with Quincy.

"And, I know you don't need a man in your life, so don't even go there. You're right Queen, you're self-sufficient in every meaning of the word, I got it, but, there's nothing wrong with being loved, Queen. And to this day, I don't think you've ever been."

"You love me, don't you Paula?" I smile and put my index finger on her nose. She smacks my hand out of her face, playfully.

"Yes, silly, I love you."

I'm lost in thought as the lights in the room dim and Quincy's friend takes the stage. I am shocked when I hear that his poem is dedicated to me from Quincy. Paula smiles and says, "Maybe this will be the sign your stubborn ass has been waiting for."

Angelo's words are carnal and sensual. I close my eyes and just listen to his voice and allow my mind to daydream about Quincy.

"Please allow me to swallow, of nectar so sticky and sweet."

I exhale as images of Quincy kissing my neck fills my mind.

"The animal in me yearns for the gratifying liquid of your loins, along my thighs, wrapped around me, on my tongue."

My mental picture switches to Quincy's head between my legs as I run my fingers through his hair and guide his mouth and tongue deeper inside me.

"That one thing is you, Queen. The cherry on top of my Chocolate covered dream."

I smile. I've never had anyone serenade me before, except for Quincy, and I'm flattered, once again. The poem is alluring and I can feel myself blushing with each word. Who would have thought I'd be courted by a white man, let alone be receptive to one.

The room fills with the sound of fingers snapping when Angelo finishes speaking, and Paula actually stands up, "Now that's what I'm talking about." She yells mid air. I can't help but continue smiling at the fact that the poem was made just for me. I begin to sway back and forth in my chair chasing the feelings that are running through my mind. My thoughts range from giving myself to Quincy to having Quincy as my man. I look at Quincy. Wow, it took a lot for him to put himself out there like that; exposing his feelings for me to all in the room. Our eyes are connecting and I can feel him asking for my approval even though his lips do not say anything from across the room. Not many brothers would have stepped out and been so vulnerable to a woman, especially one like me who has her guard up. Yet Quincy did. I have to admire that. He's leaving me with few choices.

Our eyes linger on each other for a moment and I see him get up from his chair. I can only guess what will come next and I am unsure of my next move. My stomach is in knots, but why? Everyone in the room, including me, already knows his intentions; he had them stated over a microphone for all to hear. So why do I care what others think? I shouldn't, but I do. With each step that brings him closer to me, I feel my heart race just a little faster. He seems to glide across the room with an air of confidence I have not witnessed in a long time. *Lord help me, he's fine.* My clit throbs in anticipation of him. Mental note: Do not invite him home. My mind tells me I'm strong, and that, hey, no problem, I can handle it. But, my heart speaks a different language, it's telling me that I want him, and that I haven't admitted it to myself. I tell both my heart and my mind to shut the hell up so I can concentrate on my Adonis as he moves smoothly across the room like a Sean John model.

Look at him walking over to me. He's a sin and a damn shame. Quincy seems to be in sync with the music. His stride is in rhythm to the bass. Long legs seem to move in slow motion as he approaches. My eyes leave him for a moment and I see the ladies at damn near every table follow his every move, just like I am.

A black woman spins her head all the way around like the scene in *The Exorcist.* She's scoping hard, and just as she is about to get up and step to him, he quickens his pace, while totally disregarding her. Something about that turns me on crazy.

I want to scream with my arms wide open, "Come on, Baby!" Yet, I remain quiet, scared, nervous, elated and I simply stare.

I pray God will guide me and direct me whether to follow my heart or my head. Paula sits and stares at each of us with a grin on her face drinking in a speechless moment of romance before whispering to me, "I think Quincy wants a piece of his chocolate covered dream." She giggles like a school girl as he finally makes it to our table.

"My feelings for you were delivered from his lips to your ears...beautiful lady, please tell me, now have I earned a dance?" He licks his lips and reaches his hand out for mine.

Unlike the first time he asked for a dance, this time I can't resist. The poem and his persistence warranted at least a 'yes' from me, so I accept.

With the boldness of a cobra he confesses, "Excuse us, Paula. I'm taking *my wife* to the dance floor."

He leads me to the dance floor and pulls me in close to him with a strong, masculine grasp. The warmth of his arms around me feels so natural and comforting that I find myself melting in his arms. With each breath that I inhale, my senses are engulfed with his smell. I can't quite place what cologne he has on, but it is pleasing and enticing to me.

Bill Withers' classic *"Use Me"* boldly plays and the speakers make their presence known. Quincy pulls me closer to him and sings, "Baby, baby, baby, baby, when you love me I can't get enough." I close my eyes and lay my head on his chest just to get a closer whiff of him. I have to do something to prevent myself from inviting him home tonight. Because in about thirty seconds, I swear, I'm going to throw caution to the wind, say fuck all this racial shit, and tell him to come home with me tonight. As I lay my head on his chest, he holds me tighter against him and the muscles in his chest, products of his workouts, provide me with a sense of comfort. He rubs his hands up and down my back and begins to whisper in my ear.

"I can be all you want me to be Queen, if only you let me." His speaks slowly, yet deliberately, breathing hard between each word. His breath against my ear is warm and provocative, sending goose bumps down my arms.

Ten seconds and counting...

A slow jam comes on next, adding a magical touch to an already magical night. He slow dances like an old-school G, and his two-step is driving me wild.

"I know it's complicated, but it doesn't have to be. I can give you the world Queen, if only you let me." His lips touch my earlobe and I feel my nipples harden, yet I don't say a word. I just allow my body to grind with his. With each sway of our bodies side to side, the space between us gets narrow. My eyes are closed and I can only imagine what others must be thinking watching us dance with one another.

Damn, I'm having trouble thinking. He smells so good and his body against mine is turning me on in the worst possible way. I nestle my face deeper into his chest and run my hands up and down his shoulders and arms. Damn, I want to lick his nipples. *Shit, this man is buffed.* I've always been a sucker for a man with nice arms. I ask myself the question again, *Why does he have to be white?* Things would be so much easier without the handicap of his skin color, I think to myself as I inhale him once again.

"You look beautiful tonight, Queen."

Five seconds…

"Queen, doesn't this feel good? Doesn't it feel right?" He lifts my head from his chest and looks me directly in the eye. Damn those blue eyes. They force me to answer, even though I don't want to.

"Yes, Quincy, it does." I try to look away, but he won't allow it. He holds my face directly in front of his.

"Stop caring what others think Queen. I can't change the color of my skin, but I can be all that you need. Deep down inside, I think you know it Queen."

He's right. I can feel the connection between the two of us, but am I strong enough to lay down my own racial preference? Don't I owe it to my race to stay on my side of the line? Wouldn't crossing over and intermixing be a slap in the face to them? My head continues to race until I am reminded of Paula's words from a few weeks earlier, "If you don't get him, someone else will." I witnessed that less than five minutes ago with half the women in here.

"This is right Queen, allow it to happen." He runs his hand down the side of my face and I am in a trance. I know he wants some sort of affirmation from me that it's okay for him to continue chasing me, but I can't speak. I don't know what to say. Before I can answer, he pulls my face closer and kisses me and as our lips part he whispers, "You taste so sweet, Baby."

"So, you had a good time last night?" he questions me and smiles.

I'm so embarrassed that I place my head on his arm and smile. He senses my shyness and lifts my face to his.

I stare into his eyes as he pulls my body closer to his. He kisses my lips once more as we rock side to side in beat to the music that floats throughout the room.

"Tell me you like this, Queen," he demands as his lips leave mine once again.

"I do, Quincy, I like it," I smile as I return an answer to him.

"So, what do we do now, Baby?"

"I don't know, Q."

He smiles that smile that makes me warm inside.

"You called me Q."

"Yeah, and you call me Baby, so?"

"That's because you are my baby, Queen. I've been told that if you want something in life, you speak it into existence. But, you still call me Q, even though I've explained to you what that means. Why?"

"I can't explain it, Quincy."

"You're such an intelligent woman, why so few words tonight? You've overcome so much that I know you have words for days."

"How do you know what I've been through?"

"I have my sources, Baby."

I chuckle.

"I see."

"You see what, Queen?"

"I don't know."

"You see that you need to be with me. So, let's make that happen. Tell me something, Baby."

"I don't know what to say, Q."

"Ha, ha, here you go again. I'm yours for the taking, Queen."

"I do know that."

"Kiss me."

"We just kissed, Q."

"Kiss me, baby, please."

Reaching up, I land on the tips of my toes and as he grabs my face once more, I close my eyes and return to heaven. His tongue finds its way around, and as he bites my bottom lip between hot, nasty kisses, I feel everything in my body get hot. He moans, raising the pressure of the narrow space that rests between us. "Mmmm," he pants between breaths.

It's getting hot in here, so I try to break free, but his massive hold on me draws me nearer and as he pulls me into one of the most sensational kisses I've ever had in my life, I give in, as I've lost this battle.

"I can be all you want me to be and more Queen, if you just let me."

QUINCY
Annihilation

Her lips are softer than I imagined. Kissing Queen makes me weak in the knees; I can feel the destiny of our relationship within the crevices of her lips and the surface of her tongue. It's hard for me to let go of the kiss, but eventually I do. Our lips danced with the devil all night long and it felt damn good. Her hands wrapped securely around my neck. My arms around her waist. My fingertips move along the small of her back. Reluctantly, my tongue leaves her mouth once again as the music stops. I can hear Big's voice from across the room.

"Hey Kid Rock. Party's over. Romeo and Juliet, time to go home." Queen smiles as she stares at me. I return her smile. "You know, my best friend is a nut. You'll have to get used to him."

"Is that right?" she questions, looking sexy as ever.

"Yes. But you'll love Pat. He's my boy – for life."

"Looking forward to getting to know him, Q."

"That sounds promising, Queen. Sounds like you're going to be around for a while?"

"Time will tell."

She smiles once more. "You know your friend Big has a point. We're the last ones on the dance floor." My arms don't leave her waist and her arms keep their firm hold on me. I look around and confirm Big's statement. As we walk back to her table, the DJ announces the last call for alcohol and I know the club is getting ready to close. I'm not ready for the night to end; I'm ready for our life together to begin. Having tasted

Queen's lips, I want more, so I pull her close to me with my hands around her waist, leaving her little room to move.

"The night's still young, how about we go somewhere for a drink or a bite to eat."

"The only thing open at this time of night are women's legs, Quincy, and I plan on keeping mine shut." She winks at me as she leans down under the table reaching for her purse. I can't help but to notice the plump, round ass staring back at me as she leans down. She's so sexy.

"It's not like that at all." I can't help but laugh at her wit, as I watch her fumble with her cell phone checking the time. Her face becomes alarmed. "What is it? What's wrong, Baby?"

"I'm still getting stupid text messages from some idiot that thinks mind games are funny." She stares me directly in the eyes. "On second thought Quincy, I think I would like you to follow me home."

"Anything to make sure my future wife is safe." I help her put on her jacket and she tells Paula she'll see her in the morning. I grab her by the hand and lead her to the exit.

"Oh, you just gonna leave the boys Q without even saying bye?" Big is practically shouting across the room. He's right, since I stepped out on the dance floor; I had forgotten all about the fellas and only had Queen on my mind.

"You're big boys…you'll find your way home, bitches." I holla back at Big, not missing a beat in my stride with Queen to get out of Jasper's. Luck is on my side and Queen's car is in eyeshot of mine. Slowly, we walk hand in hand as we make our way to her car through the brisk night air. Something about her being on my arm is so satisfying to me.

"You're holding my hand in public, Queen, I'm proud of you."

"Ha, ha, ha. You're very funny. That's because you have a gun to my head," she replies, smiling, never letting go of my hand.

"Yeah, well, I can't wait to pull the trigger," I tell her hoping she'll read between the lines.

"I can't wait either."

Oh shit. Okay, be easy.

We arrive at her truck. I open her car door and tell her that I will follow her in mine.

"It's only about twenty minutes from here, try and keep up?" She winks at me as I head toward my car.

I kiss her on the cheek and she surprises me by pecking me on my lips.

"Keeping up with you is on top of my list of things to do." I wink back and head to my ride which is just a few feet away.

Behaving like a love-sick fool, I break down and call her. I really shouldn't, considering we're both driving, but I place my earpiece in, and speed dial her. She picks up on the first ring.

"This is Queen," she answers the phone professionally.

"You do look good from behind, you know."

"Ha, ha. Oh yeah?"

"Yeah."

"You're naughty, Quincy. So, tell me, what does it look like?"

"Looks good enough to eat."

"Right."

"Looks like you have a lot to offer too, Baby."

"I admire your persistence."

"Me, persistent, no way," I laugh out loud.

"Yes, you couldn't say that with a straight face, I know."

"Baby, watch those deer to your left. They're coming up."

"Wow, thanks Quincy. They're beautiful to look at but can cause major damage. Thanks for looking out for me."

"Anytime, sweetheart."

I can hear music playing softly in the background. "Who are you listening to?"

"Oh, just Maxwell."

"Is that right?"

"Yes, why?"

"Nothing."

My mind goes back to when Paula gave me all the insider tips about Queen. I remember that if she listens to Maxwell, that she's feeling sexy.

"What is it, Q?"

"I'm just so happy to have made a connection with you, Queen. That's all."

I lie. What I really want to tell her is that I want to break her back tonight, giving her all I got and then some. That I want to fuck her face to face until she comes all over me. I laugh out loud. I want to tell her that she could sit on my face anytime, any place…But, I keep my cool and remain a gentleman.

"Me too, Quincy. But don't tell anyone that. K?"

"I'll be your dirty lil secret, Baby. No problem," I laugh.

Her neighborhood is quiet and well kept, as we pull into her driveway, I admire the landscaping and the beauty of her home. She has good taste, at least from what I see on the outside and I try to think of an excuse to get inside.

As I walk her to her front door, I notice a cop coming out of the car right in front of her home. He approaches and my defenses are up.

"Are you okay, Ms. Thomas?" he questions as he walks near.

"Oh sure, everything is well. This is Dr. Quincy Hughes, officer. He's with me."

"Great, Ms. Thomas," he says then returns to the patrol car.

"Do you mind if I come in and use the bathroom?" My excuse is generic, but all that I could think of at the moment.

"Now you know I'm not falling for that Quincy. That's just a line to get in my house. I already told you, ain't nothing open this time of the night but legs, and if I let you in, something tells me you will be trying to open mine."

"You want me to, don't you?" I ask, beaming from ear to ear.

"That's not the point, Q."

I move in closer to her, placing my hand in the small of her back leading her towards her front door. "I really do have to use the bathroom. Besides, I should check out the inside of your house just to make sure it's safe and that nobody is waiting in there for you. You never know what's lurking inside and you never can be too careful. Honey, you mentioned feeling uneasy about those text messages, why don't you let me at least complete my bodyguard duties by making sure that your house is safe for you to be in alone." I give her half grin, hoping she's buying my excuse. She's right I don't have to use the bathroom, but I do want to make sure she is safe. I can see her mind processing my words as we walk the few steps to her door.

"Quincy, you can come in, but only for a few minutes. And don't you try anything funny." She waves her finger in the air at me like a scolding parent. How cute!

"That leaves a whole lot of other things that I can try." I smile as she opens the door. She looks back at me through the sexiness of her hair. The lights in the house are on timers, so as we enter, exquisite lamps in the foyer light our path. The ambiance in her home is soothing. I envision myself coming home after a hard days work to my beautiful wife and our happy home. For a few moments, I daydream of what life would be like married to Queen and coming home to the womanly comforts of a house like this.

"Well, are you just going to stare, or are you going to look around to protect me? You would make a lousy security guard Q, if someone was here to get me, I'd be dead by now." She jokingly nudges me in the shoulder as she places her coat and purse on the table in the foyer. "I guess since you are here, and you were so nice to follow me home, the least I can do is offer you some coffee. Would you like some?"

"Pretty lady, whatever you want to give me, I'm willing to take." I respond with a sinister smirk as I make my way to the living room.

"So, what's the cop for?" I ask, as my eyes scan her living room which connects to her den.

"Paula got a judge to approve security for me. You know, with the Bevens case and all," she tells me as she moves closer. She looks at the pictures on the wall, right along with me.

"I didn't follow that case closely, due to my hours at the hospital and clinic, but I thought that guy was guilty as sin, honestly."

"Yes, you and the rest of the county. But justice prevailed, so I'm happy."

"You're a very skilled litigator, Queen, and I'm proud of you."

She moves in behind me, wrapping her arms around my waist. Her pretty face rests on my shoulder. "But, I still wonder how you got him off. I mean damn, Baby, Bevens killed those girls, right? Or is that attorney-client privilege?"

Placing her hand on her hip, she pokes out those pretty lips and gives me the evil eye. If she's trying to look mad, it's not very convincing, she's more adorable than anything, but I play along.

Laughing out loud, I question, "Is that your mean face?"

I kiss her forehead.

"Yes, aren't you terrified?" she laughs.

"You're adorable, Baby," I tell her as her eyes leave mine.

"You always wanted to be a lawyer?"

"Good question, Dr. Hughes. I think so. I remember being on the highway with my Dad in Jersey. I remember the look on his face, the change in his body language and, well, I can still picture the image so vividly. We were pulled over by the police. We were in our new Toyota Corolla. I believe it was a 1983 Corolla, all white. We were taking our father-daughter trip to the beach down on the Jersey shore. I had never seen my Dad so petrified. The officer asked him about the car, how he got it, and just a whole bunch of questions that made him uncomfortable. I think that, along with my Mom telling me to take care of my Dad, somehow made me into this nut of a lawyer. Like I have to save all black men or something weird. I don't know. My Dad told me, after the cop left, he said, "Queen, this is the cross that the black man has to bear." I'll never forget it. I guess things from our childhood do help to shape us into who we are later in life. What about you, Doctor? Tell me about your journey from Quincy to Dr. Quincy Hughes."

"I suppose you're right, Queen. Actually twenty years ago, I lost my brother."

"Oh Baby, I'm so sorry."

"Thank you. My brother Quinton, he died. I saw how the paramedics couldn't save him. I saw the look in my parents' eyes, the heartache, the pain. They couldn't save him. He shouldn't have died. Not so young. Not when I needed him to be a son to my mother. Not when I needed him to guide me as an older brother should. He died, right in front of me. He was seventeen and I was fifteen. No one should stop living at seventeen."

I witness Queen holding back the tears so I change the energy in the room.

Noticing the record player, and the crate of old albums next to it, I know for sure she is a lover of good music, much like myself. My eyes notice pictures of some of the greats on her wall. Billie Holiday, Miles Davis, Marvin Gaye, and more, all in exquisite frames, perfectly planted on her wall. "You love real music too, huh?"

"Absolutely. What about you Quincy?"

"Me too, Baby. From Al Green to Notorious BIG, to Prince to Jimi Hendrix, I love good music. So there, we have something else in common."

"Yes, we do," she reveals, her arms still holding on to me. I'm afraid to move, as I do want this moment to last a lifetime.

There's a great photo of Nas and some other Hip-Hop giants on the wall too, which lets me know how deep she really is. "What you know about Hip-Hop Queen?" I question, jokingly. "I know more than you, I'm sure," she tells me as she kisses me on my cheek. She removes her hold on me. I want to tell her, "No, hold me again," but that would make me sound like a bitch, so I remain silent.

"I love rap music, the blues, jazz, shoot, I just love music, Quincy."

"Who's the greatest rapper of all time?"

She smiles and looks at me crazy. "What do you know about rappers, Quincy?"

"Honey, Big and I would spend our summers outside with his radio blasting, and best believe, we came in the house every afternoon to watch Video Music Box with Ralph McDaniels. We listened to Cool DJ Red Alert every night, girl. I've loved Hip-Hop since its inception."

"Notorious BIG would be the greatest rapper of all time. Although my fav is Redman. Jay-Z is in a class all his own, and his music sets the theme to my entire life. I love him for everything he stands for. He's a genius, really. But let me not forget my girl, Miss Lauryn Hill. Can't forget the ladies; Latifah, Eve, and MC Lyte, definitely can go toe to toe with some of the best of them. Yes, I'm a feminist."
"Redman is the truth, for sure. And, yes the Lyte is definitely taking names."

"So, Quincy, who do you think is the greatest?"

"KRS-One, no doubt," I tell her as we walk to the oversized window. The skyline is beautiful. "And why KRS?"

"Because my Queen, Knowledge Reigns Supreme."

She laughs. "What am I going to do with you, Dr. Hughes?"

We look out her window and the view of the ski lodge and beautifully lit mountains is breathtaking. It's a view I wish I had at my own home. She stands in front of the window, pretending to be sincerely interested in those mountains.

Seductively, I grab her from behind as we gaze at the stars together.

I notice a full-length mirror to our left and I move her body towards that direction. We look in the mirror together. She, somewhat shy about the reflection the mirror delivers. But she doesn't move from my arms. I kiss her on her cheek. She looks at me and smiles through the perfectly polished glass.

"You know love is blind, Queen. Love sees less of what we see because it sees more."

"Quincy?"

"Yes, Baby?"

"Something about this scares me."

"Why? Because I'm white?"

"Well, honestly, that part is becoming less of an issue, although, it still is one."

"So, why then?"

"Something about this feels too right and makes me nervous."

"Love is never painless, Queen," I tell her as I hold her tighter. The sight of the two of us in the mirror is picture-perfect. "Don't we look good together, Baby?"

She smiles. "Yes, we do, Q."

"Ut-oh, you called me Q again. So, whatchu saying?" I chuckle.

"See, that's the level of comfort that scares me Q."

I turn her to face me. Placing my hands on her face, my tongue once again finds its way into her mouth. Her lips, moist and soft, her breath, sweet and warm. She returns my kiss with more passion than she ever has. My hands rub along every crevice of her shapely body and she wraps her arms around my neck. Seductively, I bite her bottom lip and my dick rises. I'm nervous about what she might feel if she senses that I am only here for sex, so I back off.

"Is Paula your only friend?"

She chuckles. "No, she isn't but she is my best friend. Women are so catty and competitive. Don't get me wrong, I've got old college buddies and nice legal associates, but Paula is my one true friend. I've come to learn, the hard way, that if you have five cents more or weigh five pounds less, women will become fighting mad at you. It's usually the ugly ones, with deep insecurities that try to make life a living hell for you. And when I say ugly, that could be physical or emotional, either way, it's visible."

I find her words comforting and disturbing at the same time. She's a straight-shooter, but I can tell she's been wounded and that her guard is up.

"You're brutal, Queen."

"Honestly, I'm not, Q. I've been the nice girl, only to find that most people will smile in your face, but you can't turn your back to them. If a woman detects your flaws, she'll point them out to you and the world, viciously, but will never work on herself or look in the mirror, and when she's long gone and has forgotten about the damage she has caused, you're still holding on to the mess she made. I just got fed up with it. Paula and I love one another, unconditionally. I know she has my back, and I have hers. And I know that she was sent from God to be in my life. I'm cool with that."

"I assume Big is your best friend?"

"Yes, baby, he is. A lot of what you said applies to our friendship also. Besides, a lot of men nowadays gossip and I can't stand a gossiping man. Might as well have a skirt on."

"You're silly, Q. But you're cute!"

Finding the remote, I turn on the TV and as I mindlessly flip through the channels, I notice a massive hand-painted portrait above the fireplace. The kind you see in museums or Southern mansions. It's exquisite and the craftsmanship is unlike any I have ever seen before. I assume it is Queen and her parents from when she was a little girl. The details are magnificent and I walk over to the painting unable to resist touching it to feel the detail of the paint. Queen walks up behind me and hands me a cup before beginning to speak.

"That's my most cherished possession. It was painted right before my mother left. Daddy let me have it when I bought this house. It was his housewarming gift to me; and it does just that, it warms my house and my heart. It's one of the few pictures I have of my mother, and seeing all three of us together reminds me of both their love for me and of just how much I miss her."

My eyes are fixated on Queen's mother. "She's very beautiful; did she die shortly after the painting was done?" My curiosity is piqued.

"Actually, she went into the hospital about a year after this was done if I remember correctly, and I never saw her again. I miss her so much. Sometimes I yearn just to hear her whisper in my ear like she did when I was a child. But daddy did a very good job of being both mother and father to me and I always felt loved."

We move from the painting to the sofa. Queen sits close to me and has one leg tucked underneath her. She has taken removed her boots and I love the comfortableness she finally seems to have around me and the sight of her manicured feet is sexy to me. I can be a jerk at times and one of my pet peeves is ugly feet on a woman. But not my baby. Her toes are blood red in color and visually appealing to my eye. My focus deters for a moment as I imagine her pretty feet resting on my shoulder as I dig deep inside of her. I watch as she leans forward with each sip of her coffee and I notice that her hair hangs in front of her eyes as she does. She has a sexy habit of swinging her head to the side to move the ringlets from her eyes. It's a subconscious gesture on her part, but one that's sexy as hell and does not go unnoticed by me.

"So you and your father are close?" I get cozy on the couch and inch closer to her.

"I couldn't imagine my life without him. I wish my mother were still around because girls need their mothers in their life, but daddy didn't do too badly. Actually, now I think he needs me more than I need him. A few months ago, I was in a horrible car accident and when I woke up in the hospital, the first face I saw was his. I have never seen him so worried or scared in my life. I think he thought he was going to lose me, like he lost momma. With her being gone, I don't think his heart could take it if I were gone too."

"You were in a car accident? What happened? How bad was it? You seem like you are fine now." I rub my hand along her leg for reassurance and for a chance at a cheap feel.

"I'm fine now. The accident was pretty bad, I had to stay in the hospital for a while and a friend of mine died. The whole thing was and still is a nightmare for me to think about." She begins to tremble and I reach in to hug her.

"I thought I told you not to try anything funny Quincy. Is that all you came here for? A piece of ass!" Queen puts distance between us.

"I just wanted to comfort you. I don't like to see sadness on your pretty face." I run my hand along her face for emphasis.

"I'm sorry Quincy; I didn't mean to snap at you. It's just that the whole incident is something I like to try and forget."

"I understand, no need to apologize, I am always here for you when you need to vent." I rub my hands up and down her arms and lean in to kiss her but she stops me.

"Quincy, what is this?"

"What's what Queen?"

"This. Us. What are we doing?"

"I think we are following our hearts Queen." I kiss her on the neck allowing my nose to linger close to her earlobe.

"I can't help but wonder if this is a game for you Quincy. How do I know this is not about you busting a nut in some black pussy? Show me I am not just some part of a jungle fever experiment orchestrated by you." She gives me 'that' look, the one women give when they don't trust a man.

I lie back on the sofa and pull Queen on top of me, placing her head on my chest. She doesn't resist and I run my fingers through her hair as I speak.

"I want you to be my wife some day Queen. I know I must sound like some kind of lunatic, but I'm keeping it real with you. You are more to me than a potential booty call. I could get sex anywhere, trust me when I say, that's not what this is about. From the first moment I saw you, I wanted you to be a part of my life. This is about more than sex to me Queen; it's about my future, OUR future. A future where I see you and me together as husband and wife. Queen if this was about sex, to be honest, I wouldn't put this much time and effort in chasing a piece of ass. You're beautiful and intelligent, but ain't no piece of pussy worth me humbling myself for. The only thing, no...the only person I would humble myself for, or chase after, is you. Pussy comes a dime a dozen for me. Soul mates and future wives are rare. I see the beauty of you enveloped in us, and I knew it from day one. This isn't about sex for me Queen, it's about us and our future." I mean every word and I pray I have delivered my feelings in a manner that she can appreciate and accept.

She exhales and I can feel her smile against my chest even before she speaks.

"Quincy, I think you appreciate how hard this is for me. I have deep feelings for you, but before I take a step to let you into my life, I have to know that it is right. Everything about you and us goes against the grain. Everything I have done all my life says don't give you a chance. But I'm feeling you, and if I am going to go against all that I have told myself was right all my life, I need something more from you to convince me. I desperately need to know this is my destiny. Then and only then will I be able to go against the grain and have the strength to weather the storm. Because you and I will have to weather storms, I'm sure of it. If you're in for the long haul Quincy…prove it to me first, and then I can prove it to myself."

"I feel you and from my point of view, everything about you and me is totally right Queen. It may be wrapped in an interracial package that all may not accept, but that does not lessen its beauty, that does not make it less right. In fact, in my eyes, that makes it stronger that makes it more the worthwhile fighting for. Give me a chance Queen. Give our love a chance. I think we both owe it to ourselves to at least roll the dice and see where they fall." I rise up and in doing so, I move Queen from my chest. I gracefully roll her over on her back and put myself at her feet. The lovely feet I have been eyeing all night and she does not resist my actions.

"I know this is real. I've never, and trust me when I tell you, I've never felt this way about anyone in my entire life. This is my proof. Wow, I've just revealed my innermost thoughts with you. I feel a lil silly now. But I'm glad I said it. Can't take it back now anyway."

"I'm glad you said it, Q."

"Well, tell me something Queen. I just put myself on front street, why don't you tell me what's on your heart."

"Honestly, Q, when our eyes first connected at Jasper's, my soul--down to the aching in my chest- thought you were the one for me, my eternal soul mate, my everlasting love; something about you – my spirit instantly connected with yours. I didn't admit it to myself for some time. I kept fighting the feeling. I was coming out of something. You're white, it just wasn't right. But I've thought about you every day since that night. And I do mean, I've thought about you quite a bit."

"You sure know how to play hard to get."

"I had to."

"What were you coming out of?"

"Well, I don't want to talk about it much, but it got abusive. He started to hit me. Derrick Simmons. He's a corrections officer. I met him while working. The love had died a long time ago, if you can call that love. I don't know why I stayed. I never really made time for a boyfriend in my later years; I've been too focused on building my practice. He came around. It's was just something to pass the time, now that I think about it. I think he's the one sending me those stupid text messages. He's part of the reason that cop car is outside."

"He'll never get the chance to hurt my baby again. I swear on my life, he'll never hurt you again. You hear me, Queen?"

"I do."

"Just let me love you."

I place her big toe in my mouth, seductively sucking and tasting every inch of it. "This has never been about me Queen." Raising her leg in the air, I run my tongue up the side of her foot and alongside of her heel.

"It's always been about us…been about you." I circle my tongue around her ankle and kiss her calf.

"I left ME at the door a long time ago, and invited YOU into my heart." I continue along the path up her calf to her left thigh, sucking it passionately, yet gently as I raise her leg into the air and admire the beauty of it as I wipe the saliva building in the corner of my mouth.

"My actions are not my own Queen, they are dictated by you, whether you realize it or not, you control me. You control all that I do." I spread her legs with both my hands and slowly remove her thong from its foundation as she allows me to pull them from their perch.

Placing my nose into her warmth, I inhale, take a deep breath, and breathe in her aura, hardening as her scent moves my senses. My tongue escapes me, landing on the surface of her love.

"You smell so sweet, Baby."

"Quincy, this is moving too fast."

"Do you like it, Queen?"

"I don't know if I can do this with a white man, Quincy, I'm sorry."

"Queen, does my touch make you feel good? Do you like it?"

"Yes."

"Then, let me love you."

I see her move her head backwards in anticipation and relaxation and take that as a sign to proceed.

The sight of her voluptuous thighs, dipped in butterscotch, makes me solid as a rock.

My tongue has a mind of its own, and I allow it to lead the rest of me. Its target is the lips of her pussy and I am more than willing to oblige. Tasting her juices has been calling my name for some time and I am ready to feel her juices on my lips. I can feel the heat of anticipation on my tongue as it finally has the chance to indulge the gateway to her ecstasy.

I reveal, "It's so pretty, Baby," and I roll my tongue slowly along her pussy lips at first, witnessing my dick harden as I do so. After an initial first appetizer of Queen, my body yearns for the full meal that is her. As she arches her body in approval of my actions, I decide I want to be a superstar; I want to hit a home run in appreciation of all fans of the sport of pussy eating. My initial slow licking becomes a more lingering sucking. I let my tongue search and conquer every corner of her pussy, hovering over the lips and becoming a squatter on her clit. Damn...she tastes so good. All you can eat buffets have nothing on the delicacy that is her. I enjoy...I become a glutton in my endeavors, and I revel in satisfaction of pleasing her. As I lick and suck her until I feel the trembling of her thighs to a point that she is moments from crushing my skull from her own personal enjoyment, I am pleased at my skills in pleasing her. It is and always has been about pleasing her.

Smacking her ass, I give her a slight sting to keep the juices flowing.

"Quincy," she softly yells, as she pulls my hair.

My tongue fucks her repetitively, in and out, out and in, as she releases her nectar on my lips. Watching her reach orgasm satisfies me. Feeling her cum heightens my hard on, yet her satisfaction is enough to gratify me. As she screams out my name in intervals between sexual orgasmic indulgence, all I can do is whisper in her ear, "I'm so into you, and pleasing you is what I want to do."

Her heart beats louder and louder and I feel a sense of accomplishment. I want to follow up eating her with feeling my dick inside of her, but I know this is not the time or the place. Tonight was not about me, it was about her. If I want to have her forever, I need to make tonight hers. I rub my dick and tell it, "Down boy, your time will come."

As she lays on the sofa under me, trembling in pleasure, I take a mental snap shot of her pleasure and allow it to be enough for me right now.

"You look so good when you come, Queen." Queen grabs me by my shirt collar and says, "Quincy, please, I need it, now." Her pussy is ready, her guard is down, and her juices are flowing. Any other man would cease the opportunity. "Baby, I don't ever want you to look on this moment and lump me into a category with all the other men you had encountered in your life. I want you to remember me. I want you to have a memory of this moment and marinate on it as a time when your man put you above his own needs; as much as I want to feel myself inside of you, around you, and in you." All things in due time, I say to myself as I reluctantly stand up.

"Quincy, please, I need you," she begs in a soft whisper.

Yearning to be set free, her body calls me, whispers my name, screams for me to provide deep penetration into her love, and her heart.

"I want you so bad Queen that I'm in pain right now from not feeling myself inside of you. But as I told you today...none of this is about me. It's about you. And I want to please you, and only you. Queen, you need to be loved. You need someone to put you first and recognize you for the prize that you are. I, on the other hand, need you. I need you to see that about me. I need your love. I need your acceptance. I need you in my life. It's funny, but both our needs revolve around you. So for tonight, blue balls and all, I am going to leave because YOU need to know I am here for you and only you, and I need you to want me." I grab my jacket and walk towards the door.

She gets up, removing her skirt and her sweater, I witness her in full rare form and undeniable beauty. Full breasts with chocolate perky nipples invite me back to her sofa. I try to move closer to the door but my feet stay stuck in this one spot.

"Quincy, don't do this to me, please. I want you now. Please, make love to me," she tells me as she pulls me into a passionate kiss. My hands caress her naked body. As I place my hands between her thighs, I feel the heat of her righteousness. She's so hot. I want to love her so badly.

My fingers land on her clit and I rub it vigorously as my tongue licks her lips. Her mouth is so warm. She's going to make me bust.

In between lust-filled breaths, she tells me, "Quincy, fuck me, please, baby. You don't have to go."

She pulls me back to the sofa, and I'm having trouble maintaining my composure. Removing my shirt, Queen kisses my chest gently, and runs her fingers along my nipples.

"Mmmm," I moan in pleasure.

The touch of her lips makes leaving a harsh reality.

"Shit, Queen, you're making this hard for me."

"Good."

Sweet kisses glide across my abs and lovely, lusty, flickers of her tongue find a place on my neck as she gently bites it.

"Queen, I have to go. We can't do this right now."

"Baby, you want me don't you?" she questions as she lays on her back on the sofa. Spreading her legs, I witness her play in her pussy. It's calling my name; screaming for me to empty myself inside of it. Begging for deep penetration; crying for me to hit that spot with all the force I can find.

"Queen, I'm not fucking my chance up with you. We have time." *I feel like such a bitch.*

"Kiss her good night, Q. You tell her you don't want her," she waves her finger at me, gesturing me to come face to face with my sweet temptation.

Placing my hand on my hips, I stand and look down at the floor. I'm trying to concentrate. She breaks my thoughts...

"Quincy. Don't leave. Baby, please..." she tells me as she spreads her legs wider.

Getting on my knees, my face once again finds its rightful place between a set of thick thighs. I kiss her pussy, and lick it passionately. Ravenously, I bite her inner thighs as soft skin brushes up against my face. I suck her pussy like I would an ice cream cone. I can't help myself.

"Queen, I want to fuck you so damn bad right now," I confess between luscious licks.

"Oooh, right there, Q. Please, baby, fuck me, now."

Taking my hands, I spread her pussy open, and suck on it like a champ. The heat rises from her and I can taste the warmth with my mouth. Introducing my fingers into her goodness, I move them all around as I lick her sugar walls with passion.

I suck my Queen with my soul, like if I suck her long enough, maybe; just maybe she will be mine forever. My tongue dances around inside her goodness in a way it never had before with anyone. I've never given a damn about a woman's pleasure before, but tonight, all that matters to me is Queen. Holding onto her thighs, I love her with my spirit. In and out, out and in, my tongue finds every inch of her and has the audacity to introduce itself as her new comforter, her new man, her king, her protector, her one and only. Kissing her pussy lips, licking them slowly, admiring the juices that flow uncontrollably makes everything inside me emerge to the surface. My heart, now vulnerable and naked, is now on my sleeve. This woman, this woman lying here with me...damn...she's all the woman I'll ever need.

Her juices flowing, her legs trembling and her continuous sultry moans cause me to slow my pace. Somehow I've managed to escape into my own world, because I can no longer hear her sounds, her moans, and her pleasure. I slowly move up to face her. She welcomes me back into her arms and kisses me softly.

"Oh, baby, right there. You're going to make me..."

As she releases all over my mouth and fingers, I once again reluctantly make my way to the door. My head tells me to walk away and leave a lasting impression. My heart tells me to remain, take my lawful place as her man and annihilate that ass like it's going out of style. To dig so good and so deep that she'll never look at another man as long as she's alive. I turn around and witness her in complete satisfaction, yet she's yearning for a piece of my love. My head wins as I tell her, "I know I licked that pussy good. I know I put my name on it. I know I am in your veins where you scare in mine and where I want to be in yours. If I did all that I know I did, then tonight will place me deeper into your psyche and I accomplished all that I needed to do. For me, it's never been about busting nuts...Queen; it's always been about you."

QUEEN
Meet Me in Paradise

His tongue resuscitated my soul and lulled me to a place of satisfaction I have not visited in a very long time. Tempting, tantalizing and taunting – his touch, revived my belief in love, that it does exist. He's so sweet. Quincy. His was the face I went to sleep to and his is the face I wake up to. I could get used to this. My body's natural alarm clock jolts me on cue as always and as the sun's rays whisper its wake up call, I arise finding myself in the same spot he left me in. Wet. I'm wet, wild, waiting still.

Sleep eluded me last night. Played a sick game of hide and seek with me. Couldn't seem to catch it, only in sessions, and I swear the next time sleep comes anywhere near me, I'm fucking it up on site. I thought about him all night…

Mesmerized, I was. He left me wanting. Needing. Longing, he left me, deficient, lusting. Remembering the condition my body was in as he departed – aching. I had no strength... it left me when he walked out the door. I pleaded, "Quincy." I needed to take flight. I had no pilot. I was ready to be his faithful concubine. He had me. Turned me into a woman I didn't recognize. I wanted to get to know her. I was hungry, aching, needing, in pain. Roaring flames consumed me. In him lay the extinguisher. The fire down in my love, endured. He left. I was nuts. It was wrong. He was wrong – for me. It was right. He's right. He's white. It was all right. I needed orgasm. The fragrant walls of my sex begged for invasion. I moaned, played with myself. I wanted to come. Crying, I called him, he didn't respond. He whispered to me, deliberately, his face, I imagined it as he told me to come. I tried. Wanting him to take me to nirvana, I called out to the heavens, begged Quincy to take me there. Sticky, succulently soiled fingers dialed his number. No answer. "Pull the trigger," I begged. I needed to come. But he left me – sacrificed me, for me. I pictured his erection, it was an enigma. I wanted to fellate him, capture his release with my tongue. My sex, my walls, my pussy demanded Quincy, told me I needed him – needed to come, needed orgasm. Made me crazy. Craved his tongue on my nipples. I licked them. He turned me into that chick. I wanted to know her. He brought me back to life. The dead had arisen. His whispers resurrected my being. My screams brought me back to existence. Emboldened by his essence, I relished in being his conquest. The absence of him, his rod, his staff, his dick made me cry. I wept remembering his pants, hot heavy breath on my neck, between my thighs. I whimpered memorizing the movements of his mouth. I heard him tell me to come all over him. Following his instructions, I obeyed his commands. But my orgasm played games, mind games, my sex needed his penetration. Got caught in the rain. My fingers replaced the absence of my king. I came without him, but he was there, he told me to come. I listened.

Wow, that man has skills, I say out loud to myself as I begin picking up my clothing and underwear from the floor and head towards the shower. The red light is blinking on my answering machine. Funny, I didn't even hear the phone ringing last night. Pressing the speaker button on the machine, I stand in place, waiting for the messages to play. While doing so, Quincy runs through my mind, his stature becomes present in my thoughts and I smile. Quincy put it on me good last night with that tongue of his. But, it's more than that and he and I both know it. Never in my wildest dreams would I have thought this would be possible – me in love with a white man, and a white man in love with me.

"Message 1," the automated lady reveals.

"Baby girl. You must be having a good time with that cracker. I'ma let you think you having a little fun. The minute that cop gets from in front of your house, it's on, like hot butter popcorn. You still mine, Baby girl, and ain't nothing gonna change that. You hear me? You still belong to me, Queen. Yeah, I know I acted up but you still love me…"

"Uggh!" I yell out loud. The thought of Derrick repulses me and I feel like I want to throw up. I skip to the next message. I'm sincerely not interested in anything Derrick has to say.

"Message 2. Hey Queen. Sweetie. How's my princess? It's Dad. Just calling to check on you. Call me when you can and let the old man know you're okay."

I smile.

"Message 3. Baby, I know it's late. I'm having trouble getting to sleep. You don't know how many times I wanted to head back over there and…damn girl. I'm so into you. I wanted to check on you, make sure you got to bed okay. I guess you did since you're not picking up. Ha, ha. Sweet dreams, sugar."

Mmmmm. I guess this is what it is all about. Quincy. Glancing, my eyes regain their focus and I see that I'm going to be late this morning. I have to move quickly to get my ass in motion and to my office. But rushing has never been so satisfying or so worthy.

I make a pit-stop to the nearest mega shopping center to pick up a box to place Quincy's gift in. Actually, I'm going to buy a gift and box all at the same time. I thought of him on the way to the office and decided to throw caution to the wind, like he always says. I let my heart lead me this morning and I couldn't be more satisfied. I smile, when I think about him. He's so damn sweet and so good to me. Letting my guard down has me nervous, excited, scared, elated and confused, all at the same time.

It's a beautifully brisk morning and I'm feeling exceptionally sexy and alive. My attire reeks of confidence. From the business skirt suit and new Nine West pumps, I look good today and feel even better. God is good, and the blessing of life, even with all of its complexities, is something that I don't take for granted. A power surge of positive energy shoots through me as I pull into the parking lot of my office building.

The fact that the day brings a world of possibilities into my life is encouraging to me. I could potentially defend another innocent person who has managed to land on the wrong side of the law. Or I could pick up a pro bono case where I could save someone's life. Although, the latter is not financially rewarding, it does something for the soul. Having a purpose in life, something to contribute to mankind is big on my agenda. It is something my Dad always taught me – to make sure that my life has some type of meaning. Not only to myself, but for those around me, to make certain that my life affects positively, someone near me, so that the energy always has life and spreads.

As I make my way out of my car, my phone rings. I check it, only to see that Derrick is still playing games. I still haven't figured out how he's managed to send me texts from other numbers, but like I told Paula, he only wins, if I play the game along with him. So, I read his text, but I will ignore this, just like I've done the others.

Can't wait to see you today. The text reads. "Whatever," I say out loud as I make my way to my office.

When I get to the office, the doors are still locked which is unusual. I open up, flip on the lights in the front offices and proceed back to my office only to see the red light flashing on my phone. The only message is from Paula letting me know she is running late, which is no big deal since I have a few things to take care of myself before actually seeing clients. I kinda knew she would be late this morning given the fact that we were out so late last night. I put my bag down, place Quincy's gift and card on my desk, and begin sorting through the mail and pulling the files of the clients for the day. I notice that Paula has already begun the billing for the Bevens case so I review the hours and sign off on the final bill details for her to arrange for the last consult before putting his records in the completed case files. My calendar shows that the first client for the day is not supposed to come in for another hour and thirty minutes so I decide to make some coffee. Quincy runs across my mind again. His tender lips, and that endearing smile. Mmmm. As I walk toward the reception area, I hear someone moving.

"I thought you said you were going to be late? I'm glad you're here, you make the coffee much better than I do. You do everything so much better than me, girl." I yell out to the empty area trying to welcome Paula.

"Excuse me Ms. Thomas; I was hoping to speak to you before you got too busy."

I stop in my tracks only to see Michael Bevens standing at Paula's desk.

"Oh, good morning. What are you doing here Michael? What can I help you with?" He catches me off guard and I'm confused as to why he's here. Although I don't like being in the office with him by myself, I continue to walk around Paula's desk giving the impression that I am still at ease.

"I've been doing really well since the trial Ms. Thomas and I wanted to come and thank you again for giving me a second chance at life." He's smiling and I can see he is sincere. Michael's not a bad looking brother. He's certainly stepped up his appearance since the trial ended. I'm happy to have played a part in saving his life, because, he was looking at doing some serious time.

"Well, you have thanked me enough Michael. Seeing you free is thanks enough." I walk toward him and try and use my presence to gently persuade him towards the front door, but he just stands his ground, staring at me. He's too close. I think he knows it and is getting off at making me uncomfortable.

"Ms. Thomas, do you think the jury would have found me not guilty even if you hadn't gotten me off on a technicality?" His head leans to the side awaiting my answer.

"It could have gone either way Michael. Lucky for us, we didn't have to take a chance of putting the case in the hands of the jury."

"If you were on the jury Ms. Thomas, would you have voted me not guilty?"

He seems to be following me around the small reception area, asking question after question.

"I believed in your innocence then Michael and I still do now. But you are really going to have to leave; I have a client coming in a few minutes. Is there something else I can do for you?"

"Yes, Ms. Thomas, I just came for a copy of my paperwork saying I'm not guilty and that I am free." His eyes are pleading to me.

"Michael, I told you at the trial that you would have a copy of everything at our final consult. There's really no reason for you to be here right now. So I'm going to have to ask you to leave."

"Hello Mr. Bevens, good to see you again." Paula walks in the door and I'm glad for the company. Her eyebrows are freshly arched and raised as she looks at me as if questioning why Michael is present.

"I was just telling Michael that he will get a copy of all his paperwork at our final consult with him later in the week. Paula please put him on the calendar; I have to get ready for my next client."

Looking at Michael, I tell him goodbye in the nicest way possible. "Michael, good seeing you. We'll talk more at your final consult." I leave Paula to deal with him. His just being here is uncomfortable to me and I don't have the energy to figure out if that is because he's creepy or if I'm just edgy right now. I think it's because I'm caught off guard. I watch Michael's eyes penetrating me as I close the door to my office, chickening out by making Michael Paula's problem instead of mine. Thank God for Paula, sometimes she has a way of doing the ugly work that I don't want to do and she's good at it. It takes a few minutes, but almost on key, she walks in my office and closes the door behind her.

"So?"

"So, what?" I chuckle to myself.

"So what happened with Quincy after you left the club? Did you give him some?"

"Damn, you don't waste any time trying to get to the details do you girl?" I almost choke on my coffee.

"Quit stalling Queen! What happened? And how was he?" Paula is practically leaning over my desk screaming in frustration. It's kinda cute, if I do say so myself, not to mention I can't wait to share what happened last night with someone. Underneath all of the legal mumbo jumbo, Paula and I are giddy and silly best friends at heart.

I smile.

"Girl, I can't believe it. Everything about him was wonderful." I lean back in my chair closing my eyes trying to remember how he felt.

"I told you that all you had to do was give him a chance. So what was "it" like?"

"If by "it" you mean sex, I didn't actually have sex with him, although that wasn't because I didn't want to."

"Awh shit. You mean to tell me that you wanted to have sex and he didn't? Damn, how the hell did that happen?"

Paula sits down in front of my desk and I know I have to get to the juice before she pops.

"Well let's say he worked his tongue better than most men work their dicks."

Paula gives me a high five and begs for more.

"Tell me everything, Queen, and bitch, don't leave out any of the details. I want to know everything. And I do mean everything."

"I can still smell his breath on my thighs Paula. I've heard people say that white men really know how to eat pussy, and Quincy is proof that the myth is true. He ate me out like he was starving for the taste of my juices. It was as if he traced every letter of the alphabet on my clit with his tongue. He did this little flicker thing in between sucking my pussy that made me scream. I don't think I have come so hard in my life."

"Shit, you making me jealous Queen, I might have to go and find a white guy for myself."

"Well, I highly recommend being a buffet for a white man. But Paula, stick a fork in me, I'm really done."

"What do you mean?"

"Paula. He's got me. I'm not sure if I'm so intrigued because he's white or what it is, but what I can tell you for sure is that I've never felt this way about a man. I'm gone. I'm done."

Paula smiles and raises her arms in the air.

"Thank you, God!" she yells and I laugh out loud.

"Is it like that Queen?"

"Yes, Paula."

"You know Queen, I'm not surprised. He treats you like a Queen, no pun intended. The way he looks at you. The way you look at him. I've been told that when it happens, you know. It may not make sense, because love sometimes doesn't make sense, but once you know, you know."

"Call the coroner, Paula. He's got me. He makes me think nasty thoughts. He makes me want to drink him all in, like I'm in some type of weird trance. Girl, I can't sit still."

"Queen, I'm gonna cry," Paula tells me as she gets sentimental.

"Paula. He is so sweet and so good to me. I feel so alive when I'm with him. When I talk to him I feel good. When

I see him, when I'm in his presence…girl, I think I'm in love," I reveal as I swirl around in my office chair.

"And I know that sounds stupid, especially coming from a hard ass like me, but honey, he's got me. Maybe too much, too soon, but not to Quincy, he says that we are following our hearts. I can't believe I'm admitting this, since he's white and all, but baby, I'm in misery when he's not around."

"Damn, girl. Well, shit, does he have a brother?"

"Oh Paula. His brother, Quinton, died when they were teenagers. To hear him speak of him is so endearing. It just made me love him even more. Me and him have so much in common. He lost someone way too soon. Girl, he loves Hip-Hop, too."

"Oh Lord," Paula chimes in, smiling from ear to ear.

"But I am afraid. Just when I want to totally give in to his delicious ass, I think about him being white. I think about slavery, and my mind goes to places that are dark. I think about work, and how I'm fighting for equality. But, he's so sweet, damn."

"Hold that thought Queen let me see who that is." She goes to the front office and before I know it, I am swinging around in my chair. Just thinking about Quincy and last night has me a little giddy, and I'm loving it.

"Look at what I found lurking in the front." Paula says between a wink and a smile. I stop spinning long enough to see Quincy standing in the doorway with a single white rose in his hand.

"I'll leave you two alone." Paula announces as she closes the door behind her.

"Well, somebody seems to be in a playful mood." He says as he walks up to me and plants a kiss on my forehead while handing me the rose.

I smell it while trying to once again look professional. "Thanks for the flower Quincy, you're so thoughtful."

"I've been thinking about you all night. Have you been thinking about me?"

"A little." I lie.

Quincy smiles. "Only a little? I think I have to work on that." Quincy leans down to me and begins kissing along the side of my neck and I can feel my nipples harden.

Quincy's all blue scrubs match his eyes perfectly.

"What are you doing here so early, Baby? Aren't you supposed to be working?" I question as I place my arms around his neck.

"The ER is quiet this morning so I snuck out. You have no idea how hard it was for me to leave you last night Queen. Driving home with a hard ass dick should be listed under cruel and inhumane torture. It took everything in me not to turn around and come back."

"Well, why didn't you? You know you left me wet and waiting."

"Because I wanted you to know that I am into you and only you. Last night I needed for you to see that I would do anything to please you."

"You definitely pleased me Quincy."

"I tried my best. Queen I want to please you in all that I do. I want to make you see that you and me are meant to be."

"We're meant to be? Just how do you know that, Q?"

"How does the sun know it's supposed to shine? It just does."

He pulls my face close to his and kisses me gingerly.

"How do the seasons know when its time to change? They just do."

Placing his hands around me, he lifts me up until my butt rests softly on the desk top with him between my legs as he begins running his hands up and down my thighs.

"How does a mother know to love and protect her child? She just does."

He kisses me again, this time deeper and longer than before.

"I have no answer for what to call it Queen; all I know is that it's instinct. You and I are meant to be."

"Quincy. Tell me something."

"Yes, darling?"

"What happens when either you or I get ridiculed or get hate because of this? I mean people of your race hanged people from my race from trees. How do we handle the hate?"

He kisses my forehead. "Baby, stop it. They talked about Jesus, if I'm correct. People are talking about you now, because you got that man off. Some are loving you and some are hating you. Shit, people are talking about me. A black woman loves me right now because I saved her son's life. Point is, people talk, Queen. Who are you living for? Other people's words? You deserve happiness. We're not on this earth to make everyone else happy while forgetting ourselves in the process. Do I make you happy?"

"Well, you're becoming harder to resist, that's for damn sure, Quincy."

Quincy's eyes peer over to my desk and he notices the card with his name on it and the box the card sits under.

"For me, Baby?"

I snatch the box, playing around with him.

"Maybe."

He smiles.

I watch him open the card, while taking in the sensuous smell that he emotes. My eyes go to his crotch and see the bulge that rests firmly through his scrubs. I remember last night, his touch, his smile, his lips, his mouth. I remember how hungry he was. I remember the passion.

He smiles as he opens the card. He reads the words out loud.

"In your eyes, I see my dreams. Your care for me is like the river flowing. In your smile, I feel your love. In your arms, I found my world."

As he leans in to kiss me, he tells me, "You're so special to me, Queen. Thank you for this."

I hand Quincy the box and he smiles more, bright, big and wide. His lips are so pretty, with that gorgeous mouth and pearly white teeth.

"What's this Baby?"

"Just a little something for my man," I reveal as I exhale. I can't believe what I just said.

"So, I am your man, huh?" he questions as he opens the box.

"I think you've earned that title, Q."

Quincy pulls out the "Muddy Waters" CD by Redman. "You're funny, Queen. I love it, thank you," he tells me as he kisses me on the lips.

"There's more, Quincy."

He pulls out the "Criminal Minded" CD by Boogie Down Productions. "Oh Baby, I lost this CD and never replaced it. Thank you, Baby. You're going to make it hard for me to leave you alone, Queen."

"I don't want for you to leave me alone, Q."

"Good, because I don't plan on going anywhere."

"You forgot one last thing in your box, Quincy." I tell him as I chuckle out loud.

"What, Baby?" he questions as he raises the tissue in mid-air.

"There's only tissue paper here, Sweetie?"

"No, Quincy. That's a napkin."

He smiles.

"For what?"

"For you to wipe your mouth with, Quincy."

"Oh you got jokes, huh, Baby?"

"I do."

"Well, you weren't laughing last night. All I heard was "oooh" and "right there Baby," he tells me as he laughs.

"Well, wasn't nothing about last night funny, Quincy. You made me feel so good and I can't thank you enough."

He moves in closer to me. "You know, I smelled you all over me last night. My fingers, around my mouth, on my shirt, you were everywhere. I didn't wash my hands until I had to this morning when I got to the hospital."

"Really, Q?"

"No doubt, Baby. Hey. I'm leaving the hospital around 3pm today. Headed to the gym afterwards. What time do you get off?"

"Whatever time you get me off, Q!" I tell him as I trace my finger along my thigh.

"That's a loaded statement. Keep talking like that and I'm going to have to provide you with something long and strong for you to get off on."

"Is that a threat?"

"No Queen, it's a promise. Trust me."

"Sounds good."

"La Frontera, tonight. I'll pick you up around 7pm, okay?"

"How did you know that's my favorite restaurant?"

"Queen, I'm your man. You just said so. And a real man always knows what his woman wants."

"I brought you a gift too, Sweetheart," he tells me as he hands me a white envelope. "What's this, Q?"

"Just read it, Baby."

I unfold the document and the top reads, Quincy Anthony Hughes, his date of birth, January 15, 1972, social security number, and a whole bunch of medical stuff.

"Baby?" I question.

"Go to the highlighted portion."

My eyes scroll down the page to the highlighted portion of the document. I figure it out. These are the results from Quincy's yearly medical examination, it says it right here. I guess he has to be checked out regularly in order to be a doctor at Mountain View. A yellow box highlights the words, HIV negative. I smile and look up to him. Neither one of us say a word, but we both know that we have the green light to take things to the next level if we so choose. I appreciate his responsibility, and admire him for being so thoughtful. I switch gears as not to harp on the subject.

"Quincy, your favorite food?"

"Peach Cobbler, baby. Well, that is second to eating you, of course."

"You're cute."

"I'm glad you like, Queen. Because if you like, you'll keep me around, right?"

"I'm not letting you go anywhere, Quincy."

"Good. I need you too badly."

His words touch me like no others and my thighs quiver even though I try to hide it. Could this be as good as it feels? Instinctively I pull Quincy closer to me and I feel him grinding up against me as we kiss and he grasps my ass and thighs under my skirt. I want him so bad, but this is not the right place or the right time. My mind wants to stop what I know is going to happen, but my body does not want him to leave me again with that "wanting" feeling.

Not needing to convince him of anything doesn't stop me from telling him how badly I want for this to go down. "You know I can be more than a lover, more than enough for you." I feel so free, liberated in his presence. What else could explain my heart rate climbing.

"I had to only give you a taste of me yesterday Queen out of recognition of the power you have over me. I wanted you to know that you need me just as much as I need you. You need to be treated special Queen and I wanted you to feel that way."

He kisses down my neck and I hear him removing his pants. Instead of saying what I know I should say, which is 'no', I find myself helping him out of them.

My heartbeat is racing. "Quincy, I've never been with a white man."

He smiles, kisses my lips gently.

"You're getting ready to get a good taste," he tells me as he spreads my limbs across hemispheres.

"Let them hate, baby. Now, take it, Queen. It's all yours."

I gently grab his manhood, and he cooes as I guide him inside me. We both softly yell, "Ooooh," upon initial penetration. He smiles. I feel myself release all over him as he delves deeper into my love.

"Is this enough dick for you, Queen?" he questions softly as he pulls my hips closer to him. He gets deeper.

"Yes," I delicately yelp.

"You're so hot and so tight. Mmmm, I love it. Fuck me like you love me, Queen," he demands as he sucks on my neck. I give it to him with everything I have inside of me. He's turning me on like crazy and I feel myself about to explode. Quincy's strokes come with a new history behind them, and with each stroke delivered by Quincy I understand more and more what he was trying to say, there's no clear answer why either of us feel the way we do, but as I he digs harder and harder inside of me, I know Quincy and I are instinctively meant to be.

Holding on tight, the lust gets the best of me and he knows it, I guess he knows his pussy so well, already.

"I've been dreaming about this all night, Q," I manage to whisper through sensuous moans.

"That's right, Baby. Come all over me, Queen. It's all yours."

I climax.

"It's been so long."

As sweet come pours fluidly from my love onto him, he softly whimpers in ecstasy. "Please Baby, don't give this to anyone else," he begs as he goes deeper.

"Is it mine, Queen?"

"I'm all yours, Quincy."

�������

"Do you want me to come in and escort you out, Sweetheart?" Quincy questions. My fingers gently part the blinds in my living room and I see Quincy outside in his truck, an all black Navigator. Very nice and classy. He parks.

"I can come out, Baby. Besides, I learned my lesson last night, letting you in."

"I do need to use the bathroom, Queen." I laugh.

"Yeah, right. Use it at the restaurant."

"Can't blame me for trying, right?"

"I'll give it to you Quincy. You don't give up."

"Not when it's something I want."

"I'll be right out, Q."

"Don't make me wait too long. Oh, Queen?"

"Yes, Dear?"

"The temperature is supposed to drop tonight, so bring a warm coat. We'll get back late, okay, Baby?"

"We're just going to dinner, Q. But sure, I'll bring my coat, of course."

"I have a surprise for you afterwards."

Smiling from ear to ear, I skip across the living room in an attempt to find my pumps.

"What am I going to do with you, Q?"

"Just love me, Queen. That's all."

I smile. My heart skips a beat.

"I'll be right out."

Grabbing my purse, I stop at the full length mirror in my den. I remember Quincy and I staring in this very same mirror. His arms wrapped securely around me, made me feel so safe and warm. We do look good together. This is so new to me, so unfamiliar that it makes me very nervous but something about Quincy is so right, he is so right.

Running my fingers through my curls, I loosen them a bit, and smooth my black dress in place with my hands, and admire the picture staring back at me. I do look good tonight. Good for Quincy. He makes me feel like a Queen and I don't feel like I have to go the extra mile for him, but I did tonight. A form fitting black dress, low cut, of course, with a single strand pearl necklace and matching bracelet, thigh high sheer black pantyhose, and patent leather pumps makes for a seductive yet classy look for our dinner date at La Frontera. Besides, as good as Quincy looks, I better be right, and look the part on his arm. Seems as though I'm officially his woman, although it's hard to admit it. I just remember what Paula has been telling me all along. To love and be loved the way I deserve to be. She tells me I'm worth it, and to not deny myself true happiness. And happiness is what God has placed into my life. He makes no mistakes, so I'm trying.

Checking my lips, my Mac lip glass shines to perfection. Just a tiny spray of Jasmine, in honor of my mother, and I'm done. As I spray, I speak to her. "Mom, I so miss you and your smell. Did you send this angel named Quincy to me? I wonder about you sometimes Mommy. This feels so right. I've never felt like this before in my life, Mom. Was this the whirlwind Dad speaks of when he talks about you? I love you, Mom."

Exhaling, I glance in the mirror once more, pick up my purse and coat and make my way out the front door. Placing a bounce in my step, my stride is cloaked in arrogance as I walk to Quincy's truck. His eyes don't leave me as he exits the driver's seat, and meets me at the passenger's door.

"Damn, you look good, girl. My lady looks hot tonight," he tells me as he opens the door. Wow, he looks like a million dollars in that navy blue suit. No tie, just a blue silk shirt and a thin gold chain around his neck. His chest looks firm and masculine. "Why, thank you Dr. Hughes. You know you could button your shirt a little more. I don't want to have to beat some woman's ass tonight," I tell him as I stare him deep in the eyes.

"Jealousy, counsel?"

"Not jealous, doctor. I just don't want to have to fight for something that rightly belongs to me."
He pecks me on the lips as he closes the door.

"I likes," he tells me as he makes his way back to the driver's side.

The smell of new car clings to my nostrils. I admire the cleanliness of his ride. I remember him again from last night and I smile.

"What are you smiling about, Baby?"
Turning to my left, I look at Quincy and smile again. "Nothing, just enjoying myself, that's all."
"Good."

Inhaling his essence, I'm forced to question the origin of his scent. "Q, what are you wearing? You always smell so good."

He smiles. "Oh, just some shit I had on my dresser, Baby. You like it?"

"You're so silly, and yes, I love it. It's addictive."

"You're addictive, Queen."

"Is that right?"

"Yes, it is, Baby. I'm going to need to check into rehab if I get too much of you too soon."
He rubs my thighs and sends a tingle up my spine.

"Sounds like you may have a problem. Addiction is not a good thing," I jokingly expel. "You have to wean off of me slowly."

"Oh, hell no. I'm an addict and the first step is admitting it, Baby. We all gotta die from something. If it's from falling in love and being addicted to you, then my life would have been worth it."
Oh my God, he's killing me softly.

Embarrassment covers me and I know he can both sense it and see it as it must be written all over my face. I smile, but try to cover it delicately with my hands.

Through Fendi shades he watches me between looks at the traffic. He questions, "What is it baby?"

"Nothing, baby." I lie, and he knows it.

"Queen, you're a horrible liar. What is it baby? Why are you smiling?"

"Just thinking about earlier."

Cloaked in his own infamy, he owns it and wears it well as the dimple in his cheek – well, I could fit a quarter in it right now if I wanted. And those pearly whites are all a glow as he smiles. "What about earlier?"

I nudge him on his thigh. "You know, Q, stop playing. And, thank you."

"So, did you like it?"

Exhaling, I reveal, "Absolutely. Couldn't you tell?"

"I'm happy you did. Kinda nice that we had to sneak it in, in your office and all. I thoroughly enjoyed myself. Gonna be hard getting rid of me, Queen, just forewarning you, baby."

"Getting rid of you? No way. You gave me what I wanted, and what I needed, and to be honest, you felt so good, I thought about you all day, and I was pleasantly surprised."

He looks delicious as he laughs out loud, grabs my hand and kisses the back of it. "Why were you surprised?"

We both know why, but I guess he'll take delight in hearing me say it. He knows he's the bomb, and revels in me realizing it.

I laugh. "Well, I haven't been with a white man, and well you know the rumor."

"Ha, ha, ha, ha," he laughs harder. Kisses my hand once more.

"I see we're going to have a lot of fun together, Queen, getting you past your racial biases and tendencies. Baby, I'm almost six-foot-four. Am I enough for you?"

My puppy dog eyes bat as he looks at me through those designer shades, he awaits my approval and I give it to him.

"Yes, Q, more than enough. I'm happy, satisfied, definitely."

"Well, you know there's plenty more if you want. I'm yours for the taking. You know, your sweet expression and the way you gave me that sweet love earlier was all I'd been dreaming about, for a good while. I'm definitely satisfied, Queen. So happy you're mine now."

Maxwell's "Submerge" plays softly in the background and we head to La Frontera's for dinner. Quincy reaches in the backseat, and hands me a bouquet of magnolias. A red box with a silver bow accompanies.

"Wow, thank you. These are beautiful, Q. You're spoiling me, you know."
"Open the box, Baby."

As I open the box, my heart flutters and Quincy smiles and starts to hum to the tunes of Maxwell. He drives like one of those boys in the hood, the kind I grew up with in Newark. Right shoulder cocked to the side. Left hand on the wheel. A serious old school gangsta lean. But it doesn't seem forced. This is who Quincy naturally is. I admire the fact that he is so authentic. It is a confidence that is to be admired. From the outside looking in, one would think that Quincy is trying to be something other than who he is, but after getting to know him, the truth is revealed. He is genuine in his appearance. His swagger is bona fide.

I finally get the box open. Luminous and exquisite, a diamond necklace sits perfectly in this box. Winding gently along a path of what appears to be platinum, a princess cut diamond sits beautifully. A traditional symbol of true romance. God, he's going to make me cry, but I refuse to punk out, so I force the tears back inside, and I smile as I admire how it sparkles vibrantly.

"The gift is from my heart and is an expression of love only for you, Queen."

"I love it, Quincy. I really do. Thank you so much." I lean over to give him a kiss on his lips.

"No one has ever done something so special for me," I tell him as I remove my string of pearls.

"You want to wear it now, Baby?"

"Absolutely, Quincy."

We pull up to La Frontera, and the valet takes the keys from Quincy. Quincy slides him some money and opens the door for me. I take his hand and step out of the ride. Turning around to look in the car window, I place the necklace around my neck. Quincy steps closely behind me, sweeps my hair to one side and secures the clasp on my new diamond necklace. It rests perfectly on my chest and shines so brightly. He kisses my neck. "What am I going to do with you, Quincy?"

"I told you, I'm yours for the taking, Sweetheart."
I see Quincy through the reflection of the truck window and he hugs me from behind. I smile.

"I really do love it, Quincy. Thank you so much."

"You deserve much more. If you keep me around, I plan to show you how deserving you are."

"I'm not going anywhere, Quincy."

I turn around and take Quincy's hand and we walk into La Frontera's. The hostess' eyebrows raise as we approach. Quincy notices and pulls me closer to him. "Do you have a reservation?"

"Yes," Quincy responds.

"Table for two, Dr. and Mrs. Quincy Hughes," he boldly reveals and goose bumps run up and down my arms.

"Sure, follow me."

As we make our way to our table, which sits alongside a large bay window and overlooks the mountains, I notice all of the stares that come from other people in the restaurant. Music plays softly in the background, creating a seductive backdrop, one that sets the tone for me and my King, yet, I feel uneasy as I take my seat. Quincy sits across from me, and I admire his style. My uneasiness is written all over my face.

"You know, Queen. They could be looking because you look so beautiful tonight. We do look good together. Try not to think about anything but you and I, okay?"
I smile.

"How do you know me so well?"
"Because you're my lady."

A nice looking black woman with short curly hair and glowing skin approaches. She smiles and I can't read her intent. Women are so fiercely competitive, and I'm use to receiving both the hate and love from the black woman, but this time, it's different. I don't know where she's coming from. Why do I care? I just do.

"Good evening, welcome to La Frontera. My name is Carla. Can I start you off with a glass of our vintage house wine?" Quincy looks at me for approval and I give it to him.
"Yes, thank you, we'll have two glasses."

As Carla leaves our table, she gives me a thumbs-up on the low and I smile. My confidence just shot through the roof. My hand finds its way to my neck again and I trace my necklace with my fingertips. "You really are going to spoil me, Quincy." The moonlight shining in through the window lands on his face and body in an enticing manner. His diamond stud shines to perfection, as well as his chain. The navy blue suit offsets his eyes perfectly. He looks like a star, a leading man in a blockbuster movie on its opening weekend.

"Quincy!" a weave-wearing, ghetto hood rat screams as she walks up to our table. She has to be about a size ten or twelve, with a long, shiny, horse-haired weave that is not very well put together at all. Her breasts are popping out of the two sizes too small t-shirt. I wonder who she is as I watch her place her hand on her hip. She begins to roll her neck, and I smile.

How the hell did she get in here is question number one.

My man smiles, hard and wide, and his face is red. He puts his hand on his forehead and shakes his head. Leaning into me, he tells me, "Baby, I apologize. Excuse me for one minute. I'll be right back."

He kisses me on my lips.

"I know you didn't just kiss this bitch!"

With a curious look, I hesitantly respond, "Okay, sweetie."

"Sweetie? Quincy, I know this high-falutin' bitch did not just call you, Sweetie!"

She called me a bitch, but I will let that slide because we're in a public place. She's lucky though. First, she knows my man, very well, it seems and secondly, she's loud and ignorant, playing right into the hands of those who think we're all that way, like somehow we all misbehave in that fashion. She needs a good ass whooping.

Quincy grabs her arm and pulls her forcefully to the side. Onlookers are entertained by this white man in a love triangle with two black women. I must admit, I'm finding this hilarious. While I should feel threatened, I don't, not one bit.

Thrusting that neck round and round, back and forth like a hood rat in rare form. Yuck, she's popping gum and wagging her finger in mid-air as she tells my man a thing or two. Everything in me tells me to get up and get in her ass, but, I need to remain a lady. I'm about two seconds from slapping the hell out of her, not only for stepping to my man in this manner, but for behaving this way in public. Where's her Momma?

I hear him tell her, "Look. I'm here with my woman tonight. Have respect for her, and have some respect for yourself, Tina."

"Look, Q…" He cuts her off.

"Look, Tina, I don't give a damn what you think. Right now, I'm here with my lady, I don't have time for this shit. I told you it was over, and I mean that. I said it a while ago and I'm saying it again; It's over. Look at my woman. Do you think you have a chance? Look at her, Tina. Now, get to stepping and stop making a fool of yourself."

He releases her arm and throws it to her side, and walks back to me, smiling like he was just busted.

I smile. "I'm not worried, Baby. And, I am not saying anything."

He laughs. "Good, you have nothing to worry about. And, Baby, I'm sorry about that."

"We'll talk about that later, Q, I'm not letting you get away with that."

We both laugh. "Hey, we all make mistakes, Queen, right?"

"Yes, sir, we do."

Reaching into his jacket pocket, Quincy pulls out a white envelope and slides it across the table. "Open it," he commands. And just like a love sick puppy, I pry the envelope open. "We'll head out right after dinner, Baby." Two tickets to a midnight performance of Mos Def in Manhattan.

"Quincy, how did you pull this off? I have depositions in the morning."

"First, you're a big girl; you can stay up late, right? Second, I have connections baby."

"Yes, I'm a big girl, smart ass and thank you, Sweetie."

❧❧❧❧❧

The concert was live. It was on and poppin'. I'm so damn tired right now but loving every minute. I can't remember a time in my life where I've been so happy. I feel so alive with Quincy. Quincy found a spot in New York City and we took photos. As I admire the 8x10 photos of the two of us, I wonder what's on Quincy's mind. He opted for smooth jazz for our 2 a.m. ride back home, as we cross the George Washington Bridge. The stars are shining bright, illuminating the night, making the ride home, sexy and uneventful. Once again, I go through our photos and can't seem to identify which one is my favorite.

Glancing over to Quincy, he seems lost in time and space somewhere off in a distant land. He looks tired, so I rub his thigh, in an attempt to gently revive him. "I had a great time tonight, Quincy. Are you okay?"

"Yes, sweetheart, I'm fine. Just loving the place I'm in right now."

"Me too."

He smiles and chuckles out loud.

"What's so funny?" I question with curiosity.

"I'm remembering how Big and my boys told me I'd never be able to get you. You know, I love my man, Big, but he told me in the nicest way possible that I'd never get you. I'm so glad I didn't listen to him. I never gave up."

I laugh. "Is that right? I wonder why they would say that. I mean, I've never heard of that before. I white man having trouble getting a black woman."

Quincy smiles. "Well, Queen. Everything in life is not centered around race. It's obvious why they said it."

"Is that right? How's it so obvious, Quincy?"

"Because you're beautiful. You're like a big time celebrity lawyer. Big said you are the poster child for affirmative action. I'm just so damn happy they were wrong. But like I told you before, I knew from the first time I saw you that we were meant to be."

"Wow, it's amazing to hear what others think about you. I had no clue. Well, honestly Quincy, I can't lie, I do think about your race, but there's something about you that makes me feel so good inside."

"Probably the way I work my tongue," he laughs.

"Well, that could be part of it, but it's more than that. You remind me of my father. And I can't explain why. Something about your spirit, your kindness, your care for me."

Taking off my shoes, I recline in my chair and enjoy the gorgeous night and the beautiful scenery as we make our way back home to the mountains.

"I'm surprised you don't know Big. He's from Newark, just like you and we're all around the same age."

"Well, don't forget, me and my Daddy left Newark when I was young, so while Newark will always be my home, I've been in the Poconos for some time. But I'm a brick city baby to my heart. I know you spent a lot of time there, right?"

"Yes and Big spent a lot of his summers with me in Jersey City. We had a good time."

Quincy grabs my hand, and I let him with no resistance. He kisses the back of my hand and that sends a quiver through my entire body. "Thank you for taking a chance on me Queen."

"Quincy?"
"Yes, Baby?"

"Have you been with a lot of women? A lot of black women?"

"What constitutes a lot?" he laughs out loud, and I snatch my hand away from him.

"You know you're so spoiled Queen. I can tell. Don't be frustrated with me. I've been with women. I spent eight years in college, I had fun. Nothing really substantial. I've been with black women and white women. Nothing outrageous, though. I'm the average guy."

He looks at me and I can tell he senses my aggravation. "You need to put your bottom lip back in Queen and stop pouting. You lived a life before me, and I can't be mad if you slept with other men. This is the reason I don't ask. I don't want to picture anyone else having been with you in any fashion. You're my woman now, hopefully the last woman I'll ever be with in my life, so that's all I'm concerned about. You need to look at how bright our future together is and let go of the small stuff. Living in the past and worrying about things you can't control only causes unnecessary stress."

"Okay, Doctor. I will follow your orders. But just to let you know, the only reason I ask is because you're fine as hell, you're a doctor, no children, no baby mamas. I'm just trying to figure out if I'm really blessed to have you or if you're some serial killer in witness protection?"

He laughs out loud. "Shit girl, you're something else. No I'm not in witness protection. Ha, ha, ha. I hadn't met the right woman until now. I listened to my Mom and Dad talk about their love. They always said when you know, you know and when you find "the one" everything will come into focus. It's all in focus now. I found what I need and what I want in my life. That's all that matters. Come home with me. I don't want this night to end."

"You don't want this night to end? I don't either baby, but I do have depositions in the morning. Besides, I know what us being alone together in the middle of the night will lead to."

"Baby, come on. Come home with me. I promise to let you get a little rest before you have to go to work. I promise I won't try anything funny. I mean it's hard as hell not to touch you, but I'm a big boy and can control my emotions. Can you?"

I laugh. He takes my hand. Kisses the back of it. I rub his thigh. "Come home with me, Queen."

"Okay, Quincy, but just know that you won't be getting any tonight, okay?"

"Alright, Queen, damn baby, I'll keep my hands to myself. We'll have a drink, curl up, watch a movie and do what old married folks do…we'll cuddle."

৵৵৵৵৵

"Right there, Queen?"

"Oooh, right there, baby!"

"Is that it?"

"Yes, Quincy, that's it baby, oooooooh!"

"I love to give it to you right there, Queen…damn, you feel so fucking good."

"Q, you're going to make me explode…mmmm."

"Ooh, I've been dreaming about being inside of you, Baby, damn, girl, you're too sweet."

We sing the same tune. Different octaves. Glorifying sounds of sensuality. We moan. Music in the air, a sexy melody of orgasm pending.

"Love me just like that, Queen…shit."

"You like it like that, Q?"

"Oh, hell yeah."

I roll my hips, grabbing Quincy's tight, muscular ass, pulling him deeper inside of me. Digging, I leave scratches along his entire back. *Oh my GOD, he's so good…*

"What happened to cuddling?" I question through pants and heavy breathing.

Smiling through the pleasure, Quincy tells me. "Mmm. I rather be deep into this sweet pussy. Do you wanna cuddle, Queen?"

"No, Baby. You fuck this pussy too damn good, Q. Mmm, don't give it to nobody else, please." I beg. I can't stand to look at him too long, he's so sexy.

"This is all your dick, Baby. All yours."

Wet. Soaked. Hot. Sweat. Sweet. Sex. Me – laced in sweat, patent leather pumps and a new diamond necklace. Him – adorned in lust, sweat, a chain, diamond stud in his ear and a smile on his face. Naked. Nasty. Naughty. Midnight grinding. Heart rates climbing. Hands on my hips, he pulls me close to him, in so deep, like he's constructing Hip-Hop beats. Rhythmic, rumbling, round and round, right, so right…he revels in my righteousness. It's raining, thunder and lightning, on the inside of my love.

The flicker of a flame provides the only light – just enough to see his chiseled silhouette as the moonlight shines, making an appearance through the bedroom blinds. Hovering over me, his strong arms hold him up as he creeps further into my love. Glancing at his chest – it's so strong and masculine. His diamond shines bright, offsetting the amber color from the vanilla scented candle. Luther Van Dross plays softly in the background, sets the tone for this erotic encounter.

"Don't you give my pussy to anyone. I don't want nobody close enough to smell it. You hear me, Queen?"

"Yes."

Digging deeper, his blows are bold, blunt, forcing me to whelp. I wanna cry. He's so good.

"Yes, what, Queen?"

He thrusts harder.

"Quincy, yes, I hear you!" I cry in ecstasy, as he hits my G-spot out of this stratosphere.

"Nobody else, Queen." Biting my neck, my lips, he licks them, digs deeper into me.

"Nobody else, Quincy. I'm all yours."

"Good girl."

Apparently, the alcohol diluted my inhibitions and revealed my inner-most thoughts, carnal in desire, longing, needing, lusting for him. I wanted to feel this passion and desire once more in a manner only Quincy can deliver. Oooh, I want to scream. I want to yell to the heavens, "Thank you God, for this white boy with his sweet, nasty ass." Euphoria is rising. Quincy, covered in a serious fuck face, that life-altering state where euphoria meets nirvana as the titans clash. He's like cocaine, a drug, my drug of choice, keeping me high, scary, invigorating. He's seducing my body, one whisper at a time. I'm coming hard, in succession in response to his revelations.

"You know I could fuck you all night, Queen," he murmurs in delight as he closes his eyes, leaning his head back.

"You're so sexy, Q…"

Deep, deliberate, desirable strokes penetrate my world, as his eyes watch every moment, every caress, every in and out like a sadistic voyeur.

"Damn, I want to come all over you, Queen."

Each thrust becomes harder with intention as he makes me bounce – he rocks and rolls me, in rhythm to his beat.

"You like the way your pussy looks, Q?"

I can't believe I just asked him that.

"It looks so damn good, Baby, and I love the way your tits bounce," he whispers as he glides his tongue across the right one. They perk up and stand at attention. Sucking with purpose. Swallowing my scream, I whisper in satisfaction. "Quincy, you're fucking my head up." Heel marks from pumps leave traces of our encounter on his wall, documenting this love making.

"I want to kiss you, Q," I whisper through the satisfaction.

"Kiss me, Baby," he demands as his tongue finds its way back home into my wet orifice. He licks my lips, hot, sweet breath escapes him softly as I bite his bottom lip, my tongue lands and glides down his chin, onto his neck, I bite it, suck it, lick it, love it.

"Mmmm," he moans in pleasure, closing his eyes for a moment. He bites my neck, whispers in my ear, "You're so good, Queen, I love everything about you."

Once again releasing, I dig deep into Quincy's back as I softly yell in gratification, "Quincy."

He moves away from me and I'm momentarily paralyzed.

"Quincy…No," I whisper as he removes my pumps. I hear them crash to the floor.

Grabbing my feet, my left lay in his right hand and he grabs my right with his left. He towers over me, and I'm anxious as to what he has planned. But I'm feeling desperate, wanting him to enter me once again.

"Quincy," I softly yell. He spreads my legs far and wide. My big toes enter his mouth alternately. He spreads my legs further apart.

"Quincy…I can't take this. Fuck me, please."

As the tip of his rod bounces against the surface of my love, I swallow hard, my nipples harden even more. Unable to break free, Quincy continues to lick my toes, one by one this time, my legs – spread so far apart. His dick, teasing me as it glides across my clit – it's knocking at my door.

"Grab the headboard, Queen." He commands and I reach back, my arms above my head, hold on as he instructed. I look at him – my feet still in his hands, my legs still far and wide. His length, still taunting me.

"Quincy. Baby, please."

As my toe leaves his mouth, he asks me, "Do you like it?"

"I love it Quincy. Please…"

In a rush, his head travels down my thighs and quickly lands on my righteousness, he licks it, full, wide, kisses it once more, makes his way back up to my toes, both of my legs still wide apart.

"Quincy," I beg.

"Close your eyes."

My eyes slowly shut and he moves my legs further apart. His dick moves in circles across the surface – gently, yet deliberately. He's marking his territory. Branding the letter "Q" into my love, embedding this moment in my memory. Showing me who the boss is, the conqueror, the master of my domain.

His dick bounces against my clit, then he gives me the tip quickly.

"Quincy," I beg. "Please, don't do this to me."

"You want it, Queen?"

"Yes…"

"Take it."

I open my eyes and reach for him – his rod. I reach.

"Close your eyes. Picture me, Queen."

I reach again. He pulls away.

"No hands. Take it."

"Quincy, please, just give it to me."

"Take it. Let me watch you take this dick baby."

Eyes closed, heart beating fast, hands on headboard, I motion my body to take what is mine. My hips roll frantically, as his length touches my walls. I can't get it. I roll harder, faster, reaching up, my legs shake.

":Quincy! Please, fuck me!" I softly yell as his tip glides across my clit.

"Take it, Queen."

I growl. "Give it to me, Quincy."

"Take it."

"Fuck me, Quincy."

"You look so good, Queen."

"Quincy, I…"

"That pretty hole looks like it needs some deep dick, baby."

"Then give it to me, Quincy."

"It's your dick, baby."

"Give me my dick, Q."

"You called me Q."

I smile.

"Are you going to be my wife?"

"Yes."

"Good girl. Now, take your dick."

I roll my hips with everything I have in me, trying to capture it.

"You're stingy, Quincy."

"You're greedy, Queen."

"Give it to me, Q!" I yell.

"You're spoiled, baby."

He plays with me more. I can't move. I reach for him.

"No hands."

"Quincy, you give me that dick, now, or…"

"Hush," he yells softly in my ear as he rams deep into me. *Lord, have mercy.*

He swims deeps down, then comes upstream, pulls out, over and over again. He goes deeper with each blow.

"Damn you, Quincy."

A greedy grin glides across his guilty face.

"Best pussy I've ever had."

"Best dick…oooh, best dick baby, I swear This dick don't have to be this damn good, Quincy."

Slowly, sadly, sorrowfully, he withdraws from my love. Logic and lust collide with lust winning the game of hearts. My lover, my man, moves further away. I want to cry. Not now. More. Please. My eyes, the size of silver dollars, inquisitive in nature, curious by design, I plead, as a sensual rage overcomes me, I beg, "Quincy," as I levitate off my back. I reach for him, grab him, pull him close to me. Extending my arms, my heart, my love, I expel, "I need you."

"Shhh, Baby, it's not over, I promise you."

He kisses my lips, then finds his way down to my inner thighs – kisses them, sucks them.

"Baby, I'm too excited, I need to calm down, just give me a moment. I don't want to come yet," he reveals, his tongue tracing my inner thigh.

"Let me taste it," I confess, surprising myself, elating him.

"Damn, Queen, I want you to taste it." He kisses my lips. Biting his bottom lip, I confess, "I can't wait to taste you, Q."

"Mmmm. I wanna see your pretty lips…mmm."

Although his erection had found its way and made a home inside my tender walls, I had yet found the courage to view it, hadn't the strength to visit foreign territory. Wet walls take precedence when rhyme and reason crash and burn. I see it. Witnessing his phallus in full and rare form. Uniquely wonderful. First hand knowledge. Wondering for a moment who wouldn't give up a paycheck to keep it, selfishly, must have been a crazy bitch who occupied this place before me. His manhood, rigid, unbending, taut, hard, unyielding, lay solid and erect against the firm, flat six-pack of his abdomen. It's gorgeous. I want to give it a standing ovation, an Oscar even, for his performances as of late. Not having more than a handful of men who could claim journey into my abyss, I doubt there is a man alive with a dick so wonderfully and marvelously designed it could showcase in *The Louvre* as a wholly, perfectly produced symbol of manliness and masculinity.

Never in a million years would I have ever thought that fellating a white man would be on my list of things to do and that I would take pleasure in doing so. Yet, tonight it is my honor to give my man this type of attention. I hate to blame it on the alcohol, but it sure has helped me with becoming less conservative in the bedroom, that and the fact that Quincy is so desirable has made me let go of all inhibitions.

Taking delight in witnessing my expressive love for him, he stares at me while in complete and utter ecstasy. I devour it; make it my ice cream treat for the night. Quincy spanks me on my ass, he commands, "Look at me, baby. You're so fine, Queen."

I look up to him while I carefully and meticulously love every inch of him.

"Come on, baby. I'm not done with you." He tells me as he gets up.

"Quincy? Can I finish?"

Grabbing me by my arm gently, he turns me over. "You're done."

"Quincy?"

"Lay down, baby. I need to be inside of you."

I smile. This man knows how to give orders and I love obeying. It's more than sexy, the way he takes control.

My breasts meets the sheets, and I hear Michael Jackson's "Lady in My Life" playing softly in the background. Quincy's chest lays firmly on my back and I can feel his heart beating. He leans in and whispers softly in my ear, "I need to come now, Queen. This is too good."

Exhaling, I anticipate him entering me once more and my body relaxes. Spreading my legs gently, Quincy runs his hands along my inner thighs. He enters me from behind and lays directly on top of me. He nestles his face into the back of my neck, and cooes, "Oooooh, Queen. You're so wet, baby. Damn."

His movements are bold, and deep, slow and deliberate. He thrusts in me so good, so hard, so powerfully. I know I'm going to reach heaven in record time.

I need to cement my presence in Quincy's thoughts. I need to make sure that he doesn't have a reason to go any where else. I need to become a permanent part of my man's psyche. I need to make this dick my own and put my name on it.

Moving in and out of me, he kisses my shoulders, licks the back of my neck.

"That's my spot, Q. Oooh."
Michael sings about putting my trust in Quincy's heart, and meeting him in paradise…

Nestling his face once again, I feel him exhale and I know he's ready.

"Quincy, can I come on you, baby, please?" I ask, knowing my next round of questions and comments are going to do the trick.

"Yes, baby, please, come all over me." His movements are slower. He exhales.

"Gimme that tongue, Q." I command and he leans in. I turn my head slightly and our tongues play around with the other's. I lick him good and he moans.
Michael sings to us, "Stay with me…"

"Mmmmm, Queen, baby, I have to come. It's too fucking good."

I beg. "Quincy, no, please, I need more."
He exhales. Kisses my shoulder. Swallows hard. His movements are staggered. His moans get louder.

"Quincy, its so delicious, baby. Please don't stop fucking me."

"Mmmmmmmmm…"

"Oooh, Q, right there. Oh God, you fuck me so good, Quincy."

"Grrrrrrr…," he growls. He's ready, I know it.

"Queen, baby, I can't hold it. Please let me come now. I have to."

I whimper. "Q, no, baby, please. Please fuck me. Your dick is too good, Q."
He exhales again. Movements are slow. I can feel my splendor as it journeys on the sheets and on his thighs. He's taken me to nirvana once again and I know he can feel the warmth.

"Queen, you're so spoiled. Baby, I have got to come, please Queen. I'm gonna bust."

"Quincy," I whimper, just faint of a cry.

"Baby, your loving is too good. I'm gonna bust. Queen, please, I need to."

"Quincy. Do you like it?"
His thrusts get harder. He's pulling all the way out and sliding all the way in me, over and over and over again. His heart is racing.

"I love it, Queen!" He yells softly in my ear. Licks my earlobe. Hot, sweet breath on my neck.

"I love coming all over this sweet dick baby. Q, your dick is so good, baby. Please tell me it's all mine Quincy."

"It's…it's, oh God, Queen, it's all yours…all…your dick, baby…oooh…I…swear, it's all yours. Shit, I gotta come, Queen, please…"

"More, baby. Let me suck it some more, Q."

He exhales, swallows hard and whispers, "Queen, stop TALKING like that, please, I can't hold it." He begs, he's out of control.

"Quincy!" I yell as the rain pours down.

"Quincy, nobody can fuck me the way you do, baby."

Silence. Quincy's dick has hardened to a point unfamiliar to me. Quincy bites my shoulders, kisses my back, smacks my thigh. Nestles his face into my neck, licks it, sucks it. Lustful, hot heavy breath on my back.

"Gimme those sweet lips," he commands. I turn, he licks them, bites them.

"Quincy. Oh God! I wanted to fuck you from the first time I saw you, baby. Give it to me just like that, baby!" I cry, I scream, I beg.

He doesn't say a word.

"Quincy. You love this pussy don't you? Because this pussy loves you, baby!"

He exhales. His right palm slams against the bedroom wall. His left hand grabs the bedpost.

Moving in and out of me, he thrusts hard and long, and my rain continuously pours down.

He yells, "Oh, Queen!"

I scream, "Quincy! Baby! Oooooh! Baby!"

"Never leave me, Queen."

"I won't baby, I promise."

"Aaaaaahhhhhhhhhhhhhhh," he exhales once more. Face nestled in my neck, breathing heavy and labored. His cold tongue glides along my back. I feel his heart beating so fast.

We forget about tomorrow as we lay in total satisfaction, engulfed and gratified in each other's pleasure.

"Queen, don't leave me."

"Oooooh, baby. Never."

QUINCY
Feeling Froggy

Night after night, shit, in broad daylight, I'm always yearning for a drop of her time, a piece of her mind. Between the hospital, the clinic, the gym and occasional time with Big or my parents, Queen has taken up all of my time. She controls every move I make. I am her slave, her menial, her laborer, her lover by design, willingly, her servant. From dinners to mid-week house calls from me, to catching an early morning lover's breakfast, Queen has become my life—this is what I've been wanting. Damn, she was so hard to find. She's perfect in every imaginable way. Our whirlwind romance has taken on a life all its own and the time, well it's flying by. Seems like just yesterday, I found my Queen that night at Jasper's. We've been spending every waking minute together it's hard to imagine that time has passed. It's almost Christmas already. Wow.

Queen is so sexy, with little effort. And not only am I attracted to every inch of her, her mind has a hold of me. I love her intellect. Her compassion. How she prepares for trial, the care she has for her clients. I love her wit. She's a smart ass, unafraid to go toe to toe with me when need be. She's strong and holds her ground. Not to mention, she's a shit-talker, especially in the bedroom. She loves the New York Giants. I'm in heaven.

My beautiful lady surprised me with tickets to see the Giants and we went to last night's game. She rocked a pair of skinny jeans, high-heeled Timberlands, a brown fur jacket which matched her hair to perfection, and a low-cut, form fitting Giants jersey. After I picked her up yesterday, I wanted to tell her to forget about the game, and let's stay in. It takes days for her to leave my psyche, and I'm loving every minute of it.

Holidays are not my favorite time of the year, since my brother's death, I haven't thoroughly enjoyed Christmas the way I should, the way I know I would if Quinton were here, however, there's something magical about the weeks in between Thanksgiving and Christmas this year. The cold air outside is welcomed and embraced by the festive feeling of love from family and friends that surrounds everyone like a warm hug of cheer. This Christmas is the first Christmas in a long time that I'm actually looking forward to. I grab the frame from my desk and smile. It's the picture of Queen and I. We took this photo after our midnight rendezvous – Mos Def's concert. I remember this night so well. Having her on my arm that night made me feel complete. Although I would never mention it to Queen, she is a trophy to me in some respects. She has it all— brains, beauty, body, and my heart. Stick a fork in my ass, because I'm done. Tracing the picture frame, I love the elegance of it, of course my baby bought this for me, and she has good taste. Look at her, that warm smile, she's so pretty.

Haven't seen my baby since this morning. After the Giants game yesterday, we went out to dinner, and of course, it was on once we got back to her pad. My dessert was Queen and a full bottle of baby oil. Leaving her house around 4a.m. to get ready for work has me a little groggy at this time of day, but the tiredness, I'll take any day if it stems from me loving my lady all night long. She's so familiar to me, something about her makes me feel like I've known Queen all my life.

I call her. The phone rings.

"Hey Baby."

My angel sings, "Q, I did it again. I'm sorry."

I smile because she doesn't sound sorry about anything. I'm anxious to hear what she will say next.

"Oh yeah? What did you do this time?"

"I've been a bad, bad girl."

"Ha, ha, ha. Yeah?"

"Really bad, Q."

Looking at her photo, I smile hard. She's full of shit this afternoon and I'm almost afraid to hear what's gonna come next out of that pretty mouth of hers.

"So, how are we going to handle this, Queen?"

"I don't know baby, I'm sorry. I promise not to do it again."

"You're not getting off that easy. You've been a bad girl. I'm gonna have to teach you a lesson. Let you know that you can't get away with that shit."

"Oh baby, I've been really, really bad. You're gonna have to show me - punish me real good, baby."

I laugh out loud. "Don't make me leave this hospital early today girl."

"You try it, you may like it. But baby, all jokes aside. Have you eaten yet?"

"No baby, I'm sitting here at my desk, looking at your lovely face. Why? You got something for me to eat?"

"Always, sweetheart. No big deal, I was just curious."

"Okay, baby. But no, I haven't, not yet. I have patients to see anyway."

"Alright, Q. I'm gonna grab a bite. Gotta get back to the office. I have trial this afternoon. Murder. Oh the joy!"

"Gimme some sugar."

"Muah. Bye, Q."

I watch the nurses decorating their station with holly and miniature Christmas trees and breathe a sigh of relief that I only had to work the morning and afternoon shifts. Hopefully I can do some holiday decorating of my own with the real woman in my life as opposed to the ones sniffing after me here. It's only been a short time since Queen came into my life, but it feels like an eternity. Life before her is just a blur and I want it to stay that way. I'm grateful that this Christmas I will have someone I love to spend the holidays with as opposed to just an available piece of ass near the tree as has been my practice in the past. Or sulking somewhere, thinking about Quinton.

"Time to rock and roll." I say to myself as I pick up the first set of records on my desk and try to familiarize myself with the patient's history. Through the blinds on the full-length glass door in front of me, I can see the nurses eyeballing me but I pretend not to notice since it seems like the holiday spirit has them all sweating me like dogs in heat. Carmella is the worst today; I can smell she's up to something. Her uniform is unbuttoned a little lower than usual and I can tell she has on more makeup than she normally does, if that's possible. Carmella could easily be a poster child for makeup and how not to wear it. She giggles to one of the nurses and heads in my direction. I wish I had somewhere to run, but I don't. I glance up for a brief second only to witness her stride—it's forced, contrived like she's trying to be sexy. Those skinny snake hips leave little to the imagination and either she has recently gotten implants or has a padded bra on, either way, it'll never be enough for a man like me – a passionate lover who likes women who are well-equipped with more than enough to offer. I'm gluttonous that way. She knocks on the door and sticks her head in.

"Dr. Hughes, can I speak to you for a minute?" She smiles and is closing the door behind her before I can even answer.

"Yes, Carmella, what can I do for you?" I barely take my eyes off of the records in front of me. Not because they are that interesting, but because I am avoiding eye contact. Her long red hair is pinned up in the back with ringlets hanging in her face. If I liked her type, I would have to classify her as looking good today; but she's not my type. She doesn't do it for me like Queen does. She looks me directly in the eyes as she walks closer towards my desk.

"I was wondering if you have a date for the hospital Christmas party next week. I'd love for us to go together." She walks as seductively toward me as she possibly can, but her best effort is tired to me to say the least and not even the slightest bit enticing. She's just not my type, far from it. Galaxies from being anything close to what I'd ever want. If I were lonely and horny, on my deathbed, and about to get castrated, she might be able to catch a lick on a desperate night. That's a big fucking "might." I'd have to be drunk, well over the legal limit. But I am neither of those things and I have Queen, so all of what Carmella does falls on deaf ears and blind eyes concerning me.

"To be honest with you, I hadn't given much thought to going. Really, I had forgotten all about it." I try to give her a little bit of eye contact, but it's minimal, I don't want to engage her at all, but feel it's the right thing to do.

"Wow, Dr. Hughes, I hadn't noticed before but I love that goatee you're growing in."

I look at her and don't respond.

"What would it take to make you reconsider going to the party with me?" She licks her lips trying to look sexy and I can see the hope in her eyes. I pity her for not catching a clue that she doesn't have a chance in hell with me.

"Nothing personal Carmella, but I usually don't get into the holiday spirit enough to really get into the parties here. I'm going to take a pass on this one." I make sure she knows I am adamant about not going to the party and even more persistent that I ain't going to the party with her.

"I wish I could change your mind about the party Quincy. Are you sure I can't persuade you?" She runs her fingers down the front of her uniform and almost makes me look twice. Almost. I want to laugh out loud. She does not hold a candle to my Queen, so I can't fake the funk of interest in her. She has her hands behind her back and I'm afraid to even guess what she wants as a consolation prize for me not going to the party with her. I should've stayed my ass in bed this morning.

"Well, if you won't go with me, do you mind at least coming over here right now?" She says, as she stands near the door using her pointer finger to beckon me closer to her.

"What's this about Carmella? I have patients to see. And you're borderline inappropriate at this point." I can see the other nurses sitting at their station, yet staring through the blinds of my office and giggling amongst themselves. Something's up. I don't know what, and to be honest, I don't fucking care.

"Please indulge me Doctor Hughes, I promise to be brief." She bats her eyes, but I am not impressed or swayed by her attempts. However, I do want her to leave my office so I reluctantly walk over to her in order to get whatever game she is playing out of the way so she'll leave. As soon as I am right in front of her, she brings her hand from behind her back and I can see she is holding a small twig of some sort.

"What are you doing Carmella?"

"Tis the season to be jolly, giving and loving Quincy. This is mistletoe. You do know what mistletoe is, don't you?" She has one hand holding the green and red plant and one hand around my neck trying to pull me closer to her.

Did she just call me Quincy?

"Yeah, I know what mistletoe is Carmella, but you have the wrong one if you think you are using that on me." I place both my hands between us, trying to break her grasp.

"Come on Quincy, you can't break tradition. Be a little loving. Be a little giving. Let Carmella taste a little of your Christmas cheer. Besides, it is almost sacrilegious if you find yourself under mistletoe, not to give that person a kiss. I swear it's a written rule somewhere Doctor Hughes, I'm sure of it, so you HAVE to give me a kiss." She lowers her hand from around my neck, pushes me against the door, and tries to force her tongue down my throat as she slowly begins to close the blinds behind us.

"Carmella…what the hell is wrong with you? I'm sorry and I don't want to be mean, but this is not about us; this is not about you. I have somebody in my life and I am not messing that up for you or anyone else right about now. Let's just act like this didn't happen. I won't say anything if you can keep your mouth closed. If you need to, then save face with the other nurses by calling me a prick, but this isn't going to happen. Not today, not at the party, not ever. I've found what I want and need, and I'm sorry to say this to you, but I'm no longer looking and no longer searching. Hopefully you will respect what I am saying. And Carmella, if you don't, trust that if anything like this ever happens again that you will lose your job." I do my best to be honest without sounding condescending or rude, after all we do have to work with each other every day, and I don't want any tension between us. I see her searching her mind of what to say, what to feel.

"I'm pissed Quincy, but your honesty makes me want you even more. Good luck with your girl. I'd be lying if I said I hope it works out. But I will say, if the relationship crashes and burns, please know I have no problem with retrieving her seconds." She makes her comment as she kisses me on the cheek, winks, and opens the blinds on my door. I see the other nurses sitting at attention waiting to see what happened and I don't envy Carmella of having to find a way to explain being shut down. She walks out my door blowing as kiss to me as she closes it behind her. I walk back to my desk without looking at the circus act going on at the nurse's station. I could care less what she tells them or what they think.

I'm sure that for the rest of the day I will be subject to stares and ridicule.

"He ain't all that." I hear more than once, yet I ignore them.

"He ain't nothing but a Robin Thicke wannabe," Lucy, the Spanish one of the bunch pronounces. I know it's her by her thick accent, not the one from Spain, but from Brooklyn. She's just mad that I didn't give her the business when she tried a couple of months ago.

"Ha, ha, yeah, Matthew Mcconaughey always coming in here like he's The Mack. Like he Hollywood or something," Angel remarks, and laughs with the rest of the hens.

It's sad to know these are women who aid doctors in saving lives. They could start their hospital version of *The View* out there some days.

A whiff of Jasmine comes over me. I swear I smell Queen. Now I know it's definitely time to get out of here. My baby is calling me, speaking my name. I'm out.

"Carmella, tell Doctor Sorenson to take my load today. I have three patients, they're on my desk. Pull the charts and give them to him. Have a great day."

As I make my way out, I feel the holes burning in my back. Laser beams of heat from horny bitches looking for some dick, some rich dick at that, my dick. It ain't up for grabs. I have my woman, she doesn't need my money, shit, Queen may go toe to toe with me in the area of dollars and cents. I'd never ask, and even if she did make more than me, she would never flaunt it. She is a woman in her own right. And, she doesn't have her hand out, which is the type of woman that has entered and exited my life. That woman. I've gotten more gifts, more love, more care from her than I have with most women of my past combined. She's so giving, so generous and doesn't mind spoiling her man. I have a feeling Queen is a ride or die chick underneath all the intellectual lawyer stature.

It's crisp outside and I stop when I pass through the sliding glass doors of the hospital to zip up my jacket. When I look up from my zipper, a large black man stops me in my tracks.

Scoping him up and down, his frame is big, muscular, he's a rugged dude.

"You in a rush Doc? What's your hurry?" He uses his body to force me to stop.

"Do I know you?" I give him half a stare and continue to walk towards the parking lot and to my car.

"Not really, but I know you. You the punk ass white boy that's trying to steal my girl." He's taller than me, slightly, and I can see anger in his face so I mentally prepare myself for battle. He's pretty cut and his arms look like they can deliver a hell of a punch, but my trips to the gym have me in better shape than him, and I'm sure I can take him if need be.

"Look, I don't know what your problem is man, but you don't know shit about me, so you need to get out of my way." I look him dead in the eyes to make sure he knows I won't be punked by him.

"Who you talking to like that white boy? Just because you've tasted Queen's pussy makes you think you got balls now?" He folds his arms in front of him trying to stare me down. He looks familiar to me; I know I've seen him before. I never forget a face, and this big, badass brotha is no exception, I just can't place where I've seen him before. But in any case, I'm not going to let him think he can scare me.

"Don't let the white skin fool you. If you're feeling froggy, then jump, otherwise, it would be in your best interest to walk away before you need help doing it."

"And it would be in your best interest to leave my girl alone." He's so close to my face that the smell of alcohol on his breath is turning my stomach.

"Your girl? Ha, ha, ha. Since, I'm tapping her ass instead of you, seems like she's my girl instead of yours. How the fuck you let that go anyway? Shit, you must be a crazy motherfucker. Don't you miss those long ass nights? Ha, ha, ha, you need to step, bitch. If you can't hang, don't hate the player hate the game. Now, excuse me, *my wife* is waiting." I brush his shoulder with mine allowing the swagger of my walk to show him I mean business. As I walk away I ball my fist up to prepare for a sucker punch I assume he will throw, but one never comes. I'm ready now to fuck his ass up since he claimed my woman as his girl. He just stands there watching me walk to my truck. Once I am inside I breathe a sigh of relief. I'm a lover not a fighter, and even though I just talked a good game about whooping his ass, I really was hoping I didn't have to back it up. But I would've, no doubt.

A rush of adrenalin bubbles over in my veins and after turning the ignition switch and putting the truck in gear, I press speed dial on my cell as I leave the parking lot. I just had my first test as Queen's man and I want to let her know I passed with flying colors. I can't wait to tell my baby about how one of her ex's just got punked, I want to hear her laugh right along with me as I speak of my victory in protecting our relationship, I want to suggest a little congratulatory sex, but she does not answer and I get her answering machine instead. So I leave a message.

"Hey sugar. I just gave one of your ex-boyfriends a taste of what kind of man I am, and I would love to come by and give you a taste of me as well. Call me baby, I need to see you."

No gym for me today. Queen's been working her man out like crazy and my body needs a break. I decide to stop by Big's place. It's Monday afternoon and I know he's off work. Since starting his own construction company, he's a believer in extended weekends, every weekend. So, I know where to find him on a Monday. Fat ass is probably sitting on the couch, watching something he ain't got no business watching and eating something that shouldn't be within ten feet of him. But that's my boy.

I pop in the CD Queen gave me some time ago and enjoy the sounds of Redman wildin' out on my way to Big's house. "Soopaman Lover" blasts as the bass kicks in, making the ride a live one. As I pull up, I see not only flurries coming down, softly, just to signal winter's arrival, I see Big's truck in the driveway which confirms my suspicion that he is home.

The crisp Poconos air will bite a hole in your ass if you're not dressed properly. Making my way up the stairs, I ring the bell and give him the finger through the peephole as he asks, "Who is it?"

"Who the hell else would be coming to see you?"

"Take a number; I'm in high demand prick." Big opens the door and we give each other a pound and some brotherly love.

As I make my way to the couch, I further confirm what I thought all along. Noticing the foil from the sandwich he devoured, I shake my head. Americans no longer treat themselves on occasion to a good ass sandwich and some fries. It's become the every day norm, and we eat healthy a few times a year. I know, I used to do the same thing until I started pronouncing folks dead in droves from massive heart attacks.

"Where's your manners Big, can't you at least offer your house guest a beer?"

"You're no guest; go get it yourself, Vanilla Ice."

"Fuck you. Don't you want to know why I came by?"

"Not particularly, but from that big fucking grin on your face, something tells me you are going to tell me anyway." Big flops down next to me and takes a sip of his beer.

"Just shut up and listen." I begin reliving my encounter outside the hospital and Big gives me a high five for manning up and holding my own.

"Yeah, Big, so his big black ass steps to me like I'm some punk ass white boy."

"You are a punk ass white boy, but I'm the only one allowed to say that shit. You should've cold-copped his ass."

"Man, I wanted to so damn bad. But shit, I couldn't tell if ole boy was crazy or not. Now that I think about it, I wonder if that's the same man Queen said was beating her ass?"

"What? He was hitting on her? Man, you need to fuck his shit up."

"I don't know, but I do know that somebody started getting physical with my baby."

"Your baby?" Big questions, and rubs those sausage fingers together again like he's in need of details.
After a few jokes and me getting my own beer, I get serious.

"Big, I'm really feeling her. Today wasn't about me proving my manhood against some bully; it was about protecting what is mine. It was about marking my territory; it was about making sure I have a future with her."

"Damn, you're serious man. I haven't heard you talk like this before about any woman." Big's eyes widen and I can tell I am shocking the shit out of him.

"I've never been so serious about a woman in my life. I want to spend Christmas with her. I want that to be the real beginning of the rest of our lives together."

"Ain't nothing wrong with a little holiday humping Q. Go for it."
Big leans in, a shit grin comes over his face.

"No offense man. I still can't believe you got her. She's pretty as shit, Q. Is the pussy good, man?"
I nudge him upside his head, but because he's my boy, I give him just a little bit to keep his attention.

Leaning back on the sofa, beer in one hand, I expel, "Maaaaaaaaaan. Whew. No joke. I'm still trippin' as to how I got in the door. Don't get me wrong, honeydip made me work my ass off, for sure. I was spending hundreds a week on flowers, man. Writing love letters and shit. Last man must've really tore his ass and fucked up major league. Sort of like how bad Bush fucked up the country so bad that we had to give Obama a chance!"

"Dayum! Is she that good?"

"Shit, bro, I'm tellin' you. I ain't goin' nowhere. I'm really feeling her. I've heard people talk about soul-mates before, and I really believe she's mine. No way to know it, if you haven't experienced it before. Those people weren't lying. I love her man. I do. I'm in love with her. I love everything about her. She's has a big heart, she's sweet, kind, she cares for me. I've never felt like this before. And before you start with the jokes, let me say, "Go to hell, Big.""

"Awe, see, white boy, I wasn't going to say anything. I don't remember a time that you've ever said you love someone. Never. Damn, I'm speechless, Q."

"She does this thing, man. This thing with her tongue…talks that shit. Whew, shit, man. Big, she has the prettiest toes – red toenail polish. Soft skin, like butter, damn. She begs me not to come. She starts talking all sweet and shit, begs me to hold on, tells me she needs more, tells me she loves it too much. Meanwhile, I struggle cause Big, I'm tellin' you, I never had pussy this good in my life. She gets so fuckin' wet man. For real. Always tight, always wet, wet as hell."

"Well, she got a sister?"

"No Big, only child. Sad story though, Mom died when she was young. She's a daddy's girl. But she's so fucking sweet, Man. Smell good as hell. Hmmph."

"You know what? I'm happy for you. You've had some real stank bitches in your day. I'm happy for you. Just don't forget about your best friend."

I give him a few playful taps. "You my boy, that ain't never gonna change."

"Well, what's that thing she do?" Big questions, waiting for the dirt.

"Just trust me. I couldn't ask for more. She treats me like a king, for real. Cooks for me. You called me yesterday and I'm just seeing you now. Wanna know why?"

"Yeah, motherfucker. I almost forgot about that shit. Where was yo ass yesterday?"

"Did you watch the Giants game?"

"Yes, bitch, we do every Sunday. Me, you, Raj, and Lo. Yo white ass was missing in action."

"Well, man, she got tickets. We were at the game. And she looked good as shit. Low cut Giants jersey, big titties sitting nice and pretty. People stared as we made our way through the stadium. Her hand in mine. I walked through the crowd proud as hell leading her the way. She even got an autograph request, someone recognized her from that big case she won some time ago. I guess it went national. I know she still has an issue with me being white, but I just encourage her to give me a chance. I appreciate her honesty about the race thing. Anyway, she surprised me with tickets to the game. We went out to dinner afterwards. She paid, man. Came home to her place. Damn. Yeah, man, she's got me."

"Okay, so I ain't never heard you talk about Christmas like this. Wassup? Some holiday bumpin' and grindin'?"

"It's going to be more than a holiday hump Big, it's going to be about showing her I love her and about making her my wife."

Big almost chokes on his beer. "Your wife? Aren't you moving a little fast Q? Don't you think you need to think about this more before taking that step?"

"Big, all I need to know at this point is if she can make a mean peach cobbler. Better than my mom's and better than your auntie's. If she can, it's a wrap!"

"Whoa…well, if she does, let me know. You like black folks and their potato salad when it comes to peach cobbler. I know you serious now, man."

"You're my brother, Big, which is why my ass is sitting here talking to you about all of this. But, time waits for no one Big. I don't need more time; when it's right, you just know it; and I know it. This is right Big, I can feel it. Now more than ever, I am convinced to make her mine, for a lifetime. I've had my share of one night stands. Had the around the way girl. Dealt with the hoochies and gold-diggers. Been there, done that. Big, given all that I just told you, would you let her go?"

"Hell no, Q, I wouldn't. Shit, you let a Queen come around these parts. You know Quincy; do your thing, man. I got nothing but love for you. If this woman makes you this happy, I have no choice but to be happy for you. Matter of fact, I can say for sure, I have never seen you like this. And I know you like I know my rusty ass. I know I better be the best man, that's for damn sure."

"Oh, no doubt. I'm playing my cards right and carefully, so time will tell, Big."

Big interjects. "Man, here's a quick test for you. Can you imagine anyone else with Queen? I mean, if you saw her on the street or at Jasper's with some other dude, would it matter?"

"Man, the thought of it makes me lose my appetite. I don't ever want to not be with her and I don't *ever* want to see her with another man. I can't think about her fucking someone else. She's mine, that's all to it. And, I plan to do whatever I have to, to keep it that way."

My hip vibrates. It's my pager. I pull it from my side and see that it is the hospital with an emergency. A severe emergency.

"Big, I have to go. Hospital's calling. Something urgent."

"Damn, hope no one is dead. Be careful man."

"Thanks, I'll holla," I say as I make my way out the door.

QUEEN
Inhaling Redemption

My feet are moving faster than my brain can process. My heart races so hard, beats so fast, I can hear the rhythm in my eardrums. My heart ascends to my throat as I make my way back to my car – with a swiftness.

A tear manages to escape my right eye as I open the car door. While littering is not something that I make a point of doing, today calls for it. I drop the bag of lunch to the ground in the parking lot of Mountain View Hospital and start my engine.

My heart flutters as I begin my journey back to my office to pick up my work to go to court today. I pop in India.Arie's CD and forward to the song, *"Good Mourning."* No other song, no other words make sense to me right now. Her words, as if they came straight out of my mouth are befitting for my mood right now – I'm sad. I normally don't let emotions take a hold of me in any fashion, but damn it, that man – Quincy.

The tears begin to pour down my cheeks, heavy, fluidly, profusely, they pour. I grab a tissue and blot them for fear that I'll crash this car due to blurred vision. "Quincy," I say out loud as India sings to me, "Good morning to the harsh realities of life and good morning to the fact we're not husband and wife." The words settle down deep into my soul, and the tears continue to pour, and land on my coat. I exhale and let out a wail, a scream, I cry, for Quincy, because of him, my need for him, my love for him.

"You're so stupid, Queen. Stupid for falling in love with a white man in the first place." I tell myself as I blot more tears. "You knew he was too good to be true."

I press the speed dial button to my home voicemail and check the messages. The first three are a mixture of telemarketers, one of heavy breathing, and one from my baby, Quincy, *"Hey sugar. I just gave one of your ex-boyfriends a taste of what kind of man I am, and I would love to come by and give you a taste of me as well. Call me baby, I need to see you."*

Struggling, I smile, although it's difficult, I love to hear his voice. I love to see his face. I'm a damn fool for falling so hard, so quickly, I knew this was a sick game his white ass was playing with me, and I fell right into his little sneaky white trap. But, I'm flattered that he stepped to Derrick, I presume. Who else is fool enough to say something to Quincy? Only Derrick's insanity could own confronting my baby. I have a funny feeling that Quincy won't take any shit, not even from big, black ass Derrick. However, I can't believe what I just heard. Did some bitch really tell him to kiss her? Quincy seems too smart to indulge in office affairs. I'm so hurt. One lesson I've learned is that I will never surprise anyone with anything, ever again, whether it be lunch, dinner, or a bar of soap.

As I ride through the mountains, the winter-kissed scenery is beautiful. I'm still shocked that Judge Perkins hasn't closed the court today, I mean, tomorrow is Christmas Eve and I should be home, enjoying a hot cup of chocolate in front of the fireplace, while Quincy…

"Damn, Quincy." The tears resurface, and have come back with a vengeance. I have wrapped at least ten presents for Quincy, and was looking forward to spending Christmas with my baby. I blot more tears and I pull into the parking lot of my law office.

I check my face before reaching my office door, because Paula's here, she knows me like the back of my hand and hers, and I just don't feel like any questions from her ass right now. She's my best friend, and I love her, but being on her witness stand today is not in the plans.

As I open the door, I peek in to see where Paula is. Damn, she's sitting at her desk right in front of me. Hopefully she's online or doing something she has no business so she won't notice me, better yet, she won't see my face.

I walk in and brisk by Paula, until she interrupts me, stopping me in my tracks.

"What's wrong, Queen?" *Damn, she knows me so well.*

"Nothing, Paula."

"You're lying." Funny, she doesn't even look my way.

"I'm fine, Paula. Just came in to grab my work for court today."

"It's on your desk. What's wrong?"

"Surprised Quincy with lunch."

"That's a good thing."

"Not really."

"Why?"

"Some bitch was in his office. We're done, I'm done with him."

"What did the girl say to you?"

"Nothing. I didn't see her, she didn't see me, Quincy didn't even know I was there."

"So, you're done with Quincy and Quincy doesn't know it?"

"Right!"

"Well, what did the girl say?"

"She told Quincy to kiss her."

"Well, did he?"

"I don't know, I don't think…I don't know, Paula."

"Before you jump to conclusions, you need to talk to Quincy."

"Quincy is too good to be true, Paula, I'm gonna let this go."

"You're a coward, Queen," she tells me, still staring at her computer screen.

"Paula!"

"Queen, you're scared to be involved with a white man. You done stringed that man along, and you know how much he loves you and now, because you think something else is going on, you're not even going to give him the courtesy, Queen…"

"You don't get it, Paula."

"Oh, I get it. I get all of it. You're emotional this time of year, every year anyway. Speaking of which, I'm coming by tomorrow to drop off your Christmas gift."

"No problem, Paula. I'll be there."

"I hope Quincy will be there too, Queen. You never know what the day will bring, right?"

"Right, Paula. His loving is so damn good. I wish he were there, I love him so much," I tell her, as the tears pour again from my eyes.

Paula doesn't move from her chair, she never looks at me, she just stares at her computer screen, fumbling with the mouse.

"Fix your face, wipe your tears, and kick their asses in court today, Mami. You got about ten minutes to get to the dance floor."

I laugh through the tears, "Okay."

Of all the days to have to go to court, why is today one of them? I really wish I could just go home and drown myself in my sorrows from my lunchtime excursion, but I can't. Life has to go on. Instead of thinking about what just happened, I have to begin laying a foundation to save Jonathan White from going to prison for murder. Thank God for small favors that I had enough foresight to prepare all my briefs last night. I'm emotional right now and would have a hard time winging it if I wasn't prepared for this hearing. Realizing the power of harnessed anger and fueled by a need to chew someone's ass, I remove my case file from my brief case and decide that Cletus and his zealous prosecution of my client would be the recipient of built up anger and frustration.

I strut my ass to the defense table, walking down the aisle, cloaked in audacity, arrogance, and empowerment. My form fitting business suit and three inch heels makes the bailiffs stare. My flat bangs, and flat-ironed, straight shoulder length hair rests softly on my shoulders. I look down at the diamond necklace Quincy bought me, the one I haven't taken off since he put it on, and I feel the tears about to come down again, but I stop them. No one ever sees me like this, no one, except for Paula and my Daddy.

"Ready to rumble again beautiful?" Cletus whispers in my ear, walking by me on his way to the prosecution table.

"Hopefully you're prepared for more than a round of boxing because I plan on bringing you a war."

"Humph, someone's feisty today. But I like it when you're like that." Cletus winks, unbuttons his Armani suit and sits down. The new, fresh set of waves in his hair shines, just like his Stacy Adams shoes. The man has style.

"I could give less than a damn how you 'like me' Counselor; I just hope you are prepared. I plan on making my last spanking of your ass seem like a love tap compared to this time around."

"Oooh promises…promises…talk dirty to me baby. I like it when you play rough." Cletus blows me a kiss and mouths the words in my direction as he turns to confer with co-counsel at his table.

"Funny Mr. Jackson, I don't seem to need co-counsel." I smile as I give him that one to grow on.

We are at the cat and mouse game portion of the trial that jurors don't get a chance to see because they are not present. Judge Perkins takes the bench to hear pretrial motions from me and Cletus as to what evidence should be presented to the jury. It's our time for each of us to put our scent on the case, our time to show the judge that we each run the dog pit, and I'm determined to make my scent stronger. Stoic in his mannerism, I can tell that Judge Perkins is in a no-nonsense sort of mood, and so am I. I pity Cletus knowing that he is going to get it from both sides from the judge and me. I can smell it, and I am out for somebody's blood today, it might as well belong to Cletus.

"I'm ready for your arguments Counsel. Mr. Jackson, we'll start with you. My time is precious, so don't waste it." The judge sits back in his chair and begins twiddling his thumbs as a sign to hurry up and deliver.

"Your Honor, the State would like to enhance the charges from Murder Two to Murder One with intent." Cletus smugly announces his motion as if his mere speaking the words makes them gospel.

"On what grounds?" I smugly reply, sipping in air at the arrogance of my colleague.

"Your honor, this is nothing more than an attempt on the Prosecution's behalf to use community attention in this case as a publicity tool to further his own pursuit for political ambitions. The Defense's case rests on the fact that my client is innocent. The State barely had enough evidence for an indictment, and now they want to pad their image in the media at the expense of my client by enhancing an already blown-up charge. This case has already gone before the Grand Jury and Mr. Jackson has had his bite at the proverbial justice apple and he chose to seek Murder Two. If he felt he had enough for Murder One, he should have sought it at that time, not now, as an after thought to how much better Murder One would look on his resume. Barring any new explanation or evidence not presented, this case should proceed as charged and indicted. It is the Defense's position that Mr. Jackson is trying to sneak a higher charge as a politically-charged, witch hunt in order to advance his own career at the sake of my client."

Judge Perkins looks at me with raised eyebrows and Cletus has the look of someone who has been suckered punch. I'm in attack Pitbull mode. I can feel the saliva of a mad dog building in the corners of my mouth. I'm armed, dangerous and out for blood. I smell it, the Judge smells it and Cletus can smell it and fear it. It's obvious he is unprepared for a rebuttal.

"Mr. Jackson, Miss Thomas has a point. Do you have any *new evidence* that was not presented to the Grand Jury that would warrant escalating the charge?

Cletus sighs, rolls his eyes and tries to use begging as a persuasive argument.

"Well, your Honor, I don't have any new evidence to present, but the fact that the State did not push for a higher charge with the Grand Jury should not be a roadblock to justice now."

"Is that the best you can do Counsel? " Judge Perkins looks at Cletus with frustration. "If so, the motion is denied."

I smile. "Strike one." I use lip sign language to warn Cletus as I wink, raise one finger for significance and proceed on with two other motions to weaken his case. Like a pitcher on a pro baseball team, I strike him out, one by one, with motion after motion, coupled with convincing arguments that Judge Perkins has no choice but to sustain in my client's favor. I'm in rare form, the room has my dog pit scent on it. Slowly but surely I lay my foundation while watering down the groundwork of the State.

Cletus never saw me coming. Poor guy, he was blindsided and I almost feel sorry for him concerning the way I'm man handling his ass and his case right now. It's not his fault I am pissed and empowered. It's not his fault I need an outlet for my aggression and he is the unlucky one to be my prey. But all is fair in love and war. My lunchtime errand to the hospital showed me that concerning love. Cletus gets to be proof positive in court concerning war.

Having humiliated Cletus enough for the day and feeling slightly vindicated in my anger, I begin to pack up my briefcase and call it a day concerning the "White" case. My job here is done for the day and I'm happy with my performance. Fear of the fact that I am letting my emotions for Quincy fill my head and direct my actions, I am still happy with today's outcome. The words of Maze come to my mind, "Joy and pain, like sunshine and rain." That's been my day today. Joy and pain. The hook from the song dances in my head when I see him. Michael. He's walking toward me from the back of the courtroom. *"What the hell is he doing here?"* I whisper as he approaches.

He claps his hands together with each step as he steps to me.

"Bravo Miss Thomas. Bravo." The smile on his face is a mile long, yet it troubles me.

"Are you following me Mr. Bevens? What are you doing in court today?" I try and ask the question without letting on my apprehension at his presence. I make it like a joke.

"I heard about the case on TV and just wanted to see you in action from the other side of the courtroom. I had an appreciation of your skills as your client, Miss Thompson, I just wanted to see if I would have that same appreciation from a different chair in the room, and I do. You really are quite brilliant Queen. The best at what you do." He continues to approach me, running his finger along the tops of each pew in the courtroom, as he gets closer.

Did he just call me Queen? What happened to calling me Miss Thomas? When did we get this casual? And, he seems different. His appearance, clean, polished, his suit is tailored, nice, stylish, his watch, while not expensive, looks decent, even his shoes.

"Thank you Michael, for the compliment. I try to do the best for my clients."

"And that you do." He moves past the portion of the courtroom that separates the galley from the parties in the case and is closer in my space than I am comfortable with.

"Looks like you are on your way to helping this killer walk Queen. Money well spent for him I'm sure."

His comments anger me. It's like he is assuming Jonathan is guilty, even though I am convinced to the contrary. "Well, it's not about the money Michael. Just like it wasn't about the money with you. I do what I do because I believe in my clients Michael."

Michael smiles and stops in his tracks and begins to turn around. "You believe in your clients with an undying passion that is normally only seen in parents. Against the odds, against the truth, and against the evidence. It's noble Queen, just as noble as the parents of the two little girls in my case. They wanted to think their daughters didn't suffer; they wanted to feel like their innocence hadn't been taken. Against all the odds of how much they suffered and how much they screamed, those parents wanted to believe that things weren't as bad as they knew they were deep down in their hearts. Those parents wanted to reach out and hang on to the hope of an easier reality, one that is not so demonic or evil, and you do the same concerning your clients; Queen." With that, Michael begins walking toward the door to the courtroom whistling with each step. I watch him confused and trying to recognize the song on his lips.

Where's the shucking and jiving? Where's the "you talk so good and white" verbiage that came from him during his trial? Where's his braids and the ignorant slave mentality that he displayed? He's well-spoken today, language is fluid, sentences actually make sense. He's using above-average talk. A flashback of his trial crosses my mind. I remember one witness saying that Michael was like night and day. Which one is he today?

My concentration is broken by Cletus grabbing my arm, and I think to myself, Damn, will the madness of this day ever end?

"I'll give you your props girl. You caught me with my drawers down today. I wasn't ready for you and you took advantage of that. Must be that white super sperm you're digesting lately." His usual cockiness seems to be replaced with combativeness.

"Take your ass whooping like a man Cletus, this is only the beginning." The courtroom is just about empty so I make sure to hold my own against Cletus, I refuse to let him smell fear on me.

"Word on the street is that you have a case of reversed jungle fever Queen. Is that what has you so full of yourself today? What's that white boy done to you, and is this why you are taking on the cases of deadbeat black men? Does it make you feel okay Queen? Does getting them off make your relationship justifiable?" His words are hurtful, yet I can't let him see that. I know it's all a set up for the game we are playing with this case and I won't give him the satisfaction of thinking he is getting to me.

"Call it white boy super sperm or whatever other label you want to place on it Cletus…just know it's potent enough to help me kick your ass. It's good enough to have my ass rushing out of court today to get to."

"Oh, it's like that, Queen? Why didn't you give me a chance? You know I've been trying for some time now. What, am I not your type? Does the bluest of eyes only float your boat? I'm sure that white boy's great-grandfather would be spinning in his grave if he knew his blood was knee deep in some black puntang. You should have gotten with me, Queen." I smile through the viciousness of his words and begin walking, switching hard as hell so that he gets a good look at what he's missing.

I turn around, smile seductively through my hair. Cletus stands still, just like I thought he would. "Baby, the way you let me spank your ass in court leads me to believe that I'd have to spank your ass in every other aspect of our lives. Me, personally, I like for a man to be the man, and if that man comes and delivers, and it's an interracial package that all may not accept, then so be it. I have a real man at home, not one that needs a spanking. But oh how he spanks it so well, Cletus." I use part of Quincy's line and feel good as hell about it. Although sadness, torment and confusion cover me, I grab my briefcase and head out the door. "Merry Christmas," I yell as I make my way out.

I just want and need to get to my car and take my ass home. Amidst a victorious moment, I'm feeling violated. Violated by Quincy, violated by Michael, and violated by Cletus. I need to reenergize myself. And then he shows up. The last face I wanted to see as I stroll to my car.

"Where's your ivory-colored bodyguard Queen? Tell him he's slipping in his duties." Derrick walks up behind me and follows me as I quicken my stride.

"That's none of your damn business Derrick, what I do is no longer any of your business, and by the way, Go to hell!" Maybe it's the victory today, or maybe it's the fact that I am just tired of bullshit, but in either case, I'm too tired to deal with more bull shit.

Derrick pulls me close to him and sniffs up the side of my neck. "You smell like you always do. Jasmine. My favorite." He bites me softly on the ear and my purse falls to the ground. "Does that punk as white boy make your spine tingle in the same way that I do Queen? Be honest, you know he doesn't."

I pry myself loose and pick up my purse and fumble for my keys.

"Wouldn't you like to know?"

"Come on Queen, that pencil dick can't possibly satisfy you like I do. I should have done both of us a favor and got rid of his ass when I had the chance, just like I did Sherri."

Anger builds up inside me. I feel my hand bawling into a fist before I even know it, but I exhale before throwing a blow. He's not worth it.

"Next time you're laying next to that wet-dog smelling ass white boy remember that he is alive because I allowed him to be Queen. I know you're angry with me right now because of some of the things I've done in the past, but you will get over it. You always do. And when you come crawling back to me, I don't want you to be mad at me for fucking up your little ice cream fantasy. Don't get it twisted Queen; I did you and me a favor by not kicking your boyfriend's ass."

I look Derrick in the eye for the first time in a long time, armed with confidence instead of fear.

"Derrick, I've never liked a sore loser, especially a cocky one; and right now, you're both. We're through Derrick. Say what you will, believe what you will; but keep in mind, it's over between us. If my chasing white dick bothers you; get over it. If you think I've lost my mind for dating a white man; get over it, whatever you feel about Quincy and me; get over it. Bottom line, Derrick, I'm through with you, there is no love between you and me, there is no future, there is no us. If you don't hear anything else I say, hear this…Get over it!"

"We're never gonna be done, Queen. You know that. You know that white boy ain't gonna be around long, and I forgive you and I'll be waiting for you when you come back to get some of this good black loving."

"Ha, ha, ha, ha. Derrick, please. First, you need to go back to the drawing board in the area of love making. My man, no excuse me, my White man takes very good care of me, and I do mean VERY good care of me."

I open the door to my car, turn the ignition and inhale redemption.

Derrick jumps in front of my ride just as I'm about the pull off, and I'm tempted like hell to run his black, crazy ass over. It is only by the grace of God that I don't. I don't believe in an eye for an eye, because I'm confident that Derrick will get everything, and I do mean everything that's coming to him.

Rolling down the car window in disgust, I yell, "Derrick, would you move? As bad as I want to run your dumb ass over, you're not worth my freedom!!!"

Running like some type of freak out of a circus, he quickly reaches my driver's side window, and reaches in. Frantically, I press the button to roll up the window, and his arm gets caught half way. His massive hand reaches around my neck, so I step on the gas. Derrick tumbles to the ground. For a person who tries to follow the letter of the law, I should remain and call the cops, but instead, I look at his big, black, dumb, abusive, psychotic ass laying there on the ground, through my rearview mirror, and this time, I inhale a small dose of redemption, and whisper to Sherri, "I'm going to get him. You did not die in vain."

QUINCY
You've Changed

"**D**r. Hughes? Dr. Hughes?" As I open my eyes, panic settles down deep. I'm still in the hospital. I wasn't supposed to sleep this long. Looking up, I wipe the cold out of the corners of my eyes. "Thank you, Carmella," I say through a hoarse and reluctant voice. I am immediately on guard when I see her face. This is the same woman who made aggressive passes at me yesterday. I don't want any trouble from her right now. I'm too tired to fight.

"What time is it?" I question as I sit up slowly.

"It's still early in the day Doctor, but its Christmas Eve, get out there and enjoy the holiday season. As long as you have worked at this hospital, I have never seen you take off for Christmas and New Year's. I still can't believe you finally did it. So I figured I'd wake you up instead of allowing you to sleep right through the holiday."

I smile, stand up and stretch. Other than the crook in the back of my neck, I feel pretty good after such a nerve wrecking night.

"Thanks, Carmella." All of a sudden his eyes flash in my mind. So much pain at such a young age. I think to myself before asking for an update. How's the boy?"

She smiles, walks over to me and pats my shoulder. "He's fine Doctor, he pulled through. Thank God."

"That's great; I was hoping and praying that he would. You know, before he passed out, he told me the bus driver was texting."

"My goodness, that's a shame!"

"Yes and I called the authorities."

"Good. You know it was very heroic of you to come back and work the ER all night. It's because of you that we only lost one. Unfortunately, the boy's dad passed away, but you saved his mom, his brother and his sister. It's a miracle any of them survived at all, considering that tour bus crashed into them head on. I didn't think any of them would be alive to see another day, but thanks to you most of the family made it. You really are a talented and brilliant doctor." She stares at me like a lovesick puppy and the room is instantly full of an awkward air.

"Thanks, Carmella. Who's covering for me today?" I try to keep her focused on the hospital and not on me.

"Doctor, don't worry about any of that. Enjoy Christmas and your much needed vacation; you deserve it. Although we will miss you, we'll be fine."

I take that as an opening to get away from her, so I walk over to the chair, grab my coat, my bag and make my way out of the ER at Mountain View Hospital.

The wind chill creeps into my bones as I walk to my truck. It's crisp and very cold today, but neither the weather nor the patient I lost last night will dampen my mood or my spirit. It's Christmas Eve, and I'm headed to my Baby. It just doesn't get much better than this. I retrieve my cell from my hip and dial Queen. She must be out shopping or running errands because the voicemail picks up so I leave a message.

"Hey Baby. Sorry, I couldn't get to you last night and I apologize for not calling. I was tied up at the hospital all night. There was a horrible accident; you probably saw it on the news. A bus collided with a car; it was a really bad scene. Anyway Sugar, I'm coming to my Baby today. I'm headed home to take a shower, and I'll be right there. Call me if you need anything, Honey."

"Merry Christmas," A resident says to me as we cross paths in the parking lot.

"Merry Christmas to you too," I reply as I quicken my pace.

The drive through the mountains is tranquil and relaxes me. I pop in some smooth jazz and turn on my heated seats for added comfort and decide to give Big a call to see what he's up to. He picks up on the first ring.

"Man, you had me worried."

"Awe Big, you sound a little gay," I respond jokingly.

"Hey, I ain't gay man, but you left out of here on some emergency, now it's the next day. Wassup?"

"Bad, bad, car accident, Man. The mother and children involved are fine, but the father didn't make it. Sad thing is, the tour bus driver was texting when the crash took place."

"Damn, that's really fucked up. It's Christmas, Man. No one should have to go through this on Christmas."

"Yes, I know. I reported it to the authorities. I thought the little boy wasn't going to pull through, but thank God he did."

"Yeah, thank God. So, Merry Christmas white boy! What you up to today?"

"Man, I slept so hard at the hospital, I'm just now leaving."

"Damn, Man; better you than me."

"Yeah, so I'm headed home; gonna shit, shower and shave, then head over to my lady's."

"I hear that. What's up for tomorrow? Doing our usual run down to Jersey?"

"Of course. I'm not about to start breaking traditions now. But remember, this is my first holiday with my girl, so I'll be running late, if I have my way."

"Man, I'm jealous. You gettin' all that sweet ass, and good lovin' on Christmas and I'm getting, what?"

"I got you a gift, Man."

"You need to bring me a Queen; I want a gift like the one you got. All jokes aside, I'm happy for you."

"Thanks, Man. So check it, I'm gonna holla at you later. I'm home and I need to get to my baby."

"Aiight. Peace, Fam."

"Peace."

જીજીજીજીજી

The hot shower, combined with this tall glass of orange juice, is just what I need to give me the last bit of energy I require to get me going for the day. I must have been exhausted as hell to have slept that hard. Trying to look good for my baby, I throw on a Sean Jean ivory turtleneck sweater, matched up with some Sean Jean blue jeans, some new wheat Timberlands, a mean belt, and I make sure I generously spray on the cologne Queen loves to smell on me. Hey, I just might get me a little Christmas Eve action today.

Putting on my jacket, I carefully tuck away one of Queen's gifts into my pocket and zip it securely. There are boxes and boxes of gifts I had wrapped at the mall the other day, and I begin to load them into my truck. Buying her everything that I could find that I thought she would like, forced me to spend a pretty penny. But she's so worth it. I can't wait to see her face when I walk in with this spread fit for a queen. Red boxes, white boxes, red bows, white bows, silver bows, gold boxes, everything. Diamond earrings to match the necklace. A diamond bracelet to match the earrings and necklace. A Jasmine gift set. Music, Hip-Hop, of course. Some gift cards. I even found a white Fox waist-length jacket on sale. The recession apparently forced the store to go out of business. Too bad for them, lucky for me. It was marked down by more than half. I know it's going to look beautiful on my baby. A sophisticated, yet feminine look that will brighten the dullest winter day. I can see it on her now, the color of her skin blending with the color of the coat, on a bright, winter morning. Damn, my girl is beautiful.

As I close the trunk, I reach for my cell phone and dial Queen again. Still, no answer. I try her cell, no answer. Is this what love's all about? That sick, empty pit in your stomach when you can't reach the one you love? I've heard of it before, but never had the chance to experience. I know love is never painless, as I hear my Mom say it all the time, and this part of love, I can do without. My nerves are getting the best of me because of the recent events in the ER.

I hop in the truck and make my way over to Queen's. I press the speed dial button on the way over and call Mom and Dad.

"Quincy. Hi, son," Mom says as she picks up on the first ring.

"Hey, Mom. How's my favorite lady in the world doing today?"

"Oh, I'm fine dear. Your Dad and I are just decorating the house. Are you coming by tomorrow?"

"Of course, Mom. I have something for you."

"Now, Quincy, you know I don't need anything."

"I know, Mom. Tell Dad I said, "Merry Christmas Eve.""

"Will do, Son."

"Love you, Mom."

"Love you too, Quincy."

"Oh, Mom?"

"Yes, Dear?"

"How did you know Dad was the one for you? I mean, how did you know that Dad was the love of your life?"

"Oh, Quincy. I knew that I loved your Dad with all my heart and soul when one day I felt like I couldn't breathe without him." I smile at her words. They are the comfort I needed. I rub my hand across the box in my jacket pocket and smile.

"Thanks. Love you Mom."

ȣȣȣȣȣ

As I pull up to Queen's house, I see her truck in the driveway. There's no cop car parked out front which alarms me since her house is supposed to be watched all the time due to her Ex and those nutty murder trials. I pull into the driveway behind her to give me quicker access to her door, while carrying my packages.

With boxes of gifts in hand, I finally make it to her front door and ring the bell. The outside light comes on, and I hear her unlocking the door. I see my baby; finally, as it feels like it's been an eternity since I've looked at her pretty face. She opens the door.

Dressed in a silk red robe, Queen looks delicious and I instantly wonder what's underneath. Her pink furry slippers always make me laugh but I keep the laughter to myself. As I glance up to her face, I look deeply. Her hair is wild, natural, like it has been freshly washed. No makeup, her face glows naturally, and she smells like she's been soaking in Jasmine all night, and immediately my senses are penetrated. She's so sexy, even without trying.

But, as beautiful as she is, Queen looks sad, her lips are red, as well as her cheeks and even in the midst of her beauty, she looks like she's been crying.

"What's wrong, Baby?" I ask as I lean in to give her a kiss. She turns her head and walks down the foyer. I step inside; using my shoulder to close the door behind me. Making my way into the living room, I see that Queen has done a hell of a job decorating the house. The tree is lovely, everything in sight is festive and the house smells like warm baked goods. I walk over to the tree and place the gifts down, and as I get up, I see my name written on at least ten different boxes.

I'm unsure as to what mood my baby is in, so I tread lightly. She hasn't said a word to me since I walked in. That's not like her. Removing my coat, I lay it on the sofa and toss my boots to the side by the tree. I look at her; she's gone off to the kitchen. I make my way there as I follow her I question, "Where's the cop?"

She doesn't turn to face me, as she prepares her tea.

"I told him to take the week off; it's Christmas."

"The cop is supposed to be here for your protection, Queen."

"I know that, Quincy."

The cold shoulder has never been delivered to me in such an icy fashion. She walks away from me, and I follow the sway of her luscious build, her body commands my attention, so I follow her as she steps into the den.

The sounds of Billie Holiday penetrate the atmosphere. Sorrowfully, Billie sings, "You've forgotten the words, I love you." A flashback comes to my mind. I remember Paula telling me that if Queen is sad, she'll listen to Billie Holiday. She's barely speaking; she's given me no sugar, not even a hug. It's Christmas Eve, and she's not saying a word. Something is definitely wrong.

"Queen, look at me," I tell her as I grab her arm. She turns around to face me, taking a sip of her tea. If looks could kill, I'd be on the floor right now, dead.

"What's wrong, Baby?" I kiss her on the cheek.

"You tell me, Quincy." Her voice is dry and sarcastic.

Oh boy. Is this part of the bargain? I have to play mind reader now?

"Nothing's wrong. It's Christmas Eve, and I'm with my Baby." I remove the cup of tea from her hand and place it onto the coaster on the coffee table. Grabbing her by the waist, I pull her close to me and kiss her neck. "Merry Christmas, Baby," I whisper in her ear.

She looks me dead in the eye and doesn't say a word. I rock her from side to side.

"Merry Christmas, Queen." I repeat myself, hoping for a response.

"Thank you, Quincy."

That isn't the response I was hoping for. She's cold as ice and I haven't the slightest clue as to why. Maybe because I was at the hospital all night? Guessing that might be the reason, I remind her of the fact that I was in surgery all night. She walks away from me and sits on the sofa. I follow her, and sit next to her.

"Queen, didn't you get my messages? I'm so sorry I didn't reach out to you last night, Baby, but I was in surgery all night long. I apologize. I wanted to be here, but there was a bad car accident. Please forgive me." I once again kiss her cheek. Taking her hand in mine, I rub it, and then kiss the back of it. She's so stiff, so cold, there's a sadness I can't cut through.

"Queen, Talk to me. Tell me what's wrong? Baby, let me fix it for you. What's the matter?"

"Nothing, Quincy," she snaps at me as she snatches her hand out of mine. Moving from the sofa, she gets up abruptly and walks back into the living room. Turning up the volume, I've figured out the tune that sets the mood today. Billie Holiday's, "You've Changed." I remember hearing my Mom play this song when I was younger.

Graciously, she glides from the living room back to the kitchen, and checks what's in the oven. Her ass pokes out deliciously as she bends over, and I can't help but to get heated. I wonder what's under that robe.

"You smell so good today, Queen."

No response. Something is wrong. Walking closer to her, I grab her from behind, wrap my arms securely around her. Her ass rests firmly on my manhood, and I back up just a bit, so that she doesn't feel my erection as it gradually takes place. Inhaling the fresh smell of her hair, I pull it to one side, and whisper in her ear, "Did you just wash you hair?"

Feeling her exhale, she's tense, and I don't know why.

"Yes." She replies curtly to my question.

Turning her to face me, she gives me a sad look, and I need to know what's wrong.

"Baby, I'm sorry. The bus acci—"

"Its fine, Quincy. Besides, I thought you may have had other plans."

She once again walks away from me and her smart-ass comment intrigues me more than a little bit.

"The only plans I have are to be with you, Queen. This is the first time since being at the hospital that I've ever taken Christmas and New Year's off. I didn't do that for something else, I did it to be with you," I explain as I follow her back into the living room where Billie Holiday sings, "You've changed, you're not the angel I once knew. No need to tell me that we're through. It's all over now, you've changed," I can still hear Billie's voice in the backdrop as I pour out my being to Queen.

"Funny thing is. I fell asleep at the hospital. I was so tired. Carmella woke me up, told me to enjoy my holiday." Queen's face has been despondent, until now. I see anger cover the softness of her eyes.

"You've got a lot of fucking nerve, Quincy." Queen tells me as she begins to yell.

"Baby, what the hell is wrong? What did I do?"

"Nothing, Quincy, I think you should leave."

Okay, this must be a bad dream, unless I'm the biggest jerk in the world and don't realize it. My mind searches for clues, anything that will lead me to understand the enigma that is Queen. Placing my hands on my hips, I look down at the floor, I think, quick, fast and in a hurry, I wonder, think, imagine, what could be wrong.

"Queen, I don't want to go. Please, baby, tell me what's wrong. Are you on your period?"

"No! And if I was, it would have nothing to do with this!" she yells and she makes her way to the front door.

"Quincy, get out!" she screams and the lump in my throat becomes heavy. She can't do this to me now, not now, we've made it, we've jumped the interracial hurdles, she's perfect, we're perfect together, not now, Queen. I don't know what to say.

"Queen. Look, I have no clue what the hell is going on here, but I'm not leaving you. Not now! Why are you doing this?"

As she walks up to me, I can see her nose becoming redder. She's flushed and I know she's mad and she's ready for war. Taking her hand, she nudges me in the forehead and pushes my head in. "You make me sick, Quincy."

My neck slams to one side and I hear it crack.

"Queen, what the fuck is wrong with you?"

"Don't play stupid, Quincy. You know what? I knew this was too good to be true."

"Oh, here we go. This is good! We are good!"

"Apparently, I'm not good enough; right Quincy?" she questions, with an evil look on her face as she walks back to the door.

"You are enough for me, Queen."

"I thought so since you can't seem to keep your head from in between my thighs."

Low blow, but I maintain my composure.

"I love being in between your thighs Queen," I respond softly.

"Yeah, I know, you're always there," she spits back.

"Shit, I'm not complaining; are you? I can't even get to the gym like I want because I'm always over giving it to you, "right there," I point down toward her delicious mound which is hidden from me behind the robe.

She wants to throw blows, so can I.

"Awe, wa, wa, boo-hoo, you can't get to the gym, huh? Fuck you, Quincy."

Oooh, I could just bite her sassy ass.

"You've fucked me, Queen."

"No complaints out of you, Quincy."

"You damn right, no complaints. I love being with you."

"Leave, Quincy."

"No! Not until you tell me what's wrong!"

Placing her hands on her hips, she cocks her neck to one side.

"Quincy, this is not going to work. Black men want me, and I should be with them. You're white; Quincy and I just can't do this."

"What? You're fucking joking right? Yeah, I met your black boyfriend, you're better off with me, Queen, trust me!" I feel anger rising in me. I know that we are not back at square one.

"Oh, now you're talking about black men, huh? You know what, Q, I'm not your slave!!"

"You're such a fucking racist, Queen."

"Go to hell, Quincy."

"I'm already there, Queen, thanks."

Walking back to the sofa, I put on my boots, grab my coat and put it on. Walking towards the front door, I feel like I'm dying inside. I turn around to witness Queen drinking her tea as she watches me walk away. Reluctantly, I grab the doorknob and dread what waits for me on the other side; a cold, lonely night and another Christmas without Quinton, now without Queen. This can't be right, yet, it is what it is. The cold air bitch slaps me in the face.

"You know. This is the first time, in a long time, since Quinton's death, that Christmas ever mattered to me. You managed to fuck that up, Queen. Have a great life."

"Quincy. For the record, she'll NEVER love you the way I love you."

Slamming the door, the glass sounds like it's going to shatter. I turn around. Look at Queen.

"What? Who the fuck are you talking about?"

"Don't play stupid, Quincy!" she yells and places her tea on the coffee table. She's ready for war and I'm not ready for battle. I turn around, grab the doorknob again, and she comes up behind me.

"Like I said…Carmella will never love you the way I love you."

Did she just say Carmella? No, Carmella? Carmella…hospital…Carmella?…My nurse…What the hell? Queen, Carmella, love, what? I'm confused. Nuts, torn. I'm crazy. Carmella…Queen…mind is racing…Queen, love, she loves me?…Carmella, but…Damn, no…Queen…no, I think…no…can't be…not Carmella, damn, Carmella, yesterday, the hospital…mind is racing…heart beating too fast, can't breathe, Carmella, the hospital, yesterday, God damn Carmella…not my baby, I remember…Carmella, "Kiss me Quincy"…Shit, I smelled her, Queen…she was there…she heard, no, she heard Carmella, damn it!

"Yeah, see that's what I thought. Busted. How could you do this to me, Quincy?"

"You think I would risk what we have for some tired ass piece of meat? Nothing happened Queen. Nothing! She came on to me, I pushed her away. I don't know what you saw or heard, but that's what happened. Queen, I've jumped through hoops to get to you. If I wanted her, I could have had her a long time ago, but I don't want her, I want you. Do you think

I'm stupid enough to chase trailer trash when I have a Queen? Come on now, give me a break, or at least the benefit of the doubt. Nothing happened."

"So that's your story and you're sticking to it huh? Typical!"

I hear the pain in her voice. I'm mad. I'm confused. I see her in pain. She wants to cry, too stubborn to let a tear fall. My baby is in pain because of me, because of fucking Carmella, I'm mad!

Taking my jacket off, I throw it on the floor, and walk quickly over to Queen and my nerves get the best of me. I knock down a lamp, it crashes to the floor, and breaks into a million little pieces. I'm becoming excited. There is hope for us yet. This is not an issue of black and white, but jealousy and desire that has birthed her anger. I need to hold her.

"Quincy!" she yells as she backs up quickly. I've frightened her.

Quickening my pace, I reach her. She backs up more, she's startled, frightened. I need to hold her. She'll know that it's just me and her.

"Go be with her, if that's who you want!" she yells, frantically as she attempts to escape me. I would never hurt her, but her fear lets me know that someone else has wounded my baby.

I become gentle for a moment. "Who has hurt you, baby? Why are you afraid?"

There are tears in her eyes when she whispers in a scream, "You have hurt me, Q."

My anger rises up again. How do I break through this wall that she has built? What the fuck is she talking about?

The aroma of the room penetrates my nostrils. "And what the fuck is in the oven, Queen?"

"Peach cobbler, you bastard!"

"Who the hell are you making peach cobbler for, Queen?"

She stares. I can tell that the realization that she is safe has occurred to her. She folds her arms in front of her.

"Get your ass on that table!" I command as I follow Queen into the dining room. I need to know if she will. I need to know that I can still make this right. I need to taste my Queen.

"You're crazy, Quincy," she yells. I see her nipples rising through the red silk. They're screaming for me. They need me.

She needs me. My baby needs me. She loves me. Gotta make this right.

"Get your ass on that table, now!"

Queen, covered in pain, joy and euphoria props herself up on the mahogany table, her slippers fall to the floor, her toes, freshly manicured.

"I can smell your pussy getting hot. I smell it, Queen. Why is your pussy hot, Queen?"

Her breathing is heavy and labored. She stares at me with confused, but excited eyes. Her Tootsie-Roll nipples are at full attention. Deliciously, she's propped on her elbows, she's waiting for me, I know it.

Walking up to her, taking my right hand, I reach and grab her by the hair, tilting her head back. She exhales a passionate sigh. Biting her neck, I kiss it, suck on it, leave a passion mark on her, marking my territory like a savage beast.

"Is it hot for me, baby? I know it is. It's got my name all over it."

She's angered and then cooled. She's conjured up this fire down in my soul and only she can quench the thirst that she has caused. I'm not thinking straight, not properly, I want what I want, and I have to have what I need, and that's her.

With my left hand, I remove her robe and toss it on the floor. Just as I had assumed, she was naked underneath it. Her silky skin smells so good. My hand travels down to her sweet, wet, cave. I place my hand over it, and feel the heat rising.

"Quincy." She barely has the strength to fight me back. She whispers, "Quincy, I..."

Biting her bottom lip, I prevent her from saying another word. My pants hit the floor and I remove my sweater.

My mouth finds its way to her sugar walls and I take in a mouth full, biting her clit in the process, she yells in ecstasy, "Quincy, please..."

Moving up to her face, I taste her lips, tongue kiss her like my life depends on it, and at this moment I feel that it does. My life depends on this moment.

"Didn't I tell you I wasn't going anywhere?"

"Quincy!"

"Who do you smell on my lips, Queen?"

"Quincy, please..."

"Who do you taste on my lips, Queen?"

"Me!"

"All I want is you, Queen."

Taking my fingers, I place them into her love, vigorously, I move them around into her goodness until they become saturated with her luscious liquid, her juices cover them. I bring them to my mouth, taste them, I suck them, put them into her mouth, she licks them.

"Who do you taste on my fingers, Queen. Carmella?" I question with anger and lust.

My dick has become the Rock of Gibraltar now, and I slither into her with strength and vigor. She screams, "Quincy!" in ecstasy.

I hear her let out the most tantalizing moan I've ever heard in my life.

I can't take it any longer. With one thrust, I'm inside her. I cry out. She cries out. Damn, my baby is so sultry; searing, scorching and sweltering with lust and love. I can't believe that I am inside of my baby, my Queen once more. I thought I'd lost her forever. I can see her nipples getting harder right before my eyes. As her body shudders, I go deeper.

Hearing her sensual sounds of pleasure makes me try harder than Avis.

"Tell me I'm not your man, Queen! You can't, can you? You better not ever tell me I'm not your man."

An unfamiliar feeling runs through my being. The magnitude of this moment takes over me. I hold her tight as I somehow climb higher. Somehow dig deeper. She's so wet and so soft that I feel her walls of comfort give way to each of my blows. Our solaced spirits emanate Earth-shattering harmony – a melodious blend of worship and devotion as I rise to depths unbeknownst to mankind. Having my share of sex in abundance, I've done this plenty of times but I realize now, this is the first time I've ever truly made love. I'm making love to my baby, my woman, my future, my wife.

This woman has been in my soul, my dreams, my nightly talks with God – no way in hell I'm losing her.

As my manhood slides in and out of her love, I witness my dick glisten as a result of her excitement. She's so wet, sopping, soaked and her desire is evidenced each time I look down at her pulsating pussy and the remnants of lust it leaves on me.

Coercing me into demanding confirmation, my lust and love is fueled for and by my lady and overwhelms me, has me struggling with rhyme and reason.

As Queen's warmth turns to heat, her wetness drowns me so good, devours me, takes me to a place that I don't recognize, but I love it, I love her, everything about her. She has her legs wrapped around me so tight pulling me in deeper and deeper. Taking her mouth into mine as if on cue and with so much determination, makes my heart race faster, my emotions climb, my feelings for her grow more and more with each stroke.

Unfeigned love empowers me as I stroke her with every inch of my body. Powerful, blunt force impacts take me to deeper plains. Making love to her face-to–face, mouth-to-mouth, soul-to-soul becomes too much for me.

Queen's so sexy and sweet that I feel myself spiraling into a cosmic free-fall of intoxication. My head spins, and the air in the room seems thin. Sweat runs down my head and I'm dizzy. My body jerks. I try to pull out. I can't. I won't. She refuses to let me break free. Sugar walls clutch on to me, grasp me tight, hold me captive, seize the movements, paralyze the moment.

Slowing down with my thrusts and my strokes; I need to rest in all this deliciousness. Needing to love her, I want this to go on for hours. I need to be inside of Queen for as long as I can. Nothing else in my life makes sense anymore, aside from me loving her, making love to her and giving her all the love that she's deserved for so long.

Queen's warm body, her soft skin, her scent, her touch even, makes me feel like I've died and gone to Heaven, enjoying some sort of paradise. True love in its most deep and purest form; I've been missing out on this all of my life, but now its here, she's here, I've found what I didn't even know I was looking for, needing, longing, and at this moment, I've discovered the tenderness of sweet affection in my baby.

Her drenched core grabs a hold of me. We both cry out in unison as our bodies combine deeper, harder – passion overwhelms me. Feeling how drenched she is, I know it's going to be hard for me to hold on, but I can't let this go.

Sounds of Queen ascending to a higher place of emotional serenity forces me to question her. I need her, I love her.

"I told you I wasn't going anywhere. Didn't I?"

Queen moans and quivers as I move in and out of her. I pull all the way out and go back in, over and over and over again. The sensation her pussy leaves on my shaft is indescribable, it's so good. Like a hand in glove, I'm destined to be here, as my world fits perfectly into hers. Her drenched core has a hold of me, and I can't hold on any longer. She reaches heaven. With desperation, I whisper in her ear, "Tell me you love me, Queen."

"Yes," she replies as her head falls, she closes her eyes. Her mood shifts, I feel her sadness, it penetrates me, down into my soul. Slowly, I withdraw.

This spiritual magic has been absent from my life for so long. I can feel it. I know this is love, the real thing.

"Baby?" I question and she doesn't lift her head. Kissing her forehead repeatedly, I tell her, "I know, Baby."

I hug her.

Placing my hand on her chin, I lift her face into view. She slowly opens her eyes. I can see the tears formed but they don't fall. I kiss her forehead.

"Look into my eyes, you'll see happiness and all the lovely things you are to me, Baby. You mean everything to me, Queen."

Queen places her hands on both sides of my face, begins tracing my profile with her fingertips.

"You know sometimes I watch you when you sleep. I kiss your lips, and you smile. I wonder if you know that it's me kissing you."

"I know, Baby." I kiss her hand.

"I live in misery when you're not around, Quincy."

I place my hands on her face and gently kiss her lips.

"You just came into my life and I wasn't ready, Quincy. I'm scared."

"Baby, it's okay. I'm not going anywhere. Do you understand that?"

One tear escapes her, and I brush it away with my thumb.

"I can't breathe without you, Quincy."

"I love you too, Queen. I love you..."

More tears fall from her eyes, and I wipe them away as soon as they appear. A teardrop kisses her lips, and so do I. I kiss her tears, her forehead, her lips.

"I love you so much, Quincy. Please don't ever leave me. I can't live without you."

"I love you, Baby. I love you. I'm here. You're my baby?"

"I'm your Baby."

"You got to be good to me, Queen."

"I'm gonna be so good to you, Baby."

"You got to love me right, Queen."

"Baby, it's gonna be right. I promise. I'm gonna be good. So good to you. I made your favorite – peach cobbler."

"Good girl."

I bend over to pick up the red robe, and put it on. She smiles. I slide my feet into her warm, fuzzy, pink slippers and walk away.

"She's only a nurse at the hospital. That's who Carmella is, Queen. She's fifty years old and looks like Flo from the TV show, *Mel's Diner,* you know."

"Where are you going, Q? I want you…"

I turn around to look at her as I make my way to her bedroom.

"You want me? You come and get me."

QUEEN
Thirsty

My eyes hungrily follow his every move as he slowly walks away from me. Laced in my red silk robe and my fuzzy pink slippers, Quincy, makes me want to laugh out loud, instead, I simply smile. He turns around to look at me once more, blows a kiss and tells me, "Come on, Baby."

Sliding off the table, my feet land on the floor and I begin to walk toward my bedroom, I follow him, until he vanishes. I hear the sensual sounds of Maxwell, calling me, he along with Quincy, beg me as he sings, "were you embarrassed about the way you freaked," coming from my bedroom as Quincy sets the mood, he plays, *"Til the Cops come Knocking,"* one of my favorites.

He yells, "Baby…you want me?"

I smile as I walk. I'm naked in everyway imaginable, without clothes and without walls or barriers to my soul. Yet I've never felt so comfortable in my life. The closer I get to my bedroom, the more my heart flutters. Almost to the point of embarrassment, I chuckle out loud at my behavior. Quincy pulls out the best and worst in me, as I can't seem to recall a time when I've ever been a jealous woman. And here I was ready to give up my future with my king on the count of a fifty something hag.

"Yes, Baby, I want you," I answer his question.

"Come and get me!" Quincy yells back.

"I'm coming, Baby, I'm coming." I giggle to myself at how many times I have said that phrase since getting with Q.

Making a pit stop in the kitchen; I quietly remove ice cubes from the freezer and make my way into my bedroom. Standing at the bedroom door, I watch Quincy, as he lights candles all around. I smile.

He spots me as he makes his way back to the front of my bed. He sits down, still wearing my robe and slippers.

Quincy looks at me. He looks at me, the way only he looks at me. He's so fine. That delicious goatee he's growing in makes him the image of some hot Hollywood star. Now that I think about it, Quincy could pass for that actor, Eric Dane.

I remain in the doorway, with my arms folded behind my back. I smile. He's so sweet. Quincy returns my smile, reaches out his hand to me.

"Come to Daddy."

Slowly, I approach, until I reach my man, my lover, my king. He gazes lazily up to me and smiles. My eyes don't leave his. Mmm, those damn blue eyes. I never imagined that blue eyes on white skin would attract me—astound me—love me— really see me. They have that power over me—the power to make me weak in the knees. Blue eyes have turned me into a woman I don't recognize. Blue eyes turned me into that chick. I want to know her. I love her. White skin brought me back to life. Made me crazy. Quincy – delicious in appearance, perfect in design, territorial, flawed, like me, but mine, my man, my king, my lover – he's perfect in my eyes.

Standing in a Wonder Woman stance, I place my body directly in front of him; Quincy kisses my belly button, and inhales, breathes in my scent. "You know I love the way you smell."

"Thank you, Quincy."

He moves back, sits up straight and just stares. I joke with him.

"Are you gonna take my robe off, silly?"

He smiles.

"All I want to do is look at my naked wife. You are the most perfect Christmas gift, Queen. I'm so happy right now."

I can feel my emotions bubbling again inside of me. Just the thought of losing him, coupled with the fact that he's mine again makes me anxious, makes me happy, scared, and through it all, overflowing with joy.

"Just let me look at you. You're so beautiful, Baby. I need you for a lifetime." He kisses my navel, licks my abdomen, creeps down, and kisses the top of my righteousness.

"I don't think you realize how much I love you, Queen."

"I know, Baby."

Looking up at me, he confesses, "I love you. More than you'll ever know. Its scary being this vulnerable to you, but it's invigorating at the same time. I couldn't stop myself from loving you if I tried. I am a slave to your love. And, if there's a cure for this, I don't want it."

I smile and the waterworks resurface, but I refuse to let the tears fall.

I feel the ice melting in my hands; so I move closer to Quincy, order him to lie down. "Lay back, Baby," I seductively demand. He smiles and leans back on the bed.

Quincy covers his growing phallus so that I won't see what I already know – that's he's ready, been ready, to be inside of me once more.

"You want me, don't you?"

He smiles. "Yes."

Getting on my knees, I place my face close to his erection, and remove the robe with my teeth, brushing it aside with my face. The full view of his manhood is pleasing to me; I love the beauty of it and could look at his dick all day. Deliciously, it entices me, standing at full attention, firm, bold, erect, waiting for me and only me. Kissing the tip, I lick it; glide my tongue down the side.

"Is this my Christmas gift, Baby? Because I love it if it is," he whispers through the anticipation.

"No, Baby. I planned on doing this anyway, because you're my man and my man deserves this kind of attention, but this here, this is your real gift," I tell him as I put the ice cubes on his phallus.

He laughs out loud, as he begins to shiver. "Shit Baby, that's cold!"

"I know. It's meant to be." I love the sexual sadistic nature of our foreplay.

Alternating between him and the ice cubes, I suck with purpose. Love him like he deserves to be loved and make sure my technique is unforgettable.

"Baby, that's too cold!" he yells as he shivers more. He's so cute when he's like this. He smiles nervously, and laughs while I continue on with my mission.

"This is what you get for breaking my heart, Quincy." I say to him feeling a tad bit dominatrix in design.

"Baby, I promise not to ever hurt you again." He says in submission.

"Good! You better not. Next time I might not be this nice."

Standing up, I remove what's left from the ice cubes and toss them into the waste paper basket in my bedroom. Walking back to Quincy, he reaches out his hand for me and I approach taking his hand in mine. "I want my Christmas loving now, Baby."

"I want to give it to you." Teasingly I say the words as I run my fingers along his thighs.

"Come to me you lil racist. Ride me." He's almost begging and I'm loving every minute of it.

"Ask nicely, Q."

"Baby…please…please…baby, I can't wait any longer, please, Queen."

Straddling Quincy, he grabs my hips to position me.

"Put it in that sweet pussy, Quincy," I command, he looks up to me and smiles.

"I love it when you tell me what to do, Queen."

"I'm going to remind you that you said that down the line."

My perfectly manicured fingers look good as hell as they grab hold of him, helping to guide him into my pretty pink hole once more. I slide down onto him and the pleasure we've been seeking all night greets us once more. I can barely say a word and neither can he.

"Ooh, Quincy."

"Queen, ride me good, baby. It's your dick, baby, I promise, all yours."

"It better be all mine."

"It is, Baby, all yours – now, get Daddy's dick nice and wet like only you can."

I oblige and ride Daddy nice and slow allowing him a sensual visual of his sweet pipe in and out of my delight, over and over again. He grabs hold of my breasts and plays with my nipples with his tongue between soft bites, which bring my nipples to a hardness I have never experienced before. He holds on to my hips as he delves deeper and deeper into my love.

"Queen, I love you."

He strokes me deeper.

My head tilts back.

"Queen, I love you so much."

He goes harder, deeper.

My back arches, head falls back again.

"Queen, I love you, baby."

I release all over him, bringing my face back into view where the tears roll down my cheeks.

"You don't have to cry any more, Queen. I love you."
He kisses my face, my cheeks, wipes my tears away. I kiss his lips, his forehead, his nose.

"I love you so much, Quincy."

✌✌✌✌✌

"Oh my God, the peach cobbler!" I yell through blurred vision and morning breath. My heart races in a panic. As I attempt to get out of the bed, Quincy nuzzles his face into my neck, as he spoons me. His massive hold on me is both serene and comforting, and I can't break free. I urge him to let me check the cobbler, as I know it's burned and I pray the kitchen is not on fire. Its morning and I see the sun creeping up.

"Relax, Beautiful." Quincy whispers in my ear, and kisses my neck.

"Baby, did you take it out of the oven?" I ask as I stretch, barely able to move.

"Yes, Baby and it was good. I ate half the pan last night."

I smile. "Did you?"

"Yes, Baby. I'm greedy, Queen."

I laugh out loud. "I know you are. I love your greedy ass."

"You gotta stop loving me all night like this. I have to get back to the gym. You cook too good for me, Baby. I'm gonna get fat and lose this six pack that you love." He slaps his stomach.

I lay still and take in the moment. "What's up baby doll? You're happy this morning, right?"

I smile and lean in to Quincy's chest. He welcomes me with his embrace.

"Yes, baby, I'm happy. You know, you have changed me in a way I can't explain."

"Some things don't need explaining, sweetheart." He kisses me on my shoulder.

"Merry Christmas, Quincy."

"Merry Christmas, Queen."

Quincy rolls me onto my back and climbs on top of me, tickling me, kissing my neck, kissing my face. I laugh out loud, hard, as he's found my spot.

"Quincy, stop, I'm ticklish."

"I love your morning breath too." He laughs as he kisses my lips. He's a sinful combination of peach cobbler, cologne and early morning funk. His hair is wild, blue eyes bright, teeth, pearly white.

"Well, let me go take a shower, Quincy, ha, ha, ha, and stop tickling me like that!"

"Okay, Baby."

I make my way out of the bed, and my eyes instinctively search the room for my robe.

"Baby, where's my robe?"

"I ate it," he jokes. "Besides, who needs pesky clothes, we've got love. So do daddy a favor and let me watch you walk to the bathroom."

"You're so nasty."

"Yeah, and you love it, Queen."

"You're right, I do, Quincy."

Walking towards my master bathroom, Quincy throws the robe at me, and I turn around.

"You're so naked, Queen, with your jealous, spoiled self." He laughs out loud.

"I'm not spoiled, and I didn't know I had a jealous bone in my body, until my life was threatened." I wrap the robe around me, pulling the belt tight.

"What do you mean?" Quincy is genuinely confused and not following what I am trying to say.

"When I heard Carmella in your office, I wanted to die, Quincy. I was done, too through for the entire night. That hurt me."

"You could have just asked me, Queen. I'm not fucking this up Queen for anything or anybody. You're going to be my wife, whether you realize it or not."

"I would like that."

"Would you?"

"Absolutely." I blow him a kiss and walk faster.

"You know I love you, don't you?"

"Baby, it was only when I really looked into your eyes that I saw my Paradise, and every woman wants that. But then, I realized that you are my Savior in disguise, so it's not wrong for me to love you, because I do, I love the hell out of you, Q."

He smiles and I can't believe the words that just came out of my mouth.

Reaching the bathroom, I look in the mirror, and smile. I have a happiness set deep into my face, my body, my being – a happiness that only Quincy can bring. I brush my teeth and rinse my mouth and start the shower. Removing my robe, I drop it to the floor, and hop in. Pouring a handful of the Jasmine shower gel into my palm, I allow the hot water to aid in the lathering as I smooth the sweet smelling bubbles all over my body. Closing my eyes, I place my face under the water, and allow the beads to run down my face and body. I smile as I sense him near. My body tingles in anticipation of what he will do next, what he will say. I welcome the butterflies in my stomach.

"You know I want to fuck all the good sense out of you." Quincy tells me as he enters the shower. His manhood presses against my back and his hands rub up and down the sides of my body. I release all pretenses and lean my body further into his.

"Quincy, do you ever get enough?"

"No, Baby. Not of you."

My man speaks the words that set a fire in my heart. Damn I love this man.

He turns me around and kisses me as the water runs down my back. "You're so sweet, Quincy." I open my eyes, only to see he's wearing the platinum chain I bought him for Christmas.

"Baby, did you open your Christmas gifts?"

He smiles. "Not all of them, just this one."

I smack him on his arm. "Baby, you were supposed to wait! We were supposed to open our gifts together."

"I couldn't help myself. You were sleeping so soundly, resting so peacefully, after I put your ass to bed, ha, ha. Baby, I was in the peach cobbler, I saw the gifts, I just opened this one, that's all."

"Okay, Baby. Do you like it?"

"I love it. It's perfect…just like my Queen. Thank you, sweetheart."

In the background, I swear I hear something ding or ring, so I question Quincy. "Baby, did you hear that? Is that the phone?"

"I don't know. Want me to check?"

Wow, I hadn't thought about that until now. Quincy is my man, and sure, he can answer my phone. There's no shame in my game or any regrets about belonging to him, I don't care if the world knows that we belong to each other. Hell, maybe hearing a strong male voice answering my phone in the morning on Christmas will stop the prank phone calls. I have no problem with Quincy marking his territory.

"Yes, baby, get it please."

"Sure." I can hear in his voice that he knows, just like I do, that we have reached a milestone in our relationship. The significance of me allowing him to answer my phone is a sign of another hurdle that our love has conquered. We both know it, yet we pretend we don't.

Quincy steps out of the shower, and I smack his behind. Most white men lack cushion on their asses, but Quincy's is just right for me. Must be all those trips to the gym. He laughs on the way out and the playfulness of our moment makes me smile as well. Sinfully, I watch the way he wraps the towel around his waist. The beads of water hold on to his chest and back and he glistens. He looks back at me and smiles.

"You better go get the phone before I invite you back in this shower, boy. Looking all good. You look like a bacon-egg-and-cheese, baby."

He laughs as he walks out of the bathroom.

Moments later he returns. "Honey, are you coming out?"
"Yes, Quincy, right now, actually."

As I make my way out of the shower, Quincy hands me my terrycloth robe that hangs on the back of the bathroom door.

"Thank you, sweetie." I say as I take the robe from his hands. He's thoughtful in everything he does, even the little things. I like that.

Quincy dries my back softly and tenderly before helping me get into the robe, then he kisses my shoulder and hands me the phone. I take it, and before I speak, I tell Quincy, "I like my eggs scrambled with cheese, make sure they aren't runny."

"Girl you are something else, but I aim to please. Anything else for my baby?"

"Some hot peppermint tea, and you, later." I wink as he walks out of the bathroom.

"Merry Christmas," I say as I put the phone to my ear, clueless as to who is on the other end of the line.

"Hey girl. Merry Christmas." It's Paula. I smile.

"So, I see you two kissed and made up, huh?"

"Girl, did we ever! We made up over and over and over again. I can't tell you how many times God was called! Honey, he put my ass to bed, but you know what? I haven't slept so well in a very long time. I mean, I didn't wake up in the middle of the night, no crazy dreams about my Mother; it was just some really restful, peaceful sleep. And, as usual, you were right. The girl at the hospital is a non-issue. Q says she looks like Flo from the TV show Mel's Diner, girl, he is so stupid!"

"I'm so happy to hear that, and yes, your man has a sense of humor! Damn, remember, "kiss my grits?" Shit, girl, you got me dying laughing over here! Listen, sweetie, I love you and you're my girl, but I'm not interrupting the flow today for you. I've had you for a lifetime, and if Quincy makes you as happy as I think he does, then he can have you for today. I'll come by tomorrow. We can do our thing anytime. Make today about you and your man."

"Are you sure, Paula? It's not a problem. But I have to warn you, he ate half the peach cobbler I made, so I'll have to make more."

"Damn, he eats like that? Are you sure he's white? Tearing up Peach Cobbler is a black man's trademark, not a white one."

"Girl, yes, he eats like that in more ways than one."

"Ooooh, Queen!"

"Yes, Paula. I'm gonna be happy, fat and pregnant, messing around with this man."

"Ain't nothing wrong with that, go for what you know girlfriend."

We both laugh. "Okay, my friend, Merry Christmas again. I'll shoot by tomorrow. Tell Quincy I said, Wassup!"

"Bye, crazy girl."

Turning on the blow dryer, I dry the back of my hair, and fluff it into a make shift style just for the morning. It's funny how exhilarating it is to have a good man in your home, loving you, pampering you, and laying pipe that makes your toes curl. As I try and put much effort into making my appearance look effortless, I tickle myself at my need to please him. Wow, that has to be an element of love; the need to care about what another person thinks about the things done behind closed doors has to be a sign of love. I'd do *anything* for him. That scares me, yet I welcome it. It's time. It's my destiny. And deep in my heart I know he would do the same for me. As I make my way out of the bathroom, I smell peppermint tea, the fireplace, and eggs cooking and I nod in recognition that he would. He's doing it now, putting a lot of effort into making me think that his actions are effortless. That's love. That's what he gives me, and he gives it unconditionally. As I near the kitchen I see that Quincy has managed to put on some smooth jazz, Joe Thomas, for the morning's theme music.

I approach the kitchen and living areas, smiling to myself, thinking how I could get used to this routine of waking to Quincy's presence around me, in me, pampering me. He knows how to treat a woman and I whisper a prayer to my heavenly father to pinch me and show me that what I feel is real. Why he's not married, or have some insane groupies chasing him? I'll never understand. But, hey, he's mine now, and while I never thought I'd need a man in my life to complete me, Quincy does, he completes me. As I get closer to the kitchen, I hear Quincy talking. Who the hell is he talking to? A neighbor? Oh shit. Wait a minute. It dawns on me.

It's Christmas morning. He could only be talking to one person. The person that I spend each and every Christmas morning with. Oh fuck...how could I forget? Christmas mornings are spent with Daddy.

Daddy! Oh my God, is Quincy talking to Daddy? My Daddy and Quincy are talking? Shit...this can't be happening. I'm not prepared for this. I haven't prepared either for this moment. Daddy...Quincy...hell, I didn't tell him, hadn't had the heart or the courage to do so...Daddy...Quincy...he's white...Daddy...he's black...didn't tell Daddy...what will Daddy think? I love Daddy, but can't I have Quincy as well. Shit....I should have laid some groundwork; will Daddy hate me for crossing that racial boundary? Shit...this can't be happening...But I love Quincy, love the hell out of Quincy, love me some Quincy, but...Daddy...Daddy...me...his baby girl...with a white man...Daddy...Daddy...gotta explain...stand my ground...Lord, come by here, I need you.

Quickening my step, I secure the belt on my terry cloth robe and walk into the living room. Daddy's smile is bright and wide. Not what I am expecting. He looks at me. Stares his baby girl in the eyes and somehow lets me know everything is okay. He seems extremely comfortable in Quincy's presence as Quincy hands him a cup. He's sitting on the sofa, in front of the fireplace and the two talk as if they have known each other for years. I watch them, confused, yet appreciative.

"Hi, Daddy," I say nervously as I approach.

"Hey baby girl. Merry Christmas," he stands, hugs me and kisses me on the cheek as if the moment at hand was not as confrontational as I am expecting it to be.

I can't stop fiddling with my thumbs, I'm so nervous right now, I'm close to getting sick. Quincy senses it and walks over to me, grabbing me by my waist, and kissing my cheek. On instinct, my man senses my apprehension and begins to take charge to make everything right in my world. He does not say a word, only offers the comfort of being by my side at a moment he knows is confusing and hard for me. He keeps his arms tightly around me, knowing I need to feel him for comfort. Damn I love this man.

"Sweetheart, it's a small world," Daddy reveals as he stands, looking extremely proud.

"Uhm, Daddy, this is Quincy. Dr. Quincy Hughes as a matter of fact. Uhm, Daddy, well, I'm just gonna be honest and put it all out on the line. I love him, Daddy, and I hope you can accept that. He makes me happy, he loves me, and I love him with all my heart."

Daddy smiles and walks closer to me. Quincy lets go of my waist so that I am free for the other man in my life, my father, to hug me tight.

"Queen, I know who this man is. I'll never forget his face as long as I'm walking this earth. I'm surprised you don't remember?"

"Remember, what, Daddy?" I'm clueless.

"Queen, this is the doctor who saved your life when you were in that terrible car accident with the young lady who died."

What? Quincy…no…Oh my God…It can't be true. Quincy was the one who saved my life? I'm shocked beyond words or emotions…tears form in my eyes. I can't see, can't think, can't breathe, need to sit down, I sit on the sofa, stumble in my movements, Quincy sits next to me, rubs my back.

"Baby, I didn't even remember myself, until I saw your father. I don't remember you, the night, or anything else about it. You've seen me at work. I see so much at the hospital. Too much quite frankly. There's so much death, despair, accidents, it all becomes a blur after awhile and I function on instinct to save lives, I rarely visualize a face since my goal is to make sure they live. I'm always in the ER, you know that, but I never put two and two together that I treated you at one time. But I remember it now. You were so badly bruised that night. You didn't look anything like you look now…your face alone was so…" He's grasping at the right words to make me understand even though it's clear he does not understand it all himself. As I listen to him, my mind tries to accept the reality that but for Quincy, I might not be alive now. Finally, he stops trying to speak and touches my face, running his fingers along the outline, while tears pour from my eyes, down my cheeks. I'm having trouble breathing again.

"Baby, your face was so bruised. I didn't even know your name."

A deep, heavy sob escapes me, as I cry profusely. My Dad comes over to console me.

"I'll never forget this man Queen. He saved my baby's life. Love him if you feel it's right, just know it's okay with me."

Through the tears, I tell him, "I do love him Daddy, and I don't care what anyone thinks about it," my sassiness returns with a vengeance even through the life-altering revelation.

"You shouldn't care. You're happy; right?"

"Yes, Daddy. I am."

"Then, I'm happy," he says as tears well up in his eyes. I kiss Daddy's forehead.

Quincy returns with a cup of tea. "Baby, a splash of milk and honey, just like you like it."

"Thank you."

Quincy returns to the seat next to me, and kisses my cheek. "I told you we were meant to be."

"I believe you," I laugh out loud, as I wipe my tears.

Quincy walks toward the front door. "Quincy, are you leaving?" I ask as panic settles into my heart.

"No, Baby, but since you're Dad is here, I have something I need to ask him." He leans down and whispers something in my father's ear. Daddy's face begins to glow and he nods his head up and down without saying any words. The reaction of my father pleases Quincy and he smiles then reaches into his jacket pocket and comes over to me with a red box in hand. He takes me by the hand, and raises me to my feet. Looking at my Dad, he faces him man to man.

"Mr. Thomas. I love your daughter, like I've never loved anyone in my life. I can't breathe when she's not around. I refuse to live without her. I need her like I need the air I breathe."

Daddy smiles. "Tell me how you really feel, son."

I laugh out loud.

As Quincy gets down on one knee, I begin to shake and tremble and have trouble standing. The tears come once again and I don't even bother stopping them. He looks up to me and smiles.

"Baby, when we first met, when I first looked at you, I knew you were the one for me. I fell in love with you as soon as our eyes connected. You told me that day, you said, "thirst of any kind is an awkward need," but yet, I'm thirsty. Thirsty for your love, your touch, you – Queen, I need you so desperately." He grabs my leg and hugs it. "Queen, I need you. I love you and I can't live without you. Baby, please, for a lifetime?"

He opens the box and pulls out a princess cut diamond ring and slides it onto my ring finger. He laughs out loud, "I'm so happy it fits."

Looking up to me once more, he smiles. "Baby, nothing else matters in my life but you. The meaning of love is so clear to me when you're wrapped in my arms. Queen, please, will you marry me?"

"Quincy."

"Queen, be my wife. Do you love me?"

"You're like winter turning to spring, Quincy," I manage to get those words out through the tears.

"Baby, your eggs are burning. Will you marry me?"

"Yes, Quincy, I will be your wife."

As he rises to his feet, he grabs me by my waist, and pulls me into a sensational kiss. "Thank you, Baby."

My hand runs alongside his cheek. "I love you, Quincy."

Moving swiftly from me, Quincy shakes Daddy's hand and heads to the kitchen.

Yelling from the kitchen, Quincy says, "Mr. Thomas, come have Christmas breakfast with us. Queen already told me how she likes her eggs. I made some potatoes, and some bacon too. Come on," he says as he sets the table.

Daddy walks over and jokes. "Son, you better get her eggs right. I remember when she was a little girl, I had to get her scrambled eggs with cheese right, or she'd sit there and pout. Made me late many days for work and made her late for school if her ponytails weren't lined up perfectly."

We all laugh in unison.

"See Queen, I told you that you were spoiled rotten, you know how to work your men."

"That she does." Daddy says patting Quincy on the shoulder. My heart is full of love seeing the two men I love comfortable with each other.

As we sit at the table, we all talk and reminisce and Quincy and I plan our life together, with Quincy taking the wheel. "Queen, if your Dad doesn't mind, I'd like to take you to Jersey today. Big and I always visit his family on Christmas. It will just be a few hours, I want to show you off on my old stompin' grounds."

Dad jumps in. "Sure, you all have a good time. I haven't been down to Jersey in a good while. What part, son?"

"Newark and Jersey City. My best friend Pat—Big is what we call him, grew up in Newark and I grew up in Jersey City. So we go back home every Christmas to spread some cheer."

"Queen and I lived in Newark for some time before heading up to the mountains. Her mother would be so proud knowing Queen is going to marry a man from that area. Bella always loved that area. Today, she would be proud; she would love this day if she were here to experience it. Bella and I used to talk about this day and what it would mean to us as parents. Too bad she is not around to be a part of it." His face is somber and supportive all at the same time. I knew he was missing momma. I could feel it in the way he said her name.

"Your wife was a beautiful woman, Mr. Thomas, just like Queen."

"Yes, Queen looks just like Bella. Sometimes the resemblance is too much for me to handle. Bella was beautiful and so is "our" Queen. Like mother, like daughter, beautiful inside and out. "

I look over to Quincy, and he seems to be lost in heavy thinking mode. The wheels are turning in his head and I don't think I have ever seen him so focused on a conversation before. His hands are on his chin, deep concentration and analyzation of Daddy's words. He seems to hang on each syllable as if he were being told the secrets of creation. I stare at my man, and I wonder what's on his mind.

QUINCY
The Circle of Life

The satisfaction in her face delights me. It's a thrill I have never experienced before, yet I hope to never be without again. I could live a lifetime rewinding the moment of where I am right now. Saving lives at the hospital gives me a sense of gratification each time I see the tears of joy in the eyes of a parent whose child's life I just saved. I always thought that feeling was enough for me. It was; that is until today. But now, even that feeling fails in comparison to being in love and seeing the sunshine through her eyes. I now know how much of life I was missing; how much substance my life lacked before now, before her. Life was fulfilling before Queen; now it is complete, I'm truly satisfied. The joy in Queen's eyes when her father accepted me as her future husband, coupled with the warmth and comfortableness of the time the three of us spent together, fills me with a sense of completeness, a sense of closure of finally being whole. Well, almost. My work in solidifying this relationship is not totally done, not yet. I now have a clue to complete the circle of both Queen's life and my own. There's one detail I have to unravel. One more thing I can give to my baby as a Christmas present and a token of my love and commitment to her. One more sign of my undying love. I gotta bring it to fruition, and if I can…the world is my oyster and Queen is the pearl inside.

As my baby gets dressed, I make a few phone calls, making sure everything is in place. It all has to be exactly right. It all has to gel. If it does, Queen and I will both have our happily ever after. I seek that ending. I need it, and so does she. My baby deserves it, and I want to deliver it to her on a silver platter. Pursuing it is my goal, fulfilling it, my destiny. Queen has agreed to give me the best present a woman can give to a man; the promise of spending her life with him, giving him a piece of her soul, at the very least I can give her back a bit of her past. As I hang up the phone, I feel a sense of completeness and accomplishment as I confirm my suspicions. I look at the gifts Queen has given me today and get a lump in my throat. She spent a pretty penny on me and each gift is a sign of her love.

"Thank you God. This is what love is all about." How did I go through life this long without this feeling? How did I exist without truly receiving unconditional love? As I stare at her tokens of love, I recognize I will never be as good as she is, but all I can do is try.

She dresses for our day, aware that her appearance matters. She matters. Without my suggestions or assistance, she emerges in a manner as only she can. Magnificent, fabulous and enchanting; exactly what I would have chosen for her on a day as special as today. One word describes her and that word is perfection. She looks fabulous, flawless, fantastic. She always does. That's my baby and as I take in the beautiful vision that she is, I know exactly why she's my choice to share my last name. I am undeserving of having her as my own, but thankful and grateful that she is mine. God has blessed me with Queen, and as she tosses her head and flips her hair to one side to add the finishing touch of the earrings I bought her, I point upwards towards the sky and give God props for the unique and precious gift He has given me. I am eternally grateful.

My eyes look at my own clothes that are laid out on the bed and I smile. I watch her as she carefully irons my clothes, matching my pants with an appropriate sweater, even down to the socks and boxer briefs. I remember just moments ago, as I headed out of the shower, I simply watched her iron and handle my clothes with meticulous care. We are not officially a union, but even our choice in clothes matches, all due to her creativity. She has on a winter white ensembles with chocolate accents. Eloquent in design. She smells of class with a hint of city sass that screams character of a woman who knows who she is and isn't afraid to show it. I love the contrast of the white color against her skin and the scarf she has draped around her shoulders is the perfect added touch. It is unusual, brown with gold accents, very regal, very Queen.

"Beautiful scarf honey, I've never seen you wear that before."

"I haven't, worn it until now. I've never removed it from my hope chest. But as my hopes and dreams begin to come true, I wanted to put it to use. It's one of the few things that belonged to my mother that I still have. It's very special to me. It's only fitting that I wear it since she could not be here to give my hand to you in marriage, wearing this is my way of showing her approval for me to give myself to you. I am wearing this today Q, to show you that all of me; including my genes; accepts, welcomes and loves you Quincy. My mother can't be here to say those words, but through her possessions, through one of the tokens of love of hers that I have, I wanted to show you that even she welcomes you into my life."

How is she able to do that? Just when I think there is nothing more she can do to capture my heart, Queen does little things like this to make me fall in love with her all over again.

Walking over to her, I witness her smile as I put on my winter white Sean Jean, Jacquard sweater which accentuates my chest and arms quite nicely. Thank God for all the weight work at the gym. I add my brown, Hamilton embroidered jeans with matching leather jacket for an overall "polished without trying" look. She bought me all of this and more for Christmas. I didn't have to go home to change clothes, to brush my teeth, to get dressed, as my baby has everything here for me. She treats me like a king. When Queen puts on the jacket I bought her, it's on. Everything falls into play. We both look like we are on our way to a photo shoot for *Vibe* magazine.

My eyes follow her every move as we walk towards the front door. Through her signature move, she looks back at me through that soft brown hair. I think Queen knows that gets to me; that she has a way of seductively crawling under my skin. "Put the alarm on, baby," she commands and I follow instructions, just like a husband would. I am, willingly, a slave to her rhythm.

My right hand embraces her left one as we walk down the stairs. Her diamond glimmers in the early afternoon sun. "Do you know I've gained ten pounds since I've been with you, Queen?"

She smiles. She's so soft and gingerly today, like the weight of the world has been removed from her somehow. "Really? I think I've gained five, Q. My dad told me that when he and my mom first courted that they both gained weight. He said it was happiness settling in."

I receive her words as confirmation as such; happiness.

"I usually go to Quinton's grave on Christmas, usually around the end of the day. Do you mind?"

"No, sweetheart. I want to be a part of every aspect of your life. I want to be there for everything that you do, for all of who you are, Quincy." She pecks me on the lips as I close the passenger door to my ride.

I swiftly move to the driver's side. "What do you feel like listening to today, baby?"

"Got some Marvin Gaye?"

"Sure, sweetie." I take her hand and kiss the back of it.

I put on Marvin Gaye's greatest hits. She looks over to me.

"What is it baby?"

"I don't know, Q. You mentioning Quinton's grave makes me yearn to go to my mom's, but dad never wants to go. He never even told me where she's buried. So I talk to her, almost daily, and see her in my dreams. That's my way of communicating with her. Do you know, since you've been in my life, I can actually sleep? I mean, good sleep, no crazy dreams sleep, so once again, thank you."

"Oh, baby, I didn't know. I'm glad you're now resting. No need to thank me, that's what I am here for."

While in the truck, I hold her hand on the way to my parent's house. The engagement ring sparkles between our intertwined fingers. "Not a bad choice of rocks." I say to myself admiring the Princess cut diamond.

"Q, do you think your parents will like me?" Queen's words break my concentration.

"They'll love you; who wouldn't?"

"I'm serious Q, what will they think about the differences in our race? Will it bother them that you're marrying a black woman?" I can see worry in her face. She's being vulnerable again and I find it endearing.

"Some of the women I've dated in the past were black Queen, my best friend is black. My parents know I'm partial to dark meat." I laugh and raise her hand to my lips, kissing the back of her hand.

"Oh, so I'm just another piece of meat huh Quincy?" She gives me a snide look in a flirtatious way.

"Yeah, and a tasty piece of meat at that." I wink and lick my lips while Queen gives me a slight push on the shoulder.

"They're going to love you Queen."

"You promise Quincy?"

"I promise with all my heart."

❧❧❧❧❧

As I get ready to push the doorbell, Queen stops me.

"How do I look?"

"You look beautiful as always." I reach for the bell once more. She stops me again.

"Wait a minute." She closes her eyes and inhales deeply.

"Queen, don't be nervous just be yourself and they will love you just as much as I do." I push the bell before she can stop me again. My father answers and gives me a big bear hug.

"It's about time you made it home. How are you doing, son? Merry Christmas."

"I'm fine dad; I brought a little gift with me." Mom walks up before I can say anything else.

"Hello Quincy, it's good to see you. Merry Christmas. Who's this lovely lady?"

"I was just telling dad that this lovely lady is my gift. Mom, Dad, this is Queen…my fiancée."

"Fiancée'? Well, aren't you full of surprises today son?" Dad's tongue hangs out of his mouth as he sizes up Queen. "My boy! My boy!" He says in approval.

Queen stares at my parents like a frightened child and my mother is speechless for a few seconds.

"Well, you sure picked a pretty one to marry Quincy; didn't you? How about both of you come on in out the cold?" My mother grabs Queen by the hand and walks her into the living room and as the girl chat begins between them, I smile seeing the nervousness leave Queen's face. Mom seems to like her from the start. She asks question after question getting to know Queen. She makes her sit near her and is impressed with her background. I can see that Queen is at ease and I love seeing the two most important women in my life enjoying each other's company.

After about an hour of small talk, coffee cake and gift exchanging, I interrupt. "Mom, we have to go. We just stopped by on the way to pick up Big. We're going to Jersey, but Queen and I will be back before New Years Eve."

"Quincy thanks for stopping by and thanks for the gift of meeting my future daughter in law. You had me scared for a while. I was wondering if you were ever going to settle down and make me a grandmother."

Queen's eyes widen at the mention of children.

"I was waiting for the right one." I say as I help Queen put on her coat.

"And is this the right one Quincy?" Mom looks me directly in the eye with a stare only a mother can give.

"She is mom, she definitely is." I reassure her with a kiss on her cheek.

My mother places hands on both of Queen's arms.

"If my boy says you're the right one. Then you are. Welcome to the family." She hugs Queen and then hugs me before waving us out the door. "Now you two be safe and tell Patrick he owes me a visit."

"Will do. Love you mom."

"Love you too Quincy."

As we walk down the sidewalk to my truck, Queen exhales and grabs my arm putting her head on my shoulder and snuggling in close.

"Your mother is really nice; I think I am going to like being part of your family."

"OUR family Queen. Ours!"

"I stand corrected. "Ours!"

"I'm glad to hear you say that because this is only the beginning Mrs. Hughes. I can't wait for you to finally really meet Big and my adopted family in Jersey."

"You're just going to show me off all day like some trophy?" She laughingly asks as she snuggles even closer to me.

"That's the plan honey. I want the world to meet my future wife. Once they get to know you, I know they will love you as much as I do." I kiss her and help her into the truck.

We ride to Big's, the next stop before Jersey. Queen has seen Big in the club, but they've never actually met. Big is my boy, an extension of who I am. I want Queen to like and accept him. I need her to. He's my blood; she's my future. I pray those two worlds can coincide.

Big throws a bag in the door before getting into the back of my truck. He looks at the back seat as if he's never seen it before. He's use to being in the front passenger seat, but he knows Queen now owns that seat.

"So you are the one that has my boy's nose wide open." He says to Queen.

"What's wrong Big? Feeling threatened? Are you a believer in bros before hoes? Is that your philosophy?" Queen laughs as she takes a sip of bottled water. She brings it to Big and all three of us smile at the game being played between the two of them. My role is chauffer…I let the players play.

"My boy has some real feelings for you, so it's all good in my book." Big says as he moves things around getting comfortable in the back seat.

"I have no problem sharing my man with you Patrick, just make sure he's home by curfew and he's all yours."

"Awh, snap Q; you got a curfew dog?"

"Shit man, look at her. If you were *forced* to come home to that, wouldn't you willingly accept the command?" As I say the words, Queen strikes poses in her seat.

"Hell, yeah man. I ain't going to lie and I ain't mad at ya! And, if you get in trouble, at least you know you have Miss Johnny Cochran on your side." Big gives me dap and settles back in his seat.

"Treat my boy right Queen, that's all I ask."

"I plan on whipping it on him something fierce Big. You know what they say, 'Once you go black, you never go back.' I plan to make Quincy the poster child for that." Queen winks at Big. They connect. I smile.

I raise Queen's hand, and show Big the ring. "No your white ass didn't get engaged?" Queen and I laugh out loud.

"Yes, we did, Big, and before you demand it, yes, you are my best man."

"Oh, I wasn't hardly worried, not hardly. Ain't gon' be no wedding, if I ain't standing by your side man."

We laugh again.

"Congratulations. I'm happy for both of you," Big tells us.

Queen reminds us that she hasn't been to Jersey in years, so Big points out spots of interest as we drive through the city. The cold weather doesn't detour the street vermin and some are hanging out on the steps of Auntie's home as if they are just chilling on a summer's day. They are dressed warmer and huddle near the front door without missing a beat in their regular activities. As we pull up and get out of the truck I notice a couple of the hood rats eyeballing Queen and one makes a comment about her coat. I pull her closer to me in protect mode and Big loudly announces, "It sure would be tragic to have to kick some ass on Christmas Day." Big has my back by dishing out menacing stares and brushing shoulders as we make our way up the stairs.

"Hey fat boy!" The crackhead with the micro-braids yells at Big. He ignores her.

"Hey fat boy! Where's your Christmas Santa suit? Your fat ass needs to have kids sitting on your lap today!" All the crackheads start laughing out loud.

"What's the matter? You can find nothin' to smoke today you lil crack pipes?" Big adds and laughs.

"Fuck you fat boy!"

We can hear the familiar sound of piano playing before we even get to the door. Auntie's place has always been the spot for Christmas Day. Even Big's cracked-out cousins seem to pull it together for the holiday. The aura of family love soars throughout the place on wings of music being played on the piano by Big's uncle, Pretty Ricky. Ain't a damn thing about Uncle Ricky that's pretty, but he seems to think so. Auntie meets us at the door and she gives Big and me a hug. After our embrace I smile at Auntie. The smell of candied yams greets us as we move further into Auntie's apartment. Christmas lights all around set the décor.

"Is this her?" Auntie says putting her arms around Queen.

"Yes, this is her." I stand still for a moment, watching Auntie examine Queen before I continue, "This is my wife to be, this is my Queen."

Auntie hugs Queen very tightly with an embrace that lingers a little too long for Queen's comfort level. I can see it in her face. She's confused and seeing the tears rolling down Auntie's face confuses Queen even more.

"Quincy, I love you like a son, are you sure she's the one?"

"Auntie, she's my morning, my noon, my night; my life. I'm sure."

Auntie runs her hands down the side of Queen's face. "You're more beautiful than I imagined. Your name fits you and you look just like your mother."

Queen's face begins to tighten and I feel the need to step in, I look at Auntie, "Which room?" I ask her.

Big steps into the kitchen, gives me a thumbs-up. Everyone is on edge behind my revelation, but they don't show it. Pieces of a puzzle coming to fruition has butterflies in my stomach.

"The one on the left." Auntie loosens her grip on Queen and I take her by the hand.

"Q, what is going on here? That woman seems a little off. Why does she act like she knows me when I haven't seen her a day before in my life?" Queen stares at me as I begin walking her away from Auntie.

"It will all make sense in a few minutes Queen."

"Where are we going?" I can tell Queen's patience is fleeting.

"To the bedroom." I try to give as little details as possible.

"The bedroom? What's up with that Q? I know you don't think we are getting busy here at this Christmas party. You're so nasty baby." She chuckles and I smile as we make it to the closed door.

"Queen, I have one last Christmas present for you."

"You do? Damn, I thought you had spoiled me enough. What is it? Where is it?"

"It's in there Queen." I turn the knob and open the door motioning for her to walk in while I stand at the threshold. "I love you Queen." I whisper and nudge her forward gently.

"I don't know what this is all about Quincy, but I'll play along. And for the record, I love you too." She says as she walks in the room.

My baby's scent mixes with her's. The smell of Jasmine becomes stronger and fills the room. Ms. Belle walks toward Queen. Ageless beauty meets infinite splendor.

"I'm sorry to interrupt you ma'am, my fiancée' is playing some sort of joke on me." Queen turns and begins to walk toward me but stops in her tracks as she hears Belle begin to sing:

"Whisper something sweet to me.
Whisper something sweet to me.
Mama loves her baby.
Mama loves her baby.
From the sunshine to the night.
From the darkness to the light.
Queen loves her mommy.
And Mama loves her baby.
Whisper something sweet to me."

A tear rolls down Queen's face as she looks at me and she places her hand over her mouth. She's confused and she looks at me and shakes her head "No."

I can't move. This moment is hers; I have to let her have it without me, so all I do is shake my head "Yes."

Queen stops in her tracks, she doesn't move, she just stares at me, continuously shaking her head, "No."

I mouth the words "Yes" to her as I nod my head up and down.

She walks toward me, reaching her hands out, she needs me, wants me to save her from this emotional reality. I have to let her stand on her own. I love her too much to do anything else.

Queen turns and faces Belle.

"How do you know that song?"

"Because I used to sing it to you every night." Belle rubs her hand across Queen's head allowing my baby's silky hair to run through her fingertips. "My scarf looks better on you then it ever did on me."

Queen's legs buckle and she sits down on the bed. Belle sits down next to her as Queen's sobs become louder and she rocks back and forth hugging herself in disbelief. Belle's wrinkled hands cup Queen's face and she wipes her tears with her fingertips. Then she hugs Queen, placing her lips next to Queen's ear and begins singing again.

"Whisper something sweet to me.
Whisper something sweet to me.
Mama loves her baby.

Mama loves her baby.
From the sunshine to the night.
From the darkness to the light.
Queen loves her mommy.
And Mama loves her baby.
Whisper something sweet to me."

Almost instinctively and through her tears, I hear Queen whisper in a childlike voice, completion of the song,

"I love you mommy."

They wrap their arms around each other and the room suddenly seems brighter as if an indoor cloud has been lifted. The lump in my throat grows and I fight tears of my own as Auntie comes and places her arms around my waist giving me a hug.

"You did good Q. You did real good. God sure knows what He is doing. You found her and didn't even know it. Belle always talked about wishing she had the courage to reach out to her daughter. We've talked about it for years. Thank you for putting it all together and making this happen."

"When I suspected something, I kept ignoring my suspicions but I could no longer ignore it. I love her, how could I not give her this moment?"

I watch the mirror images, one polished with time over the other, spitting images, beautifully exquisite, wonderfully unique; they stare at each other without words. Each strokes the other's hair and face as if they both want the moment to be engulfed by all their senses including the one of touch. The first words come from Queen, "After all these years, you smell just like I remembered."

"Jasmine. My favorite." Belle smiles through the water works captivating her face.

"It's my favorite too. In tribute to you." As the words slip pass her lips, Queen's face changes.

"Where have you been? Why did you leave me? I thought you were dead! How could you let me go through that?" There's anger in Queen's words, in her face. Queen stands and breaks the physical bond she has with Belle.

Belle stands and grabs Queen, holding her tightly with everything in her soul screaming not to let go.

"You'll never understand Queen. I don't quite understand it myself. But I had to disappear. It was the right thing to do for you and your father."

"Don't you mean it was the right thing to do for you? What about dad? He was so sick without you!"

"No. This was never about me Queen. I have schizophrenia. Back then, I did not know what it was, all I knew was something was taking over my mind. I was afraid I would hurt you, hurt your father. I heard voices, I would lose time. Slowly but surely, I was neglecting you I was having a hard time distinguishing reality from fantasy. I loved you both too much to make you go through the monster I was becoming."

Queen listens. I can tell she's receiving the closure she needs. She lets her mother continue.

"One day the thoughts were too much. I did not recognize myself, fearing for you and your father's safety, I just ran. I left the city, just fled, I ended up at all strange places from shelters to clinics. I came back here and friends got me medical help, but that was after years of searching and trying to stay alive. It was a long journey to becoming sane, but over the years I finally learned to deal with my illness and recognize it for what it was. By that time, I knew I had hurt you and your father too much to just waltz back into your lives. You were better off without me."

"I needed you. How could you think I was better off?" Queen's words sting, but they are less harsh.

"Because you were better off." Belle grabs Queen's hand and walks her over to the bed. She reaches under a pillow and pulls out a hatbox. "Here's my proof that I made the right decision." She hands the box to Queen.

"I never stopped loving you. I've been watching you grow from a far for years."

Queen opens the box and slowly flips through its contents. Her whole life lies in the confines of the four small walls of the box. Graduation announcements, Awards from college, newspaper clippings of her most prominent cases. Queen picks the articles up and hold them to her chest. Even from the door I can see her exhale feeling her mother's love. The love that my baby has been yearning for all of her life was there, she just didn't know it.

Belle looks at me as she begins to hug Queen again.

"I never stopped loving you, I was just afraid talk to you after all these years. But Quincy gave me the courage to make a comeback in your life."

Queen finally looks at me, and her eyes say what her mouth is unprepared to say.

"I know baby." I say as I blow her a kiss.

A tear escapes my right eye and I quickly wipe it away.

My Queen looks at her mother. "How do you know my Quincy?"

I look at my Queen and smile. She's something special.

Ms. Belle smiles, and kisses her daughter's forehead. Queen leans in to the kiss, her mom's embrace and takes in the moment, the meaning of this moment. She inhales the comforts of her mother's touch.

"Queen, I watched your Quincy grow up. You've got a winner, he's definitely a keeper, Queen. That's my lil Quincy. I remember when he was just a teenager."

I smile at Ms. Belle's words. "While every teenage boy was in love with Farrah Fawcett, I was in love with Ms. Belle!"

We all laugh.

"I'm sorry I left you Queen, but I had to, it was the best thing for you. Please forgive me, I never stopped loving you. You're my baby girl and I've always loved my angel."

Queen stares her mother in the eyes for what seems like an eternity, then she leans in to Belle's ear and barely audible through her tears says, "Like you did so many years ago, whisper something sweet to me."

Queen lays in her mother's lap, places her head on her thighs. Ms. Belle rubs the side of her face and runs her fingers through her hair.

Glancing to my left, I see Big crying. He looks at me. "Man, this is a Christmas sent straight from God. But, I'm too sexy to be standing here crying. Let's eat."

Big, Auntie and I make our way out of the bedroom.

Ms. Belle rocks side to side as she rubs Queen's back, her face, she begins to sing again:

"Whisper something sweet to me.
Whisper something sweet to me.
Mama loves her baby.
Mama loves her baby.

Elissa Gabrielle

From the sunshine to the night.
From the darkness to the light.
Queen loves her mommy.
And Mama loves her baby."

QUEEN
The Queen of My Heart

Be careful what you ask for because you just might get it. My childhood was riddled with anticipation of wanting my mother to share my life and needing to see her again. Quincy. Wow…Quincy. I stare at my future husband, my soul mate, grabbing his hand; I think how wonderful this man is that he has made it all come to pass. Who would ever have thought that some white boy from Jersey would find a way to bring this black girl's life full circle? Definitely not me.

I stare at my man, and he looks at me every so often and smiles. I'm still in disbelief really; in love with a white man? Yet, this white man, is colorless to me at this point. He is simply my man. Had it not been for my man, my life would have been filled only with legal triumphs, but no true sustenance; no one to run home to, no one to cook for, to pamper and certainly, if it had not been for my heaven sent angel, I would not know the meaning of true love, would not be able to fathom that someone could love a person with every fiber of their being, nor would I have ever been reunited with my mom.

When I look at Quincy, my heart melts. He's so good to me, and he deserves a standing ovation, not only for his care of me, his love for me, but also for the way he holds me down. He is unafraid of my success, it doesn't even faze him. He is successful in his own right and is strong enough to let me have my shine. I get hot and bothered when I look at him too long. A champ in the bedroom; I swear, I'll fuck a bitch up if they tried to step to my baby. That is so not like me, but Quincy has managed to introduce me to things about myself I never knew before. I'm anxious getting to know who I really am.

Soon as I'm done spending much needed quality time with my beautiful mother, it's on. I have to thank my man for all that he's done for me, for all that he means to me, for making my life complete. I plan on thanking the hell out of him tonight. I hope he's ready.

Big met up with some hood rat from Jersey from back in the day, so he decided to stay down there for some old school Christmas ass. That man is funny as hell and I see why Quincy and Big are best friends. They fit perfectly into each other's world, no matter how it looks from afar.

I stare at mom as she sits in the back seat of Quincy's truck quietly observing the scenery, lost in her emotions and thoughts. What's she thinking? Is she feeling what I'm feeling? As our eyes connect, I recreate all the moments we lost over the years. When I look at her, I see a reflection of me. From the lips to the flowing hair to the honey skin; there's no denying it, this woman, Mrs. Anna Bella Thomas, is my mom.

Big had us rolling on the floor when he put the pieces of the puzzle together in his own mind. I remember him from just a short time ago. He said, "Miss Anna is Ms. Belle to us, and Mrs. Belle sometimes, but who's Bella?" Quincy jumped in with his silly self. "Man, Bella is what Queen's father calls Ms. Belle, dummy." Big threw his hands up. "How is anybody supposed to figure this out!" We all laughed and it was a good laugh, even at my mom's expense.

My mind is in rewind mode and replacing every significant moment that my mother missed with a mental insertion of her being there for each and every one. My cheerleading matches, graduations, and courtroom triumphs are all being replayed in my head only this time I have her witnessing them from the front row. Instead of being absent all those years, in my mind she is at every one of them leading the cheers.

"Thanks for coming back home with me." I break the silence in the car.

"It's my pleasure; you don't know how long I have wanted to be able to see first hand how you are living." She says with a smile that lights up the truck.

"Well, from now on, you will know up close and personal as a mother should."

"I don't plan on missing another event in your life. I'm just happy to have my Queen back."

"And I'm glad to have my mother back."

"The timing couldn't be more perfect. I'll get to be here for your wedding."

"I know you don't think you are getting off that easy. You won't just be here for it, I'm going to put you to work helping me plan it Ma." I give her a playful smile.

"Yeah, that's my Queen, always running things." Quincy says as he pats my leg.

"And you know that's one of the things you love about me Quincy." I reply with a wink.

"Yeah, I'm a glutton for punishment." Quincy laughs.

"Oh, so you got jokes honey? I'll show you some punishment all right." I lightly tap Quincy on the back of the head.

"Hey now Queen, don't abuse him until 'after' the ceremony." Mom says waiving her finger at me in a scolding parent manner. It's a chastising I've been yearning to see for years.

As we get closer to home, Quincy announces that he is going to drop us off at my house so we can have some girl time alone. We pull into my driveway and as Quincy gets out, he tells me, "Baby, I'm going to let you and mom reconnect, okay?"

He takes our bags into the foyer of my house and I begin to feel a pain in letting him go. There's an aching in my chest. I'm almost heartbroken that he's leaving me, but I understand why. The last two days have been magical for me and I have my man to thank for it. Mom walks around my house by herself while I say goodbye to Q.

"You're too good to be true." I put my arms around my man as he puts the last bag down.

"I could say the same about you Queen."

"Quincy, I can't thank you enough for this Christmas, it's the best one I've ever had." I start singing *This Christmas* in his ear.

And this Christmas will be...a very special Christmas for me.

I nibble on his ear as we sway side to side.

"Baby girl, you're worth every minute. Pleasing you pleases me." He taps my ass and I grab his.

"I'm going to leave you with your mother. The two of you have some catching up to do." He puts a little space between us so he can look me directly in the eyes. "Reunite, resolve your differences and reconnect. It's time for you to get to know your mother again, and as you do, you will get to know another side of yourself. As much as I hate to leave you right now, you two need to bond." Quincy puts his arms around me pulling me closer to him. His hug is non-sexual; it's only wrapped in love. Just what I need right now. Damn, I love this man. He knows just what to give me in the manner I need it.

"I love you Queen, I'm going to the gym to work off all this holiday food, but I'm always just a phone call away, just holla if you need me and I'll appear."

I kiss him. "You'll appear huh? Just like my Prince Charming on a white horse, you'll come and save me baby? I bat my eyes flirtatiously.

"Well, I'll arrive on a horse only if I can put some 22's on that bitch." We both laugh. "Seriously Queen, you are getting ready to go through a lot of emotions. Accept them all because they are necessary and they are all validated. As you get to know your mother more, also get to know yourself. You are flesh of her flesh, take this time to bond and if you need me baby, just call and I'll come running."

I squeeze him tighter.

"I love you Q."

"I know baby girl, I know."

"You're coming back after the gym baby?" I give him puppy dog eyes, while running my fingers up and down his back.

In true Quincy fashion, he places his hands on his hips and looks down to the floor. It's his "thinking" stance. I know he wants me to have my time with my mom, but I need my baby with me too.

"Quincy, don't do this to me."

"Queen."

"Baby?" I bat my eyes.

"Queen, are you sure?"

"Baby, I need you in my bed, no, I need you in our bed tonight. It's Christmas, baby, please," I whisper.

Smiling like a Cheshire cat, he agrees, surrenders to my wishes. "Okay sweetheart. I'll be back, but it's gonna be late, okay honey?"

"K, baby."

He kisses me softly on the lips and places his thumb and pinky finger to his ear mimicking a phone and whispers, "Call me" and then he walks out the door. My eyes follow his indescribable white boy swagger, and I place my hand to my lips and blow him a kiss. Mom walks up.

"Oh my gosh, is that sickening or what?" We laugh as I close the door behind Quincy.

She places her arm around my waist and I accept her embrace.

"Don't hate Ma! Besides, I thought you said you've always like Quincy, even when he was a little boy."

"I did. I do. But that doesn't stop me from ragging on the both of you. Besides, it's fun."

I love seeing this side of my mother. I'm digging her playful interaction with me. I've missed this connection. I welcome it now.

"So are you going to give your mother a tour of this mansion of yours?"

"It's not a mansion Ma, It's really not that big."

"Oh yeah? While you were playing kissy, kissy with Q, I got lost. I almost had to call you from the West wing to tell you to send in a search party to bring me back."

I laugh.

"You're so crazy Ma!" *Shit, what did I just say? Damn, did I just call her crazy?* Open mouth and insert foot Queen. I instantly regret my words and hope I haven't offended her.

"No, I WAS crazy for a lot of years. Now I'm medicated, very sane, blessed and thankful."

"I didn't mean it the way it sounded." I hang my head in shame.

"I know baby, lighten up. We don't have to walk on eggshells around each other. Even though we barely know each other, we're family. Nothing will change that, we just need to blow off the dust to get to the shine underneath."

I smile...thinking to myself; this is what I've been missing. This is what I need. "Well Ma, I have my dust buster out and I have a surprise for you."

"A surprise? For me? Haven't we both had enough surprises for one day?"

"All of this would be incomplete without one more ingredient. Quincy did us a favor by giving us an appetizer; I'm continuing where he left off and making this a full course meal."

"Queen, you are talking in riddles, break it down for an old woman. What are you saying child?" It's cute to hear her motherly chastising once again.

I look at my mom as I take her hand and lead her into the kitchen. I see, no, I remember now, where I get this rack from. Wow, mom still looks good and is still built to perfection. Albeit, and older version of me, mom still has "the goods."

"I'm saying that bringing you here was just the beginning. Tonight, we complete the circle. I'm making dinner tonight, but not just for you and me, I want to invite Daddy."

Her face turns almost white instantly. I don't know what to think or feel right now about her reaction. Ahh. The Daddy factor...we hadn't discussed him yet.

"What did you tell him Queen? Her words are inquisitive as her eyes search my face for an answer. I know this is a part of the fantasy she hadn't addressed in her head.

"I didn't tell him anything, except for Merry Christmas. We spend Christmas morning together every year."

"You didn't tell him that the surprise was me, did you Queen?" I am saddened by her nervous eyes. The realization that she didn't just leave me, but she left him too, hits me like a ton of bricks. "You know you are playing with fire on this issue; don't you?" She shakes her head side to side.

"Well, Ma, I didn't know I was playing with fire. You mean to tell me he doesn't know where you have been all these years?"

"Why would he? When I walked away, I just broke clean. All he knows is I disappeared years ago. I never contacted him again."

"Wow that explains a lot. When I think about it, he never said you were 'dead'. He never used 'that' word. He just said you were 'gone'. I always thought you died when I was around five, but he never did say you were dead. Now I know why."

"Over the years, I wondered what he told you about me. I feared that he would make you hate me. That he would hate me."

"He never put you down. He would never do that; he loved you—he loves you."

"Queen, always the romantic. He probably doesn't want to see me after all this time."

"Ma, don't be concerned. We'll ease everything back into your life, slowly but surely." I see worry in her face, but I won't feed that emotion.

"Did your Dad remarry?" I smile and walk up to her. Although Mom is a spitting image of me, well, I am of her, she's about two inches shorter, so I lean in to kiss her forehead. I inhale her smell. I will never forget my mother's scent.

"No, he never did. Matter of fact, I've never seen him with another woman. And trust me, they try."

She smiles. "Your father was such a handsome man. We fell in love instantly," she says as she makes her way to my masterpiece – the painting above my fireplace. She delicately touches the painting while admiring the exquisiteness of it.

"You've always been in my heart, Mom."

"And you have always been in mine. Even when I was at rock bottom, I always prayed for you and your dad. Always. Please forgive me, Queen."

"Mom, please, I forgive you. Let's start fresh. I want to cook for you Ma, I'm going to the grocery store to pick up a few things for tonight. Make yourself at home and get comfortable in the guest bedroom next time to mine." I grab my keys and head for the door.

"Oh, and Ma, not that you have to put any extra effort into it because you are beautiful, but make sure you look extra good while you're here, a man likes it when a woman cleans up nicely for him."

"Oh, so you're giving your mother advice on men now Queen?" She folds her arms in front of her and gives me a look. Wow, that's my signature move. Must run in the blood.

"Well, I don't know if you are rusty on these types of things, so I thought I would give you a pointer or two."

Like a little girl who fears divorce, I pray all the way to the grocery store that my parents will get back together and we can be a happy family again. The next days have to be special, and I am going to do everything in my power to make sure it is.

As I ride through the mountains, I press speed dial on my phone and call my baby. Now that he's mine, I plan to make it my mission to keep it that way. He picks up on the very first ring. "Baby, everything okay?" he questions with concern.

"Yes, baby, everything is fine. You know I miss you already. And I know I sound like a spoiled brat, but I do, I miss you already baby."

"Ha, ha, ha. Well, you are a spoiled brat but you're my brat so that's all that matters. It'll be our dirty lil secret. Can't have your clients knowing that you need a good spanking every now and then. Baby, I'm gonna get my workout on. I just got to the gym. The parking lot is damn near empty so I'll have the gym to myself. I'll be home soon."

Mmmm, something about the way he said he'll be home makes me anxious.

"Q, I don't want you giving out any autographs at that gym tonight with your fine ass. It's Christmas and I don't want to have to whoop any hoochie's ass today."

"Shit, girl, it ain't that type of party. I'm yours baby. Now, I should be worrying about you since you're such the celebrity lately. I know you have a fan club."

"Nah, Q, I ain't going anywhere baby. Never."

"Good girl. Baby?"

"Yes?"

"Where are you?"

"Going to get groceries for dinner. I want to cook for my mom. I want to have dinner ready for my man. You want something special baby? Wait, I know…more peach cobbler?"

"That's what I love about you, you're so thoughtful. Yes, baby, that's fine, sugah, but get some butter pecan ice cream to go with that cobbler. Baby, let me go. I have to work out. I told you, I'm gonna get fat being with you."

"I love you, Q."

"I love you, baby."

The store is quiet and relatively empty for this time of day. Most people are basking in the afterglow of Christmas morning, eating leftovers, not running to the grocery store. But

I'm on a mission. I decide to not surprise mom with dad tonight, it'll be too much. I walk through the produce section trying to select the freshest vegetables for tonight when I hear a familiar voice.

"You look like you know what you're doing when it comes to choosing the firmest and ripest things." His body is too close for comfort for me and I have to put the tomatoes in my hand in between us to add some space.

"Wow, Michael, what are you doing here? I didn't know you lived on this side of town. Merry Christmas." I take a few steps moving toward the bell peppers to continue my shopping.

Out of the corners of my eye, I see Michael has on hospital scrubs. Maybe he got a job in the medical field? I wonder. But why wear them to the grocery store on Christmas? He's a strange cookie, that's for damn sure.

"Well, actually I don't, I was just in the area and decided to stop in here for something from the bakery to take home to my mother. Merry Christmas to you too." He follows me to the bell peppers and hands me a produce bag to put my peppers in.

"Thank you. Well, how was your Christmas?" I make small talk as I keep it moving. I notice a diamond stud in his ear. Kinda reminds me of my Quincy. Funny, he's never had one on before, an earring that is.

"As good as can be expected. I spent it with my parents. It would have been nice to spend it with my girl, but that didn't happen. But I won't complain, at least I'm on this side of a jail cell, thanks to you."

"You're welcome, yet again Michael, but I was only doing my job." I walk towards the onions and he follows me. "Oh, and I didn't know you had a girlfriend, that's wonderful Michael." I feign interest as I push my cart forward down the aisle putting space between us.

"Yeah, well I do. I have a very special woman in my life, but she's been a little shy in showing her real feelings, but I'm patient, I can wait. I know she wants me, I see it in her eyes, I saw it the first time we laid eyes on each other. I just have to wait for her to build up her courage. It's the trial and all. I think she is nervous about being seen with me because of all the publicity. But I'm persistent. I don't give up easily. I'll just help her slide into our destiny, into our future. All good things are worth waiting for, so I can wait for her." He smiles and helps me pick up the dinner rolls I am eyeing.

"Well, that's wonderful Michael, sometimes patience is all that is needed to make love happen." I think about Quincy and how patient and persistent he was in pursuing me. My baby's sweet smile doesn't leave my psyche. "I wish you luck." I say to Michael after thinking of my own man, my king and his actions towards me.

"Thanks Queen, coming from you, I take that as a huge vote of confidence that anything is possible."

"It is Michael, it is." I push my cart toward the meat section, feeling seafood for the night; I eye the shrimp and lobsters. Michael is still in tow.

"You look like you just walked off a runway, Queen. Nice coat! Was that a Christmas gift?" he questions.

It's none of his damn business honestly, but I try to be nice.

"Yes." I sweetly reply.

"So Queen what do you have planned for New Years?" Michael innocently probes.

"You know, I haven't given it much thought. Lately, I have told myself not to be so rigid, not to make so many plans, to just let life happen. Maybe I'll just have an intimate night at home. Typically, family and friends will pop through. I like it that way. No hoopla, no fanfare, just loved ones walking through my door helping me recognize the beauty of the season."

Michael has a smile on his face almost as big as when there was a mistrial in his case. I'm not sure why, but I don't give a shit, I just want to get my groceries and end this conversation.

"Just let things happen and let loved ones walk through your door."

"I love that philosophy Queen. It's thoughts like that which make you such a special woman."

"Thanks Michael. I appreciate you saying that." I try to be cordial. I want to say, that my man agrees and show him my ring, but I think twice. I just want him to go away, so I stop myself from giving him anything else to use for conversation.

"Well, Queen, it was nice seeing you today, I'll let you finish your shopping in peace. I've taken up enough of your time for now."

"It was good seeing you too Michael. You look good. And good luck on that girl of yours. Don't stop pushing for what you want especially if you can tell that she wants you too."

I didn't think it was possible, but Michael smiles even wider as if I have given him the blessing of the Pope.

"Thank you Queen. You have no idea how much your words mean to me. It's the courage I need and the inspiration I desire. Thank you for that. And I wish you a New Years filled with unscripted visits of love walking through your door."

With that Michael begins whistling and places his hands in his pockets and walks away seemingly satisfied from something I said. I have no clue what has made him so happy, but I'm thankful he is no longer sharing the same air I am breathing. That's the downside of vigorously defending clients, sometimes they think they are your family or your friend when really is that they were just another case to you...just another case you NEED to win. I believed in Michael's innocence and I did my job to the best of my ability to help others see that. But he is neither family nor a friend. His case was a challenge, and I like challenges and I usually excel to the best of my ability in order to win. Michael is like some of the other clients I have had, they see me as more approachable than I care to be to them. But it comes with the office. I can't save a person's life and then expect them to just forget me, so I wait out my time. Time heals all wounds and all infatuations. Michael Bevens is no different. I'm just glad he has some woman on his mind. Maybe that will lessen the times I will have to be 'nice' to him, because it's getting old.

Enough of Michael, he's gone...I need to prepare for tonight. I think to myself as I choose the best shrimp and lobsters for my mom. Still can't believe, I'm preparing dinner for my mom. I'm reminiscent of a song, when I see her face, my face – she will always be the girl, the number one girl in my life, for all times. I don't know how I lived this long without her.

Lord knows I love that woman.

❧ ❧ ❧ ❧ ❧

Placing my key into the door, I turn the knob and bring the groceries inside. I yell, "Mom?" I don't know why but I'm scared. I panic as I think she may not be here, like somehow today was all a dream. Mom snaps me back to reality, when I hear her reply, "Yes, Queen, I'm here in the living room."

I smile. "Okay, Ma. I'll be right there."

As I make my way to the kitchen, I look to my left to see the fireplace lit, and music plays softly throughout the first floor of my home. It's old school, one of the greats, Sarah Vaughn. "Mom?" I question as I place the bags down.

I walk into the living room, only to witness my mom cozy and comfortable on the sofa. She has a blanket covering her legs, and I see her toes peek out. She's flipping through the channels until she stops at an old episode of *Law & Order*.

I am definitely my mother's child.

QUINCY
Get Your Sweet Ass Home

It's hard walking down Queen's cobblestoned driveway to my car without her, but she needs to be with her mother right now, so I know I am doing right by her in giving them time to be alone. Nevertheless, I can't help but feel like a kid who just got the toy they always wanted and then realizing that they have to share it. I'm selfish in that regard, but who wouldn't be with Queen as the prize? At least I do what is right and keep my selfishness in check and don't show it. She will be mine from now on. My wife till death do us part. I can let her mother have a little of her time today. That's what being in love is all about. It's giving, unselfish and unconditional and I'm glad to be experiencing it.

It's funny how the trees, the sky and even the street lights all seem brighter to me as I drive to my house to change for the gym. Love somehow makes my view of life more alive. More crisp. The jasmine smell of both Queen and Bella has engulfed my truck from their presence on the drive back from Jersey, and I inhale it deeply one more time before exiting for my door. It's the smell of comfort and reminds me of all the happiness the last two days have brought to my life. I should be tired after all that has taken place, but instead, I am a nervous ball of energy needing a release. I'd much rather relinquish this energy while making love to Queen, but the gym will have to be my alternative. Throwing my overnight bag into the corner of my bedroom, I quickly change into my gym attire and grab my weightlifting gloves. Normally, I like to run on the treadmill at the gym, but given my state of mind today, I'm in the mood for a hard lift.

As I pull into the parking lot of the gym, my baby calls. She tells me she misses me already; that she needs me to be with her. I can taste her pussy on my tongue – hot Christmas pussy, wet, juicy and sweet. I meant every word I told her – I can't wait to get home.

Testosterone fills my nostrils as I walk passed each of the men with their chest poked out trying to look more buffed than the person next to them. I make my way to the smaller weight room in the back of the gym after passing displays of nutritional bars and muscle milk with insecure men around them.

"And they say women are vain." I chuckle out loud to myself as I find a weight bench and lay my towel on it. There are only about four people in the room and I place the earpiece for my iPod in my ear for solace. Mos Def enters my earlobes as I begin placing the desired weight on each end of the bar. As I put on the weight gloves our eyes meet.

What the fuck is he doing here? I think to myself as I see him giving me a snide look. Ignore him and just get your workout on. I remind myself of my promise to have patience. I lie back on the bench and begin pushing the weights in the air in repetition. Derrick strolls over to a bench next to mine and eyes me as he puts weights on his bar. I try to ignore him, but I can smell trouble brewing. Over the music in my IPod I hear him comment out loud, "They'll let anybody in here nowadays."

Because I realize this is a crazy motherfucker, I continue with my reps and continue to ignore his ass.

"Yeah, but then again, yo' punk ass needs all the weight training you can get." He adds.

I close my eyes and turn the music up louder to try and drown him out.

"I don't know what Queen sees in you, especially when she could have a real nigga like me. She must be desperate or something"

Sitting up from the first set of my reps, I can feel the burn in my arms and the sting of the pain coupled with wanting to knock Derrick on his ass are both starting to work on me. If it wasn't a crime to knock a silly motherfucker out, Derrick's black ass would be on the floor right now. I remove the earplugs from my ears and begin changing the weight on my bar. Derrick jumps on the opportunity to give me an earful without the cushion of my ear plugs.

"I'm surprised you don't remember me."

"I remember you all right." I respond nonchalantly. "You're the punk that can only prove he's a man by beating up on women."

"I'm not talking about Queen. I'm talking about Tina. Remember her?" He smiles and continues raising the weights over his head. "Yeah, you remember Tina. Who could forget that tasty piece of ass? If I remember correctly, she told me that your pet name for her was Miss New Booty…damn that girl sure could suck a mean dick." Derrick licks his lips while continuing his repetitions, exhaling and grunting in between each one.

I begin searching my mind to figure out how he would know Tina. But before I can make the connection Derrick makes it for me.

"We ate the hell out of that Salmon dinner you brought for the two of you that night. Ain't nothing like a good meal after a good fuck." He grunts again.

I try to act like I am not phased by his words, but I am. The picture is clear in my mind now. Derrick was the "Attica" looking guy I caught Tina with the last night I came to her house. I knew he looked familiar all this time, but I never put two and two together until now.

With each raise of his weight bar, he digs at me a little deeper. "Yeah, that was a night to remember. I had the taste of fish you paid for in my mouth and the smell of your girl's pussy on my dick."

A man at another weight bench says, "Oh shit" out loud before trying to act like he was not listening to Derrick's one-sided conversation.

I sit down on my bench and get ready to start my next set of reps. "Well, I hope you and that hood rat have a long life together. You deserve each other. And as you know, I've since upgraded."

"Seems like Queen downgraded, if you ask me." Derrick responds.

"I don't remember asking you, bitch. Besides, you took mine, now I have yours, seems like we're even. Now…you got what the fuck you deserve and I got what was truly mine in the first place. The only thing is I got the penthouse wife and you got the bargain basement hoe. Matter of fact, only thing Tina was good for was sucking this white boy's dick. Now, if we had her on the same night, that means you sucked this white boy's dick too, right? Bottom line; Queen is mine. While you have a lil girl to play around with, I got a real woman, apparently one your pussy ass couldn't handle. But, trust and believe, I'm handling the HELL out of MY Queen." I begin doing my own grunting as I lift the bar over my head.

"You don't HAVE anything white boy. I just loaned Queen to you. I let you take her off my hands for the holidays. I hate buying bitches Christmas gifts. Putting all my hard earned cop salary on a bitch? Why spend money I don't have to? Bitches ain't worth Benjamins. You've just being enjoying other's people's property; but it's time for me to reclaim what is mine." Derrick lets out a loud exhale and I can see that the weight is starting to wear him out.

"Queen hasn't ever been YOUR property. That's what's wrong with you; you're too stupid to even know that."

"Queen was and will always be mine. Yeah, she got out of line once and a while and I had to rough her up to show her ass who was the boss. But she always came back to Daddy. This time ain't no different. I just haven't had the time to slap enough sense into that girl. Bad girls need a spanking now and then. Don't be too upset when I spank her and she comes back home where she belongs."

Derrick's nostrils flair as he begins laughing at his own words. Did he just say something about slapping MY woman around? The thought of his psycho ass ever putting his hands on my baby boils my blood.

I watch myself react to his words in slow motion. First sitting up then removing my weight gloves. Before I know it, I am off my bench and hovering over the one that Derrick is on. As he lifts the weight above his head, I grab it and push the entire bar down two inches from his throat. He tries to push the bar back off of him, but his arms are weak from all the repetitions he has been doing, and I am powered by anger. The bar remains where I want it.

"What the hell is wrong with you white boy, get this off me. You need to get a cure for that jungle fever you got. Do you get off when Queen says, "Yessa Massa Boss!" Fucking white boy!" He kicks his legs trying to gather strength to push harder, but it doesn't work.

"The last time we met, I told you not to let this white skin fool ya. I can rumble with the best of them, and whooping ass is in my blood. You should have listened to me." I press down further using my body weight as leverage.

"Fuck you! Ain't white ass good enough for you? Why don't you go and find some white trash that would love to have a doctor on her skinny arm! Haven't you motherfuckers done enough by bringing us over here on boats? Now, you gotta take our women? Or you just need a slave to make you feel like a man? Channeling your forefathers, doctor? Did your family own slaves?" His words are weak and so are his arms. I watch as they tremble trying to keep the bar from landing on his throat.

"Tell me doctor; is your dick enough to satisfy Queen? I know it can't be. You must be buying her the world or eating her pussy like you're crazy, because I know damn well you're not packing enough to satisfy that woman."

"Oh, I'm packing plenty. Enough for her to say "Yes," to being my wife. I get in there real deep, trust me. You should have treated her like the black queen she is. Seems like you've done more to hurt your race than I have. Let me be perfectly clear Derrick. Stay away from Queen. I'm tempted to whoop your ass for the pain you put her through in the past, but I'll let that slide as long as you stay away from her now."

"White boy, you couldn't bust a grape in a food fight with your featherweight ass! I bet you dying to call me a nigger, ain't you?"

"That would be a compliment for scum like you and I don't give them out easily. See, you're a punk ass bitch, Derrick. You like putting your hands on women, but you ain't fucking with me now, right? Be a man. Put your hands on me, bitch. You know what? You're not worth my time. You stay away from Queen, or I will fuck your shit up."

"What are you going to do if I don't?" He sounds pitiful as he tries to be cocky. I lean forward and apply more body weight and pressure to the bar and it lowers; it's now only one inch from his throat.

"It's your choice big man. All I am going to say is that this little incident will be child's play to what I will do to you if you ever come around Queen again. Queen is mine now, and I protect what's mine. Think back to all the bruises you gave her and picture them magnified on you, that's what will happen if you ever come sniffing behind my woman again. I could fucking kill you right now if I wanted to. That's not a threat; it's a promise."

With those words, I let go of the bar at his neck, grab my towel and start to walk away. Derrick places the weight bar on the stand above his head and begins rubbing his arms to relieve the pain.

"You and your bitch ain't worth my time!" he yells as I leave the room.

"And as long as you remember that, yo' ass is safe."

I don't look back. I'm maintaining my composure as best I can. Part of me wishes he would come after me since I'm itching to clock his ass for continuing to call Queen a bitch. With each step I whisper, "I wish he would! I wish he would!" I can feel the heat coming off the back of my neck and clocking him would be welcomed right about now. I would lay his ass out too. No joke. But he doesn't come my way. He stays where he is. Maybe he has finally gotten a clue this time. I can only hope, for his sake, that he does not force me to live up to my words.

My anger gets the best of me, so I turn around to witness Derrick staring at me as I walk away. I yell to him, "You're such a pussy ass bitch, man."

❧❧❧❧❧

Damn, it's getting late. As I make my way back down to Jersey, I laugh out loud at Derrick's big, black, punk ass. For a man of his size and stature, he's weak as hell. I can't believe I'm on my way back down to Jersey to pick up Big's horny Christmas ass, when I should be in bed with my woman.

Derrick's words replay in my mind, and I can't help but think of him being with Queen. Did she get wet for him the way she does for me? Did she have a good time? Come hard like she does when she yells my name? One time, I hit it so good, she called me "Papi." Why didn't he cherish her? She's adorable, my baby. I'm still in shock that he'd let that go, that he'd violate her in the way he did. He hit my baby! I try not to think about it, but the fact that they dated at one point makes my skin crawl. I won't bring this incident up to Queen. Not now, it's Christmas.

My eyes are getting heavy as I cross over the bridge that leads to Jersey City. Still can't believe Big got with some old school hoochie from back in the day, for Christmas loving. He did, and unfortunately, I have to play taxi cab in the process.

Placing my earpiece in my ear, I press speed dial to call Big. He picks up on the first ring.

"Big, I'm almost there. Have your ass outside. I'm cold, tired, and need to get back."

"Well, Merry Christmas again to you too white boy. You'll be happy to know that I did indeed get some lovely Christmas ass this evening."

"Good for you, Big. See, that's the problem with this scenario. You got ass, and I'm playing cab driver when I should be home with my woman."

"Awe, come on, Q. You got her, man. Shit, she's yours. You'll be home tonight. What she got you whipped or something?" He laughs out loud after the question and continues. "Damn, Q, did she whip you?" He's laughing hysterically and I know my face must be bloodshot red by now.

"No, I'm not whipped, you fat bastard."

"See, you're calling me names on Christmas. Where's the love, man? But you told me all I needed to know."
"And what is that fatso?"
"That Queen put it on you real good and that you're a whipped ass." He's laughing so fucking loud that I can't help but to join in.

"She must have some magic or you are truly in love. She whipped a damn diamond out of your playa ass! You're whipped. Damn, I never thought I'd see the day when a woman would whip your white ass into submission!"

"You know, you're right, Big. I'm whipped. She put that thang on me. Got me thanking, not thinking, but thanking. I'm done, baby. She fucked your boy's head up, Big."

"You didn't have to tell me that. I know."

"Look, come downstairs, I'm pulling up."

"Okay."

The heat in the truck blasts, as well as the heated seat which causes me to sweat. I step out of the ride, close the passenger door, and press my back up against it as I wait for Big. The cool night, winter air is welcomed to me at this point.

Securing the earpiece in my ear, I press the number for Queen on my phone, and give her a call. It's late, but she's with her mom, so hopefully she's not mad. Well, I told her I would be late. Didn't I? Damn, I have to get used to this husband and wife game. I'll take my chances. I'm calling.

There's my baby.

"Hi, Quincy." She sounds pleasant.

"Hi, baby."

"Are you okay, Quincy?"

"Yes, baby. I'm picking Big up and coming home, okay?"

"Okay."

"How's mom?"

"She's sleeping. She ate dinner, we talked, we spent time. You know, Q, she looks like me. I know that sounds stupid, but I was looking at Mom sleep, and she sleeps like I do. Oh baby, your peach cobbler is in the oven. Ice cream in the freezer and dinner is in the fridge. I'm tired baby, but I will try to stay up for you."

"Oh baby. Go to sleep. I'll go home and come by in the morning."

There's an awkward silence on the other end.

"Queen?"

"Yes."

"You're okay?"

"Yes. But I wanted to give you your final Christmas gift."

"But you're tired. I'll get it tomorrow. Besides, I'd have to wake you up to let me in, and you need your rest. It's been a long day for you."

"Check your jacket pocket."

I reach into the pocket of the jacket she bought for me for Christmas and pull out a key.

"What's this key for?"

"It's the key to my house, our house, Quincy."

I smile.

"Come home to me, Quincy. There's red lace, a bottle of champagne, red patent leather stilettos, and honey waiting for you."

"Is that right?"

"Oh yes. Come home."

"What about Mom, Queen?"

"If you don't scream, Q, I won't holler."

"Now, that's going to be a challenge."

"Come home, baby."

"On my way, Queen, I promise."

As I turn my head to the right, I see Big walking over to the truck. He opens the passenger seat and gets in. Two women are with him and one enters my back seat. I can't tell who it is. The other, a fairly attractive, light-skinned black woman walks over to me. Wearing a short winter coat with fur hood, and tight jeans, high-heeled boots, she looks like a video vixen as I can see her ass from the front. Sweet face. She's rocking a low cut Halle Berry haircut, and her lips are shining from tons of gloss. Big hoop earrings. Yes, she's an around-the-way-girl, for sure. Her face, damn, I remember her face. She walks very closely to me, and plants a kiss on my cheek.

"Hey Quincy. Been a long time."

She seductively wraps her arms around my waist and takes my hand, forces it onto her left butt cheek.

"Do I know you?" I question. Big rolls down the windows to the truck.

"Damn, Q, I know it's winter but it's hot as Florida in here!"

"You don't remember me, Quincy. Or should I say Dr. Hughes?"

"No, I'm sorry, I don't."

My guilty eyes wander down her cleavage to her small waist then down further to where her hips meet her oversized ass. I quickly move back up to her face.

She moves in real close to me, leans up to my ear, and whispers in it. "If I'm not mistaken, I think I was your first piece of pussy, Q. I didn't want you to have it then, but damn, you're looking fine now. It's me, Hanifah. Don't you remember my best friend, Lisa?"

She points to the back seat. Lisa waves. Is that the same Lisa who gave my man crabs back in the day? Big has lost his natural mind.

"Good seeing you, Hanifah." I tell her as I give Big a "what the fuck is up look."

"Going home so soon, Quincy?" Hanifah asks. I'm prepared to answer her when I hear Queen exhale in my ear.

In a very low and respectable tone, Queen tells me, "Quincy, I'm not even gonna ask any questions. Seems like you're quite the ladies' man, Q."

I look at Hanifah, then at Big and then respond to Queen.

"Baby, old friend from the neighborhood. That's all, nothing more, nothing less. I'm on my way home."

"Sounds like more than an old friend, Quincy." Queen tells me. The coldness in her voice makes me anxious to press the pedal to the floor.

"Who are you talking to Quincy?" Hanifah questions as she presses her body up against mine. She once again whispers in my ear. "What's the rush? Stay a while. Like I said, you're looking damn good these days. It's definitely time to reconnect."

I smile, as my heart races to the point of eruption. I'm nervous about Queen hearing Hanifah's words, while also flattered that Hanifah remembers me.

The shallowed-lack-of-substance-Quincy of yesteryear would be busting that pussy wide open right about now, then would forget her name two days afterwards. But no, the new-and-improved-life-has-significant-meaning Quincy declines the offer because he knows what he has at home waiting for him.

"Sorry, I can't." I tell Hanifah.

"Big, we have to leave."

Queen chimes in. "Quincy."

"Yes, baby." I swallow real hard. I know what this must look like to her. And we just got over the Carmella misunderstanding.

"Repeat these words out loud for me, right now, okay?"

"Okay, baby."

"I love you, Queen and I can't wait to get home." Queen demands.

Smiling through the embarrassment. I hesitate.

"Quincy!" Queen yells.

"Yes," I whisper.

"You say it loud, right now, or you can kiss this sweet pussy goodbye. You'll never get close enough again to smell it."

I clear my throat and look at Big. I know she senses my hesitation.

"You know what Quincy. Here's food for thought. Just imagine someone else in this bed night after long-ass night with your woman. Dipping into all this sweet nookie, over and over again; eating me and my peach cobbler; getting treated like a king. Can you imagine that, Q?" she questions.

Dayum. The thought of it makes me want to fuck something up.

"I love you, Queen and I can't wait to get home." I say it out loud and Big can barely catch his breath.

"Damn, it's like that, Q?" Big's laughter has gotten the best of him.

Hanifah rolls her eyes and places her hand on her voluptuous hip.

"And Quincy?" Queen questions.

"Yes, baby?"

"Give me a kiss, right now. You *better* make it loud."

I pucker my lips. "Muah."

"Good boy. Now, you get your sweet ass home. Right now."

"Big, we're out. Ladies, it's been real. I gotta get my ass home."

QUEEN
Talk to Me

Waking up in his arms is heaven sent and is a place I want to live in forever. It's New Year's Eve and what else could I ask for other than having Quincy as my man and reconnecting with my mother. It just doesn't get much better than this; life is good. We all sleep in late today; mom in the guestroom and Quincy and I with our limbs wrapped around each other. As the morning leaves and early afternoon arrives, we finally get out of the bed and take a shower together. It's a long process, one we both gingerly enjoy as we lather and examine every inch of the other's body. After a long romantic shower of washing each other's back, followed by some noontime can't-get-enough-of-your-good-sweet-ass-loving, we come down the stairs only to smell black eye peas and collard greens cooking in the kitchen.

This is a feeling I've been yearning and missing all my life. The sounds of my mother stirring pots and making culinary magic is something I've long desired.

"It's about time you two came down. I thought you were going to sleep into the New Year." Mom speaks without even looking up from stirring the treasures in the pots on the stove. Her soft brown hair cascades down her shoulders. Her full pouty lips smile -- she's comfortable in purple silk pajamas that I bought for her. Matching slippers seal the deal.

"I know it's been a long time Mom, but don't you remember how good it is to lie in bed with the man you love?" I squeeze Quincy tighter around the waist as I look my mother in the eyes. My question is probative, trying to fish for details about her love life before my father arrives.

"Even at this age, love is a feeling that you don't forget. So, I remember it well Queen, and I ain't mad at ya for trying to experience it over and over again." Her hazel eyes sparkle as she smiles at me between stirring the greens.

"Miss Belle, that smells like the good ole days." Quincy moves closer to look into the pots. "I hope you put a piece of ham in there for flavoring. If ya gonna do it; do it right."

She slaps Quincy's hand with the back of her spoon, and I chuckle as he pretends to be wounded. He's so fine, with his delicious white ass.

"Boy, you know how I do. There's more than just ham in them peas, I put my foot up in there too for added measure. You know you can't bring in the New Year without black eye peas for good luck and prosperity and greens as a symbol of money in your pocket for the next year. I got it covered for this family." Mom adds seasoning and tastes the dishes as she speaks.

Lovingly, she places the spoon before me; unconsciously and automatically, I lean in to taste the goodness delivered with love like only a mother can serve.

"Do you really believe in superstitions Ma?"

"I believe in not ruffling the feathers of God or Mother Nature. From now on, I'll start the traditions and you and Quincy run with them. If I don't give you two anything else, let me give you this: Always be respectful of God and Nature, do right by them, and they will do right by you, the two walk hand in hand and I don't mess with either. So in my mind it doesn't hurt to abide by those little suggestions or superstitions, as you like to call them. I do right by them and they do right by me. My philosophy is better safe than sorry. So you can best bet that everybody in this house is eating black eye peas and collard greens if nothing else…just in case. And, I'll throw on some hot, buttered, golden cornbread. We're gonna ring in the New Year with prosperity." She smiles as the doorbell rings. Suddenly, as if her mind has switched to another channel, her eyes get big.

"That's him; isn't it?" She quickly wipes her hands on a kitchen towel and runs her fingers through her hair. "Oh, I must look a mess! I'm going to freshen up." She literally runs out of the kitchen like a teenage girl who just got a text message, leaving the spoon inside the pot of beans and saying nothing more to either Quincy or me.

The bell rings again.

"What's going on Queen, who is she *freshening* up for?" Quincy looks confused at mother's sudden disappearance and he follows me to the door.

I look back at him through ringlets of curls.

"I invited Dad here for New Years." I say nonchalantly as I begin to turn the knob to the front door.

"You did what?" Shock covers Quincy's face.

I take my hand off the knob and rest both my hands in the middle of his chest and kiss his cheek, "It'll be okay Q…I can feel it."

"Well, I hope you know what you are doing Queen." He kisses me back and stands on the opposite side of the door from me as I proceed to open it.

"Hi, Daddy."

"How's my baby girl doing today?" The hug he gives me is warm and comforting like only a father's hug can be.

"I'm fine Daddy, you look really good."

"Thanks honey." He turns towards Quincy. "Are you taking care of our girl?""

"Today, tomorrow and always sir." Quincy smiles and taps Daddy on the back as he walks in the foyer area.

"So Queen, why did you want me to come by so early? New Year's celebrations don't usually jump off until it's dark outside. Why did I need to be here so early?"

"Well, I have a surprise for you that will lead into the New Year and a whole lot of new beginnings." I help Dad from the foyer towards the couch in the living room.

"What kind of surprise are you talking about Queen? I am an old man, I can't take too many surprises. Oh Lord, don't tell me you're pregnant already." Dad chuckles as he takes a seat and I admire his choice of clothing. He's always sharp and today is no different. His rustic sweater and jeans look good on him and is age appropriate. Quincy stares at me. I can tell Quincy has no clue on how to help me break the news. I'm all alone on this one. I sit next to Dad and rub my hand across his. I can feel the veins of age and wisdom in each vein that my fingers run across. As I prepare myself to deliver a blow, I wish I possessed an inkling of the age and wisdom contained in my father's hands, but I don't. I search my mind and realize that the only way to get through this moment; a moment that has to be lived; is to just do it.

"Well, Daddy, I don't really know how to say this." I begin before I am interrupted.

"How about I say it for you?" Her words shock both my father and me. My mother cuts me off while walking up behind us in the living room. Her face is all aglow and I swear she looks like a runway model, even in her older years.

"Hello, Frank. Remember me?"

Her words seem to pierce my Dad's soul, and with each syllable uttered from her lips, my Dad's eyes momentarily close as if he is inventorying the sound for recognition purposes. He lowers his head until it is hanging lifelessly in remembrance.

I squeeze his hand tightly for support.

"Bella? Bella; is that you?" His voice is weak and shaky in disbelief.

"Yes, Frank, it's me."

He loosens his grip from my hand, reaching into his coat pocket first and then into his wallet as he slowly rises and walks towards her. The way my mother stares at him makes me anxious.

"You can only imagine how long I waited for this day. I knew you would come back to me. Your letter said you would, and as stupid as it seemed for me to keep the faith, I did just that, because your words told me to." He pulls out a yellowed piece of paper; a note that he has seemed to handle with care over the years.

I watch them together; my mother, my father, my parents, in the same room in a sight I never thought I would see.

"You kept it all this time Frank?"

"Of course I did, it was all I had of you." For the first time my father raises his eyes to meet hers. I watch as his wrinkled hands unfold the piece of paper that has been folded at least four times in order to fit in a side compartment in his wallet. He holds the paper in front of him as if he is going to read from it, but it is clear that the he has memorized its contents from reading the words over and over as the years passed, thus not needing to look at it to reveal what it says. Holding the paper in front of him as only a means of security, he recites the words contained therein in a rhythmic manner reminiscent of a skilled poet as he speaks.

Dear Frank,
This hurts me more than words can say, but it has to be done. I am leaving. The demons in my head threaten not only me but also those I love. Rather than tear down all that we have built, I choose to leave our love--our life, in tact in the purest form possible, one that my insanity cannot crush. You and Queen mean the world to me, and because of that, I need to exit your lives before me and my condition ruin it. My heart breaks when I think of leaving my precious angel and you, the love of my life. Take care of my baby girl and take care of yourself. The two of you will always be in my heart and once I have conquered my demons, our hearts, which are temporarily separated, now, will once again be united in the future. I never meant to hurt you or Queen, but if I don't leave now, continually hurting the two of you is what I will do. Don't hate me, because this is the most unselfish act I will ever do in my life, and I do it now because I love the two of you.
Goodbye my love,
Belle

As he recites the last words from memory, his hands finally stop shaking, ultimately finding steady ground.

"I really never meant to hurt you Frank. I left because I loved you. I loved you and my angel so much, Frank, please believe that."

"I know Belle. Although you did hurt me, I always understood the reason why. I didn't agree with your leaving, but I know you thought it was for the best. I just wish you would have let me help you. I was your husband, I wanted to help you."

"You still are my husband."

My mother moves in closer to my father, cupping his face with the palms of both of her hands. He hangs his head and moves in closer to her as a tear falls from his eye. Quincy and I cuddle one another as we watch my mother slowly kiss along Daddy's face in a manner that seems to soothe him like no other action I have seen in my life. With each butterfly kiss delivered from her lips along his forehead, then his eyelids, along his nose, over to his cheeks and finally on his lips; I see my father in a new light. One I might have seen before as a young child but had not appreciated the beauty of before. I see him in the manner of a man that is finally whole. As her final kiss lands on his lips, he drops the yellowed paper to the floor and grabs my mother intensely and returns her simple butterfly kiss with a passionate counterpart, and suddenly Quincy and my presence seem improper. Q notices it before I do, and he grabs my hand leading me to the kitchen. As I follow his lead, I turn back watching only the actions of them embracing one another, yet I can't help but want to stay and witness this sight for as long as it endures.

"Come on Queen, give them some privacy. I know how to preoccupy your time." He pulls me close to him.

"Oh you do, do you?"

"Yeah, I do. If I remember correctly, you like it when I kiss you here." He kisses the back of my neck. "And here." His lips move to my earlobe. "And finally here." His lips finally find a home on mine and we passionately kiss. I tell him, "You're trying to make babies, huh? Or you're just trying to turn me out? Which one is it?"

"And you know Queen, you're gonna have to stop looking at me the way you do. I'm warning you, you're turning me into a real addict."

I am lost for a moment when I hear a sound outside the kitchen window. I break our kiss.

"Did you hear that Quincy?"

"All I heard was my dick getting harder." He laughs and tries to start kissing me again. "Girl, you're gonna make this man lose his natural mind."

"I'm serious Q, I heard something outside the window. I think there's somebody out there." I try and look passed his body to see if I can see anyone.

"Queen, it's probably a cat or something. Calm down."

"You're probably right. I don't know why I am on edge, but I am."

"Well, I have just the cure for your ediginess; it's prescribed by a doctor, one you know well." He laughs and pulls me closer.

As we begin to kiss again, the doorbell rings.

"Who could that be, everybody I want to see is right here in this house already." I break loose from Quincy and walk towards the door.

"Maybe it's Paula, Queen. You know your sidekick is probably going through withdrawal by now since she hasn't seen you in a couple of days." Quincy laughs and walks over to the refrigerator.

"You're right, I haven't seen my girl in a few days, it would be good if she could spend New Years with us." I stop short of opening the door and stare back at Quincy and smile as I watch him removing iced tea from the refrigerator. Something about seeing my man so at home in my kitchen gives me a warm feeling inside. The bell rings again.

"Coming." I announce before opening the door. "Paula, I was hoping you would come by..." Derrick grabbing me by the neck interrupts my words.

"Wrong answer bitch. This house call ain't from that nosey-ass, loud mouth friend of yours...Paula." He pushes me up against the wall and my feet dangle in the air. "You know, I always hated that high-yellow cunt. She could never seem to mind her fucking business. I plan to take care of that ass real soon." I struggle to make a sound, but one cannot be heard because of his grip on my throat.

"A new year is beginning Queen, it's time for you to come on home to Papa. I let you have a little fling with that white boy, but let's not get it twisted, you're mine and it's time we tighten our shit back up like it used to be."

I utter a few syllables trying to tell him to let me go, but it does not work. No one can hear me.

He licks me along the side of my neck and I can smell Hennessey on his tongue and on my neck. I look nervously toward the kitchen hoping to see Quincy, but he's not there.

"We both had a little vacation to Booty Call Island. You had a taste of some new loving, and so did I. But I forgive you for your little indiscretion. I know that you don't know any better, so I forgive you for that. No biggie...Consider it window shopping. I let you look, but yo' ass ain't buying shit.

All this marriage to that white boy talk is nonsense. It ain't happening. You belong to me. Besides, you a real woman. You need a real man to handle that ass; not some white boy who can barely keep up. Now let's forget this little time-out of ours ever happened and get our thang back on schedule like it used to be." He's drunk, but I can tell he is serious. This nigger actually thinks that all he has to do is tell me he has accepted me back and that will make it so.

His grip on my neck gets a little tighter and breathing is harder for me. My eyes roll toward the kitchen and I try and will Quincy to see me in danger and come to my side for help.

Derrick runs his alcohol soaked tongue down the other side of my neck before speaking. "The way I look at it, you can either be with me Queen, or you can be with no one. There aren't any other options, and that stupid white boy of yours is not part of the equation."

"I got your stupid white boy right here!" Quincy announces before he comes flying into the room landing a left hook along Derrick's cheek as he finishes his sentence. Derrick falls to the floor but only momentarily. The alcohol, mixed with his own self-arrogance, has him fueled to a point I have never seen him before. Not even the night of Sherri's death compares in his anger now. That night scared me. Today scares me more. This all started with him killing someone, will New Year's Eve be a repeat?

I watch the two of them tussling on the floor with fist flying and I want to intervene, but I can't. I'm in shock. I can't relive Sherri's death just with a different body. I am frozen with fear. Sherri's death laid the foundation, Quincy and Derrick's fight right now solidifies it.

I scream, "Stop it!!! Stop!" But they continue fighting.

My ears hear threats, promises, insults and body blows. I still cannot move. My feet are in quicksand of denial. Finally, I hear her voice and I feel myself moving closer mentally to the situation at hand.

"What the hell is going on?" My mother screams at the type of her lungs, and my father runs over to the men and using his male strength, even though elderly and fragile, to try and break up the men and their mayhem.

"This needs to stop! This is stupid." My father grabs at Derrick.

"Get your hands off me man. This fucking cracker needs to know who is boss." Derrick swings aimlessly at the air as Quincy bum rushes him again.

"And this steroid-sized monkey needs to know Queen is mine and I'll kill a rock over her. I told you to stay away from her, didn't I?" Quincy continues to land blow after blow to Derrick's rib cage.

My father uses all his might to try and pull them apart and take charge of the situation at hand. I watch it all, frozen in shock and fear and in the midst of it all, I look at my mother, I see her eyes and watch her running towards me in slow motion.

What's going on? What's happening? I see her move, watch her lips moving, but I have no clue what they are saying.

And then I hear it.

A sound I thought I would never hear in my life, up close and personal.

It's a gunshot.

How did Quincy and Derrick get to this point? I don't think I can live with the fact that I am at the middle of either one feeling the need to point a gun at the other. It's too much for me. I can't handle it. I refuse to. I retreat instinctively and take a watcher's role to all that is happening.

I think these thoughts as I finally process the fact that neither Derrick nor Quincy need to be on the receiving side of a bullet. I wouldn't wish that on even my worst enemy. In slow motion I hear the shot and visualize that neither of them is on the end of the bullet. They both are safe….my mother is not.

Quincy and Derrick tussle, they shout, they argue.

I hear him, Quincy, my king, he screams, "Get the fuck outta our life!"

Derrick laughs, an evil, dirty laugh, "Never white boy!"

"Mommy!"

A shot is heard and I hold my breath at the outcome.

My mind replays the moment before the shot lands.

It has to.

I need it to…

The picture is crystal clear, even though I tuned out to other things. The bullet's shot, entry and final destination is crystal clear to me. My mother lies on the floor with blood coming from her body. Inside I scream, "No! No!" My mouth forms the words, "Mom! Mommy! No! No!" I scream at the top of my lungs.

My eyes search for Quincy. He's calling 911 and Derrick's scratching his drunken head.

What the hell just happened? I hold my mother in my arms waiting for the ambulance and try to make sense of her being the one bleeding instead of anyone else. My Dad drops to his knees next to us. My Mom's body is becoming lifeless as she lies in my lap. My Dad is almost unconscious from crying so hard. He yells, "Bella! Bella! No! No! Bella, please!"

Again, I ask myself what happened, then I rewind the moments that I was an observer, instead of a participant. My mother lies bleeding in my arms and I finally accept what happened. I see it all in my eyes now, as if reliving it in real time instead of in rewind. It's so translucent, so lucid, I see it all.

I see her. I see them, I see him.

Derrick and Q are fighting. I can't intervene. Mom has left the security of Dad and followed the commotion in the foyer. She does what mothers do. She tries to make things right. Dad gets in the middle of Testosterone drama.

I watch it all in disbelief.

Then I hear her. I snap out of it. I try to help. But her words echo the room before I am able to bring myself to action. Her words. I still hear them sounding off in my head. Mommy's words replay over and over in my mind.

"HE'S GOT A GUN!" She screams it in a blood curdling volume that would wake the dead.

As her words register with me, I turn my head to the left and see the bullet moving in slow motion, all the while seeing my mother leaping in front of me to protect me. I hear her scream "Nooooo!" as she uses her body to shield mine. Then I feel her body absorb the shot that was for me as she falls into my arms in the process.

As we both hit the ground, my body absorbing the fall of hers, I suddenly realize and relive what happened only moments before. My mind pushes replay and I rub her forehead waiting for the police as I am awakened in my mind to what transpired only moments before.

From the kitchen, I heard her screams.

"Someone's out there." She whispers it the first time but repeats it louder the second.

"SOMEONE'S OUT THERE!" Her whisper becomes a scream.

I look in the direction she's pointing; I see a shadow through the front window as I listen to the fight in front of me. Is all this going on at the same time? My mind tries to process it all.

She's right! Someone is looking through the front window of the living room. Watching the brawl in the foyer. Watching my parents, watching me.

Mom saw it all. She was the only one in the house thinking right. My mother saw HIS anguish, HIS pain, HIS need to end it all; and she tried to spare me. She tried to correct it. She tried to be my protector so that I did not have to endure.

She watched him watching us.

She saw him through the window. Hiding in the shadows, waiting for his turn, staring through the windows, rubbing his head, scratching his itches and raising his gun in frustration. And when he pulled the trigger, she tried to protect me from its blow.

Now she lies in my arms. Taking it all with her as she lies in my elbow pits--bleeding.

Leaving my life as quietly as she had entered it.

Daddy; he can not distinguish anything. Nothing is clear to him. His wife lies here bleeding, dying.

Quincy? My eyes search frantically for my man. Quincy? I look around, then shift my focus to Mommy.

I rub her scalp, kiss her cheeks and look at the perpetrator of her pain as I await the police to arrive.

Michael stares at me.

"Queen, this is not how this was supposed to end. But you gave me no choice. You seemed to beg me to prove my love. You wanted me to Man up, so I did. I just couldn't stand it anymore. You were playing with boys. I had to show you I was a real man. Your man. If I couldn't have you no one else would. Those other two are fucking toy soldiers. I had to show you I was a real man. I'm sorry your mother got hurt, but maybe this is what you needed in order to know that those other motherfuckers ain't what you need. I am."

I look up at him through my own agony. I scream for Quincy. I need him. Michael has the nerve to stand over me, trying to give me comfort at my mother's wounding. An injury he caused. He shot her. He meant the shot for me. Yet he stands before me trying to convince me that his actions were done as a means to an end. A way of showing me he was the only man for me. I want to holler. I want to beat his ass. But instead I comfort my mother who lay bleeding in my arms. I see Michael. I heard his plea concerning his actions…then I saw passed him and looked towards my man. Quincy. The Doctor. My savior. I needed him to make all this wrong shit right.

"Quincy, you have to fix this. Quincy! Help my mother. Please, Quincy! If you ever loved me, make this right baby. Make it right. Save my mother." I plead with my man and move to the side. He rushed back from the kitchen with towels. I don't have time to deal with Michael, the sirens in the background reassure me that the authorities will. I watch the blood shooting out of my mother's veins and just want everything to be all right.

I look at her and half-heartedly convince her that things will be okay as I stare in my man's eyes for reassurance.

Her eyes are weak as they stare at me. My Dad is beside himself.

"Mom, it's gonna be okay. Alright, Mommy?" I rub her face and kiss her forehead.

"Queen, you were the only one who believed in me. Even when I killed those little girls, you're the only one who cared. I know you love me and I love you too Queen. But if I can't have you, no one else will," Michael tells me as he stands there, gun in hand.

"Do you love me Queen?" Michael questions and I have no words.

Quincy moves closer to her and mechanically moves me out of the way as he takes on a persona that I am told I have seen before in him, but one I only know exists but can't remember first hand. He is in doctor mode. My mother's fate is in the hands of my savior, and wrapped around the fingertips of my king.

"Help her Quincy. Help my mom. Don't let this be it Q." I cry loud hard sobs. I scream, "I just can't take it if it is.

You gave her to me Quincy. Don't let her be taken from me again!" I yell the words without care of how needy I sound. I want, no, I need my mother. And my only hope lies in the hands of my man. "Quincy!" I plead, I beg. He's working on her, telling her, "Miss Belle, talk to me. He rubs her face as he applies pressure to her wound. Miss Belle, speak to me." She doesn't say anything.

"Quincy! Please, baby! Please, Quincy!" I yell. He calmly replies.

"Queen, I did too much to bring the two of you together. This shit isn't over yet. I refuse to let it be. But Queen, I need you to calm down. Take care of your father." Quincy reassures me as I stare at my broken window and Michael starring at me and pleading his case between gasps of air from my mother.

"Those two were fighting for what was rightfully mine, and all the while you were letting them think their cock fight would give the winner the prize. A prize, which was rightfully mine. I watched it all Queen, but I couldn't take it anymore. Neither one of them deserved you. I did. I sent you the flowers; I sent the text messages but you never responded. And the calls. You never returned my calls. I was the one you were supposed to be with. I dressed like that clueless Doctor, I sent you tokens of love that Derrick wouldn't even think to do. I did it all. And in the end you let today be about a fucking cock fight between two contenders that didn't deserve it. I just couldn't take it. I watched all of this shit from the backyard. The backyard Queen!"

Michael begins pacing back and forth. The guns taps against the side of his head.

"The fucking backyard! A place I didn't deserve to be. You love me, right? I know you do. You rubbed my hands at trial. You stroked my hair. Told me you cared. You believe in me! And when you allowed those two bitch ass punks to fight for what was mine, I decided to even the playing field and take them both out. I'm sorry your mother played hero. But maybe that is God's will. It wasn't your time to go. He kept you around because now you and I both know that you are supposed to be mine."

I stare at this motherfucker in disbelief. He is not worth my time or my attention. Sirens get louder, closer, comfort takes over me slightly; the police are here. I search for Michael. I need to see him in handcuffs. I need to see him put away for life.

The police have arrived and I welcome their intrusion. They handcuff Derrick as Quincy points him out to the officers. Michael's voice. I still hear it but I don't see him. Michael continues to plead his case to me as Derrick is placed in the back of the squad car and I look once again toward Quincy.

"Do what you do baby. Make this right. Save her life! This is my mother Q. You gave her back to me, Quincy!" The paramedics place Mommy on the stretcher. Quincy tells them who he is. Tells them that he'll ride with them. He speaks to my Mommy as they hurriedly walk out the front door. He rubs her face, "Miss Belle, talk to me."

QUINCY
Heaven Can Wait

It's been a long time since I've seen the inside of an ambulance; Quinton's death to be exact. Yet here I am again riding inside it with someone I care for. Queen and her father follow in her car. I quickly glance out the back windows of the ambulance and I see her face. Her eyes are pleading to me, "Quincy, save my mother." I place my fingers to my lips and blow her a kiss and mouth "I will Queen, I will", as the sound of the ambulance gets louder and louder both in reality and in my mind.

We move in one direction, and Derrick inside of the police car in the other. Thank God for small favors.

The paramedics seem to know what they're doing, but Belle is my lady's mother. I can't take any chances. I made a promise. I can't leave her life in anyone's hands except my own.

"I'm Doctor Quincy Hughes, I'll take care of her, you two just make sure we get to the hospital as quickly as possible."

The paramedics roll their eyes at me. I know they think I am throwing my title around, but I could care less right now what they think. I've got a job to do—I've got to save Belle. I couldn't save my brother when it counted, so I've got to save her.

Belle's breathing is labored and the paramedic tries to assist me by turning on the oxygen unit as I try to place the mask over her nose and mouth. Her weak hand stops me momentarily and she speaks through a cough.   Blood accompanies it.

"Save me Quincy. Don't let me die. Finally, I have something to live for. Heaven can wait." She coughs again. Her voice is barely audible.

I slowly lower her hand from mine, wiping the blood from her mouth before putting the mask back in place.

"I won't let you die Belle, I promise. Besides, you know that daughter of yours, she'd make my life hell if I did. I can't let that happen. Hell hath no fury like a woman scorned and I'm not about to start off my marriage that way." I smile and pat the back of her hand and feel a little better as she tries to smile back.

Her vital signs are weak and the machines in the ambulance indicate she is getting weaker. I squeeze her hand tighter then move my hands towards her blouse to look at her wound.   Her eyes roll back in her head, finally closing themselves as I unbutton her shirt to view the point of entry of the bullet. Exhaling upon sight, I recognize the magnitude of her injury.

"Can't you make this thing go any faster?" I yell to the ambulance driver. Then I whisper in the ear of the other paramedic in the back camper area of the truck with me. "Call ahead and tell them to prep for surgery. I need a room and staff ready as soon as we walk in the door." I instruct the paramedic on what to say and to emphasize the urgency of the situation.

"Yes, doctor." The paramedic says as he stands in the small truck and moves away from Belle. Thank God he knows how to be sympathetic. If Belle could see what we see, and know what we know about injuries of this type, she would die just from fear.

The ambulance barrels up to the front doors of the emergency room and I help the paramedics get Belle's gurney out of the ambulance. As we head to the front door, Queen and Frank jump out of her car seconds after we arrive. I motion for the paramedics to take Belle inside. Queen's eyes are blood shot red from crying.

"Make it better Quincy. Save my mother." She has both of her hands on mine and I have to pry her fingers loose so that I can get into the hospital. I raise my voice.

"Queen, I am going to take care of this. But I need you to pull yourself together. I can't take care of your mother if I am worrying about you. Be strong Queen. I need you to trust me and your mother needs you to be strong for her. Now go and comfort your father and let me do what I do best." I kiss her forehead and run through the front doors of the hospital leaving Queen and Frank to do the paperwork at the front desk.

I see Carmella first. "What room am I in?"

"Surgery room number two," she says as she helps me out of my coat mid stride. "Everything is ready Doctor, we got the call from the paramedics and staff are standing by in the operating room waiting for you to scrub up." I can see the worry in her face. I've operated on thousands of people before, but even Carmella knows how difficult it is for a Doctor to work on someone they know.

"Are you sure you can do this Doctor Hughes. We can always have Doctor Morgan handle it instead. He's the surgeon on call."

I know she means well, but I snap. "That's my future mother-in-law, that calls for more than the surgeon on call, that calls for me."

I scrub up and as I come out of the preparation room, wearing my scrubs and having placed my operating gloves on my hands, I see Queen again. I don't know how she got in this sterile area but she's here.

"Q, just tell me how bad it is. I need to know." Her eyes plead for information and even though I am pissed that she is in an area she shouldn't be in and she is delaying surgery, I can understand her need to know, and I can't lie.

"Queen, it's bad. It's very bad. The bullet is inches from her heart. One inch to the left, and she would be gone, so we are hopeful in that regard. But I have to remove the bullet, and in doing so, there is a risk that she could die because of the closeness of the bullet to her heart. The bullet has destroyed capillaries and tissue adjacent to the heart, and therefore will leave a hole. That hole could cause death if the bullet is removed. But we can't leave the bullet in her body or else she will definitely die. Removing a bullet this close to the heart will result in blood spilling out of her heart, filling up her chest cavity, and gushing liberally from the entry wound in her flesh. Her blood pressure will sink dramatically, and her heart may fail from the damage, all that coupled with blood loss can cause her to suffer cardiac arrest." I give it to her straight with no chaser. As much as I know it hurts her to hear what is going on, I need her to know the truth and danger.

She places her head in the palms of both her hands and begins to cry harder.

"No, Quincy, No!"

"Do you trust me Queen?" I look her directly in the eyes.

She tries to gain her composure.

"Yes, Quincy. I trust you."

"Then go and pray that God will guide my hands. These hands." I hold up my hands to her. "Right now we need a miracle Queen. I'll do my best to get in there, remove the bullet as fast as possible and close her up. I will do my very best to make sure you don't lose her. Trust me, but pray to God." I wink at her and head for the operating room. I've already wasted precious time, but it was necessary to make my girl feel a little at ease that her mother is in good hands.

It's abnormally hot in here, or at least the operating room is hotter to me than usual. Maybe it's the lights in here or maybe it's the magnitude of my patient, and who she is, in either event, the sweat rolls down my brow as I make the first incision.

God help me, I pray as the blade meets her skin. I need a miracle. "Guide my hands." I say to God, recognizing not only is Belle's future in my hands, but my own future as well.

I breathe hard.

Queen is trusting me to make this right. I can't let her down.

As the blade and first incision into Belle draws the sight of blood, my mind plays tricks on me and instead of Belle's face on the table beneath me, I see Quinton's. He whispers to me, "Save me Bro."

I close my eyes and try to shake it off. When I open my eyes, Quinton is still on the table instead of Belle, and this time instead of whispering, he screams, "Don't let me die Quincy. Don't let me die!"

I push the blade further into Belle, and finally feel it hit the bullet. Working on instinct alone and trying to submerge the Quinton illusions playing with my mind, I push forward doing what I've been trained to do. I let my mind work out the confusion of the patient...Quinton or Belle...Belle or Quinton. To me they are one in the same and I have to save them both.

My mind is confused, yet I do my best. As I remove the bullet and place it in the metal bowl next to me, I tell my mind, "You work out the whispers and the screams, I have a job to do." With that reconciliation, I am on autopilot, doing what is in my instinct to do.

With the bullet finally removed, I close up Belle's wound and pray for the best. Stitches conclude the procedure; prayer solidifies the outcome. As I walk out of the OR, I remove the gloves from my hands and glance back at the machines, which are monitoring her vital signs. They could go either way. But I did my best. Now all I can do is pray.

I search the hospital for her; she's nowhere to be found. It dawns on me where she might be and I head in that direction; there she is. Exactly where I would be if I were her; if I were in her situation; where miracles can be found; where I unknowingly sent my baby girl. —The chapel.

I join her. We sit in silence for a few minutes, wrapped in each other's arms; praying; waiting for the news.

Dad is on the other side of the chapel, on bended knee, pleading with the Lord for a miracle.

"Quincy, will she survive?"

"Only God knows the answer to that for sure Queen." My words offer little comfort, but they are all I can muster.

"This is my fault Q. She's on the brink of death because of me. If I'd just left her in Jersey, none of this would have happened. If I hadn't been so selfish in wanting her to come home with me, that bullet would have hit me and not her." Queen begins to cry hysterically.

"No, she's here because of Michael, not you. He's the one with the problem Queen. Don't make his illusions be yours." I think she hears me, I hope I've gotten through to her. And then she scares me. She begins singing. A tune I heard her sing in Jersey.

"Whisper something sweet to me.
Whisper something sweet to me.
Mama loves her baby.
Mama loves her baby.
From the sunshine to the night.

From the darkness to the light.
Queen loves her mommy.
And Mama loves her baby.
Whisper something sweet to me."

…. She's in a trance. She sings it over and over. After the third time through the song, she looks at me.

"Whisper something good to me Q."

Before I can try to answer, before I can lie or give her false hope, Carmella appears and motions for me to come to her. I answer the call; I leave Queen and walk toward her. She gives me the update on Belle; I listen and absorb.

Queen knows this minute means everything. She watches me with Carmella with apprehension because she knows Carmella wants me, but with anxiousness because she knows Carmella has news about her mother. She's pissed that it's Carmella that is involved in "our" thang, yet again, and that Carmella is the messenger of Queen's anticipated news, her future and her destiny.

"Thank you Carmella. I'll take it from here." I say to Carmella as I pat her on the shoulder once she whispers the condition of Belle in my ear. She nods and turns to leave, knowing that she as done her job.

Queen's eyes search mine, they pierce my soul as she moves closer, exhaling to allow room in her mind for the news.

"Whisper something good to me Q. Whisper something good to me." She says as she lays her head on my chest.

I hold Queen close, tight into my chest. As she reciprocates my emotion with a huge hug of fear of her own, I rub my fingers through her hair before delivering the news.

Epilogue

"Other people may be there to help us, teach us, guide us along our path, but the lesson to be learned is always ours." I remember my Dad telling me that all the time. I know it's some famous quote, but I have no idea who originally said it.
The lesson is always ours…

For days after mom's shooting, I spent every moment by her side. As she slowly began to recover, her weak smile was the incentive I needed to put the past behind me and finally make things right. I called Paula and asked her to meet me at the hospital.

"How's mom?" Paula hugged me tightly and her love was welcomed. I needed to have my best friend by my side. She is part of my nucleus, part of my life that completes me. Paula makes up who I am in so many ways.

"Thanks to Quincy, she's going to be fine."

"That man of yours is turning out to be a savior for you in more ways than one."

"I owe everything to him Paula. I truly do, and to think, I almost didn't give him the time of day, let alone a chance in my life."

Paula giggled, "Yeah, you were hung up a little on color for a while there."

"Yeah, the key word is *were*. I see now that I've let color blind me for way too long. It almost cost me Quincy's love and I've allowed color to protect a killer."

"A killer? What are you talking about Queen? What Killer?" Paula searches my eyes with her own.

"I've always been an advocate for the black man, you know that, everyone that knows me, knows that about me. I fought for them at all cost. And what did it get me? Nothing!

But by blindly protecting two black men, I've allowed my mother to be shot and a friend to be killed."

"Queen, you weren't the cause of your mother getting shot. That was all Michael and his sick obsession." Paula rubbed my shoulder to console me.

"Yeah, his sick obsession with ME! Michael had some crazy fantasy about us being lovers – he's sick! And, I may not have murdered Sherri, but it's because of me that Derrick killed her, and it's because of me that her killer is free. That same sick obsession ran through her killer's mind too."

"Sherri's killer? I thought her death was a car accident. What do you mean her killer? And Queen, none of this is your fault. You can't control the actions of others."

I looked at Paula's face and knew I didn't have the courage to explain it all.

"Paula, take this, it will explain everything." I gave her a micro cassette tape. "I can't let this go on anymore Paula, it's time to break the cycle and make things right, but I can't do it Paula, but I know that you can. I've got to go now. You'll do what I haven't been able to do." I kissed her on the side of the cheek, hugged her and walked away, watching her look at the tiny tape in her hand in confusion.

I knew that once Paula heard what was on the tape, things would be made right; Sherri's death would be vindicated. Paula would do what I wasn't able to do. I knew it. As she held the tape, I flashed back to the day of Sherri's funeral, that day, I knew Derrick would be there. I came prepared. I placed the mini recorder in my coat pocket. The one I had used in the past to tape my clients for my own protection. I knew Derrick wouldn't be able to resist gloating about his hand in Sherri's death. I was counting on it, so I armed myself. And being the egotistical bastard that I knew him to be, he couldn't help bragging about his actions.

*"You know, getting her to finally shut the hell up
was hard. I had to make sure I didn't wake you before I
killed her."*
I wanted to scratch his eyes out as the words came across his lips.

*"I picked up the biggest rock, well, it was more like a
bolder, and I bashed her head in. Poor thing. I had to take her*

out of her misery. Besides, I couldn't take a chance that she'd every say anything about anything, ya know?"
He was so glib as he spoke. I remember my skin crawling with each syllable uttered.

"She yelled like a baby with that final blow. What a shame."
I told him. "You're a murderer, Derrick."
"Yeah, and you love me, Queen."

Those words have haunted me since Sherri's funeral. I just couldn't bring myself to do anything about it. But I knew Paula would, and as expected, she didn't disappoint.

After listening to the tape, Paula immediately went to the police. Derrick was already in custody based on the assault on me in my house when Momma got shot…but armed with the tape I gave her, Paula had enough ammunition to ensure that Derrick would not be seeing the light of day any time soon. The police had his confession, even though Derrick had no idea his words would be the vessels to turn around and bite him in the ass at the very time he said what he said. But his very own words, spit from his lips with venom, ended up being the tools used to hang him.
The lesson is always ours…

He knew I would never give him up. He knew that my dedication to my race and not putting black men in jail, coupled with my fear of him, would never allow me to go to the police. But what Derrick never counted on was that even though I might not give him up, I had friends that would! He had silenced my voice for a long time. Fear of his fists and of his temper had put a zipper on my lips. A fact he was counting on. And for a very long time, he had been safe. But my mother's shooting woke me up to a lot of things. It made me re-evaluate my life, my beliefs, my dedications, or lack thereof based solely on skin color and an affiliation to it.

I knew Derrick was a killer and I knew Sherri's life had been cut short by his hands, but I couldn't allow myself to be the one that put him behind bars. Even though he was the devil incarnate, my loyalty to my race had sullied my judgment. That was then, but this is now. Color has a lot less meaning to me now. Racial barriers need to be blurred. The only time to separate color is when doing the laundry. I've learned that good and bad people come in all colors; including, but not limited to black and white. I had given Derrick so many chances just because he was black and I almost wouldn't give Quincy a chance at all, just because he was white. But now I am color blind and thankful for it.

Don't mistake me. There is still an unbalanced scale in our legal system and it is my life's mission to balance the justice system – put some stability into those scales. I will continue to fight for what is right.

My dad is the best example of the black man. The unsung hero in our lives, making all the wrong things right. Taking care of their families and communities and being prime examples of what it is to be a man – a real man – the black man.

I see a real man, a man I could be proud of in Cletus Jackson. Although I wouldn't give him the time of day, Cletus makes me proud and will make a lucky woman so very happy one day. I'll pray for her starting now. Ha, ha. On the real, he is so very much needed and respected.

And then there's my Quincy, my man, the love of my life. God makes no mistakes and I know that Quincy is my soul-mate and everlasting love. Another man I can be proud of.

The lesson is always ours...

I've decided that I will continue to defend those wrongly accused and will continue to roll the dice. But my life will have even more meaning soon. After the wedding, the honeymoon and a much needed break to enjoy my family, I plan protect and defend and assist women who have and still are being abused and are victims of domestic violence. Shit, I have first hand knowledge. I was in denial for a long time, but that's what it was – domestic violence. It will soon be part of my life's mission to get in where I fit in when it comes to aiding those women who are being physically, emotionally and mentally abused and terrified.

Quincy was the primary doctor over momma during her recovery period. Many nights her hospital bed was a makeshift dinner table for the four of us. Me, Quincy and Daddy couldn't get enough of being close to her and in doing so; we began to bond as a family. It was nice watching Quincy take such good care of my mother, but it was even more fulfilling seeing my father and mother begin to fall in love all over again, as if they had never been apart. I watched him hold her hand as they giggled like school-age kids laughing at jokes and events that only the two of them shared. Mom got better.

They reconnected. Quincy and I watched it all and took notes. The whispers in my life had escalated to piercing screams. All things in life do, and in making sure Derrick was behind bars, I thought I had silenced the screams; all was well in my world. Then it arrived. As I sat at the foot of my mother's bed, eating nasty hospital food, playing card games with my parents and my husband to be and making wedding plans, I got a text. It simply read:

"Enjoy it while it lasts. You will marry that white boy over my dead body, or yours, your choice, Beautiful. You and I are meant to be."

The text was unsigned. But I knew who it was from. I had taken care of Derrick, but Michael was still out there; still pursuing me, and still making sure that every whisper I heard still had potential to be a scream.

If you are someone you know is suffering from
domestic violence, please seek immediate help.
Contact your local authorities immediately.

The Hallelujah Corner

They...

They laughed as she chased her dreams. Said she didn't *fit* the part. Told her she was unworthy of it all. They ridiculed her for aiming high. Told her to get off her high horse. They highlighted the flaws in her structure and passed them around for the world to see. They failed to see the cracks in their own foundation. They spread gossip and innuendo. Put their foot on her neck so they could stand taller. Gave her the burdens of their own insecurities. They failed to look in the mirror. Told her she'd never get there. Encouraged her to stop chasing something she wasn't worthy of having. Said she couldn't run fast enough. Said she didn't *fit* the part. They rather see her fail than to see her fly. They spoke untruths, attempted to make her feel like trash, did it over and over again, hoping the sting of the bruises would sink in. They didn't.

She...

She ran faster when they said she couldn't. She cried on the inside; washed away her pain. She wore the bruises; her skin got thicker. She became a warrior. She knew she was unworthy – of the lies and the deceit, the ridicule and finger-pointing. She kept soaring, she had mouths to feed, souls to nurture. She had a gift. She didn't *fit* the part. She carried their burdens; made her stronger. She ran out of breath chasing those dreams; gave her endurance. They didn't look in the mirror, she did; gave her clarity. She felt the sting, wore the bruises; made her undeniable. Dealt with the gossip and innuendo; gave her power. They said "No." Her soul said "Yes."

HE...

He told her; No weapon that is formed against thee shall prosper; and every tongue that shall rise against thee in judgment thou shalt condemn.

He told her; God is pleased if a person is aware of him while enduring the pains of unjust suffering.

He told her; You are fearfully and wonderfully made: marvelous are your works; and that her soul knows right well.

Enough said.

I'd like to first acknowledge and thank God for the endurance and for breathing life into my being. I am absolutely nothing without You. You know that I come well-equipped with a multitude of sins, but you love me anyway! I give you praise.

The Circle of My Life…

My life consists of a beginning, stability, and a continuation, and be it not for these things, I would not exist. I'd like to thank my Father for creating me and instilling in me all of the traits and characteristics that I so admire in him. I thank my mother for giving me life. I thank you Mom, for birthing me. You were the lifeline, my breath-taker, at the time when there was no me without you. It is my hope that one day I will be half the woman you are. To my husband for being my stability and for sustaining my life. And to my children for continuing my life. You give me every reason to keep pressing forward.

The Hallelujah Corner…

It would be easy to throw everyone I know into these acknowledgements and call it day. Rather, I'm going to acknowledge those people who are my true friends. See, it really does take a lifetime to learn who and what really matters in our lives. I challenged myself to single out those individuals who have never condemned me. Those rare and special people who never judged or criticized me; who never spoke an unkind word, rather, have always shown me love and made me view life with more depth and understanding. It's amazing how the list dwindles once criteria are set to it. I thank my true friends, the ones who take me as I am.

First and foremost, my best friend, Paula. I can't picture my life without you in any way, shape or form. I know that God blessed me exceedingly, the day we met.

To Larry: you love me, flaws and all. We're building and growing and I am so happy to be on this journey called life with you.

To my Babies: My lil Mami and Poquito. Your love means everything to me. I love you both, more than you'll ever know.

My step-mother Ruth. You are more than a mother to me, you are my friend.

My mother-in-law, Loretta. You have shown me true and unconditional love.

Deseree, Kevin, Jim DeAngelis, Vanessa, my cousin Shawna. Aunt Betty. Monique, Talon, Bianca, Darnee, Kelvin, Chynk Showtyme. My cousin Andre at www.AllAboutAndre.com. My cousin Derrell. Thanks for the love and encouragement.

Anyone that I may have forgotten to mention here; I thank you for your love, and support.

My Literary Colleagues and Literary Friends

Lorraine Elzia and LaToya S. Watkins; two of the finest women in the literary game. You breathed life into me when I ran out of gas. I'll never forget it. All the authors of Peace In The Storm Publishing; Cheryl Lacey Donovan, S.D. Denny, Claudia Brown Mosley, Jacqueline D. Moore, Tamara Angela Grant, my baby girl, Jessica A. Robinson, Ebonee Monique, Pamela D. Rice. Heather Covington of *Disilgold*. Alvin C. Romer of *The Romer Review*. ESSENCE best selling author, Kendra Norman Bellamy and The Writer's Hut. The contributors to *The Soul of a Man*. Linda R. Herman. Marie Antoinette, my fellow Jersey girl. Tifany Jones and Sistah Confessions Book Club. OOSA Online Book Club. APOOO Book Club. Authors Supporting Authors. Joey Pinkney, book reviewer. Dr. Linda Beed. Peron Long. Crystal Nolden, book reviewer. Marc Lacy. JIHAD, ESSENCE best selling author, for the guidance and encouragement. Brian Ganges, a man of excellence. LaLaina Knowles of LadyElle Publishing; you know "we're here" girl and I love you!

To all of my readers, I thank you for being you and for enjoying my work. I especially thank Dona Florence Mosley and Angela Coleman, two readers who have now become friends.

Off the Wall

On January 18, 2009, my beloved sister Jodi passed away at the tender age of 45. I remember growing up, looking up to my sister Jodi. When I was a young girl, I thought she was the prettiest woman in the world. She had the best of everything, I thought. She was pretty like Lisa Bonet, and Halle Berry, pretty in her younger years like all of those pretty women I would see on TV. I remember watching her put on mascara in the bathroom mirror, at our home in Newark, New Jersey. I admired the way she would "feather" her hair. She would dance so well to what is known as "house music." Those of you reading this, from the tri-state area know what I'm talking about.

I remember being at Jodi's funeral. We had over 300 people in attendance and the one recurring theme was "Oh my God, your daughter looks just like Jodi." She does. Some mornings it's too much to handle. It really is. She's beautiful and a splitting image of my sister.

Jodi would throw house parties when my Dad and Mom were on the road. All of her and my sister Monique's friends would come over, drinks tons and tons of Kool-Aid and dance the night away to Sylvester tracks and one of the crowds all time favorites was Michael Jackson's "Off the Wall" album. I was still a very little girl then, but my memories are extremely vivid. I remember Mommy taking you to a Jackson 5 party in New York City, when she was working with the group. You came home with an 8x10 of you and Michael Jackson, arm in arm, afros touching the others. I admired you even more then. I was in awe of your beauty, and bragged about you to all my friends as being "Michael Jackson's girl." Hey, I didn't know any better.

Jodi swore I had a knack for acting, and would force me to do commercials and dance in front of all of her friends. I was the live entertainment during these days. I never felt humiliated, though, it was just a part of growing up. All a part of what life has offered me.

Well, life has changed drastically since those good ole days of doing commercials in the living room and dancing to '70's disco music. Life has somehow managed to lose its innocence and everything is a lot more serious.

You know Jodi. Dad had a stroke shortly after you went away. He told me you came to him in a dream and that you told him you were "happy." I was happy to hear it. We all know why he fell ill. See, you're still causing trouble even from Heaven. Dad's going to be just fine. By the Grace of God, he pulled through. But I suppose you know this already. Please tell the Lord that I thank Him.

So, I thank you Jodi, for showing me how to put on my mascara, how to dance, and what it means to appreciate good music. And yes, I'll tell Paula, you said "Hi."

It is my earthly wish that you and Michael have finally found peace.

To all of my dreamers and believers; never give up and never let anyone convince you that you are not worthy. Remember; you are fearfully and wonderfully made. *Enough said.*

With all My Love,

Elissa Gabrielle
July 4, 2009
10:47 a.m.

www.ingramcontent.com/pod-product-compliance
Lightning Source LLC
Chambersburg PA
CBHW051559100726
47898CB00001B/152